THE EVIDENC

MW00459606

THE EVIDENCE OF THE SWORD
AND OTHER MYSTERIES

Rafael Sabatini

COLLECTED AND EDITED BY JESSE F. KNIGHT

Crippen & Landru   Norfolk, VA   2006

Copyright © 2006 by Jesse F. Knight

Cover artwork by Tom Roberts

"Lost Classics" cover design by Deborah Miller

Crippen & Landru logo by Eric Greene

Lost Classsics logo by Eric D. Greene
adapted from a drawing by Ike Morgan, 1895

ISBN (cloth edition): 1-932009-42-6
ISBN (trade softcover edition): 1-932009-43-4

FIRST EDITION

Crippen & Landru Publishers
P.O. Box 9315
Norfolk, VA 23505
USA

www.crippenlandru.com
info@crippenlandru.com

Contents

AN AUDIBLE CLICK:
The Short Stories of Rafael Sabatini

by Jesse F. Knight

I've often thought that if Rafael Sabatini were alive and writing today that he would most likely be a mystery or spy novelist. First, he had an exceptional story–telling gift. You pick up a Sabatini novel or story and find yourself swept away in the first few paragraphs or pages. I've spent many an evening turning page after page of a Sabatini novel or short story. Second, Sabatini had a devilishly clever mind, and he wove into his fiction some of the most ingenious plots you can imagine, frequently with a surprise ending.

Yes, he would have been a superb spy novelist, but with an elegance of style to match what would surely have been an elegance in his characters, as well. He would have been an Ian Fleming . . . without the garish undertones and with an understated, yet still colorful, taste.

Rafael Sabatini was born in Jesi, Italy, in 1875, the illegitimate son of two opera stars. Rafael's father, Vincenzo Sabatini, was Italian, and after a successful stage career, he went on to an illustrious career as a teacher, serving as a mentor to such luminaries as John McCormack. Rafael's mother — Anna Trafford was her stage name — was English and herself an opera star. With two languages in the household, in addition to living in several European countries, such as Portugal, Switzerland, and Italy, as well as England, the early groundwork was laid for Rafael's remarkable facility with languages. Eventually, he spoke and wrote fluent English, Italian, French, German, Spanish, and Portuguese, not to mention Latin.

His extraordinary linguistic skill would serve him well, for at the age of 17, in 1892, Sabatini went to Liverpool, England (at the time the world's largest commercial port), where he obtained a position as a translator of business correspondence. It was boring work, and Sabatini was so good at his job that he doubted the company would ever promote him.

By the mid-1890s, Sabatini began to ponder a literary career. From childhood he had been an avid reader in many languages, and he decided that he could write romances as well as read them.

In those days the magazine field had a voracious appetite for short fiction, so Sabatini broke into the writing field by penning short stories. By 1898 (or at least that is the earliest Sabatini story traced so far), Sabatini's stories were appearing in magazines. He went up the literary ladder fairly quickly. A year later he was appearing in widely read national English publications such as *The London Magazine*, *Pearson's*, *Harmsworth's*, and *The Royal Magazine*.

At first he wrote part-time, whenever he could snatch a few moments (he once said he got less sleep than any man in England during this time). Eventually, though, in 1905, he took the plunge and quit his job to write full-time. It was a move he, and his reading public, never regretted.

During his early years of writing, Sabatini did not pen just historical fiction, despite the impression he gave later in his career. He took occasional excursions into other genres— mysteries, primarily, but a comedy or two, a supernatural tale, a few modern short stories that might best be termed drawing room comedies, and some short stories with O. Henry-like endings.

Sabatini, after he became a naturalized British citizen, worked for British Intelligence during World War I. In what capacity is still shrouded in mystery, but with his linguistic skills, it seems a reasonable guess to say he served in some capacity in the field of translating. Whatever it was he did, unfortunately, it never found its way into his fiction— or at least in any recognizable form. Who knows? Perhaps one of these historical tales is based upon a real life escapade. We'll never know!

About the same time that Sabatini was involved with British Intelligence, he also seemed to be especially active in the mystery short story genre. It was during the 1911-1916 timeframe that he produced more than half of this collection.

Mysteries — before the days of forensic evidence and DNA testing, fingerprints and profiling — were in some respects more fun, at least for readers, if not the detectives. The solutions to fictional crimes usually had to be deduced from clues, often by the ingenuity and analytic skills of such sleuths as Sherlock Holmes. Surely Sabatini read Doyle, as who wouldn't have around the turn of the 19th and 20th centuries.

"The Red Mask" is one of the earliest stories Sabatini wrote. Mazarin of the Red Mask was a cardinal in France in the 1600s. He was a powerful and far-seeing minister of the French court, cut from the same cloth as Richelieu, who he succeeded in 1642. Mazarin served until his death in 1661. Like Richelieu, he was manipulative and insightful, constantly intriguing, with a splendid spy network throughout the country. This story concerns one of Sabatini's favorite themes: justice, especially justice that recoils against those who would seek to subvert it.

"The Evidence of the Sword" takes us back to the generation before "The Red Mask" and the time of Richelieu, a time rich in intrigue and spies, as well. The story combines two more of Sabatini's favorite topics— love and adventure, with a bit of swashbuckling thrown in.

"Judge Foscaro's Crime," the only story Sabatini wrote that takes place in his hometown of Jesi, Italy, also deals with the subject of retribution.

"The Spiritualist" and "Monsieur Delamort" are companion pieces, although they were written some four years apart and appeared in different magazines. Taking place in the early 1900s, these tales are examples of Sabatini's love of the con-man, the devious scoundrel who plays upon the all-too-common vice of greed. Sabatini called them "ingenious tricksters"— a trait the writer admired. The stories perhaps take something from Twain's "The Man That Corrupted Hadleyburg." The stories were written in 1905 and 1909, respectively. This was the time when O. Henry was writing and when the surprise ending was in vogue. However, as with the best story-tellers of surprise endings, Sabatini adds another unexpected twist beyond the one you're expecting.

"Wirgman's Theory" is a devilishly clever mystery and one of Sabatini's few contemporary stories. What makes this story interesting is that the protagonist (for there really isn't a hero) is not especially likeable. There is something of Sherlock Holmes here, with Wirgman's ultra-logical mind. But Sabatini shows how many ways logic can be used to interpret facts.

And of course, no Sabatini collection would be complete without a couple of highwaymen stories. "The Pretender" and "Ambs-Ace" are two of his finest, and like most of the stories in this collection, this is the first time they have been reprinted since being published nearly a century ago. Ambs-Ace, what we would call snake eyes, in case you're wondering, is a dice game.

Sabatini rarely used material from his own life in his stories. However, "Shrinkage" is a rare exception. The idea for "Shrinkage" no doubt came to Sabatini from his years of working in a mercantile office, corresponding about the shipment and receipt of goods. Perhaps he saw something like this himself, since he was, essentially, a clerk and worked on correspondence.

At about 20,000 words, "The Dream" is long enough to be considered a novelette. It was turned into a screenplay by Sabatini, released under the title *The Recoil* in March of 1922. Although the film has disappeared in the intervening years, nonetheless it was well received when it was released. Sabatini dabbled a bit in screenwriting, but perhaps he found the idea of creation-by-committee wearing, for after a couple of years he abandoned the field entirely and never wrote the further screenplays for any of his other stories or books.

At the crux of the crime is hypnosis, a subject that early in the 20th century was still a matter of some controversy. In some circles hypnotism was viewed with derision— "so much clap-trap," the Major says; but in other circles it was viewed with awe— "[It] is not right to mock at what we don't, perhaps, understand," says the Major's ward.

You will find in the novelette "The Valet Mystery" the rudiments of an idea from another story (not included in this collection). However, Sabatini greatly expands the original concept and moves the plot in an entirely new direction. The story is a complex one with a beautifully modulated and touching ending

that is as startling as it is true. It is as much about a moral dilemma as it is about
a mystery.

Sabatini was fond of writing about the French Revolution. Who wouldn't
be, with its colorful cast of characters, its startling dramas of life and death, its
vivid background and intense emotions and remarkable events? Sabatini wrote
many novels, novelettes, and short stories set in this timeframe. As will often
happen during earthshaking events, during times of grand drama, a tale of petty
crime unfolds. Petty crime escalates to murder, which is the basis for the story
"Duroc."

"The Mask" is an out and out spy story told in an historical setting. Taking
place in the late 1600s, Sabatini blends the political intrigue of the Jacobites with
romance and danger. Today, the spy is often times viewed as glamorous, *ala*
James Bond. But not so when Sabatini was writing. In previous centuries,
indeed even during the early years of the 20th century, the work of the spy was
not considered honorable employment. For instance, during the American War
of Independence, when George Washington needed a spy to retrieve Benedict
Arnold from New York City, no officer would accept the assignment, looking
upon it with disdain, as something a gentleman wouldn't do. When the hero of
"The Mask" is offered such employment: " 'This is catchpoll's work,' he said in
a voice of offended protest. 'You insult me, sir. I came to you seeking
honorable employment — ' " As a result, the hero of the story not only has to
deal with the moral dilemma in what he views as dishonorable work, but he
must also be concerned that his lady love will find him despicable. In fact, it is
upon her and her group of plotters that he is spying!

Sabatini occasionally took a story he had previously written, as mentioned
earlier, turned it over in his mind, and came up with a new approach to the idea.
So it is not uncommon to read a novel of Sabatini that had its genesis as a short
story, or to see a movie that began as a novelette or a novel that started life as a
play. A case in point? "His Last Chance" is an earlier version of the later "The
Mask." However, Sabatini moves the same basic story plot in an entirely new
direction with a completely different denouement.

Sabatini had a long and illustrious career during which he published a
wealth of material. Still, he wrote for over two decades before he achieved
international fame with *Scaramouche* and *Captain Blood* in the early 20s.

In the 1930s he moved to a rural part of England, near Hay-on-Wye (yes,
the town of a million books), on the border of England and Wales. There he
spent the remainder of his lifetime.

Sabatini was an avid skier throughout his life, and he took annual trips to
Switzerland. That is what accounts for the fact that after a lengthy illness, the
writer died in Adelboden, Switzerland on February 13, 1950. He is buried in
that alpine village, under a sculpture made of him by his wife.

In the 1950s *Ellery Queen Mystery Magazine* reprinted several of Sabatini's
short stories from his last collection *Turbulent Tales* (1946). The editors knew a

good mystery when they read one, and it didn't matter to them that the story came garbed as historical fiction.

Clifton Fadiman, the critic, writer, and anthologist, has written about what he considers to be the two broad categories of short story writing. There is the type of story that is open-ended. John Steinbeck, James Joyce, and Stephen Crane produced examples of this type of writing. It is, it must be admitted, the predominant school of short story writing in the 20th century. The second type of short story is closed. Fadiman writes about Somerset Maugham that Maugham's stories conclude "with an almost audible click." Sabatini was of that group of writers. His stories close with just such a satisfying and audible click.

We need look no further than this to understand why Sabatini's literary fortunes (and Maugham's, too, for that matter) have fared poorly in the latter half of the 20th century. But there is hope. The literary world, no less than the fashion world, is subject to fads. So who know what the future might bring?

Regardless of his current literary reputation, Sabatini's goal, first and foremost, was to entertain the reader, and he achieved that admirably. Like Stephen King, nowadays, Sabatini set out to provide an entertainment with a beginning, a middle, and an end. The reader is never disappointed. The ending always closes with a finality, and the reader is never left to wonder. Sabatini's fare is light, to be sure, but for that there need be no apologies. His stories are always satisfying and accomplished.

Later in life, Sabatini wrote a couple of spy novels in an historic mode and certainly several of his short stories can be considered mysteries (such as those reprinted by *EQMM*); but with "The Mask" Sabatini's major interest in mystery writing came to an end. The overwhelming success of *Scaramouche* in 1921 and *Captain Blood* in 1922 no doubt served as an impetus for the writer to focus exclusively on historical adventure, a field in which he had few equals.

If this sampling of his short fiction is an indication, then the mystery-spy genre lost a rare and gifted practitioner when Sabatini turned his ingenuity and focused his facile imagination upon other genres.

Wirgman's Theory

Whatever might be said against Roger Wirgman — and his intimates, had they been willing to speak, might have said a good deal — it was not to be denied that he was a man of marked individuality. And in this twentieth century world a man of individuality is like a rosebush in a bed of weeds. I don't know that my metaphor is exactly applicable to Roger Wirgman, for there was little about him, morally or physically, that suggested roses. He was lank of figure with the brow of a philosopher and the mouth of a satyr.

He was widely read, rather than well read; he had a passion for criminology, and murder was his study predilect. He contended — and facts offer no lack of justification for his contention — that dictum "murder will out" was found, when tested, to be as fallacious as most proverbial tenets.

"Given," he would say in his cold-blooded manner, "a man of sufficient education, with an imagination wide enough to foresee all possible issues, and intelligence strong enough to provide capably for each and every one of those issues so as completely to cover up his tracks, and he may kill with impunity.

"Think of the hundreds — indeed, I might almost say thousands — of yearly undiscovered murderers. Why are their crimes not brought home to them? Because, possessed of the qualities I have mentioned, they have successfully effaced all traces of any implicating evidence.

"Now, what is the first question that is asked when an investigation is opened? It is: Who could have had a motive for doing this? To baffle research at the outset, therefore, we must arrange that no motives shall be apparent. So that when a man is noxious, and his removal becomes a desideratum or a thing that at some future time may be necessary, we must look to it that we do not betray those feelings by ever inveighing against him and exposing our inimical sentiments. On the contrary, let us feign and protest friendship and affection for him; let us court him, and make it appear that we are his dearest friend. Thus, when some day he is found dead, with a suggestion of foul play attaching to his end, and it comes to be asked who were his enemies, none shall think of naming us."

In this fashion would he pursue his pet theme, dilating upon the contriving of accidents by land and water in a horrible, cold-blooded, logical manner that made his audience shudder.

"To listen to you," said Pegram one night after Wirgman had delivered himself in this usual strain, "one might almost believe you had actual experience."

12

"On the contrary," rejoined Wirgman with a touch of whimsical regret, "I'm afraid that I am never likely to have an opportunity of applying my theories. Nevertheless, I am convinced that should the occasion arise I could prove them sound; though, for obvious reasons, I should unfortunately be unable to lay my results before you."

"Wirgman, you'd make a nasty enemy," laughed Pegram; "and I for one am glad to rank among your friends."

"Touch wood," muttered a humourist, "to avert the omen."

"Come to think of it, though," rejoined another, "it is really his friendship that is dangerous, for the first step according to his methods entails making a close friend of his proposed victims."

At that there was a fairly general and good-humouredly bantering laugh at Wirgman and his theory, and the topic was abandoned for others in better concert with a club smokeroom.

Little did Harry Pegram dream how soon that theory was to be put into practice against himself; and still less did Wirgman think how he was to discover the gulf that lies between theories based upon human actions and their application.

The thing came about six months later. It arose from a sufficiently common cause — a woman, whom by an ill chance they had both elected to woo. She was a poor thing herself in every sense unworthy of the struggle that followed between the rivals; but then is it not in the tortuous way of things that such women as these shall have power to inspire great passions and stir up great strife?

A coolness, slight at first, but later more remarkable, fell between the two friends. They grew distant in their manner, and avoided each other in so marked a degree that their estrangement grew into matter for conversation.

Then Pegram did a mean and foolish thing. He uttered a slander calculated to harm Wirgman. When it came to Wirgman's ears and he discovered the source of it, he flew into a violent rage — self-possessed though he ordinarily was — and swore to kill the fellow. The threat was voiced in that same club smokeroom, and loudly enough to be heard by its every occupant. That he would kill Pegram they looked upon as mere hyperbolical expression of his passion — a mere figure of speech. But that his anger was deep they realised, and they implored him to calm himself. Outwardly he succeeded in doing so; but inwardly his rage boiled on, and the desire to do for that man's existence what that man had done for his character was unabated.

Had anything been needed to swell his rancour he had it a week later in the announcement of Pegram's betrothal to the lady. Wirgman had over-estimated his own attractions, her show of favour had lured him on, and perhaps justified him in building an elaborate castle in the air. He relied upon his marriage to mend his crippled resources — for the lady was well endowed. This castle of his now came toppling about his ears, and the financial crisis which he was compelled to face deepened his ill will towards Pegram, and carried him a step farther in the contemplation of that gentleman's removal.

One night in the solitude of his elegant chambers he pondered the injury that had been done him. He cursed the moment of folly in which he had threatened Pegram's life. He recalled the theory he had been so fond of expounding, and he reflected bitterly upon how grievously he had neglected to be guided by it now that its application had become desirable. Gloomily he sat and thought. He was a man of stern, determined mind, without conscience and without any principles to speak of; and he found himself dwelling upon the contemplation of murder as calmly and coldly as he had been wont to dwell upon its theoretical aspect.

A dozen means suggested themselves to his fertile brain, any one of which he might have adopted with safety had he but refrained from alienating Pegram, and, above all from foolishly proclaiming his resentment and threatening his rival's life.

With brows knit he sat on through the night, and thought with all the intensity of his subtle intellect, until at length the frown lifted, and a smile gradually stole over his strong face, and relaxed the lines of his cruel mouth. He had found a way.

He realised that it was beyond his power — and the act he contemplated must render it doubly so — to win the woman, or, in fact, to reap any advantage beyond the satisfaction his enemy's destruction might afford him. But that satisfaction he deemed more than sufficient. Introspection showed him that he hated the woman now almost as bitterly as he hated the man; and he gathered pleasure from the thought that the blow he intended to strike would be sufficiently far-reaching to wound her also. For this it was worth while abandoning England and his friends, even had not his creditors rendered such a step imperative in any event, now that he was not to have the assistance of her wealth to set him straight; and friends, after all, were of very slight consideration to a man of such self-centered interests.

Pegram was at the time staying down at Port Wimbush with the lady — whose name, by the way, was Miss Drummond — and her mother. No locality could have been better suited to Wirgman's projects than this little seaside resort.

His first step was to contrive a disagreement with his bankers, which afforded him the motive he sought for withdrawing his deposit, a matter of some three thousand pounds, representing all that he possessed.

On the morrow he left town. But before he went he took care to look in at the club, and announce to everybody likely to be interested that he was going down to Port Wimbush to administer to Harry Pegram the most complete thrashing ever one gentleman visited upon another.

What he was about to do he knew. For the manner of it he must profit by such circumstances as should offer themselves. He put up at the Swan Hotel

— having previously ascertained that Pegram and the ladies were staying at the Crown— and during the whole of the next day he kept his room.

After dinner, as dusk was setting in, he stepped across to the Crown Hotel, and, strolling into the bar, he called for a whisky-and-soda. Through the glass doors he peered into the smoke-room, and his eyes gleamed with satisfaction as they lighted upon Pegram, sitting there with his paper and his post-prandial cigar. Wirgman was building heavily upon a slender foundation of probabilities. This, the first of the circumstances he had relied upon, proved as he had reckoned. He emptied his glass, and, moving over to the office, he inquired was Miss Drummond in the house. He received an affirmative reply. She was in her sitting room. Truly the gods of chance were fighting on his side, for here was the second circumstance making good the combination he had hoped to find.

He gave his card to a waiter; then, treading closely upon the fellow's heels, he pushed into the sitting-room after him, and without waiting to be announced, for he had a shrewd suspicion that he might be denied.

As he entered he had a swift vision of Miss Drummond — a tall, fair, showy woman — standing with brows contracted in a frown, regarding his card. Her mother, he was glad to see, was absent.

"Mr. Wirgman!" she exclaimed, catching sight of him. "This is an intrusion!"

He bowed and smiled darkly.

"I confess it. But I was afraid you might hesitate to see me; and as the communication I wish to make to you is of an urgent and most important character, I am confident that you will ultimately absolve me — thank me, perhaps — for having forced my way in."

"I have nothing to say to you."

"Possibly not. It was not with the hope of hearing you say anything that I came. But I have something to say to you that you may come to very bitterly regret not having heard if you deny me. I have come down from town and gone to the discomfort of putting up at that appalling hotel the Swan purposely to render you a service. Surely I deserve a hearing?"

She was only a woman, and curiosity got the better of her.

"What have you to say?" she inquired freezingly.

Wirgman glanced significantly at the interested waiter, whom she at once dismissed. When they were alone he unfolded his mission. He opened with an attempt to refute the slander she had heard against him and followed that up by most virulently maligning Pegram in his turn, dubbing him incidentally, a liar and a low person generally.

Miss Drummond checked his invective in full flow, and desired him to leave the room, whereupon, getting adroitly between her and the bell, he proceeded, with a readiness and elegance of diction that savoured almost of preparation, to tell her with a touching candour and honesty the opinion he had come to concerning herself. Much did he tell her that was scarcely true — but nevertheless fateful to hear — and much that was perfectly true — and therefore more hateful still. He spoke with smiling lips, which added venom to his utterance; and with a master hand he fanned the lady's spirit — an inflammable one at all times — into a very blaze of passion.

"Mr. Wirgman, you shall very bitterly regret this insolence before you are a day older!" she promised him. "Mr. Pegram shall hear of it at once."

Still smiling, Wirgman moved towards the door, leaving her a clear way to the bell should she wish to avail herself of it — as he hoped she might.

"He may hear of it, and welcome," said he, with studied offensiveness; "but if he has the effrontery to address me now or at any time, I shall receive him with the most picturesque thrashing that was ever bestowed."

She looked him over with quiet scorn.

"It is like a brave man to tell a woman what he will do, is it not?" she inquired with withering sarcasm as she crossed to the bell.

"Madam, I do not *tell* you — I warn you. But send your preux chevalier to me by all means. You will save me the trouble of looking for him."

"You shall not have long to wait," she answered, and pressed the button.

Wirgman bowed and withdrew, well satisfied.

On the stairs he met the waiter hastening to answer her bell. "It will take her five minutes to tell Pegram her story," he reckoned; "five minutes for Pegram to console her and regale her with the promises of all the fine things he will perform. So that in ten minutes I may expect that gentleman to ask for me at the Swan Hotel."

He smiled quietly as he stepped out into the street.

"I may boast that I have cast my net with singular adroitness, and I am afraid you may find its toils exceedingly difficult to break through, my dear Pegram."

He stood for a moment on the steps of his hotel — a tall, conspicuous figure in his light drab overcoat and soft hat — and he leisurely lighted a cigarette. At that moment the landlord came out.

"A fine night Mr. Wirgman," said he.

"A very fine night," Wirgman agreed, adding idly: "Hardly a night to waste indoors. I think I'll take a stroll as far as the Head. See you later."

He moved away up the steep road that leads to Wimbush Head, with the conviction that he would very shortly be followed. Twice he paused on the way, and drew attention to himself by exchanging a remark upon the night, once with a couple of fishermen, and once with a policeman.

He had conjectured aright concerning Harry Pegram. Within a few minutes of his departure that gentleman was excitedly asking for him at the Swan, to receive from the landlord the information that he was gone toward Wimbush Head. After him, hotfoot and blind with fury, came Pegram now. But for all his haste he did not overtake him until he reached the edge of the cliff, where he saw him outlined against the sky.

"You blackguard!" was the greeting he had for Wirgman, as he rushed at him with stick upraised to strike.

The other caught his wrist as the blow descended, and, holding him for an instant in a crushing grip, he twisted the cane from his hand and flung it over the cliff. They heard it rattle on the shingle below. Then Wirgman spoke.

"Don't be a fool, Pegram," he said coldly, in his dominating way. "Suppose for a moment that you had struck me then as you intended? You might have killed me!"

"You would have been rightly served."

"Quite so, my dear fellow, quite so; but you would have hanged for it. And it can hardly be worth that to you."

Pegram cursed him and raved in an almost theatrical manner. But Wirgman's stronger mind gradually quelled his spirit, and soothed his anger into a mere dull, expressionless resentment.

"Now go home, Pegram," he said in the end; "and if, when you have slept on it, you still feel as you feel now, come to me in the morning. I have always found a deal of common sense blossoming in the morning sun. The night, I think, was made for poets, lovers, and other madmen whose ranting needs the cloak of darkness to disguise its sentimentality."

Pegram still lingered a little while, but in the end, with a sulky threat to return to the matter on the morrow in cold blood, he turned away and was gone. Wirgman continued to stand where he was until the other had been assimilated in the night and the sound of his steps had died away. Then with a short laugh of satisfaction, he sat down and carefully thought out the situation as it stood.

By comparison with what he had achieved, his next step was simple, for it depended upon his own unaided efforts and nowise upon such fortuitous circumstances as had helped him hitherto.

Satisfied after some few minutes' deliberation, he rose again, and, flinging down his hat — in which were the initials "R. W." — he slipped quietly, over the edge of the cliff, and cautiously undertook what even in broad daylight was a difficult descent. Carefully groping his way, he reached the little creek below, and stood at last upon the shingle which the receding tide had left moist. He saw something glimmering, and picked up Pegram's silver-mounted walking-stick. He almost chuckled as he weighed it in his hand.

"Another link," he muttered.

Very deliberately he drew out his penknife, and inflicted never so slight a cut upon one of the fingers of his left hand. He smeared the blood upon the stick, and threw it down where it would lie beyond the reach of the tide. That done, he climbed over the rocks that bounded the creek, and struck out briskly along the shore towards Alwyn Bay, a watering-place some five miles along the coast.

At a quarter to eleven he was in Alwyn Bay railway-station, having rid himself of his conspicuous light overcoat on the way, and wearing a soft, black hat, of a light texture that had rendered it easily portable in the pocket of his discarded garment. He presented at the left-luggage office a ticket for a bag which earlier in the day he had left there in the name of Hodgson, and which bore the initials "C. S. H."

He caught the eleven o'clock train to Liverpool, secured a carriage to himself, and by, means of a safety razor he rid himself of his rather luxurious black beard and moustachios. Such other characteristic changes did he effect that he would have had keen eyes indeed who could have recognised Roger Wirgman in the man who at half-past two in the morning entered the name of Cyril S. Hodgson in the register of the Adelphi Hotel at Liverpool.

Towards noon next day — it was Wednesday — he drove down to the Cunard offices, and booked his passage by the liner sailing that afternoon for New York. This done, he returned to lunch at his hotel well pleased with the general trend of events.

Firstly, his disappearance from the hotel at Port Wimbush would be noticed, and it would be remembered that he had left word that he was going to the Head. The landlord of the Swan would give evidence how Harry Pegram, in an unmistakable state of excitement, had asked for him ten minutes later, and upon being informed whither he was gone, had followed like a man with purpose set. The cliff would no doubt be visited, and his hat would be found. This would arouse the suspicions of the police, and the creek below would be inspected. There they would find Pegram's stick smeared with blood and this would give their suspicions a definite goal. They would make inquiries, and discover the feud that existed between Pegram and himself. They would also hear of the stormy interview he had had with Miss Drummond that same evening. Thus his disappearance and the evidence of foul play, accompanied by the positive evidence that Pegram had been the last man known to have been in his company, and yet the evidence of motive on the part of Pegram, would draw an uncommonly tight net about his rival.

Miss Drummond — by virtue of what had passed, and knowing the spirit in which Pegram had set out — would be the first to believe in his guilt. So that even were he to escape hanging — which Wirgman doubted in view of the singularly heavy combination of circumstantial evidence — his life must become that of an outcast and a pariah, and Miss Drummond he could never marry.

In all this there was a certain sweet satisfaction. Yet Wirgman reflected with still greater satisfaction upon the fact that he had proven pet theory of his to be correct. Under very exceptional circumstances, and finding himself heavily handicapped, he had accomplished the destruction of a fellow-creature in a manner that could not possibly implicate him.

In the morning and noon editions of the papers there was no report whatever of any tragedy at Wimbush. As he was going on board at four o'clock that afternoon, he bought a late edition of an evening paper, and with this he stepped briskly toward the gangway. Already he had one foot upon it when suddenly a cheery voice somewhere behind him hailed him with:

"Hallo, Wirgman!"

Utterly taken off his guard, he looked round. Then, suddenly recollecting himself and his changed identity, he sought to assume an air of naturalness, as though his turning as the name was called had been no more than a coincidence. But a burly individual in a serge suit confronted him, and laid a singularly significant and possessive hand upon his shoulder, murmuring into his ear:

"Roger Wirgman, I arrest you!"

He started back, and his thoughts worked with the rapidity of lightning. Had Pegram by any chance suspected his conspiracy, and forestalled the discovery of his disappearance?

"In God's name, on what charge?" he blurted out.

"On the charge of murdering Henry Stanhope Pegram last night on Wimbush Head."

A ghastly pallor spread upon his lean face.

"Are you mad?" he choked.

"You had best not make a scene," murmured the detective, adding the formal reminder that anything he said would be taken as evidence against him.

Like a man in a dream, Wirgman allowed the detective and his companion to lead him away from the gathering crowd, and take him to the waiting-room, where they locked themselves up with him.

"Our train is due out in a quarter of an hour," he heard one say to the other.

Then he remembered the paper in his grasp, and, thinking that there he might find the solution of this marvel, he opened it with trembling hands, and was confronted by the headlines:

SHOCKING MURDER AT WIMBUSH
Flight of the Murderer

Swiftly his eyes devoured the bald, newspaper narrative that told how Harry Pegram's body had been discovered the night before on Wimbush Head, death being due to fracture of the skull. The dead man had been rifled of all money and valuables, and theft had at first been thought the motive of the crime. But the lady to whom Mr. Pegram was engaged had told the police a story — since corroborated — which gave rise to the theory that the theft was a blind rather than a motive. It was known that a deadly enmity existed between the deceased and Mr. Roger Wirgman, of Copmore Gardens, W. This latter gentleman had come down from town that day; and it was known that he and Pegram had been together on Wimbush Head that evening. A hat containing the initials "R. W.," and which was identified as belonging to Wirgman, was discovered a few hundred yards from the spot where the body, had been found, and, on the beach below, Pegram's stick, smeared with blood which the murderer had no doubt wrenched from his hand and used against him. He read how the police — by means beyond his understanding — had succeeded in tracking him to the left-luggage office at Alwyn Bay, and how they were on the spoor at the time of going to press. That powerful imagination which he had taken such pride in showed him now, as in a flash, how each item of evidence he had manufactured so sedulously to serve against Pegram would weigh a hundredfold more heavily against himself under the existing circumstances. In addition, there was his flight — that most damning incrimination — under an assumed name and in altered personality, to say nothing of the threats he had uttered against Pegram, and the purpose which he had announced was taking him to Port Wimbush.

He realised that he was indeed hoist with his own petard, doomed irrevocably, and for a crime that was none of his committing.

But even in that hour of supreme defeat and bitter agony he contended that his theory was still right. Here was a fortuitous circumstance which he could not have foreseen. The whole of his elaborate scheme had crumbled and collapsed because it had occurred to some vulgar thief to hit Harry Pegram over the head that he might rob him.

The Face of the Clock

Tricked out in brocaded silk of a yellow so daring that few men could have carried it with success, his wig a triumph of the perruquier's art, powdered with delicate daintiness, his wrists and throat set in cascades of priceless Mecklin, and his cravat scintillant with diamonds, René de Bardelys stepped into his admirably appointed salon, and complacently surveyed his dazzling person in the long mirror that was his closest friend.

The Vicomte de Bardelys had acquired the fame of being the handsomest fellow, the readiest wit, the most seductive gallant and the prettiest swordsman at the Court of Louis the Well-beloved. He could turn out the daintiest of verses, and sing them like an angel upon occasion; his dancing was a miracle of elegance, and showed to advantage the shapeliest leg at the Louvre; his birth was lofty, his honour unimpeachable, and his successes with the small-sword outnumbered almost his victories with the gentler weapons that are employed against the gentler sex.

With so many advantages well might it be forgiven him that he was not rich. He kept a small, but choicely-equipped, establishment in the Rue Véronique until the time when a rich alliance should afford him quarters that sorted better with the nobility of his person. His personnel consisted of a cook he had brought from Italy and a valet born in his father's service. The cook was taking a holiday that night, whilst his valet, after assisting him to dress, was gone on an errand to Passy.

Bardelys was to attend a rout that night at the Hotel de Savignon, at which he looked for a great happening — his betrothal to the marquis's eldest daughter, a lady upon whose beauty and whose chill indifference Bardelys had by no means been the only one to write verses. Yet what did it signify that a regiment of suitors should vie for her? What did it even signify to Bardelys that the lady herself should have few smiles for him? The favour of the marquis, her father, was his, and upon this he built the proud edifice of his hopes. Savignon was a shrewd man, and in Bardelys he saw one who might be destined to great things when endowed with such wealth as with his daughter he could bestow upon him. He was a son-in-law after the old man's heart; a son-in-law that might later be of pride and utility to him.

There had been trouble and to spare with the daughter. A young Provençal poet — one Prosper de la Haudraye — had for a moment threatened to send awry the plans of the father and of the favoured suitor. He was the owner of a pale, thoughtful face, melancholy eyes, and a yet more melancholy purse, upheld,

however, by the patronage of the Duke of Bourgogne, to whom, indeed, he owed
his presence at Court. This presumptuous ballad-monger, it was plain for all to
see, was desperately enamoured of Honorée de Savignon. And soon, indeed, it
became no less apparent to all that his passion was returned. To all do I say? No,
not to all — one there was who could not, would not, see it. That one was La
Haudraye himself. He loved her madly, desperately, with a love that in gloomier
moments he feared would drive him to self-destruction when he should be forced
— as forced some day he thought he must be — to pass out of her ways of life.
For though both Bardelys and Savignon, seeing what was toward, might dub him
presumptuous, yet in this matter of love for Honorée he was too humble — too
conscious of the distance between them to dare so much as to conceive the
thought that she might come to care for him.

And so in the end she came to translate his humility into indifference; she fell
to believing that he but looked upon her as a likely abstract around which to weave
the fabric of his rhymes — that for the woman in her he cared nothing.

Now Bardelys had suddenly manifested an interest in the young poet. He had
courted him, heaped favours upon him, and gradually drawn him to himself until
he came to be looked upon as the youth's most ardent patron. Then broadcast —
yet with artful secrecy — he had spread a scandalous, villainous story that had set
a damning blot upon the young man's honour. The poison did its work well.
Mademoiselle de Savignon was a lady of lofty sentiments — grotesquely lofty for
an age so lax — and with the disgust and loathing which we never visit save upon
those that once we esteemed, but have found unworthy, she now turned from La
Haudraye. And so the danger that for a moment had threatened Bardelys's suit
was averted.

That the lady did not love him troubled him no whit. Was she not well
endowed? And were not her endowments Bardelys's real desire? For the rest no
doubt she would come to love him; leastways, she should have the opportunity.
And if ever La Haudraye should learn that he it was who had spread the scandal,
what of it? Was he not the best blade in Paris? If the poet did chance upon the
discovery and demand satisfaction — by heaven he should have it, and a last home
in God's acre to succeed it.

That very thought was in his mind when in the mirror he saw the heavy *portière*
of crimson velvet lifted, and the pale face and melancholy eyes of Prosper de la
Haudraye himself. Bardelys swung round with a sharp exclamation of surprise.

"La Haudraye? How came you in?"

"By the street door. It yielded to my weight when I was about to knock. You
are alone?"

"As you see. My servant has just left me on an errand to M. de Valce at Passy."

An inscrutable smile played round the corner of Prosper's mobile mouth as he
eyed the vicomte.

"We are gay tonight," he commented easily, unwrapping his cloak. "Into what
fields of conquest does Cupid lead you?"

"He does not lead me, La Haudraye," laughed the other. For all that the poet's humour struck him as warped, and stung him never so lightly with uneasiness. "He does not lead; it is I who drive the urchin in the impetuosity of my wooing." He glanced at Prosper, and the temptation to flaunt his victory in the face of the vanquished proved too strong for his mean soul. "Tomorrow," he added, "I trust that all Paris will ring with the news of my betrothal to Mademoiselle de Savignon."

"You are assured?" asked La Haudraye calmly, without relaxing his smile.

"I am assured," answered the other with an eloquent glance at the splendid figure his mirror reflected. The poet dropped into a chair, and looking his companion straight between the eyes:

"Twixt this and dawn," said he, "much may betide."

Bardelys looked at his visitor. A vague alarm was taking hold of him and showing in his face. Then he laughed disdainfully.

"Croak on," he cried in make-believe playfulness. "Tell me of omens, of spells, of adverse circumstances, tell me even that the lady loves me not, and I will answer you that I fear all this as little as — as I fear the summer breeze."

"Yet men have died of chills for which the summer breeze was answerable."

"Oh, ca!" laughed Bardelys ironically, "behold a prodigy— a poet turned wit."

"It is high time when a wit turns Judas. They account you a wit, do they not, those fools at Court?" The intonation was ominous, and Bardelys experienced a chill of apprehension.

"You are obscure. Is this a metaphor?" he asked with a sneer. "I am afraid I must trouble you to elucidate."

"Vraiement?" La Haudraye sneered back, "and you a wit? I always held you a man of poor imagination, vicomte; yet that vile story concerning me that all Paris has listened to so avidly seems to prove me wrong."

"How know you that?" cried the other off his guard, to bite his lip in chagrin a moment later.

With a sigh that ended in a laugh of disdain Prosper got slowly to his feet.

"Perhaps it was that summer breeze you spoke of whispered it in passing; perhaps it is that you have just told me yourself what I no more than suspected. To be so careless!" he mocked him. "*Fi-donc*, my beautiful, dazzling Bardelys — *fi-donc!*"

Bardelys was thinking rapidly. What had he to fear? Did this fellow's inclinations run to casting aside the quill for the sword? He would willingly let him have his way.

"I made no secret of it," he brazened. "Had you asked me whence came this information touching your infamy, I had told you that it was of my publishing. It is high time the world should know you — "

"Stop!" blazed La Haudraye, livid with anger. "Be no more of a liar than was necessary for your purpose. You know you lied — that no vestige of truth lay in the foul calumny you have spread. Add not unto that splendid batch of falsehoods the unnecessary falsehood of affecting to have received the information and believed it. You have succeeded in robbing me of the esteem of the only person in this world that — . But there," he broke off, "what do your motives signify? As noisome are they as lies would be effete. But, *par Dieu*, your knavery shall yield you little profit."

"I am at your service," returned Bardelys, quivering with rage. Then, in a last attempt to justify himself, " You stood in my way," he said, "and had you been a man of the sword I had removed you in a more open manner. As it was, men would have said that I had murdered you, and so I was forced to adopt another means. But since you will have it so, I am at your service now."

"Aye, you count upon your sword play, do you not?" blazed the other. "I can understand that a man treading your ways of life should need to learn the trick of guarding what you call your honour. But you are wrong, my beautiful vicomte, my purveyor of scandal, my pretty traducer," he pursued, trembling in the intensity of his passion. "You are wrong, for I will not fight you."

"Why then are you here?"

"I came to ascertain whether the thing was indeed as I had conjectured from what was told me. I shall go from here to my patron the Duke of Bourgogne. I shall lay the facts before him, and I think I can promise you that before the night is out he will have vindicated me, and branded you a liar throughout Paris."

There followed a moment's pause as though the time were needed for the poet's meaning to sink into Bardelys's mind. Then with an oath he turned and took a step towards the table where lay his sword.

"*Par la mor Dieu*," he swore, "you shall not leave this house alive."

Prosper watched him a second with wide-open eyes. Then, obeying a sudden instinct, he sprung after him, and even as Bardelys's hand closed upon the pummel of his sword, La Haudraye's poniard was planted to the hilt in his back under the left shoulder-blade. Bardelys uttered a hideous, gurgling cry and flung out his arms; then he hurtled forward and fell prone, striking the table and rolling thence to the ground. Hist right hand swept the overmantel in his fall, and brought down the ormolu clock with a crash on to the hearth.

When the thing was done a cold horror crept over the slayer. With fascinated eyes he gazed down upon what a moment ago had been the magnificent Bardelys, and watched the twitching and stretching of the limbs that announced his death. His wig was displaced, revealing the closely cropped hair beneath, and on his brave coat of yellow brocade a deep crimson stain was spreading.

Next La Haudraye's horror was shouldered aside by fear. Here was matter enough to hang him, and M. de Sartines, the Lieutenant-General of Police, was as stern as he was astute. At any moment someone might come. He must go. To be found there would be fatal.

His face was deathly white, and his blue eyes were rendered black by the dilation of their pupils. Fearfully he looked about him, and his glance lighted on the ormolu clock, broken and stopped by its fall, its hands pointing to half-past seven. With a shudder he caught up his hat, and stealthily, as if afraid of waking him who lay, he tiptoed across to the door. A moment he paused in the act of lifting the *portière*, and his eyes wandered back to the thing lying by the hearth. Then in a sudden act of positive terror he dashed out of the room, down the stairs, and out into the street.

Now scarce had the crimson door-curtain fallen behind the departing La Haudraye than it was raised again, and a woman appeared, who, having raised it, seemed to clutch at it for support. A black domino concealed her dress, but the hood had fallen back, and revealed the powdered head, coiffed in a white lace mantille, and under this a face well-nigh as white, out of which by contrast a pair of startled eyes looked singularly black. A moment she stood there in hesitation or to gather strength, then letting fall the *portière* she advanced into the room, her hands — in one of which she held a mask — pressed to her agitated bosom.

With all speed had La Haudraye repaired to his lodging, and there he sat now, revolving in his turbulent mind the awful happening of the last half-hour. He took in the end the foolish resolve of seeking safety in flight, and he summoned his servant to bid him pack. But upon coming in answer to his call the fellow advanced that there was a lady below inquiring for him.

"A lady?" quoth Prosper. "Who may she be?"

"She is masked, monsieur, and would give no name."

It suggested itself to La Haudraye that this might be some Court beauty who sought to beg or hire his pen for the writing of a poetic answer to verses sent her by some gallant. Here was a thing he was inflicted with at times, and at times he consented to please them. But such a time was not the present.

"I'll be plagued by no woman," he snapped with a testiness usually foreign to his docile ways. "Bid her go to the devil."

The words were scarce uttered when the door opened, and his unknown visitor stood under the lintel. He turned upon her angrily.

"This intrusion — " he began.

"You will forgive when you learn how pressing is my business," said a voice that drove the colour from his cheek and set his every nerve a quivering. With a curt gesture he dismissed his servant, and having closed the door after him he faced her, consternation writ large upon his countenance.

"Mademoiselle, are you mad?" he cried. "I know not what business there can be to bring you here. But what of your good name, mademoiselle? Honoree de Savignon in the lodging of the Provençal rhymster, La Haudraye — a fine story that, as God lives, for every scurvy tongue at the Louvre to dilate upon."

"Monsieur," she answered very calmly, "I have come to ask you to forgive the ready ear I lent to those that traduced you."

"You have discovered that?" he cried, his joy at the thing putting from his mind both the horror of his recent deed and his consternation at her presence.

"Within the hour, monsieur, and I have hastened hither to tell you."

He took a step towards her. Everything was forgotten now but the glorious fact that she beheld him free of the stain that calumny had splashed upon his honour.

"It is like you; it is worthy of your great heart, mademoiselle," he began. Then he stopped short, and his tone changed again to mild reproach. "But you should not have come here; you should not have come,'" he protested, shaking his head.

"I had yet another reason," she answered. "The man that published this has met with — justice. M. de Bardelys is dead."

He recoiled until he touched the wall. His brows were drawn together; his eyes wide open and intent upon her.

"Merciful God," he whispered, "is it known already?"

"No, it is not known yet. His valet has gone to Passy, and could hardly return before half-past eight. It is unlikely to be discovered until then."

"But you — ?"

"I was there when he died. Listen, monsieur. I heard something this evening that set me thinking you had been traduced to me. I pondered over it, and my suspicions gaining ground, I resolved to go there and then ascertain the truth. I thought of M. de Bardelys. He was your associate, your intimate, the likeliest man to be possessed of exact knowledge, and so to him I went. I got away undetected by the garden gate, and I made my way to his house. I found his door open, and, entering, I mounted the stairs. I was on the point of stepping into the *salon*, when I heard your voice. You were just arrived, for you were telling him how you had found his door ajar. From behind the curtain I heard all that passed between you."

But La Haudraye was lost in amazement at the fact that to ascertain his innocence she had jeopardised her fair name by repairing to Bardelys. To this wonder he now gave utterance, and yet blind fool that he was — he who spent his nights writing of love, and his days dreaming of more writings that had love for their theme — he detected not the mainspring of her action, else had his wonder perchance assumed a different shape.

"You did this for me?" he kept repeating in that stupid surprise of his. Then suddenly his wonder grew a thousandfold. "And knowing what you know, mademoiselle, you have still come here to me — to me, a murderer!"

But she shook her head.

"Hush, monsieur. It was no murder. What you did you did in self-defence. Had you not seized your chance, the next moment would have found you dead."

"How good, how merciful you are, mademoiselle," he said, lifting her hand and touching it never so lightly, timidly almost, with his lips. A second she waited, but he added nothing. Had he no eyes to see, this songster from Provence? Had he no wit to discern why she came to see no murder in his deed? Alas! it would seem that he had not. And so he stood silent until she told him she must go.

"I will escort you, mademoiselle. You must not go alone."

"Let your servant attend me," she replied, raising her hood. "And now, monsieur, a word of advice. Nobody knows what has passed to-night. See to it that you do not betray yourself. Go about your business as though naught had chanced. Affect surprise when they tell you he is dead, and should suspicion fasten on you — it may, monsieur — deny your part in this affair, and leave the rest to heaven."

"Must I lie then?" he asked.

"If there be need. Think you they would believe the truth? Would they believe it was in self-defence you acted? Not they. The vicomte has powerful friends who will be but too eager to avenge him. And so, since they will not accept the truth if you tell it them, deny all knowledge of what has passed."

"But what if I was seen to enter or leave his house?"

"Shall that prove you killed him? Say, if you will, that you were with him, but be careful to add that you left him alive. Monsieur, I must go; it is almost on the stroke of eight."

At her request, and since she utterly refused his escort, he called his servant to go with her. He took up a taper, and lighted her to the door. In the moment of taking leave she turned to his valet.

"What's o'clock?" she asked. And, as if in answer to her question, the boom of the bell of Notre Dame was borne to them across the river.

"It is on the stroke of eight, madame," replied the man.

"We must hurry then," said she, stepping out.

What La Haudraye had suggested as a possibility proved an actual fact. He had been seen and recognised as he approached Bardelys's door that evening, and it was mainly upon that information that a couple of hours after mademoiselle's visit he was arrested at his lodging by M. de Sartines's police. He was resolved to make a fight for it, but he had little hope of success. He was too well acquainted with the astuteness and seeming omniscience of M. de Sartines, and in anticipation of his examination upon the morrow he spent a very restless night.

At noon next day they conducted him to the office of M. de Sartines, where he was to find how busily the lieutenant-general had been collecting evidence. Among those he had summoned, and who now confronted La Haudraye, were a couple of gentlemen of his acquaintance, another whose face was familiar to him, and M. de Bardelys's valet.

"It grieves me, M. de la Haudraye," Sartines began, when he was interrupted by a noise of voices without. The door suddenly opened, and to Prosper's amazement Mademoiselle de Savignon swept magnificently into the chamber. Sartines gasped and frowned, but before he could utter a word.

"M. de Sartines," she announced, "I am here in the interests of justice. From what I learn of this affair, I am led to think that I can afford you evidence that may be of value."

The lieutenant-general shot a keen glance at her from under his shaggy brows.

"That will be very welcome, mademoiselle;" said he. "Be good enough to close the door, Lescure Bretel, a chair for mademoiselle."

Then, calmly, as though there had been no interruption, Sartines turned again to La Haudraye.

"M. de la Haudraye, it grieves me to meet you under these circumstances, but the evidence we have collected places a heavy weight of suspicion upon you. You are charged with the murder of M. de Bardelys."

"I trust, monsieur," replied La Haudraye with self-possession, "that in the course of this inquiry you will realise how groundless is the charge."

The first evidence taken was that of Bardelys's valet, who deposed to having found his master, at about half-past eight on the previous night, lying dead, with a dagger wound in his back. Next the man whose face was familiar to Prosper bore witness that at a few minutes before half-past seven he had passed M. de la Haudraye in the Rue Véronique, and that he appeared to be going in the direction of Bardelys's house. Next the other two gentlemen both deposed that being with M. de la Haudraye on the previous evening in the ante-chamber of the Hotel de Bourgogne, it had transpired that certain scandalous rumours concerning him then current in Paris might have been disseminated by M. de Bardelys. La Haudraye, they attested, had flown into a great rage, swearing that he would see the vicomte forthwith, and that if he found true what he now only suspected, Bardelys should pay dearly for his slander.

Sartines was still questioning them closely as to the exact words employed by La Haudraye when suddenly Honorée's voice came clear and crisp to interrupt him.

"Monsieur," she exclaimed without ceremony, "we are wasting time."

Sartines's brows closed in a scowl.

"At what hour did the murder take place?"

"I beseech you," said Sartines with polite restraint, " to permit me to go about this matter in my own way."

"If you will answer my question, I have an idea that you will not need to go much further in any way," she insisted. "At what hour was M. de Bardelys killed?"

"Why, since you insist — at eight o'clock."

From mademoiselle's eyes there flashed a look of triumph; from La Haudraye's one of bewilderment.

"You have evidence of this— positive evidence?" she demanded.

"The most positive. As he fell M. de Bardelys appeared to have dashed a clock from his overmantel. This was found broken on the hearth beside him, and its face tells a very positive story. The hands pointed to the hour of eight, at which it had stopped when it fell. So that the proof is a conclusive one."

Prosper's bewilderment increased.

"Have you asked M. de la Haudraye where he was to be found at eight o'clock last night."

"Not yet, mademoiselle. We have not gone so far. Still," and he turned now to the poet, "can you answer this question that mademoiselle suggests?"

"But, yes," replied the amazed La Haudraye. "I was at my lodging in the Rue de Richelieu."

"You can prove it by witnesses?"

"My servant."

"Before I can order your release, I shall require evidence to corroborate such a statement coming from a man that happens to be your servant."

Though he should hang for his silence he could not tell those present that mademoiselle had been with him.

"It will be difficult, I am afraid," he was beginning, when suddenly Honorée stood up.

"It will not be difficult, M. de Sartines," she announced. "For that purpose I am here, having heard at what hour the crime took place, and knowing that I could give such evidence as must ensure M. de la Haudraye's release. I am that other witness you require. I was with M. de la Haudraye last evening, and I left his lodging as eight o'clock was striking from Notre Dame."

"Mademoiselle, what are you saying?" cried out Prosper in dismay.

There was a moment's silence. Then:

"You do well to ask mademoiselle that," put in Sartines.   "Surely, mademoiselle, you cannot expect us to believe this: that you were at this gentleman's lodging; that — Oh, the thing is incredible. You do not know what you are saying."

His vehemence and the curious looks of those that stood about made her realise to the full what she had done. A deep red flush spread on her cheeks and mounted to her brow. She hung her head, and for a second she was silent. Then an inspiration came to her. It was the only thing.

"I do know what I am saying, monsieur," she said very quietly. "I am telling you that M. de la Haudraye is my lover." She paused a second. Then she added: "We are to be married within the week."

La Haudraye's face was very white. With difficulty he had restrained an outcry.

The events of the next few moments were as the happenings of a dream to him, and not until the cool April breeze refreshed him, and he found himself in the street at liberty again, with Honorée beside him, did things resume their semblance of reality.

"Mademoiselle," he was saying, "you had been better advised to have left me to die, since you compel me, as a gentleman, to die now so that you may be saved the consequences of your rash words."

"What words were those, monsieur?"

"That we are to be wed."

"Well, monsieur," she asked, scarce above a whisper and stealing an upward glance at his comely, solemn face, "would you dare to give me the lie? Would you thus return evil for good, and make me regret that I changed the face of the clock by pushing the hands half an hour forward?"

And that is how it came to pass that Prosper's melancholy eyes were melancholy no more.

The Red Mask

During the last year of his reign, it was a common thing for Mazarin to repair to the masques given by the King at the Louvre.

In a long domino, the ample folds of which cloaked his tall, lean figure beyond all recognition, it was his custom to mingle in the crowd — all unconscious of his presence — in the hope of gleaning through the channels of court gossip some serviceable information.

These visits to the Louvre were kept a profound secret from all save Monsieur André, the valet who dressed him, and myself, the captain of his guards, who escorted him.

It was usual upon such occasions for the Cardinal to retire to his own apartments, under the pretence of desiring to be a-bed at an earlier hour. Once screened from the gaze of the curious, he would prepare for the ball, and when he was ready, André would summon me from the ante-chamber. On the night in question, however, I was startled out of the reverie into which I had lapsed whilst watching two pages throwing at dice and discussing the arts of the practice, by the Cardinal's own voice uttering my name:

"Monsieur de Cavaignac."

At the sound of the rasping voice, which plainly told me that his Eminence was out of humour, one of the lads sat precipitately upon the dice, to hide from his master's eyes the unholy nature of their pastime, whilst I, astonished at the irregularity of the proceedings, turned sharply round and made a profound obeisance.

One glance at Mazarin told me there was trouble. An angry flush was upon his sallow face, and his eyes glittered in a strange, discomforting manner, whilst his jeweled fingers tugged nervously at the long pointed beard which he still wore, after the fashion of the days of his late Majesty, Louis XIII.

"Follow me, Monsieur," he said; whereupon, respecting his mood, I lifted my sword to prevent its clanking, and passed into the study, which divided the bedroom from the ante-chamber.

Suppressing, with masterly self-control, the anger that swelled within him, Mazarin held out to me a strip of paper.

"Read," he said laconically, as if afraid to trust his voice with more.

Taking the paper as I was bid, I gazed earnestly at it, and marvelled to myself whether the Cardinal's dotage was upon him, for, stare as I would, I could detect no writing.

Noting my perplexity, Mazarin took a heavy silver candlestick from the table, and placing himself at my side, held it so as to throw a strong light upon the paper. Wonderingly, I examined it afresh, and discovered this time the faint impression of such characters as might have been written with a pencil upon another sheet placed over the one that I now held.

With infinite pains, and awed at what I read, I had contrived to master the meaning of the first two lines, when the Cardinal, growing impatient at my slowness, set down the candlestick and snatched the paper from my hand.

"You have seen?" he asked.

"Not all, your eminence," I replied.

"Then I will read it to you; listen."

And in a slightly shaken monotone he read out to me the following words:

"The Italian goes disguised tonight to attend the King's masque. He will arrive at ten, wearing a black silk domino and a red vizor."

Slowly he folded the document, and then, turning his sharp eyes upon me:

"Of course," he said, "you do not know the handwriting; but *I* am well acquainted with it; it is that of my valet, André."

"It is a gross breach of confidence, if you are certain that it alludes to your Eminence," I ventured, timidly.

"A breach of confidence, Chevalier!" he cried in derision. "A breech of confidence! I took you for a wiser man. Does this message suggest nothing more than a breach of confidence to you?"

I started, aghast, as his meaning dawned upon me, and noting this.

"Ah, I see that it does," he said, with a curious smile. "Well, what do you say now?"

"I scarcely like to word my thoughts, Monseigneur," I answered.

"Then I will word them for you," he retorted. "There is a conspiracy afoot."

"God forbid!" I cried, then added quickly, "Impossible! Your Eminence is too well beloved."

"*Pish!*" he answered, with a frown; "you forget, de Cavaignac, this is the Palais Mazarin, and not the Louvre. We need no courtiers here."

" 'Twas but the truth I spoke, Monseigneur," I expostulated.

"Enough!" he exclaimed, "we are wasting time. I am assured that he is in league with one, or may be more, foul knaves of his kidney, whose purpose it is — well, what is the usual purpose of a conspiracy?"

"Your Eminence!" I cried, in horror.

"Well?" he said, coldly, and with a slight elevation of the eyebrows.

"Pardon me for suggesting that you may be in error. What evidence is there to show that you are the person to whom that note alludes?"

He gazed at me in undisguised astonishment, and maybe pity, at my dullness.

"Does it not say, '*the Italian*'?"

"But then, Monseigneur, pardon me again, you are not the only Italian in Paris; there are several at court — Botillani, del'Asta, de Agostini, Magnani. Are these not all Italians? Is it not possible that the note refers to one of them?"

"Do you think so?" he inquired, raising his eyebrows.

"*Ma foi*, I see no reason why it should not."

"But does it not occur to you that in such a case there would be little need for mystery? Why should not André have mentioned his name?"

"The course of leaving out the name appears to me, if Monseigneur will permit me to say so, an equally desirable one, whether the party conspired against, be your Eminence or a court fop."

"You argue well," he answered, with a chilling sneer. "But come with me, de Cavaignac, and I will set such an argument before your eyes as can leave no doubt in your mind. *Venez*."

Obediently I followed him through the white and gold folding-doors into his bedroom. He walked slowly across the apartment, and pulling aside the curtains he pointed to a long black silk domino lying across the bed; then, putting out his hand, he drew forth a scarlet mask and held it up to the light, so that I might clearly see its colour.

"Are you assured?" he asked.

I was indeed! Whatever doubts there may have been in my mind as to Monsieur André's treachery were now utterly dispelled by this overwhelming proof.

Having communicated my opinion to his Eminence, I awaited, in silence, his commands.

For some moments he paced the room slowly with bent head and toying with his beard. At last he stopped.

"I have sent that knave André upon a mission that will keep him engaged for some moments yet. Upon his return I shall endeavour to discover the name of his accomplice, or rather," he added scornfully, "of his master. I half-suspect —" he began, then suddenly turning to me, "Can you think of any one, Cavaignac?" he enquired.

I hastened to assure him that I could not, whereat he shrugged his shoulders in a manner meant to express the value he set upon my astuteness.

"*Ohimè!*" he cried bitterly, "how unenviable is my position. Traitors and conspirators in my very house, and none to guard me against them!"

"Your Eminence!" I exclaimed, almost indignantly, for this imputation to one who had served him as I had done was cruel and unjust.

He shot a sharp glance at me from under his puckered brows, then softening suddenly, as he saw the look upon my face, he came over to where I stood, and placing his soft white hand upon my shoulder,

"Forgive me, Cavaignac," he said gently, "forgive me, my friend, I have wronged you. I know that you are true and faithful — and the words I spoke were wrung from me by bitterness at the thought that one upon whom I have heaped favours should so betray me — probably," he added bitterly, "for the sake of a few paltry *pistoles*, even as Iscariot betrayed *his* Master.

"I have so few friends, Cavaignac," he went on, in a tone of passing sadness, "so few that I cannot afford to quarrel with the only one of whom I am certain. There are many who fear me; many who cringe to me, knowing that I have the power to make or break them — but none who love me. And yet I am envied!" and he broke into a short bitter laugh, "Envied. 'There goes the true King of France' say noble and simple, as they doff their hats and bow low before the great and puissant Cardinal Mazarin. They forget my fortes but they denounce my foibles, and envying, they malign me, for malice is ever the favourite mask of envy. They envy me, a lonely old man amid all the courtiers who cringe like curs about me. Ah, Cavaignac, 'twas wisely said by that wise man, the late Cardinal Richelieu, that often those whom the world most envies, stand most in need of pity."

I was deeply moved by his words and by the low tone, now sad, now fierce, in which they were delivered — for it was unusual for Mazarin to say so much in a breath, and I knew that Andre's treachery must have stricken him sorely.

It was not for me to endeavour by argument to convince him that he was in error; moreover, I knew full well that all he said was true, and being no lisping courtier, to whom the art of falsehood comes as naturally as that of breathing, but a blunt soldier who spoke but what was in my heart, I held my peace.

With those keen eyes of his he read what was in my mind; taking me by the hand, he pressed it warmly.

"Thanks, my friend, thanks!" he murmured, "you at least are true, true as the steel you wear and honour, and so long as this weak hand of mine can sway men's fortunes, so long as I live, you shall not be forgotten. But go now, Cavaignac, leave me; André may return at any moment, and it would awaken his suspicions to find you here, for there are none so suspicious as traitors. Await my orders in the ante-chamber, as usual."

"But is it safe to leave your Eminence alone with him?" I cried, in some concern.

He laughed softly.

"Think you the knave is eager to enjoy the gibbet he has earned at Montfaucon?" he said. "Nay, have no fear, it will not come to violence."

"A rat at bay is a dangerous foe," I answered.

"I know, I know," he replied, and so I have taken my precautions — unnecessary as I think them — *voyez!*" and as he opened his scarlet robe I beheld the glitter of a shirt of mail beneath.

" 'Tis well," I replied, and, bowing, I withdrew.

In the dark and silent ante-chamber — for the pages and their ungodly toys were gone when I returned — I paced slowly to and fro, musing sadly over all that the Cardinal had said, and cursing in my heart that dog André. So bitter did I feel towards the villainous traitor, that, when at the end of half an hour I beheld him standing before me with a false smile upon his pale countenance, it was only by an effort that I refrained from striking him.

"Here is your domino, Monsieur de Cavaignac," he said, placing a long dark garment upon a chair back.

"Is his Eminence ready?" I inquired, in a surly tone. As my tone was usually a surly one, there was no reason why it should affect André upon this occasion; nor did it.

"His Eminence is almost ready," he replied. "He wishes you to wait in the study."

This was unusual and set me thinking. The conclusion I arrived at was that Mazarin had not yet opened his campaign against the luckless servant, but wished to have me within call when he did so.

Without a word to André I unbuckled my sword, as was my custom, and begged him to take it to my room, since I should have no further use for it that night.

"I cannot, Monsieur de Cavaignac," he answered; "you will pardon me, but his Eminence desired me to return at once. He is feeling slightly indisposed, and wishes me to accompany him to the Louvre tonight."

I was surprised indeed, but I did not betray myself by so much as a look. The ways of the Cardinal were strange and unfathomable, especially where justice was concerned, and I was well accustomed to them.

"Indeed!" I replied, gravely. "I trust that it prove nothing serious."

"God forbid!" cried the hypocrite, as he held the door for me to pass into the study; "think, Monsieur de Cavaignac, think what a loss it would be to France if anything were to happen to Monseigneur."

He crossed himself devoutly and his lips moved as if in prayer.

And I, infected by his pious mood, offered up a prayer to heaven with him, a prayer as fervent as any that my heart had ever formed, a prayer that the torturers might have his weakly body to toy with, before it was finally consigned to the hangman at Montfaucon.

When he had left me in the study, I leisurely donned the domino that he had brought me, and judging by what I knew must be taking place within the bedchamber that I should have to wait some little time, I seated myself and listened attentively for any sounds that might pierce the tapestried walls.

But strain my ears as I would, all that I caught was a piteous wail of the words:

"*Je le jure!*" followed by the Cardinal's laugh — so dreadful, so pitiless, so condemning — and the one word, "Forsworn!" then all became silent again.

I accounted for this by the knowledge that the Cardinal seldom raised, but rather lowered his voice, when angered, whilst André, aware of my vicinity, would probably take pains to keep his expostulations from my ears.

At length the door opened, and a figure emerged, clad in a black domino, the hood of which was so closely drawn over his head that I could not see whether he wore a mask or not. Behind him came another similarly clad, and so completely does a domino conceal the outlines of a figure that I did not know which was the Cardinal and which the valet, since they were both, more or less, of the same height. Nor, for that matter, would it have been possible to discern whether they were men, or women.

"Are you there, Cavaignac?" said Mazarin's voice.

"Here, your Eminence," I cried, springing up.

He who had spoken turned his face upon me, and a pair of eyes flashed at me through the holes of a scarlet mask.

I stood dumbfounded for a moment as I thought of the risk he was thus incurring. Then, remembering that he wore a shirt of mail, I grew easier in my mind.

I glanced at the other silent figure standing beside him with bent head, and wondered what had taken place. But I was given no time to waste in thinking, for as I rose —

"Come, Cavaignac," he said, "put on your mask and let us go." I obeyed him with that promptitude which twenty years of soldiering had taught me, and, throwing open the door of the antechamber, I led the way across to a certain panel with which I was well acquainted. A secret spring answered promptly to my touch, and the panel swung back, disclosing a steep and narrow flight of stairs.

Down this we proceeded swiftly, André first, for I cared not to risk being pushed, which would have entailed a broken neck. I followed close upon his heels, whilst the Cardinal brought up the rear. At the bottom I opened another secret door, and passing through, we emerged into the vestibule of a side and rarely-used entrance to the Palace Mazarin.

The next moment we stood in the silent and deserted street.

"Will you see if the carriage is waiting, Cavaignac," said the Cardinal.

I bowed, and was on the point of executing the command, when, laying his hand upon my arm —

"When we reach the Louvre," he said, "you will follow at a distance, lest by staying too close to me you should excite suspicion, and," he added, "on no account speak to me. Now see to the coach."

I walked rapidly to the corner of the Rue St. Honoré, where I found an old-fashioned vehicle, such as is used by the better bourgeoisie, in waiting.

With a whistle I aroused the half-slumbering driver, and bidding him sharply hold himself in readiness, I returned to his Eminence.

In silence I followed the two masked figures down the dark, slippery street, for it had rained during the day, and the stones were damp and greasy. The old coachman stood aside for us to enter, little dreaming that the eyes that scanned him through the scarlet mask were those of the all-powerful Cardinal.

He whipped up his horses, and we started off at a snail's pace, accompanied by a plentiful rumbling and jolting, particularly distasteful to one accustomed, as I was, to the saddle.

It was not, however, a long drive to the Louvre, and I was soon relieved, as the coach came to a standstill in a bye-street, as usual.

Alighting, I held my arm to the Cardinal, but, disregarding it, he stepped heavily to the ground unaided, followed by André, on whom I kept a sharp eye, lest the knave should attempt to run.

I followed them at a distance of some eight yards, as I had been ordered, marveling as I went what could be the Cardinal's plan of action.

We elbowed our way through a noisy dirty rabble, whom a dozen of the King's Guards could scarcely keep from obstructing the side entrance — used only by privileged individuals — in their curiosity to see the fanciful costumes of the maskers.

It was close upon midnight when we entered the ball-room. His Majesty, I learnt, had already withdrawn, feeling slightly indisposed; therefore, I concluded that if there was any serious conspiracy afoot, the blow — which otherwise might have been restrained by the King's presence — could not be long in falling.

Scarcely had we advanced a dozen paces, when my attention was drawn to a tall, thin man, of good bearing, dressed after the fashion of a jester of the days of the third or fourth Henry. He wore a black velvet tunic, which descended to his knees, with a hood surmounted by a row of bells; it was open in front, disclosing a doublet of yellow silk heavily slashed with red. In keeping with this he wore one red and one yellow stocking, and long pointed shoes of untanned leather.

The suit of motley admirably became his tall, lithe figure, and, in the light of that night's events, I have often marveled why he had chosen so conspicuous a disguise. At the time, however, I thought not of the figure he cut, but watched uneasily the manner in which he followed the Cardinal with his eyes, and, strange to tell, Mazarin returned his gaze with interest.

For some moments I observed his movements closely, and, certain that he was the man to whom André had betrayed his master's disguise, I drew instinctively nearer to the Cardinal.

Presently I lost sight of him in the glittering throng; then, as the musicians struck up a gay measure, the centre of the room was cleared for the dancers, and we were crushed rudely into a corner among the onlookers, he appeared suddenly before us once more.

His Eminence was just in front of me, and within arm's length of the jester; André stood motionless at my side, so motionless that I thought, for a moment, Mazarin must be mistaken.

There was a sudden lurch in the crowd, and, simultaneously, I heard a voice ring out loud and clear above the music, the hum of voices and the shuffling of the dancers' feet:

"Thus perish all traitors to the welfare of France!"

At the sound of those words, which sent a chill through my blood, I glanced quickly towards the jester and beheld the glitter of steel in his uplifted hand. Then, before any one could seize the murderer's arm, it had descended with terrific force, and the knife was buried in the Cardinal's breast.

Heedless of the soft low laugh which escaped the Judas beside me, I stood horror-stricken, yet confident in my mind that the shirt of mail worn by Mazarin would have resisted the poignard.

As I saw him, however, fall backwards, without so much as a groan, into the arms of a bystander; as I saw the red blood spurt forth and spread in a great shiny stain upon the black domino, a wild inarticulate cry escaped my lips.

"Notre Dame!" I shrieked the next moment, "You have killed him!" And I would have sprung forward to seize the murderer when suddenly a strong nervous hand was laid upon my shoulder, and a well-known voice, at the sound of which I stood as if bound by a spell, whispered in my ear:

"Silence, fool! Be still."

The music had ceased suddenly, the dancing had stopped and a funeral hush had fallen upon the throng as it pressed eagerly around the murdered man.

Contrary to my expectations, the assassin made no attempt to escape, but removing his vizor, he showed us the features of that notorious court bully, the Comte de St. Augére — a creature of the Prince de Condé. He folded his arms leisurely across his breast and stood regarding the silent crowd about him with a diabolical smile of scorn upon his thin lips.

Then, as a light gradually broke upon my mind, the masked figure beside me which I had hitherto regarded as André, moved swiftly forward and pulling back the hood from the head of the victim, removed the red mask.

I craned my neck and beheld, as I had expected, the pallid face of the valet set already in the unmistakable mould of the rigor mortis.

Presently a murmur went round the assembly breathing the words "The Cardinal!"

I looked up and saw Mazarin, erect, unmasked, and silent. From him I turned my eyes towards St. Augére; he had not yet met the Cardinal's gaze, and to him the whisper of the crowd had a different meaning; so he smiled on in his quiet scornful way until Mazarin awakened him to realities.

"Is this your handiwork, Monsieur de St. Augére?"

At the sound of that voice, so cold and terrible in its menace, the fellow started violently; he turned to the Cardinal, a look of pitiable terror coming into his eyes. As their glances met, the one so stern and steady, the other furtive and craven, St. Augére seemed as one suddenly smitten with ague; he darted a hurried glance at the victim, and as he beheld André, his face became as ashen as that of the corpse.

"You do not answer," Mazarin pursued; "there is no need, I saw the blow, and you still hold the dagger. You are I doubt not," — oh, the irony of his words! — "you are, I doubt not, surprised to see me here. But I heard of this and it was my intention to foil your purpose and to punish you, false noble that you are. Methinks, Monsieur, that you have wrought sufficient evil in your life without culminating it by so dastardly a deed as this. That you should have stooped to stab a poor defenceless valet, whom you considered below the dignity of your sword, this — fallen as you are — I had scarcely expected from one whose veins are fed by the blood of the St. Augéres. And to think," he continued in accents of withering scorn, "that you should attempt to throw upon your deed the glamour of patriotism! What harm has this poor wretch done France? Speak up! Have you naught to say?"

But rage, despair, and shame had choked the Count's utterance, and were fighting a mighty battle in his soul. So violent, that as the Cardinal paused to wait for his reply, his lips twitched convulsively for a moment, then, staggering forward he fell prone upon the ground, in a swoon.

"Call the guard, Monsieur de Cavaignac," said Mazarin to me. "That man has committed his last crime. A week in a dungeon of the Bastille and the companionship of a holy father, may fit him for a better life beyond the scaffold."

"You see," said his Eminence, an hour later, as we stood alone in his study, "if I had allowed the world to know for whom St. Augére's blow was intended, the world would have sympathised, as it always does, with a luckless conspirator; would, mayhap, have loved me less. Again, there are always fanatics ready to copy such acts as these, and had they known that what has ended in the death of an obscure valet was an attempt against the life of Mazarin — I am afraid that some murderer's knife would have cut short my existence before the appointed time.

"As it is," he went on, with a wave of the hand, "St. Augére meets the doom of a cowardly traitor; he dies, regretted by none, for a deed of surpassing loathsomeness. As for André, his death has been too easy."

"How comes it, Monseigneur," I asked, "that he gave no warning to his confederate, made no attempt to defend himself."

"Can you not guess?" he said, smiling. "When I had forced the confession of his treason from him I bound his arms to his side and pressed a gag into his mouth, which I removed together with his mask."

"But the mask?" I cried.

Again he smiled.

"How dull you are; I changed it whilst you were seeing to the coach."

"Why did you conceal the fact from me, Monseigneur?" I cried. "Did you mistrust me?"

"No, no, not that," he said. "I thought it wiser; you might have betrayed my identity by a show of respect. But go, leave me, Cavaignac, it grows late."

I made my bow, and, as I retired, I heard him muttering to himself the words of St. Augére: "Thus perish all traitors to the welfare of France." And with a chuckle he added: "How little he guessed the truth of what he said."

The Evidence of the Sword

I.

When two men chance to love the same woman, they seldom love each other.

It appears unreasonable that it should be so, for such a state of things but proves how much their tastes lie in the same direction, and, therefore, how much they are fitted to agree. Yet in spite of this, dislike, and even hatred, will oft arise between them.

Don Rafael de Molina and I contented ourselves with mutual scorn, all the more bitter on my part since I was the less favoured suitor; all the more lofty and disdainful on his, since his wooing prospered passing well.

There were dark rumours abroad concerning the presence in Paris of this sleek and courtly Spaniard. 'Twas said on every hand when he was not by — for he wielded a tolerable rapier — that he was a ruffler of the Court of Spain, who, having fallen upon evil days, had pocketed his pride and taken secret service of a not over honourable character under Anne of Austria.

I took scant interest in the knave until he had the audacity to raise his eyes to Mademoiselle de Navéry. Then, of a sudden, I began to lend an ear to those who styled him a foreign spy. And when I saw him succeed with mademoiselle, where I had all but failed; when I saw the bold glance of unmasked meaning in his dark eyes when he addressed her, and the fatuous, self-complacent smile wherewith he listened to her answers, I felt convinced that what was said of him was true.

I might have picked a quarrel with him, but I had naught to gain by doing so; for, even if I succeeded in killing him, I should have to reckon with the Cardinal, whose edict against dueling was not a thing that one might make too free with.

I might have told His Eminence, what title the Spaniard bore; but such a proceeding was too unworthy, and not to be dreamt of by Léon de Bret. And so I contented myself with hating him cordially, and invoking every evil I could think of upon his head.

We were in the month of June, and the King was on the eve of leaving Paris for Blois. It was incumbent upon me, as one of the gentlemen-in-waiting, to accompany the Court. I made bold to ask Mademoiselle de Navéry's unnecessary permission, and she answered me with scant waste of compliments and a pretty toss of her fair head, that it was no affair of hers, and that I must follow my inclinations. Yet, when I told her that to follow my inclinations I must follow her, and that, since she went to Blois in the suite of Anne of Austria, I would accompany the King, she bit her lip and dubbed me *impertinent*. Dubbed *me* impertinent, *Pardieu!* for uttering words which would have brought a blush to her delicate cheeks and a smile to her red lips had they been uttered by that graceless de Molina.

It was with a heart full of bitterness that I left the Louvre that night, and turned my steps homeward, through the slippery streets — for a misty rain had prevailed since noon, and the mud lay deep upon the ground.

Wrapped in my cloak, and a prey to thoughts that took no pleasant turn, I trudged moodily along until I reached the colonnade which borders the Place Royale. I was about to pass on, when, chancing to raise my head, my attention was arrested by the sight of two men pacing slowly to and fro in the middle of the square.

Now, as I have said, the night was rainy; moreover, had those two gentlemen in spite of that, still desired to enjoy an innocent promenade, methought it unlikely that they should choose the precincts of Place Royale to indulge their fancy, saturating their boots and risking a cold by stepping from one pool of water into another.

So I concluded that this was an assignation, and I waited to see another couple arrive, pitying the gentlemen that would have to strip in such weather.

But presently the twain stopped, and from where I stood I could just make out their voices raised in altercation, although I heard not what was said.

Then, of a sudden, they sprang apart. Their cloaks flew from them. There was a familiar rasp, and the white glitter of steel followed by a clash, as, with scarcely a word of warning, those two engaged.

Astonishment and curiosity held me glued to the pillar against which I leant, and for some moments I watched them as best I could in the uncertain light. I saw the left hand of one of the combatants drop from its upheld position. I watched it running round the waist, then pause, then rise again clutching a short shining object.

For a moment I marvelled at this, then suddenly I understood, and with a loud cry I dashed forward to prevent what I saw was about to resolve itself into an assassination.

But I had understood too late; for even as I sprang into the square, the victim stretched forward with a lunge. His opponent's sword moved not to the parry, but his left hand shot out, and the dagger it held turned the stroke aside, while simultaneously he bent forward and transfixed his man by a vigorous thrust.

Then, hearing my footsteps, he freed his rapier. Gathering his cloak about him, and lifting it so as to conceal his face, he darted a glance at me from over his shoulder as he turned to run.

"Stop, assassin!" I shouted wildly, as I prepared to give chase. But as I reached the spot of the encounter and cast a sidelong glance at the prostrate figure, something familiar in the outline drew my attention and made me pause.

I turned, and stooping I raised the mud bespattered head. A pair of eyes, wide open and mutely appealing, looked at me from out of the well-known countenance of Raoul de Navéry — Mademoiselle's brother.

Horrified at my discovery, I dropped on to my right knee, and pillowing his head upon my left, I proceeded to examine the nature of his hurt. 'Twas as I had expected. The murderer's sword had entered his breast full on the left side, close to the heart. Raoul was bleeding inwardly, and in a few moments would be dead.

I loosened his doublet so that he might breathe with as little pain as possible, and as I did so, I caught a faintly murmured word of thanks.

"Who was it, Ferdinand?" I inquired, taking his hand in mine.

"De Molina," he answered, in a hoarse whisper — "Foul stroke; he used a dagger." A spasm of pain crossed his face.

"I know it, *mon ami*," I answered; "I saw the parry. The dastard shall account to me."

He smiled feebly.

"Thanks, dear friend!" he said. Then, after a pause: "Bend lower, Léon," he murmured; and, as I obeyed, I faintly caught from the dying lips:

"He is a spy in the pay of the Queen Mother. There is a plot to poison the Cardinal. Warn him. Take care of my sister, she is — "

He stopped abruptly, and a shudder convulsed his body for a moment; then, with a long drawn sigh, he became still.

Overwhelmed by the tragedy I had witnessed and the news I had heard, I remained in my kneeling posture with my arms about the poor clay of him, who but a few moments ago, had been as strong and brave a gentleman as any in France, and wondered dimly how I should carry the awful news to the woman I loved.

But I was at length aroused from my sorrowful musings by the tramp of feet and the jangle of accoutrements, and presently I saw a body of men approaching across the square.

At a glance I recognised the uniforms of Richelieu's guards. Someone carried a lanthorn swinging on a pike, and, by the scant rays it shed, I discerned with glad astonishment — for I imagined that he was under arrest — the swart face and pointed beard of Rafael de Molina.

But even as I looked his arm went up and his finger pointed towards me, whilst in his soft southern accent came the words:

"*Tenez*, Monsieur de Bret is still there."

The next moment, and before I could grasp the situation, I was confronted by an officer and six troopers, and in their wake a morbid, curious crowd of all grades from courtiers to mendicants, which rapidly encircled us, and well-nigh drove me frantic with its babbling.

Molina stood beside the officer, and surveyed me with a glance of malicious triumph which I was puzzled to understand.

"This is a sad business, Monsieur de Bret," said the officer, with an ominous shake of the head, as, stooping, he put his hand to poor De Navéry's heart. "Dead," he muttered. "Worse and worse; and so irregular. No seconds. I am afraid it will fare badly with you, monsieur."

A light began to break upon my mind.

"*Diable!*" I ejaculated. "What do you mean?"

He drew himself up, and his foot struck against my sword. I had drawn it when I sprang to De Navéry's rescue, and I had heedlessly dropped it when stooped to tend the fallen man.

"There is a witness, Monsieur de Bret," the officer answered respectfully, but firmly. "This gentleman," he continued, indicating de Molina with his thumb, "saw you fight and recognised you when it was too late. Did you not, monsieur?"

"I did," the Spaniard answered slowly, "and I ran to summon you."

"*Ventre St. Gris!*" I cried, springing to my feet and facing them, "this is preposterous!"

"I am afraid that it is not," answered the officer coldly. "I must trouble you for your sword."

For the moment the thought of opposing him and giving my version of the story occurred to me. Then, realizing how futile this would prove and that I might but flounder deeper into the quagmire wherein I stood already, I resolved to keep my narrative for the Cardinal's ear and to deliver it along with De Navéry's message. Richelieu knew me and held me in some esteem. I might rely upon his justice.

With a proud glance at De Molina I lifted the baldrick unconsciously over my head, nor did I understand the officer's puzzled stare until I saw that from it hung an empty scabbard.

The officer looked about him, whilst the swelling crowd set up a curious murmur, and some callous ones laughed, even in the presence of the dead, at my embarrassment.

Then noting that De Navéry's sword lay under him, the officer stooped, and lifting my naked rapier from the ground returned it to its sheath.

"The evidence is complete," he muttered. and again he shook his head. "Monsieur de Bret, I pity you. 'Tis a hanging matter."

He turned his back abruptly upon me, and bidding two men take up the corpse he ordered the others to surround me.

"Way there! Make way!" cried the guards that preceded me, and with the butt end of their pikes they persuaded the crowd to let us through.

II.

Ventre St. Gris, but my position was an unenviable one! And as I sat ruminating in the dark upon my prison bed I realised it to the full. The news would be all over Paris by then that Léon de Bret had killed a man in the Place Royale.

The King would know and the Cardinal would know — which troubled me but little — and Renée de Navéry would know — which troubled me overmuch.

What would she think? Had the Spaniard carried the news to her, and had he perchance — since he accused me of killing the man whom he had killed — also accused me of his full crime? Would he dare to say that I had struck a foul blow, and that I had not merely killed Raoul de Navéry, but *murdered* him?

The grating of a key in the door interrupted my miserable thoughts and reminded me of supper — for albeit a man must die to-morrow he must sup to-night.

I turned to greet my gaoler with an oath for having kept me waiting thus long, when, to my surprise, a cloaked and hooded figure entered the dismal chamber, and I heard a woman's voice which I recognised in a moment and which set my nerves a-tingling with excitement.

"Thank you, Monsieur le Capitaine," she said; "you may leave us."

Quéniart, the officer in command of the Chatelêt, set down the lanthorn upon the dirty deal table and bowed respectfully.

"For five minutes, the order says, Madame," he murmured bowing, whilst I watched him in a dull fashion, wondering what she had come to say, and what new torture Heaven willed me to endure.

At length, when the door had closed upon him, she tore back her hood, and, removing her mask, showed me a face white and drawn with pain, and a pair of eyes red from weeping.

"Monsieur de Bret," she said in trembling accents, "what does it mean?"

I started; for in her voice I detected the old ring of the days — before that accursed Spaniard came between us — when she had not been so sparing in her favours. I was bewildered, and justly might I have asked her the very question that she put to me.

"What does it mean, Monsieur de Bret?" she repeated.

"What does all Paris say?" I asked at length.

"That you have killed my brother," she answered brokenly.

"And you — you believe it?"

"Believe it?" she echoed in amazement. "Do I believe it? Should I be here if I did?"

"Thank God," I cried fervently.

"But you were there, Monsieur de Bret, when he died; do you know who killed him."

"He told me," I answered. "It was — "

"Molina," she cried," Ah, you see I know. Am I not right?"

"You are, indeed," I said, marvelling from what source she had derived her information.

"Aye, 'tis as I thought. Oh, why did not Raoul heed my warning? I told him so often that Molina was a spy of the Queen's, and that naught would deter him from ridding himself of such an opponent as Raoul might become if he were able to prove what was being whispered everywhere — for Raoul was a cardinalist. But as God lives, I will avenge my brother," she ended passionately. "This Spanish hound shall not live to see to-morrow dawn."

"Hush, child," I cried. " 'Tis not for frail women to talk of vengeance."

"But I have no one in the world, Monsieur de Bret," she wailed, "and Raoul has no one but me to look to for justice."

"Since when has Léon de Bret ceased to be counted among your friends — yours and your poor brother's? Moreover, Mademoiselle, Raoul entrusted me with a secret before he died, and with a mission which I shall fulfill to-morrow. Then, others shall reckon with Rafael de Molina, and if he escapes the wheel — I do not know Monseigneur de Richelieu.

"But you, dear friend!" she cried. "Oh, I had forgotten your position. Forgive my selfishness. I am distraught with grief at what has happened. You are a prisoner."

"True," I muttered, "but I shall have something to say to-morrow to Monseigneur de Richelieu. If only I could prove my own innocence conclusively — " I paused abruptly as a thought occurred to me.

"I have it!" I cried presently. "*Ma vie*, but you may count upon me. I shall be freed to-morrow!"

We were interrupted by a knock, and she was forced to say farewell.

As I led her to the door, after she had readjusted her mask. "Do nothing, Mademoiselle, until you hear from me," I whispered. "Your brother will be avenged."

There was more that I might have said, but her grief commanded respect and circumspection, and so I contented myself with kissing her hand, and cutting short her grateful words by throwing wide the door.

When she was gone, I found that I had much to think of and ponder over. I had said that her brother would be avenged, and it was incumbent upon me to discover a manner wherein my promise might be fulfilled.

But I could not do it. I tried a score of times to drive my thoughts into such a channel. Unconsciously they would drift back again to Renée de Navéry, and again I would see the flash in her eyes; again I would hear her call Molina a Spanish hound.

And in the dark I rubbed my hands softly together and chuckled gleefully to myself — for love is a monstrous selfish thing — forgetting her brother's death, her own grief — which was but partly held in check by the over-mastering desire to avenge him — and all else besides, down to the very condition wherein I found myself and from which I had yet to be extricated. I remembered only that none stood between Renée and me, and gloated fiendishly over the discovery that she had but feigned a preference for Molina in order to unmask a traitor, and to defend her brother from the danger by which she rightly fancied him assailed.

I was ever sanguine, and the dawn of hope which brightened the blackness of my cell was rosy and full of promise.

She had found me gloomy, sullen, and despondent; ready for the airy death dance of Montfaucon. She had left me elated, joyful, and confident that to-morrow would restore me my liberty, my sword, and the right to woo her.

'Twas a pleasant enough dream, and it abided with me until I fell asleep.

Morning found me cheerful and much refreshed in spirit, but famished in body, for those sons of dogs who kept the *chatelêt* had left me supperless.

I was beginning to fear that the Quéniart had made too sure that I should be hanged, and with a saintly solicitude for the welfare of my soul, had deemed it best that I should fast awhile in preparation.

A praiseworthy solicitude this, perchance, in the eyes of the well fed, but one which drew from the depths of my empty stomach a score of vigorous words which took not the shape of prayers, and did my soul but little benefit.

But in the end my breakfast came. A scanty one, 'tis true; half a tough capon — from which soup had been boiled for every other inmate of the prison before it was roasted — and a *demi litre* of wine which was first cousin to vinegar. Still I partook of it, and if it did not give me strength, at least it duped my hunger for the while, and paved the way for a hearty meal which I hoped to reckon with anon.

Scarce had I finished when Quéniart returned and after a hasty toilet I announced myself ready to accompany him to the Hôtel Richelieu.

A coach was hired at my expense, for Quéniart was too well known in Paris to render it pleasant for a gentleman to walk swordless beside him.

"Hi, Master Quéniart," I exclaimed as we were leaving, "will you be good enough to bring my sword. I am indeed mistaken if His Eminence does not order it to be returned to me within the hour."

The captain's eyebrows were lifted in surprise.

"You are sanguine, monsieur," he ejaculated. Then bending his head, "It may serve as evidence," he said.

"And what of that?" I cried.

"There is blood upon it."

I started despite myself at the unwelcome news.

"When did you see the blade?" I inquired sharply.

"Last night when it was handed to me by the officer who arrested you."

He spoke the truth, I knew, and so I concluded that the blade must have received its stains whilst lying on the ground beside the wounded man. I pondered for a moment, then lifting my eyes to his face —

"Bring the sword," I said decidedly. "What signifies a little blood when there is one who swears he saw me slay the man, and a score who saw me with the body in my arms before it had gone cold."

He shrugged his shoulders, and turned to do my bidding, although he tired not of telling me how mad I was until we stood in the presence of the Cardinal.

Never was an audience granted me with such despatch. Scarcely had we been announced when the crimson portiere which masked the door of Richelieu's cabinet was lifted by an usher, and —

"His Eminence will see Monsieur de Bret immediately," he cried.

Quéniart's great fingers closed over my hand.

"Good luck," he whispered.

I pushed my way through the idle crowd of clients, and the next moment I stood in the Cardinal's presence and face to face with Don Rafael de Molina.

Richelieu, who was seated at his writing-table, raised his head as I entered, and darted a quick glance at me.

"Monsieur de Bret," said he, "I am sorely disappointed in you. What have you to say?"

"That your Eminence has been misinformed," I answered stoutly.

He perked his head on one side, and studied me attentively through eyes that wore a sleepy look — an infallible sign that he was wide awake.

"Do you mean that you did not kill Monsieur de Navéry?" he inquired slowly.

"I did not, Monseigneur."

Richelieu turned to Molina, and the words he spoke made my heart bound within me.

"I know Monsieur de Bret for a man of honour," he said quietly, "and in the face of your accusation, I looked for an excuse from him for having broken the edict, but never for a denial such as you have heard."

A deprecatory smile, full of significance and venom, swept over the foreigner's swart countenance.

"However," continued the Cardinal, "let us hear what Monsieur de Bret may have to say. Perchance it would puzzle him to explain satisfactorily how he came to he found in so compromising a position by the guard."

Briefly I told him what I have set down here concerning the affair, suppressing, however, the facts that a dagger had been employed and that in the man who returned with the guard I had recognised the perpetrator of the deed. I also omitted, for reasons of my own, Navéry's dying message.

When I had done, the Cardinal, whose eyes had been riveted on my face whilst I spoke, turned again to Molina.

"Are you certain that it was Monsieur de Bret whom you saw?" he inquired, with marked coldness.

"*Por Dios y la Virgen!*" cried the Spaniard, forgetting in whose presence he stood, "have I not said so? Think you I should accuse a man unless I were positive? Moreover, since my word appears to be insufficient, was not his sword found drawn?"

"True," mused the Cardinal, looking at me again. "Still, Monsieur de Bret has satisfactorily explained that he drew it to rush to the assistance of Monsieur de Navéry."

"Has your Eminence forgotten that there is blood upon his sword?" exclaimed Molina, with a sneer.

The Cardinal frowned, perchance at the Spaniard's tone, perchance at the fresh piece of evidence.

"There is more upon my sword than you will relish, Monsieur *l'Etranger*," I cried hotly, whereat his Eminence looked pleased, and the foreigner changed colour slightly, for he could not tell how much was known to me of the encounter.

"I dropped my sword," I continued, "when I raised Navéry from the ground, and the blood that flowed from his wound must have stained it where it lay. But we are wasting words. Since my sword has been mentioned as evidence, let it be produced. At my request Captain Quéniart has brought it with him. He waits now in the ante-chamber. If your Eminence will order it to be brought in, I imagine it will tell us something that will surprise Monsieur de Molina."

The Cardinal raised his eyebrows, and glanced from one to the other of us. Then, without a word, he touched a small hand-bell.

"Call Captain Quéniart," he said to the lacquey who answered the summons.

A moment later the burly soldier appeared.

"Now, Monseigneur," I said, taking the weapon, which, at a sign from the Cardinal Quéniart surrendered to me, "your Eminence has wielded a rapier yourself, if Fame speaks truly, and you are well acquainted with the points and virtues of the weapon."

He smiled, evidently pleased by the memories I had aroused in his priestly heart.

"It was my good fortune," I went on, "to take this sword to an armourer's a week ago, so that a new blade might be fitted to it. Will your Eminence be good enough to look closely at the edge, and see what it has to say concerning last night's doings."

I drew the sword as I spoke, and I now presented the hilt to Richelieu.

He took it from me with a puzzled air, whilst Molina and Quéniart, actuated by different feelings, went nearer than deference ordained.

Richelieu looked at the blade, then, with a slight exclamation, he rose and walked over to the window.

The sun shone through the leaded panes and fell upon the steel which glittered brightly, save here and there where a shiny patch of reddish brown had deadened its lustre. For some moments he examined it attentively, then, turning, he bent his dark, penetrating eye upon the Spaniard.

"You have been over zealous in the cause of justice, Monsieur de Molina," he said coldly. "This sword has not been used since this blade was fitted to it."

Had a thunderbolt fallen at his feet Molina could not have been more taken aback. He turned pale to the lips, and darted a furious glance at the Cardinal. There was a moment's silence, then Richelieu spoke.

"Monsieur de Bret, you are released. Quéniart, we must look elsewhere for the culprit; you may go. Monsieur de Molina you also may retire."

"Might I suggest that Monsieur de Molina should submit his rapier to a like examination," I ventured to remark.

The Spaniard drew himself up stiffly.

We do not carry swords for ornament in Spain," he answered proudly, "as I shall be happy to prove to you if you have reason to doubt the fact."

Then, before I had time to reply —

"There may be dints upon the edge. Does Your Eminence desire to see them?"

"It would be useless," the Cardinal answered carelessly. "You may go."

III

When we were alone I gave the Cardinal the fullest details of what I knew.

"I half suspected it was thus," he said when I had finished. "And he used a dagger, you say. The dastard! But what am I to do? He has killed Navéry, of that I am assured. He may be plotting against my life, that also I do not doubt. But what proofs can I offer the Court of Spain? He is a spy of the Queen's, and that makes it more dangerous still. I would consign him to the wheel if I dared, but — " He paused, frowned, and lapsed into thought.

"If peradventure, Monsieur de Molina, were to involve himself one of these evenings in a brawl, and receive a thrust in the windpipe or in low *quarte*, methinks Your Eminence's riddle would be well solved, and Raoul de Navéry most fitly avenged."

"True," he mused, " 'twould be a great blessing."

"But an unlikely one while the edict is so strictly observed."

His glittering eye rested upon me for a moment. Then he laughed.

"I understand," he said. "Well, if you know of anyone inclined to avenge De Navéry to save me from poisoning — the edict shall be forgotten for once."

I thanked him, and told him that I thought I knew of such man, whereupon he dismissed me with his blessing.

"You are a tolerable swordsman, I know," he said, as I took up my hat, "and I have every confidence in your skill. But what if he use a dagger again."

"I trust he will, Monseigneur," I answered, "I am reckoning upon it."

From the Hôtel Richelieu I wended my way towards the house of my late friend, De Navéry. Renée welcomed me with a glad cry and a smile which lighted up the sorrowful darkness of her countenance. I did but remain until I had told her what had taken place, and what was likely to follow, then, leaving her, I went to dine, grim memories haunting me of my last repast.

To take Molina at his word, and ask him to prove to me that they did not carry swords for ornament in Spain, would have meant a duel. A duel with seconds, wherein he would have been compelled to follow the rules of honourable play. That I could have killed him under such circumstances I did not for a moment doubt. But it would be too easy an end for him. To let him feel himself mastered; to compel him to have recourse to that assassin trick of his, and then, when he imagined himself triumphant, to beat him with his own cards — that would be something like revenge! And for that a brawl was needed.

Towards nightfall, therefore, I repaired to the "Green Pillar," in the Rue St. Honoré, which I knew he frequented. The gods were with me, for I found him there at play with half a dozen others.

I seated myself apart, unnoticed, and awaited an opportunity.

Presently it came.

"Come, host, another bottle of Armagnac. And let it be of the best, rascal, for we will drink to Don Rafael de Molina's safe journey home."

This was news that caused me no great astonishment.

"Does Monsieur de Molina contemplate leaving Paris?" I inquired, turning towards the party. "I am not surprised, for such an interview as he had this morning with the Cardinal is apt to make one's liver pale. I am glad to learn it in time, however; for I should have been deeply grieved had he left us without learning the opinion which I have had an opportunity of forming of this worthy gentleman, and which I imagine will be shared by all honourable men when the truth is known."

I had risen and stood facing the Spaniard, and giving him back scowl for scowl.

"You mean?" he inquired in a voice of suppressed wrath.

"That you are a liar and a murderer, Monsieur l'Espagnol," I answered coolly, "and that Monsieur de Navéry met his death at your hands."

A charming scene of confusion followed, as with a vigorous *"Madre de Dios!"* the Spaniard kicked aside his chair.

"Outside, Monsieur," I shouted, pointing to the door, and making myself heard above the din. *"Sortons!"*

And then, with many an oath and angry word, we burst through the door péle méle into the courtyard beyond.

We fought as we stood, in hats and cloaks. There were no formalities, De Molina was in too great a hurry, and I guessed his reason.

For a good five minutes I played the fellow in the uncertain light of a couple of lanthorns, and showed him that I was his master, yet forebore to press him too hard but waited, with my eyes keeping good watch over his left hand.

At last it came. The onlookers stood ranged against the wall to the right. Away from these Molina led me; retreating under my attack, and I following as if his designs were unknown to me. At last the other side of the quadrangle was reached, and in the shadow that enveloped us, he thought himself safe from detection.

His left hand dropped as on the previous night, but I saw not the glitter I looked for, and yet I knew that he had drawn his dagger. But there were many eyes upon him, and even in the darkness a lack of caution might betray his motive. He must be wary lest they should interrupt the fight in the very moment of his victory. Possibly he did not care whether he was discovered or not if only he had time to kill me before the interruption came.

I pressed him hard, and whilst I did so I loosened the fastenings of my cloak with my other hand as if I desired to cast the garment from me. Then I feinted, and lunged under his guard. My sword was within an inch of his breast when his poniard met it, and sent it past him. Simultaneously he offered me his point, a triumphant leer upon his face.

But he had reckoned without my knowledge of his ways. I had dragged the loosened cloak from my back, and held it on my arm. With a sweep of it, I dashed his blade aside.

I saw the look of terror come into his upturned face. I heard the cry of horror which burst from the onlookers. Before they could interfere, however, Don Rafael de Molina lay writhing in the throes of death.

So cautious had he been that not one of those who stood there, so much as suspected his foul play, and when they saw him fall 'neath my murderous stroke, a dozen swords leapt from their scabbards, and with angry cries of "Shame!" and, "Murder!" they flung themselves upon me.

But when I shouted to them to look at his left hand they paused to do my bidding. And when they saw the dagger which was grasped by the nerveless fingers of the dead, they sheathed their swords and hushed their angry cries; whilst when I told them that 'twas thus that De Molina had killed De Navéry, there were some amongst them who spat upon the corpse.

Half-an-hour later I stood swordless, and under arrest, in the guardroom of the Châtelêt, awaiting the officer. When Quéniart entered and beheld me, he rubbed his eyes and spluttered out an oath.

"What, *again!*" he ejaculated. "*Ventre gris*, Monsieur de Bret, but you are like to hang this time, whether the edge of your sword be battered or not."

Nevertheless, it came not to pass as he predicted, for next day I was liberated, and I knelt in Notre Dame at the requiem mass for Raoul de Navéry.

The season was not propitious for the advancement of my suit, and so I determined to accompany the court to Blois next day, and leave my wooing until I should return, when perchance Renée's grief aught have abated.

I paid her a visit that evening, and she received me kindly, and overwhelmed me with words of praise and gratitude, until I felt myself as great a historical personage as Bayard or Duguesclin. But when I came to say farewell she looked surprised.

"You are going to Blois?" she said.

"Yes, Mademoiselle, I accompany the Court."

"You craved my permission three days ago," she murmured, studying the pattern of the carpet with great intentness, "and I cannot remember granting it."

My heart beat fast and furiously.

"Will you grant it now?" I inquired.

"No, Monsieur," she said, lifting her eyes to mine, "I will not. I cannot spare you."

The Valet Mystery

As the taxicab bore him homeward from Hampstead, Carnforth's happiness oppressed him by its very completeness. He breathed the cool air of the April night exultantly, fervidly thankful to be alive.

The long struggle behind him, the dull, wearying uphill fight that had lasted through the twenty best years of his life, so bitter whilst it had endured, was now to be viewed by him from the summit with complacence and with pride. He had striven bitterly, but — more blessed than many — he had won to his Kingdom. And now that he was come to it he realized how hollow and empty must he have deemed it but for her who was to share it with him, but for the love that had come to crown his life and to make him account well-spent that past of his and all the struggle of it.

He sighed to vent some of his oppression of happiness — a happiness so full and pure that it begot in him the desire to shed happiness upon the lives of others, to make quite sure that all those who ministered to it should also share it. Naturally it was to Muriel first of all that his thoughts must turn upon such a pivot. Was she quite happy? The momentary doubt, begotten of a thought of a young Bristow, he brusquely dismissed. He knew quite well that but for his own coming into her life some three months ago, Harry Bristow would most probably have been engaged to her by now. Nor could he conceal from himself that upon the score of age young Bristow was to be considered the fitter mate for her. Bristow's also was the greater store of worldly goods, a fortune which did not depend, as did Carnforth's income, upon personal endeavour, but which was assured and beyond all need of effort.

Yet when those two advantages had been weighed, the rest, Carnforth assured himself, was all in his own favour. If he had not Bristow's youth, yet surely he was still young at forty, and equipped with an experience, a culture, a knowledge of the world that must render him a companion to Muriel such as Bristow could never have been; if he lacked Bristow's fortune, yet his earning capacity was considerable, his income abundant for their needs. And then, Muriel herself would one day be wealthy. For the rest he had to offer a name upon which his labours had shed lustre; and when all was said, Muriel's had been a free choice between himself and Bristow; and it did not seem to him that Muriel had hesitated between Bristol's youth and greater wealth and that which he himself could offer. Not all the pressure exerted upon her by her people — as Carnforth was well aware — nor her father's urgent representations that Carnforth was too old for her, had sufficed to sway her judgment once he had declared himself.

Yet he knew that he had come upon the scene barely in time, and that it had been touch-and-go between himself and Bristow. He sighed as he thought of it — sighed to reflect that his happiness must be purchased at the cost of pain to that engaging youngster; for he liked Bristow, as all the world liked him, despite such rivalry as there had been between them — perhaps even because of it, since being the victor he could afford generosity. Retrospectively he went back to that wedding-dance at which he and Muriel Tollemache had met. Until that night the thought of marriage had never occurred to him. He had looked upon himself as a settled bachelor, esteeming his bachelor condition, boasting almost that the woman did not live for whom he would forsake it. Yet he had done little more than look into her eyes to discover his mistake. He had made discreet inquiries concerning her. He had been told that her engagement to Harry Bristow was daily expected, and it was Harry himself, boyishly proud of the acquaintance of so distinguished a man as Carnforth, who had insisted upon presenting him to Muriel.

Poor old Harry! He sighed again, almost amusedly, as he wondered whether Harry had not since regretted the introduction. For it had sounded the knell of Harry's own hopes. Carnforth had ridden into the lists in his own irresistible fashion. He had gone straight to his goal, masterfully, remorselessly, insistently as was the way of him, and in spite of all opposition, riding roughshod over all obstacles to snatch the thing he coveted.

One by one he had conquered the members of her family, until her very father — the last to hold out against him — was dominated, and allowed esteem for Carnforth to outweigh his scruples.

In a month's time now they were to be married. The day was settled; the invitations had gone forth; and Harry Bristow, resigned, had shaken hands with Carnforth and wished him joy.

"You're a lucky fellow," he had said, sighing almost; "but you have the merit of knowing your luck. And since I can't marry her myself, there's no man I'd sooner see her married to than you."

It was nice of the boy. It had endeared him to Carnforth, who had answered that the compliment was one he could have returned had their positions been reversed.

He looked back to-night on that queer jumble of a life of his, on the struggles and bitterness of it, and he was glad that it had been so. The reward that was to come to him in the shape of this pure young girl whom he loved, with all that sober devotion of those to whom love comes comparatively late, was a reward that he had earned at the hands of life. The struggles and the bitternesses had been the price he had paid for the triumph and fame, which now he could toss into her lap. That fame was genuinely his own because he had bought it with tears and sorrow and sweat and suffering. It was one of his theories of life that nothing in it is secure of tenure save that which has been bought and paid for. The good we may extract from it must be purchased; and happy is he who pays in advance; the evil that we do must be accounted for, and that is a reckoning that must ever follow.

He wondered! His thoughts took an unpleasant turn. For twenty years his life, with all it's struggles, had been clean and honourable, and in it all there was nothing that he need hide, nothing indeed that he could not exhibit with pride. But twenty years ago there had been one thing in his life which he wished out of it, and never so ardently as now that Muriel was to become his wife. It was the one thing he had to conceal; that one deed committed on the very threshold of manhood, which were it known must brand him in the eyes of all honourable men, must render impossible his marriage. True, it was all dead and buried, but the ghost of it would rise up from time to time to gibber and mock him, and never so frequently as of late. It had been condoned, but it had never been paid for. Sometimes he would seek to see in the years of struggling and heart-breaking disappointment the reckoning presented by Fate. But he knew down in his heart that this was not so, for none of his suffering and striving had been the direct result of that sin. And he wondered when the reckoning would be presented; went in dread, from time to time, of its presentation.

That dread was upon him now. He realised it almost suddenly. The sense of oppression that he had attributed to his happiness was the oppression born of one of those evil forebodings to which finely sensitive and intuitive temperaments are susceptible.

He shook off his fears; he sought to laugh at them. They were but the children of another fear — a fear to which all humanity is prone in moments of excessive happiness, a fear lest ironic Fate must be uplifting us only to make our fall the greater. It was no more than a ghost that rose up to appal him; that past, twenty-year-old deed, forgiven and forgotten, was dead and buried.

The car swung into Knightsbridge, and came to a standstill a moment later at the portals of Consort Court. Carnforth, lean and athletic, and deriving from his slenderness and upright carriage the appearance of being considerably taller and younger than he actually was, leapt lightly out, paid his fare, and entered the building. Disdaining the lift he ran up to the first floor on which his flat was situated. The door was opened for him by his man Roberts, who relieved him of his hat and overcoat.

"There's a person to see you, sir," Roberts announced.

Carnforth paused in the act of turning over the letters in a silver tray on the hall-table.

"To see me — at this time of night?" said he. "Who?"

"He's been here a couple of hours, sir — party of the name of Jackson. I told him I didn't expect you back before midnight. But he said he'd wait — said that he must see you to-night, sir; that his business was most important."

Carnforth's agate eyes considered his man with something of amazement. That the impeccable Roberts should have admitted a stranger to his flat under such circumstances was something altogether incredible.

Roberts read the import of that scrutiny.

"He's from the office of *The Eclipse*, sir," he explained.

The surprise vanished from Carnforth's clear-cut face. The Eclipse was a weekly journal with which he had important relations. Occasionally a reporter or a sub-editor would come up to see him. The matter was explained.

"Where is he?" he inquired.

"In your study, sir," replied Roberts, and led the way down the thickly carpeted corridor. He opened a heavy mahogany door for his master, and discreetly closed it again after Carnforth had passed in.

Within that spacious, handsome, book-lined room, the famous author came suddenly to a halt. From out of a deep chair beside Carnforth's roomy writing-table there arose suddenly a short, thin, rather shabby man, with a clay-coloured, shaven face, a high, receding forehead, an aquiline nose, and a tight-lipped mouth. He had small, keen eyes, and his grey hair was thin and lanky. He was not at all prepossessing. The face was crafty and vulturine.

He was smiling now, and his smile was not quite nice. He held out a bony hand with enormous knuckles.

"Well, Carnforth?" was his greeting, in a slightly cockney accent. "Don't you know me after all these years? Don't you remember Ted Jackson?"

From under his knitted black brows Basil Carnforth's light eyes played over his guest. His face slowly lost its colour. It turned grey, and shadows crept under his eyes.

Almost feminine in his intuitions he realised that he had not been misled by them to-night. Here before him in the unwelcome person of Ted Jackson stood the very incarnation of that past that he accounted dead and buried.

II

Carnforth continued to stare at him in silence for some seconds, either intentionally ignoring, or else overlooking, in his stupefaction, the hand which Jackson continued to proffer.

At first, this fellow's presence here seemed to him a thing as bizarre and incredible as it was distasteful. But as the reality of it was borne in upon him he recovered his self-possession and that habitual mastery over himself from which he had derived the mastery over others and over fate which had placed him where he stood.

"And since when have you been connected with *The Eclipse*?" he asked, in a voice which if level and subdued was yet slightly rasping and unfriendly.

Jackson's face was twisted into a crooked, apologetic smile. "You'll forgive that deception," he begged. "It was necessary if I was to be admitted. It was an inspiration — came to me on the spur of the moment when your man told me that he didn't expect you back till midnight. It wouldn't have been much use my telling him I was a friend of yours. Of course, I could have waited in the street, but two hours was a longish time, and — and I knew you'd forgive an old friend this liberty."

Carnforth's face was a mask. It was stern and set, showing neither pleasure nor displeasure. He advanced slowly to the fireplace, and there turned, leaning an elbow on the overmantel, setting a foot upon the massive fender.

"How did you know of my connection with *The Eclipse*?" he asked. "It's not the sort of periodical I imagine you reading, Jackson, unless your habits have changed a good deal in these twenty years."

"Why, bless you," returned the other, "I read everything you write — everything I can find; and when once I discovered your name by accident in *The Eclipse*, I've taken to reading it regular. We are all very proud of you, Carnforth; we all of us rejoice in your success."

"All? All who?" inquired Carnforth.

"Why, all those who knew you in the old days at Piedmont and Herder's. We have followed your career with pleasure, I can tell you — with pride."

"You are very kind," said Carnforth icily, mistrustful, on guard. "And do you often see all those others?" he inquired.

"Well, now, I run across one or another of them now and again. But whenever I do, it's always the same thing: 'Heard of Carnforth's latest? Getting on, ain't he? Good luck to him!' It's always that, my boy. Always that."

"You are very kind," said Carnforth again in the same tone — a tone that seemed to place a barrier between them.

Jackson blinked, then looked round him at the handsome room, the pictures, the bronzes, the serried ranks of books in their gleaming, costly bindings.

"Nice, comfortable place you've got here," he said. "I knew you was doing well, but I hardly expected to find you quite in such princely style. And such a select locality. Rents must be pretty high about here, ain't they?"

"Rather high, I think; yes," said Carnforth.

Seeing that his host appeared to have no notion of asking him to resume his seat, Jackson resumed it uninvited.

"Glad to hear it," he replied; and he settled himself comfortably into the luxurious chair. "Glad to hear it, my boy, for it shows that you're doing well, and that's all that matters." His eye wandered to the decanters, siphon and glasses standing on a costly little Chinese Chippendale table. "Don't happen to have a drink about, do you?" he wondered.

In silence Carnforth crossed the room. There were three glasses, and one of them he perceived had already been used. But he didn't smile at his discovery; he took up the glass, poured a measure of whisky, added soda, and returned to hand it to his unwelcome guest.

"Ain't you drinkin' yourself?" quoth Jackson, as he raised the bumper.

"Not just now, thanks."

"Ah, well! Here's luck. May your prosperity continue!" He gulped half the contents of the glass, and then set it down upon the edge of the writing-table. "You haven't said you're pleased to see me," he reproached his host.

"I'm not," replied Carnforth uncompromisingly.

"Eh? You're not?" echoed Jackson, and his little eyes blinked, his countenance seemed to express that he was shocked and wounded. "You're not — not after all these years."

"We have gone rather different ways, haven't we, Jackson? I can't see what good can be done by our meeting. Tell me," he added bluntly: "How long have you been out of jail?"

Jackson's mouth fell open. He was genuinely surprised. "You knew?" he said, after a pause.

"Of course I knew — just as I always knew that you must end there. I read your trial and conviction in the papers."

There followed a fresh pause. Jackson took another drink. "It was rather bad luck," he deplored.

"That didn't transpire from the account I read," said Carnforth. "I thought you deserved it, and that you had been extraordinarily fortunate to have escaped so long."

"Oh, you did, did you?" croaked Jackson, a malicious grin upon his cadaverous face. Resentment had been simmering in him from the moment of Carnforth's entrance. It made him angry to see Carnforth so well housed, so prosperous, so famous; to find the man so polished, and to hear his cool, level voice and cultured accent. "And what about yourself? Didn't you escape once? Weren't you extraordinarily fortunate?"

Not a sign showed outwardly of the inward agony that Carnforth was undergoing. His face remained as impassive as if it were carved of stone. Then he even smiled a little, the very ghost of a smile.

"I was," he admitted readily. "I am duly thankful. Also I have made the fullest amends. The thing is twenty years old. I have lived honourably ever since."

"Oh, yes," said Jackson, with exaggerated agreement. "You've been honourable enough since. They tell me your name has become another name for honour; that you're as famous for uprightness and the rest of it as you are for your work. But it don't become you for all that to forget what's behind; it don't become you to reproach me with having gone crooked. I never had any luck like you. I never had no gifts as I could trade upon. Don't you be forgetting that, when you set up to judge me."

"I don't set up to judge you, Jackson. I don't want to judge you."

"You can't," was the sharp, almost fierce retort. "You was in with me — in it up to the neck, and but for old Piedmont's kindness to you, where'd you be now? You'd have been a jailbird same as me, and you know it."

Carnforth looked at him so sternly, those agate eyes of his so hard that for a moment Jackson thrilled with fear. He might have reminded his visitor that in that folly, that criminal folly of his adolescence it was Jackson who had led him to his fall, Jackson who had shown him how easy was that forgery and embezzlement in which in his urgent need of money — a need almost criminal in itself — he had soiled his hands. And Jackson had shared the swag with him. Yet when discovery came Carnforth had been loyal to Jackson. He had cast himself upon Piedmont's mercy. He had written to the old man a full confession of his guilt, and had implored him not to prosecute. He had sworn that he would slave night and day, and never cease from slaving at whatever work might come to his hands until he had repaid every farthing of the embezzled money — the money of which Jackson had taken half. Yet he had not betrayed Jackson; he had not sought to shield himself behind any plea that he, a mere boy, had been led astray by a man some seven years his senior. He had taken the entire burden upon his own shoulders. Jackson had a wife and children depending upon him, and he had whined of them to Carnforth, had sworn to go straight if Carnforth would not give him away. He had pointed out that Carnforth could not save himself by betraying him, and that the good action he would be doing would cost him nothing.

And Carnforth had consented, believing Jackson's repentance sincere, as he knew his own to be. He had written to Piedmont his pleading letters. He had argued in them that, whilst by prosecuting him Piedmont would ruin his whole life, on the other hand, if he were afforded the chance he implored he would not only become an honourable member of society, but he would repay Piedmont to the last penny if it took him twenty years. And Piedmont, for the sake of Carnforth's father, who had been his friend, consented to give the lad this chance, and to trust his word.

Of course, Carnforth had left that office in the city, nor had he sought employment in any other, realising that he could not push matters so far as to ask Piedmont for a character. Already he had begun to do a little journalistic work. Young as he was, and imperfect as his education had been, he had things to say and a remarkably engaging way of saying them. Now that he had cut himself adrift from the city he plunged more fully into that journalism with which hitherto he had been seeking to eke out his income. He took up authorship. He worked hard to repair the gaps in his education, to equip himself for this new career which he intended to open for himself.

And so it came to pass that his crime, by thrusting him into the walk of life for which he was naturally fitted, actually became the spring-board from which he leapt to fame and some measure of fortune.

Within five years of leaving the offices of Piedmont and Herder he had paid back the half of that embezzled sum of close upon three thousand pounds. In that same year his second book — "The Satellite" — was published, and almost from one day to the other he found himself lifted out of comparative obscurity into a blaze of celebrity. Before the year was out he had completely liquidated his debt with Piedmont, and he had written him a letter in which he attributed to the old man's generosity all that he had achieved. Among his most treasured possessions was the letter that Piedmont had written him in reply, a letter in which Piedmont had expressed himself proud of Carnforth, and grateful to Heaven for having afforded him the opportunity for doing a good action which had brought the world so noble a harvest.

In the following year, largely as a result of the disastrous bankruptcy, of a Calcutta house, the old established firm of Piedmont and Herder had been shaken to its fall, and Philip Piedmont had not survived a ruin in which — like a merchant of the old school considered that his honour was involved. He had died quite suddenly of an apoplexy on the very day that his accountants brought him a statement of his affairs.

To Carnforth it had been a source of profoundest thankfulness that the disaster had not occurred some twelve months earlier before his debt was fully liquidated and his honour cleansed of the stain on it.

Of all this he might now have reminded Jackson in answer to Jackson's taunt. But as he considered him there he was seized with a disgust that made all argument impossible.

Instead he asked him quite coldly: "Why have you come here?"

Instantly the other's manner changed. From its lurking fierceness, from its suggestion of menace almost, it became subservient and fawning.

"I've fallen on evil days, Carnforth," he replied, his eyes downcast, his bony hands clasping his knees. "I'm out of luck altogether. It ain't easy for me to get work — that is, the sort of work I can do. I'm not strong — not strong enough to turn navvy or porter; and if I try for a clerk-ship, it's always the same story. People want to know where I was last, and they want to see my credentials. Life's been hard on me, Carnforth," he said, suddenly looking up, a sorrow in those little beady eyes. "Life's been very hard on me. I'd have gone straight right enough if I'd had my chance; but things was always against me. A man in my place has no right to get married. We always have large families, and how is a fellow to bring up a large family on what won't barely keep himself alive and respectable? I wish often that I'd been a working man, or brought up to some trade like carpentering or plumbing. But clerking — Good heavens! — you know what it is, Carnforth; you know where it leads when temptation comes along."

Carnforth knew indeed. It was one of the subjects upon which more than once he had written fiercely — the abject slavery, the insufficient wages, the long hours, the deadly, monotonous grind that was the portion of the unfortunate clerk in a city office, the man who on the wages of a labourer was expected to live and clothe himself with pretensions to gentility, to present a gentlemanly appearance, and rear a family in a genteel fashion. How was such a man to resist temptation when temptation came his way? What inducement was there for such a man to keep to the narrow, soul-crushing path of honesty?

Himself too often had he debated this question, too often had he dipped his pen in gall to state the case for those long-suffering uncomplaining millions who dared voice no complaint themselves. He had pity to offer Jackson, although he knew Jackson for a thief and a rogue, although it was to Jackson that his own downfall had been due twenty years ago. His pity partly conquered his deep-rooted dislike for the man. The hardness of his face softened a little.

"I see," said Carnforth. "In what way can I help you?"

Jackson looked at him almost furtively, and then away again. He took up his glass. "What ways are there?" he asked, almost sneering, and he finished his drink.

"Your need is very urgent?" Carnforth asked him.

"Couldn't be more so."

Carnforth drew a thin wallet from the breast-pocket of his dinner jacket, and drew from it a little wad of notes — five in all; four were for five pounds each, the fifth for ten. He looked them over, folded them across, and held them out to his visitor. Jackson's fingers closed on them as the talons of a bird of prey upon its victim, his little eyes gleamed.

"There is all the money I have at hand at the moment. It's only thirty pounds, but it should see you some little way."

"Thanks, Carnforth," muttered Jackson, stuffing the crisp notes into a pocket of his greasy waist coat. "I knew you were to be counted upon. I knew you'd never have the heart to say 'No' to an old pal. Bless you, for it."

He made no move to go, such as might have been expected now that the object of his visit might be considered accomplished. He just sat huddled there, in the old attitude, a hand clasping each knee, his eyes brooding upon the Bokhara rug at his feet.

The lantern clock on the massive rosewood overmantel chimed the half-hour.

"It's getting late," said Carnforth, "and — I have work to do, Jackson."

"All right, all right," mumbled the other. "You want me to go, eh? I'm going — in a minute."

His tone caused Carnforth to glance sharply across at him. There had been a subtle change in it; that 'in a minute' had been pregnant with some meaning.

"Help yourself to another drink," sad Carnforth.

"Right-o!" Jackson rose, took up his glass, and slouched across the room to the side-table. He poured himself a half-tumblerful of whisky, added to it a very little soda, and drained it at a gulp. He set down the glass, as Carnforth was advancing to the door.

"Just a moment, Carnforth, old man, just a moment," he begged, putting out a hand to detain him. He could feel the fiery spirit coursing through him, enheartening him, giving him the courage that he lacked, drowning his fear of Carnforth, and mastering his unsteadiness under the glance of those cold eyes of his. "You've been very good to me to-night, and I'm very grateful to you."

"That's all right," said Carnforth, without cordiality, his dislike of the man once more getting uppermost, and his quick intuition feeling a danger, a menace in Jackson's continued presence.

"But" — Jackson raised his beady eyes, and fixed them upon his host's face — "but what am I to do when this money's gone? It won't last forever, you know."

"You must make it last until you have found employment of some sort. If I can help you, I will, provided that you are prepared to go straight."

"Oh, stow that, for heaven's sake!" The change in him was sudden. "I thought we understood each other. It ain't for you to be preaching at me. I want help, man, not sermons."

"I think," said Carnforth, "that you want something else altogether." Then he checked, recovered his patience, and proceeded. "I've told you I'll help you as far as I can. But you must also help yourself. My advice to you is that you should try the Colonies."

Jackson made a grimace of disdain. "The Colonies! Oh lor'! It's easy to advise the Colonies. But I've seen a lot of fellows that have come back, and the tales they tell ... Bah! Besides, I ain't got the constitution for the sort of work that's waiting out there. No, no, the Colonies ain't no good to me, nor I to them."

"Perhaps you're right. I might be able to find something for you here at home."

"Aye, but what? None of your clerkships for me! I am fed up with clerkships."

"Tell me exactly what you are looking for," said Carnforth, with almost exaggerated patience, "and I'll see what can be done."

"I will, old sport." The whisky was doing its work bravely. He stood squarely before Carnforth, and delivered himself at last of the real message that had brought him. "I want five thousand pounds to invest, so that it'll bring me in a couple of hundred a year to see me comfortably through the old age that's coming on me. That's what I want, Carnforth, old boy. And now you've got a straight answer to a straight question."

Carnforth smiled down upon him from his greater height, but his face had paled a little. It did not require such an active, piercing imagination as his to perceive the threat that underlay that straight answer.

"I quite understand," he answered, almost lightly. "The desire has been entertained by a good many. Unfortunately I can offer you no advice as to how you may gratify it."

"Sure?" wondered Jackson, leering now. "You ain't thought about it properly. Try again."

"I really think you had better go," said Carnforth, and his voice rang with a faint note of harshness.

"You understand me, I see," said Jackson. "But I wonder, do you understand me altogether. I wonder, have you considered how much you owe to me, how I've shielded you through all these years?"

"Shielded me?"

"Shielded you. And I'll go on shielding you, if only you'll be reasonable and show a proper gratitude."

If Carnforth curbed his anger, and allowed the fellow to proceed, it was only that he might learn exactly where he stood, exactly what it might be in this rascal's mind to do. "Just think of your own position, Carnforth. Here you are at the very pinnacle of success and fame, honoured and respected with an absolutely blameless reputation, moving among the upper ten and all the rest of it. And here you are just on the point of making a splendid marriage — Oh, I've heard all about it. Now, wouldn't it be a pity if all this were lost to you? Wouldn't it be worth some little sacrifice on your part to retain it? And what's five thousand pounds to you? Just a year's earnings, I suppose. Now, if the tale of that mistake of yours twenty years ago were to get about — Well, you can see the consequences for yourself. It would be a pity, now, wouldn't it?"

Carnforth looked into the other's eyes, and there was a sneer on his white face.

"So that is what you threaten, is it? That is your return to me for not having flung you out of this flat when I discovered you here, for having been moved to pity to the extent of giving you what money I had by me?"

"Pity, was it?" flashed the other. "Are you sure it was pity? Are you quite sure it wasn't fear?"

"Fear — of what?"

"Of whatever I might be able to do. We were accomplices, you know, and —"

"Get out!" said Carnforth, clenching his hands. "Get out before I do you a mischief. You miserable thief! Who do you suppose would ever listen to a word from you? Heavens man, do you imagine that my fame is so frail a thing that the first dirty, down-at-heel jailbird who comes along with a story against me can command credit? Get out!"

But still Jackson didn't move to go. "I'm not a fool, you know, Carnforth," he said. "I never was. And, not being a fool, I don't suppose anything of the kind. But if I tell you that I have proofs — absolute proofs — which I might send to Miss Muriel Tollemache, or — or to Mr. Harry Bristow?" He chuckled to see Carnforth wince despite himself. "You see, I have been looking into your affairs, Carnforth. I have always taken a very friendly interest in you. I — Here!" It was a sudden gasp of alarm. "Here! Hold off, Carnforth, curse you!"

Carnforth had seized him by the lapels of his threadbare coat and swung him off his feet. An instant he steadied him as he was toppling, livid and terror-stricken under this sudden onslaught; then he sent him hurtling back into the arm-chair that he had erstwhile occupied.

"Now, you dirty dog," Carnforth growled, "just tell me plainly what you mean."

Breathless and badly scared, Jackson sat up in the chair into which he had been flung. His livid face was vicious, his mouth set, his eyes blinking furiously.

"Now, look here, Carnforth, just you understand I've got no use for violence. Treat me like this again — just lay a finger on me — and it'll be all up with you. Understand that!"

Carnforth's every instinct was to take up one of the cut-glass decanters and beat out the fellow's brains with it. Under that cold and ever calm exterior of his he was subject upon occasion to tempestuous passions.

"What are these proofs you talk about?" he demanded, standing over his guest.

"It's a fair question. You're entitled to know, so that you may judge exactly where we are. I'm not threatening anything, you know." He blinked up at Carnforth. "Do you mind standing away from me a bit? That's better. Of course, you remember writing two letters to old Piedmont, telling him the whole truth, imploring him to have mercy on you, and promising to repay the amount of the defalcations? Of course you do. And there was another letter that you wrote five years later, in which you thanked him for having spared you and sent him the balance still owing."

"Well?" Carnforth demanded sharply, as the other paused.

Jackson slowly licked his lips. "You'll remember, of course, that I was with the firm to the end; that I was the assistant-manager. I was there, of course, when the smash came, and I went through the old man's papers very carefully. Locked away in one of the drawers of his desk I found those three letters of yours, and — and, well, you see, I didn't want them to fall into other hands. I thought of what that would mean to you, Carnforth; and to shield you I took them away. I intended to destroy them, but somehow I couldn't do it. I thought I might return them to you some day; and that's really what I want to do now."

"Upon terms, of course?" suggested Carnforth.

Jackson spread his hands in a gesture that was almost pathetic. His countenance became overcast. "I am a victim of circumstance," he explained. "That's what I am — a victim of circumstance. They say every man has his chance once in his lifetime, and God knows this is the only chance I have ever had. If I let this slip, I may as well make up my mind to starve. And what am I asking? What's five thousand pounds to you, Carnforth? Why, if our positions were reversed, I'd — "

"Let's stick to business, Jackson. If you know me at all, you should know that I'm not the sort of man to submit to blackmail."

"Here, steady on! Who's blackmailing?" the other protested.

"What do you call it?"

"You misunderstand me altogether," cried Jackson. "If I were to come to you and say, 'Look here. I've got these letters. Unless you give me five thousand pounds, I'll take them to Miss Muriel Tollemache, or to her father,

Colonel Tollemache,' that would be blackmail. But I'm saying no such thing. All I'm trying to do is to get a fair price for something of value that has come into my possession."

"And if I refuse to buy them?" quoth Carnforth.

"You'd never be so foolish as to do such a thing."

"Suppose that I do. What then?"

"I shall have to sell them to someone else, that's all. There's Mr. Harry Bristow, now. Don't you think he'd give me five thousand pounds for them?"

"I think he'd be far more likely to break your neck if you proposed such a bargain."

Jackson's only reply was a wide-lipped, cunning smile.

Carnforth took a turn in the room, thinking swiftly, struggling with the fury in his soul. At last he came to a halt again before Jackson.

"You're lying," he said. "You haven't got the letters. You are using your knowledge of what steps I took — "

"Half a mo'!" Jackson interrupted, and he fumbled in his breast-pocket. "You don't suppose I'd try to work such a swindle as that on an old pal. Just take a look at these." And he fished some folded papers from his inner pocket.

With a half cry Carnforth hurled himself upon him and wrested the papers away.

But Jackson offered no resistance. "Take them, man — take them!" he cried, yielding them readily enough. "Either you're a fool, Carnforth, or else you think I'm one. They're only copies."

Carnforth, a little mortified by his failure and his self-betrayal, opened the crumpled sheets, and read there word for word what he had written so many years before. They removed the last lingering hope. Then his passion mounted again. He held it hard, but it showed in his white face and gleaming eyes, so that Jackson, despite his pot-valiance, shivered a little as he watched him.

"Jackson," he said in a voice of concentrated rage, "if you value your dirty neck you'll go at once; you'll go while you are safe."

Jackson rose unsteadily, alarmed. "All right," he said. And he gained the door. He opened it; then paused and threw a scared look at Carnforth. "You'll find my address on the back of one of those copies," he said. "If you should think better of it — "

"Get out — get out!" growled Carnforth, advancing upon him.

Jackson sped quickly down the corridor his footsteps muffled by the heavy pile carpet. Another moment, and the door of the flat had banged upon the departing rogue.

III

It was Carnforth's habit to work from midnight until about three o'clock in the morning, rising again at half-past ten, so as to secure the seven hours' of sleep which he deemed the right amount of which his constitution stood in need.   It will readily be understood, however, that, following upon that disturbing and almost violent scene, work on this particular night was out of all question. He did not so much as attempt it. He flung himself into his desk-chair — the chair in which, from force of habit, his thoughts seemed to flow most readily; he took up his pen — again because accustomed, through long years, to think, as it were, at the point of the pen, he found that to grip that familiar tool was of assistance in the concentrating of his ideas. Idly scribbling on a writing-pad, drawing upon it in fantastic letters the names of Jackson, of Piedmont, and of Piedmont and Herder, his tortured mind wrestled for a long hour with the cruel problem that had been set him.

That problem still all unsolved, he rose at last and went to bed. But sleep did not come to him, nor did he woo it. He lay there in the dark, thinking, thinking, thinking. He saw this life of his, which he had built up so laboriously to its present eminence, smitten to ruins by the obscene hand of a blackmailer. He saw the name which he had rendered esteemed and honoured dragged in the foul mud of a public scandal. He saw himself shunned and cast off by all those who now wooed and esteemed and honoured him. He saw himself branded a thief — an embezzler and forger, his career broken and ended. For be it remembered that he had specialised in sociology. And what a mockery must it not become for him, once that past of his were disclosed, to continue to theorise, to moralise and to lay dawn laws for the good conduct of social life? He saw in imagination, the cold stern face of Greatrex, the proprietor and editor of *The Eclipse*, when the news was bruited that should lend the enemies of that eminent journal such a weapon of offence against it. And he saw other faces no less stern and cold, and amongst them the face of Muriel.

In his despair he turned at last to the consideration of submitting to this blackmail, of buying those incriminating letters from that foul creature Jackson. It was a consideration that set him in a very frenzy of rage. It was exasperating even to consider submitting to be preyed upon by that jackal! The thing was unthinkable! Yet the alternative was still more appalling. And then there was the price that Jackson had asked, five thousand pounds. It was a price altogether beyond the means at Carnforth's command. Jackson may have believed that it represented no more than the author's earnings for one year; the world in general might suppose it; but it was very far from being the actual truth. Despite his great fame his annual earnings did not amount to half that figure, and his expenditure kept pace, step by step, with his income. He had ever been open-handed, generous and prodigal. What he made he spent, as he made it, often in advance.

Just of late, with his approaching marriage in prospective, he had been more careful, and he had saved a little; but comparatively it was a very little; there was not very much over a thousand pounds standing to his credit in the bank. True, his sales to date represented twice that sum, but then he would require that and more to meet his expenses in a measure as the one and the other became due.

He might make fresh contracts, obtain upon them advances which he knew would be paid him readily enough, and so get together the requisite sum, or something approaching it. But, in that case, how was he to live, and what would remain for him for the next couple of years upon which to run a married man's establishment in that handsome house that was being made ready for them down at Chertsey?

Towards dawn, a ray of light pierced to him at last. He must take the only possible course to draw the fangs of a blackmailer. Forestall him. Himself he must go to Muriel, and make frank avowal of that hideous thing in his past, leaving the rest in her hands. He writhed at the very thought of such a course. He rebelled against the cruelty of Fate that forced it upon him, that forced him to take up again a burden of which he had rid himself by twenty years of upright, punctiliously honourable conduct. But there was no alternative.

Acting upon this resolve he went out to Hampstead early in the afternoon of the following day. But here again Fate was against him. His time was badly chosen. It was brilliant weather; one of those days on which spring gives us a foretaste of summer. He found everybody in the garden, and a set of lawn-tennis in progress. Muriel and Harry Bristow were playing against Jack Ingram and his sister.

With a wave of his hand to the players, and a quite unnecessary exhortation to them not to interrupt their game, Carnforth sank into a wicker chair beside Mrs. Tollemache. Thence with brooding, weary eyes he watched the game. He observed the lithe boyishness of Harry Bristow, his athletic vigour, his stripling shape, his skill and adroitness in the game. The sight made him feel old — far older than his forty years. It marked more emphatically than ever the gulf of age that stood between himself and Muriel; it threw into strong relief the admirable physical suitability of Muriel and Bristow for each other. Carnforth did not play lawn-tennis, nor did he play golf, nor did he dance, nor, in fact, was he schooled to any of those youthful exercises in which Muriel herself excelled. He had had no time in that strenuous life of his for games. The terms of cricket and football and hockey were to him as Greek to Harry Bristow. Although he had ever taken the greatest care of his body, keeping it fit for the sake of the mental fitness which he believed depended upon it, yet all his energies had been devoted to the cultivation of his mind to the repairing of those omissions in his early education.

And now, to-day — perhaps because he was depressed and stricken down mentally by this thing that had befallen him — he felt himself suddenly at an unutterable disadvantage before the splendid activity of young Bristow. His culture and his mental energies and subtleties seemed of no account by contrast with the physical energy and athletic talent that Bristow was displaying. He came to conceive that the success of his rivalry over Bristow had been a very slight one after all; that Bristow really had far more to offer than had he — that is to say, far more of such qualities as must count with a fine, healthy young girl like Muriel; that the aura of fame about himself had dazzled Muriel for the moment; but that, when all was said, the balance of her inclinations between himself and Bristow was most finely poised; that the least addition on Bristow's part, the least subtraction on his own must send the scales thudding down upon the other side. And what was he not come to subtract? His untarnished honour. He was come to announce himself to that clean-limbed, clean-minded girl as an unconvicted thief and forger. Could he expect her to see — as he so clearly saw himself — that he and that Carnforth of twenty years ago were no longer one and the same man. That what Carnforth at twenty had done — and from motives of unutterable ignobility — would be impossible to the Carnforth of forty? That in spite of that foul stain upon his past, he was to-day as clean and honourable as men deemed him? Himself he believed it; he knew it. But could he expect her to believe it?

Mentally he shrank dismayed before the task which he had set himself. It was impossible — utterly impossible. To do it he must be prepared to lose her irrevocably. Was he so prepared? Would he take the slender — the invisibly slender — chance?

As he posed himself that question, Harry and Muriel victorious over their opponents, delighted with each other for what each had contributed to that victory, came arm in arm, a couple of gay children, the very best of friends, towards the shade of the beech tree, where Mrs. Tollemache sat with Carnforth.

Carnforth rose to greet them. Their talk was all of the game, and of other games — the sort of talk that invariably left Carnforth at a disadvantage, left him wondering how she could have come to choose such a dullard as himself whilst rejecting Bristow, who was aglow with youth, enthusiastic in all those matters that appeared to her to be of such paramount importance, the very mate, it would seem, appointed her by nature.

Carnforth had her to himself for five minutes before he left again. He summoned strength to tell her in spite of all; but here again the turn of their brief conversation was against him.

She spoke of the house at Chertsey, and, perhaps prompted by her late occupation, her talk was of the garden and of the tennis— lawn which required attention, and of a pavilion there that was to be structurally altered.

Carnforth set his hands on her shoulders, and held her at arms' length before him, something wistful in those pale eyes of his as he turned them full upon her smiling, sun-burned face.

"You have no doubt, no slightest, lingering doubt, dear?" he asked her.

"About the pavilion?" she flashed in mockery.

"About life," said he. "About this marriage of ours?"

She frowned and laughed at once. "My dear," she said. "I thought we had said our last word on that."

"And yet," he ventured, "I love you too dearly to be a party to any wrong that you might do yourself. Sometimes I wonder whether I am doing the best for you; whether renunciation on my part would not be the highest testimony I could offer you of my affection; there is this gap of years between us — your father's one objection."

"Basil, dear," she broke in, "I'll not listen to another word. You are morbid when you talk of your age. You talk as if you were a thousand. I am sure you don't look thirty."

"It isn't what I look that matters; it's what I am."

"And that is what I am marrying you for — for what you are." She became tender out of solicitude for him, eager to show him what compensations he had to offer her for that part of his youth that was fled. "Is it a small thing to become Mrs. Basil Carnforth — to bear a name at once so honoured and so honourable?"

He winced at the word. "And if it were not so?" he asked, in a voice that shook a little. "If my name were not honourable, after all?"

She borrowed a parliamentary phrase. "I must disallow all hypothetical questions." She thrust aside the arms that held her at a distance, and came to lock her hands about his neck, looking up adorably into his grave face. "You've been overworking, Basil. You're just tired, and you're falling a prey to your weariness. You're mistaking it for the signs of age. You must stay to dinner, and give yourself a holiday. We'll see what we can do for you."

But he excused himself. He urged an article for *The Eclipse* that must go to press in the morning. There was no escaping it. She demurred, of course, but then resignedly allowed him to depart, his task unfulfilled. His courage had failed him. He couldn't bring himself to tell her, and to change all that trust and affection into a feeling that very scorn and contempt must deprive of the dignity of hatred.

So he departed with that hateful burden still upon his soul. This, at last, was the reckoning. He had always feared that he must pay one day; but he had hardly thought that the price demanded would be so heavy. Then he faced the problem once again. There remained but one way out. He must submit to blackmail. He must make terms with Jackson.

On his way home he stopped at a telegraph office. Those copies Jackson had brought him were in his wallet. He took them out to find Jackson's address, and he wired to him to come at once.

IV

Jackson, in a new suit of reach-me-downs slightly too large for him, was shown into Carnforth's study at nine o'clock that night.

"Couldn't come before," he announced. "Only got your wire an hour ago when I got home. Hope I haven't kept you waiting."

He had been drinking — to screw up his courage to the necessary pitch for this interview — and there was a certain unpleasant jauntiness in his manner and a familiarity of attitude and address which sober he would never have dared attempt.

"I thought you'd send for me," he said, smiling slyly. "I knew you'd never be of the same mind after you'd had time to think it over. And very glad I am, Carnforth, old fellow, very glad. It would have hurt me more than I can say to have been the cause of trouble to you. But we must live. Times are hard. We must do what we can."

"Sit down," said Carnforth, interrupting him curtly. "We must have a talk."

Jackson sat down, and threw one leg over the other. "There's nothing to talk about, old boy, I assure you. I've said all I've got to say — said it all last night before you were so rude to me. You always had a nasty temper, Carnforth. But there, I don't want to recriminate."

Carnforth came abruptly to the point.

"What is your lowest price?" he asked. He was standing with his shoulders to the overmantel, his hands thrust deep into the pockets of his lounge coat, for he hadn't changed since returning home.

"I told you last night, didn't I?"

"You mentioned a figure that is quite beyond your expectations, and certainly quite beyond my means. What I want to know is the actual price that you are prepared to take. I know what I'm prepared to give."

Jackson's eyes flashed, a faint colour stirred in his cheeks.

"How much?" he asked.

"Five hundred pounds," said Carnforth.

Jackson's mouth fell open in amazement and dismay. "Five *hundred*?" he echoed. "Did you say 'hundred'?"

"That's what I said — five hundred."

"But I said five thousand," returned Jackson plaintively.

"I know. Will you take what I offer or not?"

"Couldn't dream of it, old boy. Couldn't, absolutely. Why, what good would five hundred pounds be to me? It wouldn't keep me going much more than a couple of years."

"Understand me, Jackson. I am far from being as rich as you suppose. I am far from earning anything such as is generally believed. My earnings are between two and three thousand a year, and my expenditure has been fully equal to it. I am being quite frank with you. I have a thousand pounds in hand for my marriage. If I part with the half of that I am making a great sacrifice. I'll make it, but more than that is absolutely impossible."

"Oh, no, it isn't; that's where you're mistaken. I am ready to believe what you tell me about your means. But when a man is about to make such a marriage as this of yours, there's no difficulty about raising a little sum like five thousand pounds. It can be done — "

"Stop that!" Carnforth's voice shook with sudden anger. "I may have been a thief once, Jackson, seduced to it by you; but I'll see you hanged before you seduce me to it again. Do you dare to ask me to take money from my wife's portion so as to stop your foul mouth, so as to pay you to keep something from her? Is that what you dare to propose?"

Jackson huddled back into the recesses of his chair, his erstwhile assurance flung out of him.

"No, no, no. You don't understand me," he cried, and like the nimble-witted scoundrel he was he fitted another meaning to his words. "All I meant was that, with the credit you'd enjoy, you could easily raise the money, and pay it back again by installments."

"And if I didn't live to pay it back? What then?"

"What nonsense! You're sound and healthy, and all the rest of it."

"No good, Jackson. I've told you what I am prepared to do. Are you prepared to accept it?"

"Couldn't do it? Couldn't, really. Wish I could. Wish I was in a position to. But I'll make a reduction. I'll be as generous as I can be for old times' sake, Carnforth. You shall have the letters for three thousand pounds; that's just one thousand apiece. What do you say to that?"

"It can't be done. I haven't the money, and I have no means to raise it — honourably."

There they came to a deadlock, until Carnforth gave way. In a passion almost he made a further proposal.

"You shall have a thousand pounds. Five hundred now, and five hundred in a year's time. I'll give you a bill at twelve months for the latter. I've no right to go as far as that, Jackson. But it's the last penny; absolutely the last."

There was such finality in his tone that it left Jackson without any hope that this interview could with advantage be protracted.

He determined to leave Carnforth to think it over again. He got up, and buttoned his ill-fitting coat.

"Sorry, Carnforth; devilish sorry. There's no more to be said. I must see if I can't make a better bargain with Mr. Bristow."

Carnforth set his teeth, and his hands clenched. His every instinct commanded him to fall upon this vile thing, and squelch it out of all human shape.

Hesitating still, Jackson looked at him; and perhaps, finding his appearance dangerous, he edged to the door. There he paused, his hand on the knob.

"I shan't come again unless you send for me," he said. "I should be very loath to go to Mr. Bristow, for several reasons. And to be sure, I couldn't expect him to pay me the price I'm asking you. But he might pay me more than you are offering."

Carnforth controlled himself to say: "I've told you once already that Bristow will break your neck."

"We must all take our risks," said Jackson thoughtfully. "But I'll do nothing for a fortnight. If in that time you've thought better of it, and seen your way to get the needful, there's nobody'll be better pleased than me. Just send me a wire, and you shall have the precious letters for three thousand pounds. That's absolute rock bottom, Carnforth."

"One thousand, as I have said," was Carnforth's answer. "And *that's* absolute rock bottom. And should you think better of it, come and see me. But not otherwise. You'll be wasting your time." And he pressed the bell.

"Now we understand each other," said Jackson. "I'll hope to hear from you. Good evening!"

He was shown out by Roberts.

He departed confident that he left behind him a desperate man — a man driven to bay, a man who at any cost and at any sacrifice must extricate himself from the cleft stick in which he was held.

He was quite right, and yet there was no cause for his deep-throated chuckle.

A desperate, a wildly desperate man he did leave behind him, hunched into the big chair in front of his writing-table, staring with unseeing eyes straight before him, his face livid, drops of perspiration standing upon his fine brow.

Can you conceive the feelings of a man gripped and enlaced by the slimy tentacles of the devil-fish? Can you realise something of his terror, his loathing and his frenzy of rage all blending to urge him to strike and kill the foul thing that is sucking him down to death? If you can realise that, then you can realise something of Carnforth's feelings as he sat there alone, and faced this horrible situation. The instinctive need to strike down and kill this thing that held him was the only feeling left him. There was murder in his soul, a rage almost to think that he should have allowed Jackson to depart alive. He would send for him again; he would lock the door, and he would strangle him with his hands.

And hang for it? He asked himself — hang for such a thing as Jackson? A life for a life; aye — so ran the law. But such a life as his for such a life as Jackson's? Where was the equity of that?

The law would avenge him upon such a man as Jackson; it kept a stern, a pitiless punishment for men who embarked upon the loathsome crime of blackmail. But in what case was Carnforth to invoke the law? To do so he must ruin himself. What manner of vengeance would that be, what justice?

His frenzy passed. He drew out a handkerchief and mopped his brow. Gradually he recovered his self-control. His brain became ice cold, his mental vision preternaturally clear. Calmly, with a calm that was more terrible than any passion, he set himself methodically to follow out the grin trend of thought that had been started by his reflections. He bethought him of a passage in the book upon which he was at the time engaged. It was extraordinary how aptly that passage fitted into his present need.

He unlocked one of the drawers of his desk, and drew forth a sheaf of pages covered with a fine, close hand. Having found the page he sought — the lines he had written but two days before — this is what he read:

"Given a man of sufficient education, with an imagination wide enough to foresee all possible issues, and an intelligence strong enough to provide capably for each and every one of those issues so as completely to cover up all traces that might lead to his detection, and such a man may kill with impunity. No year passes in which the police are not left with a number of unsolved murder mysteries upon their hands. Why is this? Because those murders are the work of men possessing precisely the capacity and mental equipment to which I refer. The murderers who are tracked down and caught are the clumsy bunglers, usually brutish men of meagre intelligence and no education; men without the imagination to conceive, or the intelligence to execute in such a manner as to leave no trace of their own connection with their deeds."

Thus far he read what he had written. And then he sat on a thought. He dreamed rather than considered. It was like weaving the plot of a story, tracking down every loose thread in it with that lucid, lively imagination which had made him famous. It seemed to him that he had sat there not more than half an hour weaving and interweaving the grim strands of his fancy until the fabric was complete and whole and sound.

He rose from his writing-table and to his surprise found that it was five minutes to twelve. It had taken him two full hours to evolve that plot of his, which as yet was no more than a fancy that he toyed with. It would make a story — ah, what a story it would make! he reflected, with the thrill of the creator. But would it make a reality? Had he the courage?

The door opened, and Roberts came in with the decanters and siphon. He set them down, and paused to inquire if his master required anything more that night.

"Nothing more, Roberts, thank you. Get to bed. Good-night!"

"Good-night, sir!" And Roberts withdrew again.

Carnforth mixed himself a drink, raised the glass to his lips, and then set it down again untouched. He moved away from the table, his head bent in thought. Twice he paced the length of the room, and came at last to pause before a Venetian mirror. He looked into it, looked into his own lean, resolute face with its long line of jaw and strong, stern mouth, his thick, black hair that was but slightly flecked with grey at the temples, his light-coloured eyes under their straight, black brows.

Straight into that reflection did he look, and asked it silently: "Have you the courage?"

That he had the will and the power, he was assured. But had he the courage? Not merely the courage to execute. That was nothing; but the courage to live his life as before when the thing was done without qualms or remorse or any inward shudderings? Boldly he answered himself that he had that courage; that what he intended would be a thing done as much in self-defence as the slaying of a man who, weapon in hand, came seeking his life. It was a necessary, a sane thing to do. He was driven to it remorselessly by circumstance, and there was nothing in the act that need cause him the least pang of remorse, the least feeling of guilt. If he took care to cover up his tracks it was not because he took shame in the deed, but because the law — excellently framed though it might be — was yet too narrow to deal with such a case as his in the special manner which in equity it deserved.

He went back to his writing-table. He thrust away the manuscript he had consulted, with no more than a fugitive reflection upon the odd coincidence of his having written but two nights ago in a work of fiction what to-night he was applying to a work of fact. Then he sat there with his elbows on the table and his head in his hands, and coldly and systematically he went over every stage of the plot that he had woven. It was like revising a proof. He found a shortcoming here, another there. He corrected them. He revised the whole again. He was satisfied. Nowhere was there a loophole. Nothing could miscarry. Every link was provided in that perfect chain. He rose with a sigh that ended in a laugh. He was very calm, and as he now took up the glass which he had filled some time before no slightest tremor shook his hand. He drained it, and after a few minutes went quietly upstairs to bed. It was three o'clock.

When he awakened, Roberts, with his morning tea and his letters, stood at his bedside. It was half-past ten. Roberts had drawn the blinds, and the room was flooded with the golden morning sunlight.

"Your bath is ready, sir," came the usual announcement.

"All right," said Carnforth. "I'll ring when I want you."

He sipped his tea, lighted a cigarette, idly fingered his letters, but he opened none, and in the end thrust the lot aside. He reclined on his pillows, and went over that plot of his once more, tested it now with a mind freshened and quickened by sleep. It was his habit so to test his plots. And how often had not the morning's reflection brought disappointment, revealed the banality of an idea that had seemed so sparkling and fresh the night before. Not so now. This plot of his, this plot that was to be lived, not written, was close-knit and sound. He was satisfied. He might with confidence set it into action. He selected one of the letters from his pile, ripped open the envelope, extracted and unfolded the sheet. He glanced at it, and then reached out his hand, and applied his thumb to the pear-shaped bell-pusher that dangled above his head.

Thus he rang up the curtain.

Roberts entered, in answer to that summons. Carnforth dropped the stump of his cigarette into an ash-tray.

V

"I have here," said Carnforth, "a letter from Herbert & Pawle. I am not quite satisfied with the way things are going on down at Chertsey, and I should like you to be on the spot to see that my wishes are properly carried out. Time is getting short, you know. I think, Roberts, that you had better go to Glebelands, and stay there until the work is completed. I'll give you full particulars of what should be done, and I want you to look after things generally. It's the only way, I'm afraid, if the house is to be ready in time."

Roberts stared at his master in some concern. "But what about you, sir? Who will look after you here?"

"Of course, that's the awkward part of it. But I must make some sacrifice. I shall have to get in a temporary valet. It won't be very pleasant perhaps; but then, it's only for a few weeks, and better that than that the work at Glebelands should not be finished by the time we want it."

"Very well, sir," said Roberts, but without heartiness. He had been with Carnforth for fifteen years — ever since Carnforth had come into his kingdom; and he not only jealously resented the usurpation by another servant of his own office, but he was sincerely concerned for his master's comfort.

At the same time he realised the importance of the proper completion of the work on the new house at Chertsey, and he was a little compensated by the flattery of the trust entailed in this charge which his master now gave him.

After breakfast Carnforth wrote to a couple of West-End registry offices stating his needs in the matter of a new valet. Then he went out and personally visited four others. If he stopped at the fourth it was because he conceived that he had found what he required.

This office was established in a sort of ground-floor parlour of a dingy house in Pimlico Road. The insufficient daylight that filtered to it was supplemented by a feeble gas-jet, and it was furnished with cheap pretentiousness. A bulky writing-table littered with dusty papers occupied the middle of the floor. Beside it was an office arm chair for clients. Enthroned at this writing-table was a thin lady of uncertain, age, with a wonderful coppery coiffure, a sharp-featured, powdered face, and an air and utterance of infinitely aristocratic languor. She conveyed to you by her every look and gesture a sense of the overwhelming honour done in admitting you to her august presence.

Carnforth briskly stated his needs — an efficient valet of good character who could come to him at once, not later than to-morrow.

"Not later than to-morrow?" she echoed, with a stare that implied how utterly unreasonable she found him. Languidly she turned over the pages of a ledger-like volume, and made notes from it. After a time she presented him with a list of some half-dozen names.

"These are all very superior servants that we can recommend," she said. "We have none but high-class servants on our books. I have indicated the wages in each case. But I am afraid none of them could come to you to-morrow."

"I must if necessary wait a day or two longer," said Carnforth. "But I am rather pressed."

"Should I 'ear of anyone answering your requirements, I'll let you know at once if you'll kindly leave me your address."

Carnforth left his address and telephone number, paid the fee demanded and went home.

That afternoon he attentively studied the society columns of *The Eclipse* — which was particularly devoted to social matters — the movements of people of quality. He discovered that Lord Digglefield had been compelled to leave for Canada at a moment's notice two days before owing to the death there of his brother. With a view to acting upon that information, and adapting the fact to his own needs, he dined that evening at the exclusive club in Pall Mall, of which both Digglefield and himself were members. After dinner he repaired to the library and wrote a letter in a big, sprawling handwriting which none would ever have identified with his own peculiarly neat and small characters.

"I can thoroughly recommend Adolf Schwartz, who has been in my service for close upon four years. He is an efficient valet, and generally an extremely capable servant. He is trustworthy, respectable and respectful, and I part with him with extreme reluctance, compelled to it by circumstances which have just arisen and which demand my immediate departure from England. Schwartz is of Swiss nationality."

He antedated the letter by three days, and signed it "Digglefield." He placed it in an envelope, pocketed it, and left the club.

On the following morning Carnforth left home in a navy-blue suit that had seen some wear concealed under a heather-mixture overcoat that was of a fairly full pattern. He hailed a taxi, and drove to Sloane Square. Arrived there he walked down Lower Sloane Street, hailed a second taxi, and drove over Chelsea Bridge to Battersea Park Station. He purchased a first-class ticket to Victoria, and selected an empty carriage.

On that brief journey Carnforth entered upon the first stage of the only really repugnant part of the task to which he had set his hand. He altered his personal appearance. He took off the loose overcoat be wore, drew from one of its capacious pockets a pair of low brown shoes that had seen a deal of wear, and exchanged them for the enameled boots he was wearing; he wrapped up the latter, and stuffed them into the overcoat pocket. Similarly he exchanged his fashionable soft hat for an old and faded black Homburg, with a turned-down brim. He assumed a pair of plain, steel-rimmed spectacles, and a short, black chin-beard. His upper lip he left bare and shaven, not only because he knew that a false moustache will seldom look anything but false, but also because the present arrangement would best suit the character which he was about to assume. Then between his cheeks and his gums he inserted on each side and in each jaw one of those wads used by dentists when filling teeth. These caused his cheeks to bulge, making them appear fuller, and entirely changing the character of his face; also they would as entirely change the character of his voice. He removed his straight collar, and replaced it by a very low one, and assumed a well-worn black necktie. Then he greased his hair and combed it straight back from his forehead. Lastly he inflated an air cushion, and arranged it cleverly under his waist coat.

When he stepped on to the platform at Victoria, with his overcoat on his arm, none would have recognised Carnforth in this respectably seedy, rather portly fellow.

The overcoat, with its stuffed pockets, he deposited in the left luggage office, and then crossing the station he made his exit into the Buckingham Palace Road and turned westwards.

He would have avoided, if possible, what he felt was a sacrifice of dignity entailed in this masquerade. But it was essential to the success of his plan; so swallowing his repugnance he went resolutely forward. Fear of detection he had none. The simplicity of his disguise was proof against that. And when he walked into that dingy servants' registry office in Pimlico Road he had little fear that he would be recognised as the gentleman who had applied there yesterday for a valet.

He addressed the copper-haired aristocrat with a proper deference, and with a pronounced German accent, the wads in his mouth assisting him in this thickening and dissembling of his voice.

"Good day, ma'am," he said. "My name is Schwartz — Adolf Schwartz. I am a valet."

"Looking for a situation?" said the lady, taking up her pen.

"Four years ago you find me situation wit' Lord Digglefield."

"Wasn't here four years ago," said the lady.

"No? Ach! But —" He paused, a little bewildered. "I am mistake. It must be anoder office." And upon that he would have with drawn, but that the woman, seeing that business was to be done, detained him. He seemed a little reluctant to remain. It required that her nobility should descend from the chill eminence where she reigned and employ persuasion with him. At last he responded.

He explained that he had been for four years in the service of Lord Digglefield; that his lordship, owing to the death of his brother, had suddenly been called indefinitely away to Canada. That he himself was unwilling to go so far, and that consequently, upon his lordship's sailing the day before yesterday, he had found himself unemployed. Next he entertained the lady of the establishment with a catalogue of his accomplishments and finally told her that if she could find him a really good situation in the course of the next month he would be glad.

"Could you take a place, at once?" she asked him.

The supposed Schwartz didn't think he could ... He had excellent references from his lordship in his lordship's own hand, but naturally anyone engaging him would desire to communicate direct with Lord Digglefield, and, of course, that would take some time. He thought that meanwhile he would take a little holiday.

"I can find you a temporary place perhaps in the meantime, provided you could go at once. Where are your references?"

He drew out the letter he had penned last night at his club. She considered it, and was properly impressed.

"Of course, it's for my client to say whether he is satisfied with it. It seems all right. If you'll wait a moment I'll telephone."

Carnforth heard her asking for the number of his flat, and then inquiring if he were at home. When she hung up the receiver, he knew what she was going to say.

She scribbled an address in pencil on a scrap of paper, stamped it with a rubber stamp bearing the name of the office, and handed it to him.

"If you'll call there between eleven and twelve to-morrow morning you can see the gentleman — that's his name. Let me hear how you get on. Meanwhile you had better leave me your address in case I should hear of anything else."

He gave an entirely fictitious address in Battersea, adding: "Of course, it is only temporary; only until I get a situation, eh?"

She nodded, and bade him good-day; and he took his departure.

He walked back to Victoria, recovered his overcoat, and took the next train back to Battersea Park Station, again selecting, of course, an empty first-class carriage. On the journey he restored his appearance to the normal.

He lunched at his club, and when he got back to his flat in the course of the afternoon he was informed by Roberts of the telephone message that had been received from a registry office in Pimlico. Himself he rang the office up, and made the closest inquiries into the character and antecedents of the recommended servant. He smiled as he heard the answers, the assurances of strong personal recommendation from Lord Digglefield, and the rest.

The report was so satisfactory that he bade Roberts make arrangements to go down to Chertsey by the eleven o'clock train from Waterloo on the following morning; and when the following morning came he saw Roberts depart in a frame of mind between gratified pride at the charge entrusted to him and misgiving on the score of his master's comfort in his absence.

In the course of the morning the duties of the porter at Consort Court are so multifarious that he is not always where a porter should be, and it is impossible for him to see everyone that passes in and out. But at a few minutes before noon he saw a rather portly man with a slight stoop dressed in a shabby-genteel fashion, with steel-rimmed spectacles, the bridge of which was wrapped in soiled worsted, a short black beard and shaven upper lip coming down stairs. The man approached him civilly and, speaking in a voice that was something between guttural and husky, and with a pronounced German accent, put him some questions regarding the character and habits of Mr. Carnforth.

In answer to the porter's stare, the fellow explained himself.

"He hass chust engage me ass his valet. It is only tempor'y. But I did not see his regular valet to make my questions. So I hope you'll be so kind — "

"Mr. Carnforth's all right," said the porter. "Think yourself jolly lucky to have got the place, even if it is only temporary."

The fellow's puckered face seemed to grow less puckered. He smiled, and thanked the porter.

"I go now to get my dings. I come back soon to stay." And he slouched out.

We know — for he said so afterwards — that the porter considered this valet a queer sort of "cuss." But he supposed that his oddity was to be accounted for on the score of his being a foreigner.

The man returned at the end of about an hour with a very soiled and battered gladstone bag — empty and picked up for a few shillings in a Soho pawnshop. Again he had a few words with the porter before going up to Carnforth's flat. That afternoon Carnforth telephoned the registry office to announce that he had engaged Adolf Schwartz for a month at twenty-five shillings a week. That same night, having received the registry office's account he sent the august lady a postal order in discharge of it.

It was on a Friday that Schwartz entered upon his employment with Carnforth, and for a week there after Carnforth was assiduous in thoroughly establishing the fellow's identity. Schwartz came and went, contrived to get on jesting terms with the porter, went shopping for Carnforth, and made himself conspicuous in one or two places by the offensiveness with which he attempted to stand up for his master's interests.

Schwartz answered the door to callers in the afternoons. But none of them ever found Carnforth at home or disengaged. In fact, this stout and rather elderly German, with his iron-rimmed spectacles, rubber collar and black chin-beard became as well known in a week as most servants in such places can contrive to be in a year. After the first ordeal of those inquiries concerning himself which he addressed — in the character of Schwartz — to the porter, Carnforth had known not the slightest anxiety on the score of his disguise. We know that it was simple, as all effective disguises must be — for the art of disguise is more than any other an art that must conceal art — yet it completely metamorphosed him.

On the eighth day of Schwartz's brief life — that is to say on the Friday of the following week — he had one shock. Answering the bell late in the afternoon he found himself confronted by the vulturine face and gimlet eyes of Mr. Jackson.

" 'Ullo!" quoth Jackson, who had instinctively disliked the sleek, urbane and forbidding Roberts, and was, therefore, quick to note the change. "Who are you?"

"Mr. Carnforth's valet," came the other's guttural voice.

"Made a change has he?" grunted Jackson. And added, "Is he in?"

"Mr. Carnford is not at home."

"Oh, not at home, ain't he. Ah! Very well, just tell him that Mr. Jackson called. Mr. Jackson. Haven't got a card on me. Say, Mr. Jackson from *The Eclipse.*"

Carnforth closed the door as Jackson departed, and having closed it he leaned against it. He was trembling. It was the first sign of weakness, of faltering, that he had known since setting his hand to this grim travesty. Indeed, the complete calm — the calm of the man who feels himself justified in the course he is following — with which he had gone about the work, and with which, in between, he had attended to the ordinary matters of his life, was by far the most amazing part of all this very amazing business.

Twice in the course of that week he had dined with the Tollemaches, and nothing could have been more normal and easy than his behaviour.

Yet now, after those moments face to face with Jackson, he was shaken. He recovered quickly. Yet because he had been shaken he now asked himself again had he the courage to go on and to carry this thing through. If he felt that he had not, then he had better abandon it at this stage. For without courage and an iron self-control there was nothing to be done. His introspection reassured him.

He would be equal to the emergency when the hour should strike. He was in haste now to hurry it forward. He felt that now that the ground was all prepared, now that there was nothing for him to do but wait, suspense might undermine his nerve.

He could neither write nor wire to ask Jackson to come, since either of those courses would leave traces, would give rise to questions which he might be called upon to answer. He must wait until Jackson called again, and then as Schwartz he would give Jackson the fateful appointment. It was the waiting, he felt, that was going to put him to the test. But his fears on that score were quite unnecessary.

That same evening he answered a telephone call, to hear the voice of Jackson at the other end.

"That you, Carnforth. This is Jackson. I say, do you want to see me again or not?"

"Oh, yes. My man told me you had called. You gave me a fortnight, you know. Anyway, I was just going to write to ask you to call to-morrow evening."

"Don't trouble to write," came Jackson's answer. "I'll be there. What time'll suit you?"

"Oh, between nine and ten."

"Right-o! Between nine and ten to-morrow evening. So long!"

Carnforth hung up the receiver and stood immovable for a long minute, staring straight before him.

VI

At a few minutes before seven on that fateful Saturday evening, Carnforth, wearing a black Chesterfield over his dinner clothes and an opera hat slightly tilted backwards, came downstairs from his flat carrying a suitcase.

The porter ran to relieve him of it. Carnforth seemed out of temper.

"Seen that man of mine, Timbs?" he inquired.

"No, sir."

"Can't think where the deuce he's got to. I sent him out half an hour ago to the post, and told him to come straight back. Call me a taxi, will you?"

The porter sounded a blast on his whistle. From the rank a taxi manoeuvred across.

"When that fellow Schwartz comes back, Timbs, you might tell him that if a Mr. Jackson should happen to call this evening he's to ask him to wait for me, and to ring me up at the club to let me know. Otherwise, I shan't be in until about twelve. You won't forget, Timbs?"

"No, sir. Thank you, sir."

The porter gave the driver the name of Carnforth's club, and he was whirled away.

At his club Carnforth dined with a couple of men of his acquaintance. At eight o'clock he rose from table leaving them at their coffee. He thought he would go up to the library. He went up. It was quite deserted. He remained not longer than five minutes. Then he went down to the cloakroom, opened his suit-case, and drew from it a seedy ulster that he had rendered peculiar to Schwartz, and the black Homburg hat and old brown brogues, which he stuffed into one of its capacious pockets.

With this ulster over his arm, its seediness not apparent when carried thus, he left the club and drove to Victoria. Acting upon his usual plan he traveled in a first-class carriage to Battersea Park Station, and when he alighted there he was wearing the ulster over his Chesterfield, the Homburg hat, and the old brown shoes, whilst a green scarf effectively concealed his evening neck-wear.

He had stuffed his opera hat into his waistcoat, and his patent leather boots into a pocket of the ulster, and had effected in his appearance those other usual changes which resulted in the creation of Schwartz. He walked briskly over Chelsea Bridge, and in Lower Sloane Street boarded a motor-bus.

At ten minutes to nine he entered Consort Court, and made straight for the stairs, knowing that the porter would be on the watch for him, to deliver him the message which he himself, as Carnforth, had left for Schwartz. As soon as Timbs saw him he flung out of his little box.

"Here you, Schwartz, I got a message for you."

"Vat is dat?"

"You're going to get the sack, my boy. A fine temper Mr. Carnforth was in through your not being back. Where've you been all this time?"

"Mr. Carnford tell me he vas going out, dat he vould not vant me again to-night. Vat message have he left?" Schwartz went upstairs muttering guttural oaths, and let himself into the flat.

He switched on the lights, but he did not remove his ulster or any part of his disguise. He was taking no slightest risk. Possibly the porter might accompany Jackson to the door of the flat, or he or another might merely be passing at the moment that Carnforth should open the door.

He removed his hat, and combed back the hair straight from his brow; he had not greased it on this occasion for reasons that will presently be obvious. Next he crossed to the writing-table, unlocked a drawer, and took thence a small Browning pistol. That done, he sat down to wait quite calmly. Nine o'clock struck. Another five minutes passed, and then the electric bell trilled in the flat.

That trill sent a shiver down his spine. He rose, controlled himself, and went to open the door.

On the threshold stood Jackson.

"Mr. Carnforth at home?"

"Blease gome dis vay."

He led Jackson down the corridor, and threw open the door of the study. "Blease dake a chair. I vill tell Mr. Carnford." Two or three minutes passed, and the door opened again to admit Carnforth undisguised.

He was perhaps a little pale, but perfectly calm in his greeting of Jackson. He closed the door, and motioned his visitor to a chair by the hearth. But Jackson chose to remain standing.

"Well, Carnforth," said he with that familiarity of his which Carnforth found it so hard to endure, "thought it over, have you?"

"From the fact that you called yesterday it occurred to me that you might perhaps be disposed to compromise. That is why I rang you up."

"I'm disposed to compromise for three thousand pounds, all right. But that's rock bottom, old boy."

"Have you the letters on you?" asked Carnforth.

"Have I —?" Jackson laughed with relish. "Not much! What d'ye take me for?"

"You don't trust me. Well, well, it's natural enough, I suppose. But tell me; if I were to consent to pay your price, you don't suppose I should do so other than against delivery of the letters."

"That's all right," replied Jackson. "As soon as you say the word we can meet in some public place and make the exchange there. But I'm not such a fool as to come here with the letters on me."

"Where are they?" asked Carnforth.

"What's that got to do with you?" Jackson was suddenly truculent. Perhaps he was struck by the grimness of Carnforth's manner, or perhaps by sheer intuition he became aware — that some danger threatened him.

Carnforth smiled. "I think, under the circumstances, I have some right to ask the question."

"Well, you can take it that they're quite safe."

"One more question, Jackson; is anyone else aware of their existence?"

"No," was the immediate answer. "You don't suppose I'd give myself away like that, do you?"

"I don't suppose you would," said Carnforth. "Very well, then." He dropped into a chair and leaned forward as he spoke. "I'll tell you what is the utmost that I am prepared to do — the utmost, I assure you, that it is possible to do. I'll pay you every penny of ready money I have to my credit at the moment — a matter of a thousand pounds. And I will give you my note of hand for another five hundred in twelve months' time. I swear to you, Jackson, that this is the utmost I can do. No one in the world will give you a quarter of that for them."

"Not Mr. Bristow?" leered Jackson.

"Being a blackguard, Jackson, it is quite natural that you should be unable to understand the feelings of a man of honour. I don't believe he would give you a cent for them; in fact, I am convinced that if you attempt any such deal with him you'll find yourself in jail again."

"But you'd be ruined if that happened, wouldn't you?"

"Admitted. But my ruin would profit you nothing." He rose. Come now, Jackson, be reasonable. Accept this fifteen hundred pounds and let us put an end to the matter."

"Three thousand," said Jackson stonily. "You're wasting time."

Carnforth moved across the room, and came to a halt by the door.

He sighed. "Is that your last word, Jackson? No, no, don't answer me yet. Consider well what you are doing," he pleaded, and Jackson, thinking that Carnforth pleaded but to spare his pocket, listened with a sneer on his face

"Remember that that crime of mine which now you threaten to expose was committed at your own instance; remember that I shielded you when by denouncing you I could more readily have ensured my own pardon; remember that had I given you away you would have gone to jail then, or at least, you would have been dismissed, and so you would never have had it in your power to hold these letters over me. Remember that it is entirely due to my loyalty, to my compassion for you, that those letters have come into your power."

"That's enough," said Jackson. "It don't cut no ice. I'm a desperate man, Carnforth, and I've no use for sentiment."

"So am I a desperate man, Jackson," said Carnforth, in a hard voice. "You have driven me utterly to bay. I am fighting for my honour, and I'll go to any lengths to defend it. Since I can't afford to pay your price, and since you won't be reasonable I must adopt other measures." He turned the key in the door and pocketed it.

"Here! What's this? Unlock that door!" cried Jackson. He turned livid, his little eyes were dilating with sudden fear, and his hand dropped to his pocket.

Carnforth noted the movement, and concluded that he was armed, as after all was to have been expected. He was glad of it; if the thing were to end in a duel so much the better.

"I'll unlock it in a moment. When — "

"You'll unlock it now," said Jackson with an oath.

"Wait," Carnforth begged. "Hear me first."

Near the door, and standing a little forward from the wall immediately in front of the electric light switches was a tall-backed settee. Carnforth leaned now upon the corner of this.

"Listen, Jackson, as there's a God above us, I am offering you your last chance."

Jackson sneered confidently, but said nothing.

"I will go to the telephone, ring up a messenger office and ask them to send a boy here. You will write three lines telling your wife where to find the packet of letters and ordering it to be delivered to this messenger, who will bring it here. I will then pay you the money and give you my note of hand for the rest."

Leering, Jackson wagged his head. "I don't think," he said.

"Either that, Jackson, or I swear that you don't leave this room alive."

The next instant Carnforth was looking into the barrel of a revolver, which Jackson had whipped from his pocket.

"That's a game that two can play," the fellow snarled, but his voice was unsteady. Carnforth perceived that the blackmailer was horribly frightened.

"You thought you had me trapped, did you?" sneered Jackson. He walked backwards to the bell, his revolver still leveled, and pressed it with a finger of his left hand. "You move a finger, and I'll put a bullet through you."

Carnforth was eyeing him quite coldly. "Things are not at all as you suppose," he answered. "You can ring all you like; no one will answer you. There is no one in the flat but we two, and I would further draw your attention to the fact that in these well-built mansions floors and ceilings are perfectly sound-proof, and that to shut out the noise of the traffic I am equipped with double windows."

"Oh, it's like that, is it?" In spite of his revolver, and for all that he affected still to sneer, the quivering of his voice betrayed the horrid fear that had gripped him. "Hands up, then! Hands up at once, or I'll shoot you."

Carnforth's hands went up, but one of them swept in passing over the switches, plunging the room into, darkness.

Instantly he leapt aside and dropped behind the settee, and as instantly almost came a jagged blade of flame from across the room; two sharp reports rang out followed by two dull thuds as the bullets buried themselves, one after the other, in the mahogany panels of the door.

Gripping now his own revolver, Carnforth thudded his knees on the floor to simulate a fall, drew a hand with a slithering sound along the back of the settee, and emitted a groan of pain.

Jackson fell into the trap.

"You would have it — " he began in whimpering accents, then Carnforth fired at the voice. That he had missed he knew from the smash of broken glass in the bookcase. But he left Jackson more badly scared than ever.

There followed now a spell of utter and awful silence in that velvety blackness unrelieved by any faintest glimmer of light. Neither man dared move lest he should give the other a clue to his position. They hardly dared to draw breath lest it should be heard in the deathly stillness that now reigned there, and Jackson, crouching by the fireplace, cursed the thudding of his heart which he feared must betray his whereabouts.

Carnforth, on his knees, his body mainly sheltered by the settee, was leaning forward on his left hand, his right holding his pistol ready, straining his ears for the slightest sound that should inform him where Jackson stood. Jackson, in that crouching attitude which men instinctively assume when in fear, stood alert, by the fireplace, gripping his pistol and waiting, too.

Thus a spell, during which the ticking of the clock was the only sound in the room. When it chimed the half-hour it startled them both by the jarring suddenness of it, and Carnforth had almost fired at the preliminary whir of the machinery. As it ceased, he fancied he caught a stealthy movement. But before he could make sure, all was still again.

Jackson had still a card to play; but it filled him with fury to consider that he was never now to be allowed to play it. He wanted to tell Carnforth that the letters were in a sealed package addressed to Harry Bristow and that in the event of anything happening to himself his wife — with whom he had left it — had strict orders to post that package immediately. He knew that if he were to inform Carnforth of this it might make a difference. But he also knew that the first word he uttered would certainly be answered by a bullet that might silence him forever.

So he waited, resolved to put a bullet through Carnforth. He might kill him, and if so there was no doubt he would have to swing for him. He felt that he had a burning grievance; that Carnforth had behaved in a dastardly fashion in seeking to take him at a disadvantage.

So the clock ticked on, and the silence continued otherwise unbroken.

Again Carnforth thought of forcing an issue that must bring this desperate silence to an end. He exercised his wits, and devised a way to draw the other's fire. He rose very stealthily to his feet, slipped his left hand into his waist coat pocket, and drew forth his cigarette-case.

He balanced it a moment, considering, then he flung it across the room, away to his left. It clattered in the silence, like something that had been knocked over.   At the sound, Jackson swung round in panic, with a half-strangled cry, and blazed immediately in the direction of it. Instantly, aiming a little to the right of the flash of Jackson's shot, Carnforth fired into the darkness as it closed again.

There was a sharp cry and a thud, followed by a fit of coughing. Again Carnforth fired, to be answered by a second thud, and then silence.

He groped behind him, and switched up the lights.

Jackson lay on his back, staring at the ceiling. A red disc was spreading slowly on the left side of his head. He was quite dead.

Carnforth stood considering him for a moment as he lay there. Then he slipped his pistol into his pocket, and went out, closing the door after him.

He would not have been human had he not felt shaken after the ordeal through which he had passed. Compunction, however, he experienced none. He had given Jackson every chance, and every warning; and Jackson had met no more than the fate he deserved.

Carnforth passed into the dining-room, took a decanter of brandy from the sideboard and poured himself a stiff measure, drinking it neat.   Then he returned to the hall, and resumed his black Chesterfield. Over this he drew on his ulster, stuffed the opera-hat back into his waistcoat, assumed his beard and his absurd spectacles, and filled his mouth with the dentist's wads; he wrapped his neck in the green scarf, slipped on the old brown brogues, thrusting his dress boots into his pocket, and finally donned the seedy old Homburg.

Thus he left the flat and made his way below. He was by now perfectly master of himself once more. He walked up to the porter's box.

"I vill be back in a minute," said he, "but if Mr. Carnford gome back before me, blease tell him dat de gentleman is vaiting for him."

"All right, Schwartz," said the porter. "But are you leaving the gentleman all alone in the flat?"

"I haf to go out. But I gome back at once," said Schwartz.

He made his way through Lancelot Street into the Brompton Road to the top of Sloane Street, and jumped on to a motor-bus, which whirled him away to Sloane Square. Then he walked over Chelsea Bridge and boarded an electric train which took him to Battersea Park Road. He made his way to the station, and five minutes later he stepped out on the Victoria platform, once more as Basil Carnforth.

He walked a little way along Victoria Street and then, took a taxi-cab back to his club. It was then five minutes past ten. Going to the cloakroom, which was deserted, he packed away the ulster into his suit-case, which he locked. Then he proceeded upstairs.

He turned into the billiard-room, where he remained idling for some ten minutes in talk with one or two fellow-members. Thence he repaired to one of the card-rooms, and sat for awhile watching a game of auction. Invited presently to make a fourth at another table, he consented to play one rubber, as he was anxious to turn in early. First, however, he sent the card-room waiter to inquire whether any telephone message for him had been received. A negative answer having been brought him, he sat down to play. The rubber dragged out to some length, and, it was half past eleven when it was finished. One of the party happened to be a man who also had a flat in Consort Court. His name was Hammond. Carnforth and he went home together.

As they entered the mansion the porter accosted Carnforth.

"Excuse me, sir. Your man went out about a couple of hours ago, and hasn't yet come back. He said you would be home any minute, and told me to tell you if you came before he returned that there's a gentleman waiting for you upstairs."

Carnforth stared. "Do you mean that Schwartz has left him alone in the flat?"

"That's it, sir."

"And he's been there all this time — alone?"

"Yes, sir."

His face expressed annoyance. "Where has Schwartz gone?"

"He didn't say, sir. Just said he'd be back in a minute."

On his way upstairs Carnforth grumbled to Hammond. "That's the worst of chance servants. I've only had this fellow a week, and am about tired of him."

He inserted his key in the lock and lifted the latch. With the door open he stood a moment on the threshold, chatting easily with Hammond, then bade him good-night, went in, and closed the door.

Less than half a minute later he had wrenched it open again and dashed out on to the landing.

"Hammond!" he shouted.

"Hallo!" answered Hammond from above.

"Come down a moment, will you?" Carnforth's voice was shrill and excited. "Timbs!" he shouted downstairs. "Timbs!" He clapped his finger to the button of the lift bell and held it there.

Hammond descended from above; Timbs came running up from below; both alarmed by the insistence of Carnforth's summons.

"What's the matter?" cried Hammond.

Carnforth looked pale and excited, and neither pallor nor excitement were assumed.

"Just step in here, will you?" he requested them both.

They followed him into the flat, and stood at the door of his study, gazing in amazement and horror upon the scene presented there.

Then they went in and made an examination of the body; they noted the disorder of the room, the two bullet cracks in the mahogany door, the shattered glass of the bookcases, and the revolver in the dead man's hand. It was obvious that there had been a fight. Carnforth desired Timbs to tell him again exactly what had been the movements of Schwartz that evening. Timbs did so; but they appeared to leave Carnforth as bewildered as before. Finally he sent Timbs for the police.

To assist the police Carnforth made the fullest possible statement. He had known the dead man for many years, but had lost sight of him until quite lately. His name was Jackson. He had fallen upon evil days, and had lately sought assistance from Carnforth. Carnforth had already helped him a little, and was prepared to help him still further and to enable him to make a fresh start in the Colonies. He had rather expected him that evening, and had instructed his valet, Schwartz, to telephone him at the club if Jackson should come, in which case he would return. He had not been telephoned. Of the rest he could offer no explanation. He confessed he found it hard to believe that the crime could have been committed by Schwartz.

Then he stated what he knew of Schwartz; how the German valet had entered his employ a week ago upon the recommendation of a Pimlico registry office.

Search was made through Schwartz's singularly scant effects, none of which afforded the least clue to his identity, and the letter signed "Digglefield" was discovered.

Carnforth withdrew, leaving the flat in the possession of the police. Hammond offered to put him up for the night, but on the grounds of not wishing to disturb his friend he preferred to sleep at a neighbouring hotel, where he engaged rooms. In the morning he wired to Roberts, ordering him to return to town at once.

The inquest was held on the following Monday, and Carnforth, of course, attended it. He had no slightest fear on the score of the issue; his measures had been taken far too carefully; the identity of Schwartz was far too well established, and it was as clear as could be that none but Schwartz could be the author of the deed. This, indeed, was the conclusion — a foregone conclusion — of the jury.

The inquest failed utterly, of course, to reveal the slightest motive for the crime, or to discover any connection between the deceased and his murderer. But seeing that Jackson had gone there armed, and considering the information which the police were able to afford of his extremely shady reputation and his past convictions, there was an inclination to hold the view that he might have been the aggressor, a view supported to a certain extent by the fact that he must have discharged his own three shots before he was hit himself, for the medical evidence was quite positive that a man with such a wound in the lung would have been quite incapable of using a pistol.

The most important evidence was naturally that of Timbs, the porter. It was so conclusive that the only verdict possible was one of murder against Adolf Schwartz.

Carnforth was examined at length. He answered all questions frankly and readily, but none of his answers were of any real assistance in the elucidation of the mystery. He had known Jackson some years ago; he knew him to be unfortunate, but he had no idea until hearing the statements of the police that he bore so evil a character.

He left the inquest after having received the coroner's expressions of sympathy with him in the unpleasantness to which the affair had subjected him. He was pestered by reporters in quest of details that would make a story; but his answers were of the briefest, and the mystery grew daily more impenetrable.

The wildest theories were advanced in solution of it, and more than one enterprising newspaper offered rewards for information that should lead to the capture of Schwartz. This led to the arrest of one man, who, fortunately, was able to supply at once the fullest and most conclusive alibi.

VII

For a week the placards flamed with "THE VALET MYSTERY," as the affair was rightly called, for Schwartz had not only disappeared without leaving a single trace behind, but the police were alike baffled in their attempts to trace his antecedents. It was found, of course, that the letter of recommendation was a forgery, committed it was supposed by someone who had purloined some note paper from Digglefleld's club.

It was hoped for a little time that in this there was a clue that might lead to a discovery. But again it was found that, like all the other clues that had been started, it led nowhere at all. The registry office which had sent Schwartz to Carnforth was censured for the manner in which it conducted its business, for this office, it will be remembered, in its anxiety to draw a commission, had affected a previous knowledge of Schwartz, which it was now unable to establish. Finally, there were the inevitable diatribes against undesirable aliens, and there at last the matter passed into oblivion, relegated to the limbo of criminal mysteries unsolved.

But we have slightly anticipated the course of events as they more directly concerned Carnforth.

He returned from the inquest to his rooms at the hotel with a mind that was at once elated and uneasy. He had taken the law into his own hands and he had carried out what he accounted a justifiable execution. His honour was saved. He could continue to walk among men without fear that that ghost of his past would be evoked and put up for sale by any unscrupulous scoundrel. His uneasiness was all concerned with Muriel. When he thought of her, his attitude towards his deed seemed altered. From the world in general he had no slightest scruple in keeping that deed a secret. But from her? He wondered. Yet if he told her, he knew that she must shrink from him in horror, that her affection for him would be stricken down forever; that she must refuse to marry him. Knowing what her attitude must be, could he avail himself of her ignorance?

Perplexed, tormented almost, by this thought he reached his hotel. He was met in the hall by Harry Bristow, who was awaiting him.

Bristow greeted him with a curt nod, his face so extremely grave that Carnforth was conscious of a thrill of fear. The young man desired to have a word in private with him.

"Come up to my room," said Carnforth.

On reaching the private sitting-room, the door being closed, Bristow drew from his breast-pocket a stout sealed envelope.

"I want to show you something that I received by this morning's post," he said. He was rather pale, obviously ill at ease and nervous. "Please look at it."

He held out a sheet of paper which he took from the envelope, leaving obviously other sheets still undisclosed. Carnforth took the paper. Such was his self-control that he held it in fingers which betrayed no slightest tremor, although he read the following:

Sir, — Should anything happen to me at any time, the accompanying letters written some years ago by Mr. Basil Carnforth may be of service to you. Circumstances will best show you how to make use of them, but I have no doubt that you will readily perceive the value of these letters yourself, for with same in your power you will have Mr. Carnforth at your mercy. I am leaving the parcel with a friend of mine who is to post it if anything should happen to me. When you receive it, it will be too late for me to drive any bargain with you; you may think it best to hand them over with this letter to the police. If so, please remember that I could myself have addressed them to Scotland Yard, but in sending them to you I wish to show you the service I shall be doing to you personally in putting Carnforth out of your way, and I venture to hope that you will liquidate this debt to me by sending out of the wealth with which you have been blessed a sum of not less than five hundred pounds to my widow, whose address I give at foot. — Edward Jackson.

Carnforth was smiling when he came to the end of the letter but it was a smile of self-pity. He had been so confident of his imagination to plan and his intelligence to execute; and here was something that he had entirely overlooked, and yet something that a man of Jackson's astuteness must obviously have prepared. He wondered now that Jackson had warned him of this last night, and thus compelled him to hold his hand.

"What are you going to do?" he asked quite simply.

Bristow's honest young face was preternaturally grave. "Of course," he said, "I have not read the accompanying letters to which the writer refers."

"That was very scrupulous of you under all the circumstances," said Carnforth quietly, so quietly that Bristow looked up sharply to see whether any irony was indicated in his face. But he found it stern and almost sorrowful.

"It is the circumstances," said Bristow, "that put difficulties in my way. It is here implied that it was you who killed Jackson."

"The coroner's jury has just brought in a verdict of murder against my valet, Adolf Schwartz."

There was a pause. Then Bristow spoke nervously.

"Of course," he said, "my duty is to deliver these documents over to the police, and leave the matter to them. But on the other hand it is perfectly obvious that you have been in the hands of a blackmailer. So that, even under ordinary circumstances, I do not quite know how I should act. But I do know that under existing circumstances it is quite impossible for me to do what I have said is my duty. Since I must profit, as is here pointed out, by your removal, if I do anything to contribute to it it is impossible for me to be quite easy in my mind that I am not — that I am not in some sort a confederate of this murdered blackmailer. I am in quite an impossible position," he ended.

The young man's fine sense of honour touched Carnforth as nothing else could have touched him then. A sincere admiration for this lad with whom he had been friends but whom never hitherto had he taken seriously sprang suddenly to life. It resolved the doubt touching his own conduct that lingered in him. Out of the sincerity of his love for Muriel he saw that it was his duty to withdraw.

"Will it help you out of your difficulty if I tell you the truth?" asked Carnforth.

"I do not wish to force your confidence," replied Bristow.

"You will not be doing that. As things have turned out I owe it to you that you should know exactly how matters stand. I beg you, of course, to treat what I say as confidential." He lowered his voice a little. "Jackson was blackmailing me as you have supposed, and as his letter to you proves. He had purloined some letters written by me to a man against whom I had sinned some twenty years ago— letters which contained a full avowal of that offence of mine. That past I have lived down; the offence, such as it was, I have amended in the fullest way. Since then my life has been as honourable and clean as men generally suppose it. This blackmailer threatened to destroy all this; to wreck my reputation, to drive me out in shame, to render my marriage impossible, and to set an end to my career. His power lay in those purloined letters. I offered him money; fifteen hundred pounds. He demanded three thousand, and it was beyond my power to raise that sum. He was obdurate. He went so far as to suggest that I should have recourse to dishonest and dishonourable means of raising the money he demanded. I was driven to despair. I could not invoke the law against him without destroying myself. I was forced to take the law into my own hands and to deliver myself from this peril. I did the thing relentlessly and without scruple, and I give you my word of honour, Bristow, that I am vexed by no scintilla of remorse, nor ever shall be.

"In the end even my life was threatened. Though I confess that I planned to murder him, the thing resolved itself into a duel, as the evidence plainly shows. Apart from that, however, if a woman may kill to defend her honour, may not a man when it is the only way?"

Bristow remained standing, lost in thought for some moments. At last he looked up.

"I sympathise with you, profoundly," he said. He looked at the package lying on the table, and looked at Carnforth. Then he turned to the window and stood gazing out. "Who is Adolf Schwartz?" he inquired presently.

"He doesn't exist," said Carnforth. "It is a long story. But I can say no more on that score. If you are wondering whether any other man may be in danger of suffering for what I have done, let me assure you that no one will suffer. Apart from myself, one other person will profit — Jackson's widow. For I shall send her anonymously the sum mentioned there by Jackson to compensate her for a loss which she is hardly likely to account anything but a gain, poor soul." He paused. Bristow turned, and they faced each other again. "Well?" asked Carnforth. "What will you do?"

"I have given you every facility to throw those papers on the fire," said Bristow.

Carnforth started, and his eyes suddenly brightened. It was then that he finally resolved the matter that troubled him, and he was surprised at the relief which that solution brought him.

"You do not wish to compound a felony?" he inquired.

"I assure you that it never crossed my mind. I wasn't thinking of that at all."

"I didn't really think you were, Bristow," answered Carnforth slowly. "We have been — to employ the term of melodrama — rivals. But we have not at all conducted ourselves in the fashion of melodrama. I have had many doubts on the score, of my own worth, no doubt at all on the score of yours. I am so much an older man than Muriel, and the rest of it."

"If you think that those letters — " began Bristow hotly.

"I don't," Carnforth broke in. "I have much too high an opinion of you. Nevertheless, we must look things in the face."

"Very well," said Bristow. He came back and gathered up the package. "But first we will burn this." And he flung it on the fire.

"It really doesn't matter," said Carnforth. "The point is — and I have been thinking of it all the morning — that if Muriel knew what was on my hands, however broad a view she took of it, she would not marry me now. It follows, that as I am, I hope, a man of honour, I cannot let our engagement go on without telling her. Since I shrink naturally enough from that, there remains nothing to do but to place matters where they would be if I did tell her."

Bristow was white to the lips. But he said nothing.

"I love Muriel well enough," continued Carnforth, "to renounce her when I know that such renunciation is entirely for her own good. I will write to her to-day, and I will write to Colonel Tollemache. He, at least, will be relieved; for, although my friend, he never did approve of my marriage with his daughter. She may feel it a little for a time. But I depend upon you, Bristow." He held out his hand.

Bristow gripped it. "I'm sorry, old man — deuced sorry."

Carnforth smiled into the troubled, boyish face. "So am I," he said simply. "But later on I think we shall all be glad. And the future, Bristow, believe me, is all that matters always — the future and the reckonings it presents."

His Last Chance

Through the motley throng of clients in the lieutenant-general's ante-chamber M. des Favelles moved airily, a very picture of elegance, from his well-curled and carefully powdered wig down to the red heels of his shoes. Those who did not know him inquired his name; those who knew him marveled what might be his business with M. de Sartines. For what indeed should this careless man of fashion be doing in the ante-chamber of the Minister of Police?

Perhaps in some degree conscious of the curiosity he was exciting, and with a view to in part allaying it, he informed an acquaintance whom he met — in tones loud enough to be heard in the remotest corner of the apartment — that he came to solicit M. de Sartines' interest and good offices towards a young Breton cousin of his for whom he was anxious to secure an appointment in the Guards.

For one that solicited favors he was admitted to the lieutenant-general's with an alacrity that filled the other clients at once with envy and a high sense of M. des Favelles's importance.

Within the chamber, which might not inadequately be compared to the very heart of the web of espionage in which M. de Sartines enmeshed the whole of France, he was brusquely received by the great policeman. There was no talk here of a Breton young cousin, and although des Favelles retained his habitual airiness, there was a something akin to anxiety in the look with which he met the scrutiny of M. de Sartiness' wide-set eyes.

"I have sent for you, des Favelles," said the minister brusquely, "to inquire whether you have found some source of revenue that enables you to treat with contempt the appointment you hold under me, and to neglect the duties to which it binds you?"

Des Favelles was taken aback. The airiness dropped from him upon the instant, and his color changed.

"But, monsieur, of what then do you complain?"

"Of what?" snapped Sartines. "Of everything. In the first place, you are never seen here. When I require you, I am compelled to send for you. *Mille tonnerres*, monsieur, do you conceive that the government is paying you a handsome annuity to keep you in the society to which you are accustomed merely so that you may pursue the vices that have brought you to what you are? I have sent for you to remind you, Favelles, — .and it will be for the last time, — that you have certain obligations towards us, and that unless you show yourself more zealous I shall leave you to pursue the inglorious journey to the gutter which I made the mistake of arresting a year ago."

"But, monsieur, I implore you to — "

"Tush! Let us say no more. I have other business to dispatch. You are now acquainted with my feelings, choose your way. If you are minded to continue in my favor, I have an immediate task for you demanding the very greatest delicacy and tact. It will be your last chance, Favelles."

"I beg that you will acquaint me with the particulars."

"Do you know the Marquise de Longuemain?"

"I am slightly acquainted with her."

"Could you improve that acquaintance?"

"Assuredly."

"Could you transform it into — an intimacy?"

Favelles smiled fatuously. His opinion of his personal endowments was of the highest. "I might make the attempt," said he with confidence.

"Perfectly," snorted Sartines. "Now for the affair itself. Madame la Marquise is sister to the Chevalier de Chateauroux, who was banished five years ago, and who is forbidden under pain of death to return. My spies are unerring, Favelles, but their sphere of action is more or less confined to France. Chateauroux, appreciating this fact, and well aware that his sands would be run the moment he sets foot on French soil, remains abroad in the flesh. But in the spirit he is actively among us. Twice within the last month I have had letters set before me, penned by this Chateauroux, and pointing unmistakably at a deep and mysterious conspiracy which he and some kindred traitors are organizing either in Spain or Flanders. With the political aspect I will not trouble you. The fact with which we have to deal is that this conspiracy exists. Were I acquainted with its nature I should find a way of defeating it. But I am beset by the terrors of the unknown. If I even knew where this Chateauroux is at work, I should find a way to kidnap him and thus I should stamp out this spark of rebellion before it spreads into a conflagration. My ordinary agents are powerless to gain the knowledge — or, at least, to gain it with the necessary promptness. In time, no doubt, we should succeed in tracing the chevalier, but it would probably be too late when we found him. This is where I need you, Favelles."

Sartines paused and let his glittering eye rest impressively upon the fashionably arrayed young gallant. Des Favelles, who had listened in silence, bowed and the minister continued:

"You will render yourself intimate with the Marquise de Longuemain. You will gain the entrée to her salon, where you will find some of the greatest wits and some of the greatest rogues in France. These men, I am convinced, are the correspondents of monsieur her brother. Watch and inquire with caution: induce them to initiate you into their treason and make you one of them; possess yourself of the address of this troublesome Chevalier de Chateauroux, and let me have it at your earliest."

Favelles advanced a step, his lips compressed and his face very white.

"Is this the work to offer a gentleman?" he demanded.

"No," answered Sartines, with that brutality which at times he dealt in, "it is not."

"Then why do you offer it to me?"

"Out of a hope that as a secret agent you may be less of a failure than you were as a gentleman. Enough of these airs, Favelles, they are out of keeping with your condition, and you have done work of the kind before. It is your last chance. Seize it or not, as you please. If you do not, then I have done with you; whilst if you blunder in it, I shall have done with you none the less. And now go," he ended, as abruptly as he had started. "I have others to see. Let me know by midnight upon what course you have determined."

A servant entering, Favelles saw himself forced to withdraw, his remonstrances all unspoken. Those in the ante-chamber no longer saw in him an airy, swaggering gallant; they beheld a man who walked swiftly, with bent head and eyes that avoided the glances of his fellows.

Yet for all his dejected air his soul was swayed by the first truly noble emotion that he had known for years. Whatever the cost, he swore, he would not undertake this loathsome business. He would sink to the gutter, — as Sartines had said, — sooner than lend himself to such an infamy.

Thus proposed M. des Favelles, but the Fates were disposing otherwise. That night he was at the Hotel de Savignon. A rout was being held, and Chance, — that arch jester, — led him to the side of Madame de Longuemain. Out of curiosity, perhaps, at first, to see what manner of woman was this dainty relict of a gouty old marquis, des Favelles made himself pleasant in a manner which, — to do him justice, — was extremely winning. The dainty widow showed herself not averse to his attentions, and he pursued them farther. They danced together; and before des Favelles knew it, a world of mischief was accomplished. Let those who have experience of the not uncommon suddenness of such attacks bear out the possibility of my statement that at eleven o'clock that night poor Favelles, — ostensibly one of the arbiters of Parisian fashion, in reality a broken gentleman driven by necessity to become one of M. de Sartines' secret agents, — was head over heels in love with the Marquise de Longuemain.

As he feasted his eyes upon the wondrous whiteness of her skin, the fairness of her shining hair, the depths of her blue eyes, he swore that within the hour M. de Sartines should receive his answer in the negative. He would not, — he could not, undertake the task. If it had been loathsome before, how much more loathsome was it not become since he had been brought into contact with this pearl of womankind?

Leaning towards him, she bade him come and see her upon the morrow. He would find an indifferent company at her house, yet some there were with a reputation for wit, whose conversation might perchance repay him. He protested with an ardor that brought blushes to her cheek that he valued all the wits in the world at less than nothing by contrast with the joy that would be his upon again beholding her. A mighty pretty thing to say, but a mighty dangerous thing for a man like Favelles to mean. And poor Favelles meant it.

He went home with a brain fired by ecstasy and hope. M. de Sartines and his business were all but forgotten. He had done with such matters be the consequences what they might. But when he came to count those consequences, he remembered that they amounted to nothing less than destitution. Without the financial support he received from the lieutenant-general he would be a pauper, — and how, in Heaven's name, was a pauper to win Madame de Longuemain to wife? From which it will be seen that already des Favelles was looking far ahead.

That ugly thought took him as he was rounding the corner of the Rue St. Antoine, in which he had his lodging. He halted suddenly, and roundly cursed his fortune. Then, standing there and taking no heed of the keen edge of the autumn wind, poor Favelles fought out a cruel battle in his soul. He had to decide either to play a gentlemanly part, and, keeping clean hands, refuse the task that was set him and abandon with it all hope of again seeing the marquise, or else to undertake the vile business, so that he might be provided with the means to maintain his estate, and set about winning her. Of a truth, it was a parlous choice. Honor dictated a clear course. But poor Favelles' honor was a thing which, for shame's sake, he never spoke and seldom thought of. Congenitally lacking in strength of will and by circumstance become unscrupulous, he sank at last a victim to the temptation that beset him, and, — as is common with men of infirm purpose, — sat his faith in chance to bring the affairs anon to a solution more or less convenient.

That resolve taken, — not without much mental affliction, — he went home and dispatched a message to M. de Sartines, informing the minister that he consented to undertake the task imposed.

II

M. des Favelles' cordial reception, on the morrow, by the marquise, consoled him for the coldness manifested towards him by her guests. Indeed their restraint troubled him little; misunderstanding it, he set them down for a crowd, and wondered to himself how they had come by their reputation for wit. He fell prey to a little, weasel-faced abbé, all smirks and affectation, who insisted upon entertaining him with stories of the great Scarron, — in whom he was nowise interested. Mindful now of his mission, Favelles sought to draw the cleric into political topics, in which attempts the little fellow baffled him with a wondrous skill.

Madame de Longuemain had withdrawn into the embrasure of a window, where she stood talking with a powerfully-built, red-faced man, who had the air of a farmer dressed in Parisian garments. He was leaning towards her and seemed to be speaking earnestly, whilst his glance was of a tenderness that filled

Favelles with apprehension. As soon as he could shake off the importunities of the Abbé Leclerc, he made his way across to them. As he joined them, he caught from the marquise the words:

"But my dear Eustace — " Then espying him standing there, she stopped short. But the words and the intimacy they argued sent a stab through des Favelles. She presented him to her companion, — a M. Talmont, who, she informed him, was an old friend of hers that lately had been absent in Touraine, where his estates were situated. This gentleman, after an exchange of cold civilities, withdrew, leaving Favelles alone with the marquise.

Of what he talked during the moments they stood thus apart, Favelles might have found some difficulty in saying. He only remembered afterwards that he had made no mention of politics, and that from the moment of his looking into the blue depths of her eyes until the importunate little Abbé came to interrupt them, M. de Sartines was again sunk into oblivion.

As he was taking his departure she overjoyed him by a half timidly expressed hope that he would come again. He passed out into the street the happiest man in France that day, and so wonderful was his obsession that not even then did any thought of his mission intrude itself to mar the perfection of his fool's paradise.

Had he been able to overhear the things that were said in madame's salon after his departure, he might have thought less of his love and more of his task.

"M. de Sartines," the little Abbé was saying, "commits the egregious error of believing that he controls the only system of espionage in France. A still more egregious error is that of sending this popinjay into our midst."

"I think," said M. Talmont," that Madame la Marquise has acted with a rare degree of wisdom in facilitating his advent amongst us. How do you propose, M. l' Abbé, that we should deal with him?"

"I scarcely think," replied the Abbé Leclerc contemptuously, "that we need go the lengths of proposing anything. Let us leave him to madame. She will see that his time is wasted for him. Should he grow importunate, it will not be difficult to set him upon a false track. M. de Carnac, there, can write some more letters for M. de Sartines' edification."

And so while they plotted on the one side and M. de Sartines plotted on the other, M. des Favelles — the connecting link between the two — was the only person whose thoughts did not run on intrigue and counter-intrigue. The great passion that had taken possession of him was blotting all other considerations out of his life.

Daily was he now to be found at the Hotel de Longuemain, where the pretty widow with her baby face and her scheming soul was fooling him to the very top of his bent. Sartines, who was keeping Favelles under surveillance, had this reported to him, and rejoiced to see the young gallant earnestly at work at last, as he imagined.

Thus a week went by, and although already twice des Favelles had openly declared his passion to the marquise, the latter had found a way of tantalizingly evading him. Until the plot they were hatching was ripe, the conspirators desired Favelles to be kept on in this manner; once it should have exploded, they would laugh in his face and contemptuously cast him aside.

All might have gone in accordance with their desires had not M. des Favelles — who was beginning to account himself ill-used by madame — developed a jealousy which was no whit less furious than his love. The object of it was M. Talmont, of the red face and bucolic figure, whom he had overheard the marquise address by his patronymic. After smoldering for a couple of days it blazed up suddenly one afternoon in consequence of his coming upon a man's hat and cloak in the marquise's boudoir, to which he had been admitted.

"I take it," he sneered, quivering with fury, "that those garments are the property of your rustic friend Talmont?"

She looked at him out of a pair of very innocent and very widely opened eyes.

"But what then, monsieur?"

"This, madame — that you must dismiss one of us. You must choose between us. I love you, and — "

"You weary me, M. des Favelles, with your repetitions," she exclaimed. "You have told me a dozen times within two days that you love me. I have told you that you must wait. I am not a girl, monsieur. I was wed before, and it was by no means a happy marriage. Is it strange that I should, therefore, wish to deliberate carefully that I may avoid a second mistake?"

"You talk," he cried, "as though men and women loved with their wits. Does your heart say nothing, madame?"

"Hélas! Once already has my heart misled me. Let me first consider your suitability, monsieur, I beg."

Favelles sprang up, his face hot with anger.

"It is a husband that I am proposing to you — not a coachman," he blazed. "Since you will not choose between me and Talmont, I will leave the decision to Heaven. Where is the fellow? Where does the clown hide himself?"

"I am at your service, sir," came a dignified voice, and through the parting curtains that masked a doorway stepped Talmont, inquiry on his face. "May I ask your will with me?"

Now had either M. Talmont or Madame de Longuemain divined the will of M. des Favelles and the meaning of his cryptic remark that he would leave the choice to Heaven, there would have been less eagerness on Talmont's part to come forward. The moment the secret agent's eyes fell upon his rival he regained his composure, and when he spoke it was in a voice of great deliberateness.

"M. Talmont," said he, "I have asked Madame de Longuemain to choose between us; but since she finds herself unable to make the choice, I must leave it to the will of Heaven. Will you do me the honor to meet me at seven o'clock in the morning in the gardens of the Luxembourg, bringing a friend with you?"

"But why should I kill you, monsieur?" inquired Talmont ingenuously.

Des Favelles shrugged his shoulders.

"I did not suppose, monsieur, that you had brought good manners from Touraine, but I did suppose — from the fact of meeting you in madame's salon — that you were not completely destitute of them. This boasting is out of date in Paris, and is said to bring bad luck. Shall I expect you tomorrow?"

To say that Talmont and the marquise were taken aback is far from doing justice to their condition. Here was a contingency certainly unlooked for. Talmont must not have a duel on his hands in this the ripening hour of their great conspiracy. The marquise set herself to the task of restoring peace. She implored them to be calm and not to have her name on the lips of all Paris coupled with a duel. She besought Favelles to depart. But he was adamant. He would not go until he had received a reply from M. Talmont, and, what was more, he would not go save in M. Talmont's company, for he was not minded to allow his rival the advantages of being left behind. At this it was the marquise who became angry, and from intercession, passed to hostility.

"You asked me a moment ago, monsieur, for my answer to your suit. I will give it to you now — now that I have had an opportunity of judging how you can behave. I desire you to leave my house, and never again to importune me with your presence."

Favelles went white to the lips, and for a second he seemed to hesitate, and his glance traveled to Talmont. Then he drew himself up very rigidly, and, with a low and most formal bow, he turned on his heel and went without another word.

When he was gone Talmont expressed regrets which the marquise, however, did not appear to share.

"Pah!" she sneered with a toss of the head and a snap of the fingers, "What harm can he do, the fool? He knows nothing. Besides, what does it matter now? In three days the thing will be done, and, *ma foi*, Eustace, I have endured the attentions of this trifler for considerably longer than was to my taste."

"*Enfin*, we have done with him," said Talmont with a shrug, and he dismissed the subject.

But they had by no means done with him, as they were to find to their cost that very night.

III

Upon reaching his lodging Favelles had found a letter from the lieutenant-general, expressing surprise at having received no report from him since he had been entrusted with what M. de Sartines called the "Chateauroux affair." He added that from this silence he apprehended that Favelles had conducted the matter with that levity which had now come to be his chief characteristic, and he ended by saying that, unless within twenty-four hours he favored him with some definite information, he (M. de Sartines) would wash his hands of him, and leave him to starve. That letter was the last straw. Ruin stared him now in the face, and its imminence was to the luxuriously nurtured Favelles a very ugly business. He cursed Madame de Longuemain, concerning whom he had no illusions left. From the tone she had taken with him he now inferred that he had been nothing more than a dupe in the hands of that woman and of Talmont, her lover.

The "Green Pillar" in the Rue St. Honoré was the eating-house he frequented, and there he sat that evening, brooding and desperate, when suddenly a voice smote his ear that seemed to galvanize him into sudden and most violent action. It was the voice of Talmont, who had entered the house in the company of another, and who had taken a seat close by.

There were few people in the room at the time, and of those few none saw clearly what took place until they were startled by the crash of M. Talmont's fall, as chair and man went over.

"Will you fight me now?" roared the infuriated man of fashion, standing above his fallen enemy.

"Since you insist," answered Talmont, gathering himself up, "I will meet you in the morning at — "

"Not in the morning," the other interrupted him. "You had your chance of that, and you disdained it. You shall fight me now and here."

At that the landlord interfered with the announcement that he would have no brawling in the "Green Pillar." But des Favelles tossed the lace back from his wrist, and threatened to run the host through the vitals if he interfered. His wig had got awry in his excitement, and he presented a comically rakish appearance. But there was nothing comical in his attitude. His sword looked mighty dangerous, and there was an ugly gleam in his eye, which decided the host to send to the nearest *corps-de-garde* for the watch.

But long before it arrived M. des Favelles and his rival were giving a masterly exhibition of small-sword play. Talmont was the first to score, by running his opponent through the sword-arm. It looked as if this should end the encounter, when des Favelles, passing his sword into his left hand, and, utterly disregarding his wound and the blood he was losing, began to make things extremely unpleasant for Talmont. A left-hand fencer of mediocre ability is very discomposing to face, and has an incalculable advantage over a man meeting him in the ordinary way. Of this M. Talmont became more and more sensible, until, just as the hastily summoned guardians of the peace rushed into the room, he received Favelles' point full in the breast, and sank, a limp mass of legs and arms, to the floor, whilst Favelles himself collapsed, fainting into a chair.

M. des Favelles recovered consciousness in the guard-room of the Chatelêt, whither both the combatants had been conveyed. Standing beside him he found M. de Sartines, whose wontedly solemn face wore now an amused smile.

"Favelles," said he, "I congratulate you on your zeal and your adroitness. To have contrived that brawl and to have thus delivered him into our hands was the cleverest ruse for which it has ever been my good fortune to compliment one of my subordinates. How you recognized him I cannot think, for so cleverly had he outwitted my spies that I had no notion he was in France. The very letters upon which I acted were nothing but decoy documents intended to make me suppose him abroad. You have well employed your last chance, Favelles, and I shall see to it that you are rewarded in addition to keeping you in the service of France. But tell me how you recognized him. What was it aroused your suspicions?"

"I am very faint," murmured Favelles feebly, "and my wits work slowly. May I inquire to whom you are referring, monsieur?"

"Why to Madame de Longuemain's brother, the Chevalier de Chateauroux, yonder."

Understanding nothing, Favelles turned to behold only Talmont, whom a couple of men were tending. Then of a sudden he understood, and he closed his eyes lest Sartines should see in them a reflection of his astonishment.

"I must beg of you to allow that to remain my secret, monsieur," he murmured. "You asked me to discover his whereabouts; I have done more; I have found and delivered to you the man himself. I beg of you to be satisfied with that."

"Satisfied?" echoed Sartines, who was in excellent humor. "I am more than satisfied. Do you know there was a moment when I almost thought that Madame de Longuemain was leading you away from your duty?"

"There was a moment when I thought that myself," murmured Favelles, in tones inaudible to the lieutenant-general.

The Spiritualist: A Story of the Occult

In quest of local colour in that part of France that once was known as Languédoc, I spent a week last autumn in the little village of Aubepine. I stayed at the Hôtel du Cerf, whereof Jules Coupri is host, and for companions of an evening I had the village notary, a couple of grocers, a haberdasher — who was in his way leader of fashion in Aubepine — the postmaster, and half-a-dozen young farmers, who were in the habit of coming there to drink their petit-vin and exchange their ideas.

A student of human nature in my humble way, I made a point of mingling freely with them, and I am afraid that their patience and good nature drew me to talk a good deal. But on the eve of my departure I was for once cast into the shade by a young seafaring man of the better sort, who was, he informed us, on his way to Carcassonne. He expatriated upon the wonders of Greece and Italy with such eloquent picturesqueness that he monopolised the attention which hitherto I had enjoyed without competition.

But my revenge was to come. Towards nine o'clock a tall, swarthy man, dressed in black clothes, which, if seedy, were of more or less fashionable cut, and wearing a chimney-pot hat, stalked into the room, and called for the landlord. He wanted supper as quickly as possible for himself and his driver — he traveled in a ramshackle carriage — and announced to all that he must push on that night to St. Hilaire. He was evil-looking of face, yet not without distinction. The nose was thin as the bill of an eagle, and as curved; the forehead high and narrow, with absurdly long, black hair brushed straight back; the eyes were close-set and piercing; the mouth little more than a straight line above the square, lean chin. He was on the whole a striking individual, and from the moment of his advent he absorbed the attention of all present.

Seemingly aware of the impression he had created, he came over to the table at which I sat, and fell easily into conversation with those about upon small matters of provincial interest. In less than five minutes the sailor and his voyages were forgotten.

I was still speculating upon the man's business in life — for I am of those who believe that a man bears upon him the outward signs of his profession — when a young farmer happened to mention that his vineyards had been doing badly for the last three years — ever since his brother's death. The stranger's gimlet eyes were instantly turned upon him.

"What do you suppose to be the reason of it?" he inquired in a voice that was curiously impressive.

"Reason?" echoed young Pascal. "There is no reason. It is an unpleasant coincidence."

A saturnine smile overspread the stranger's face.

"So the ignorant ever say," he deprecated. "Young man, there is no such thing as coincidence in the vulgar sense." Then he galvanised the peasant by asking: "Have you seen your brother since?"

"Seen him? But then monsieur has not understood that he is dead!"

"And since when may we not see the dead?"

"Do you mean his spirit?" gasped Pascal.

"Call it by what name you will, I mean your brother."

"Does monsieur believe then in *revenants?*"

"No, monsieur, I do not. There are no *revenants;* that is to say, there are none who return, for they are always with us; here, around us, everywhere." And he tossed his arms about him, and glanced this way and that to emphasise his meaning. "It is the body only which they quit. The earth never. And their souls, no longer clogged and stultified by the obsessing flesh, are not confined to the present as are we. For them the past is clear, and the future holds no mysteries.

"They know the causes of things, the origin of matter, and its final ending. That, monsieur, is why I asked you had you seen your brother. It is clear that you have not done so. That would be foolish, were not that it is in ignorance that you have submitted to the fate which is ruining your vineyard. If you had been better informed touching these matters you would have held intercourse with your brother, and obtained from him enlightenment. Thus might you by now have remedied the evil."

Those present sat silent and awe-stricken. To many of them, in their ignorant, credulous, superstitious way, this man, who spoke so seriously of communion with the dead, must have appeared a wizard, if not the very fiend himself — a belief to which his fantastic personality would lend colour.

"Does monsieur mean that I can cause my brother to appear to me!"

"If you were enlightened you might do so. As it is— " He paused, shrugged his shoulders, and curled his lips contemptuously — "I am afraid you cannot."

"But can such things be done?" cried the haberdasher.

"Assuredly," answered the spiritualist. "In Paris they are done every day."

"Ah — in Paris," sighed one to whom nothing seemed impossible when associated with that wonderful name.

"Can you do it?" asked the haberdasher bluntly, yet with a certain awe lurking in his question.

The man smiled the quiet smile of one who is conscious of his strength.

"Have you never heard of M. Delamort?" he asked — much as he might have asked: "Have you never heard of Bonaparte?"

They were silent, from which he seemed to gather that his fame, however great elsewhere, had not traveled yet as far as this.

"I am a member of the Sociéte Transemperique, which devotes itself to researches in the spirit-world," he informed them.

Thereupon they fell to questioning him fearfully as to whether he had ever held communion with a spirit, to which he answered vaingloriously:

"With hundreds, messieurs."

At that the sailor, who, I imagined, would be nursing a grudge against this man who had stripped him of his popularity, burst into a contemptuous laugh, which acted as a cold douche upon the audience. M. Delamort glared at him with angry eyes, but the man's expression of disbelief found many an echo, and from one or two I even caught the contemptuous word "Charlatan!"

"Fools," cried the spiritualist, his voice like a rumble of distant thunder. "Crass, ignorant clods! You live out your animal lives in this corner of the world much as a rat lives in its burrow. As your minds are closed to intelligence, so, too, do you close your ears to knowledge. Derision is the ever-ready weapon of the ignorant, and because the things I tell you are things of which you never dreamt in your unenlightened lives, you laugh and call me charlatan. But I will give you proof that what I have said is true. I will let you see the extent of my powers."

He addressed us all, collectively; but ever and anon his glance wandered to the sailor, who had been the first to express his want of faith, as though to him he conveyed a special challenge.

Receiving no answer, Delamort looked about from one to another, until his sinister glance lighted on Pascal.

"Will you submit yourself to the test?" he asked. "Will you let me summon your brother's spirit for you?"

The young man recoiled and made the sign of the cross. "God forbid!" he ejaculated. With a contemptuous laugh the spiritualist turned from him to the sailor.

"Are you also afraid?" he demanded witheringly.

"I?" faltered the fellow, and a sickly smile spread over his weather-beaten face. "I am not afraid. I do not believe in your impostures."

"Excellent," exclaimed Delamort with a satanic grin. "You do not believe, therefore you are not afraid."

"Certainly I am not afraid," answered the young man with more assurance. Delamort's contempt seemed to have effectively roused him.

"Then you will submit to the test, and you shall see whether or not I have the power to raise the spirit of the dead — to render them visible to mortal eyes. You shall tell these gentlemen then whether I am an impostor. Whose ghost shall I evoke for you, monsieur?" he ended, rising as he spoke. All sat staring in horror and genuinely afraid. But the sailor's scepticism was not again to be shaken.

"I'll not submit to any mummeries of yours," he announced. "I know your ways, and I am not to be humbugged by any lying conjurer."

"It is not mummery and it is not humbug, as I shall prove. Why insult me so? Name rather some dead friend or relative with whom you wish to commune, and I will gratify your wish."

A sudden look of cunning flashed in the sailor's face.

"Can I have my own way in this?" he asked briskly. "May I select the room in which I am to commune with the spirit?"

"But certainly."

"And may I also keep it from your knowledge whose spirit I wish to see?"

His tone and manner were full of insolence and craftiness. Delamort hesitated for an instant.

"It were better that I should know," he said at last.

"There," cried the sailor triumphantly, appealing to the audience. And he would have added more but that Delamort interrupted him.

"Fool, if you insist upon it, I will remain in ignorance of the name of your spirit. But lest you should tell us afterwards that I have evoked the wrong one, I shall ask you to impart the name to these gentlemen whilst I am out of earshot. Come now, are we agreed?"

The sailor announced himself ready to comply, and Delamort left the room at once, Pascal, at the sailor's bidding, stationing himself at the door. Then the sailor set himself to harangue us.

He had seen an illusionist do such things, he announced, at a theatre at Marseilles, by means of ventriloquism and a magic-lantern. It was nothing but trickery, he swore, and if we would unite with him, we would teach this impostor a lesson that he would remember.

With one accord we all pronounced ourselves ready to conspire with him — for what is there sweeter in all the world than to trick a trickster, to hoist him with his own petard? His plan was simple enough. He would choose the room in which to receive his ghostly visitant at the last moment, and we were to remain outside with Delamort, and see that he never for a second set foot within it. Thus should he be completely baffled. Already he was labouring under serious difficulties by not knowing whose spirit he was desired to evoke. The sailor announced then to us that he wished to see the ghost of his friend Gravine who had fallen overboard on the last voyage.

The plot being laid, Delamort was recalled and informed that the sailor was ready to submit himself to the test.

"You will not tell me whom you wish to see?" he asked.

"No, monsieur. You yourself confessed that it was not essential."

"Parfaitement," answered Delamort, bowing. "Monsieur is still sceptical?"

"So sceptical that if you care to make a little wager with me — "

"This is a serious matter," interrupted the spiritualist sternly. "It would ill become me to employ my powers for purposes of gain."

"I was proposing," said the sailor readily, "that you should employ them for purposes of loss, but I thought you would refuse," he sneered, winking at us.

Delamort threw back his head like one affronted.

"Since you put it that way," he cried angrily, "I will consent even to a wager. I am a poor man, monsieur, but I will stake every penny that I have about me that you shall not be disappointed."

He took out his purse, and emptied a cascade of gold on to the table.

"Here, monsieur, are fifty napoleons. When you have covered that sum I shall be ready to begin the *séance*."

At that the sailor was taken aback. He looked about him pathetically. Then he drew from his breast-pocket a coloured kerchief, and carefully untied it. From this he took six gold pieces, which he placed very quietly and humbly upon the table.

"I am only a sailor, monsieur, and I am very poor. This is all that at the moment I am possessed of. It seems, sir, that for want of money I am only to earn six of your napoleons?" He paused, and his eyes wandered timidly over the company. Then he sighed. "It is a sin that where fifty napoleons are to be picked up, only six should be taken."

At that, up leapt Pascal, and slapped two louis upon the table, announcing that he would wager that amount against M. Delamort. He was followed by the haberdasher with four louis; then came another with three, and another with five, and so on, until forty napoleons stood against the spiritualist's pile of fifty. And then, lest he should retain the ten napoleons that had not been covered, the landlord ran upstairs and fetched that amount himself. I was the only man who had taken no part in the wager. I was not altogether so sure that the seafaring man was right. I had heard strange things concerning spiritualism, and whilst I had not heard enough to induce me to attach any appreciable degree of credit to it, still I knew too little to dare to disbelieve utterly.

Delamort, who had been looking on with an anxiety which heightened the saturnine expression of his countenance, observed this fact, and now that the money was all there, he gathered up the hundred napoleons, slipped them into his purse, and handed this to me.

"Monsieur is a gentleman," he said, by way of explaining why he selected me as the man to be entrusted with the stakes. "Also he has no interest in the money. Will you keep this, monsieur, and afterwards either deliver it to me or divide it amongst these good people should I fail?"

"If it is the wish of all — " I began, when they at once proclaimed their unanimous consent.

"And now, M. Delamort," said the sailor with a leer and a swagger, "I have announced to the company whose is the ghost I wish to commune with, and I am ready. Come with me."

"But whither?" inquired poor Delamort, who appeared by now to have lost the last shred of his magnificent assurance.

"To the room I have chosen."

Delamort bit his lip, and a look of vexation crossed his face; whereat those good fellows nudged each other, grinned and whispered. But the spiritualist made no objection, and so we went upstairs to the room in which the sailor was to sleep. At the door he paused and turned to us.

"Remain here with M. Delamort. I will enter alone."

"I only ask, monsieur," said Delamort — and his tone seemed firmer again, as though he were regaining confidence — that you sit without light of any description, whilst here, too, we must remain in the dark, if you please, gentlemen. M. l'Hôte, will you have the goodness to extinguish the lamp? I have no directions to give you touching the arrangements of your room, monsieur," he continued, turning to the sailor again, "but I must ask you to leave a sheet of paper on the table. I will command the spirit to inscribe his name on it, so that all here may be satisfied that your visitor is the one you have desired to see."

At that a thrill of doubt ran through the audience. Much might be done by ventriloquism and magic lanterns — as the sailor had assured them — but of the magic lantern they saw no sign, and, in any event, neither magic lantern nor ventriloquism could write a name on paper. The sailor himself seemed staggered for a moment.

"I will do so, monsieur," he faltered.

With that he went within and closed the door, turning the key on the inside. A moment later the landlord had extinguished the light, and we were left in utter darkness. The last glimpse I had of Delamort, he was crouching by the door of the sailor's room.

A silence followed, which seemed to last an eternity. The only sound was the occasional whispering of the spiritualist and the breathing of some twenty men in whose hearts doubt was swelling to fear with every second of that uncanny expectancy. Ten minutes had perhaps gone by when we heard a rap on the door, and from within came the sailor's voice.

"How much longer am I to wait, M. Delamort? I must ask you to fix a limit. I have no desire to sit here in the dark all — "

The voice ceased abruptly. There was a dull thud, as of a body hurtling against the door, and with it there came a groan of fear. The groan almost found an echo in the gasps of the waiting company. Myself, I plead guilty to an uncanny thrill, and I might entertain you with my creepy sensations at some length were not my story more concerned with other matters.

There followed a silence of some few seconds, then we heard the sailor's voice raised in a blood curdling scream.

"Don't come near me, don't come near me!" he shrieked. "Let me out, Delamort! Let me out, for God's sake, monsieur!" There was a rustle as of someone moving. Then a long-drawn wail of "Jesu!" That was followed by the sound of a heavy fall, and then silence.

The landlord was the first to recover the use of his wits; the fear of a tragedy in his house rousing him to action. He pushed roughly through to the door.

"Here, someone," he begged. "Help me to break in."

There was a groaning and cracking of woodwork and the report of the bursting door. Simultaneously a maid appeared with a lamp. I took it from her and hastened into the room in the wake of Delamort and the landlord.

Stretched on the floor, his eyes closed, his face ghastly pale, and distorted by a fearful grin, lay the sailor. That and a smell of something that had burned was all that we noticed at first.

The rustics remained on the threshold, their faces pale and scared, asking whether the sailor were dead. Delamort, who had been on his knees beside him, reassured us. It was only a swoon. And presently, when he loosened his neckwear and sponged his head and pulses, the man opened his eyes and groaned, but was clearly no worse for whatever he had undergone. The villagers now crowded fearlessly into the room, and some were already plying the sailor with questions as he sat on the floor with Delamort supporting him. Suddenly a diversion was created by Pascal, who uttered a cry that was almost a shriek. Turning quickly to seek the cause of this, I beheld him pointing to something on the table at which he was staring in an awe-struck manner. I approached and beheld a sheet of paper on which had been burnt, as if with a red-hot iron, the name "Gravine."

Such in brief was my first introduction to spiritualism. M. Delamort left Aubepine an hour later, and pursued his journey to St. Hilaire. But the sailor was not himself until the following morning, and even when he had recovered from the shock occasioned him by his unearthly visitant, he sustained a fresh one when he realised that he lost his wager and his six louis.

I was at Angeville a fortnight later, staying with a cousin of mine who resides there. On the evening of my arrival my cousin took me round the old-world town, and in the course of things led me into the Peacock Inn. As we entered the general room, a familiar voice assailed my ears with familiar words.

"Fools," it cried. "Crass, ignorant fools! You live out your lives in this wretched corner of the world much as a rat lives in its burrow, and as your minds are closed to intelligence, so, too, do you close your ears to knowledge. Derision is the ever-ready weapon of the ignorant, and because the things that I tell you are things of which you never dreamt in your unenlightened lives you laugh and call me charlatan."

It was, of course, M. Delamort. As I craned my neck to catch a glimpse of his lean, cadaverous face, I heard a sudden and contemptuous laugh, with which I also seemed familiar. I turned in the direction of the sound, and there, surely enough, I beheld my friend the sailor, baiting the spiritualist as he had done at Aubepine.

I was on the point of denouncing them as a couple of impostors and swindlers, when for some reason or other I held my peace. I had a sort of feeling that would be like taking vengeance upon them for having fooled me in common with those others at Aubepine. I am rather ashamed to confess it, but I turned and quitted the Peacock Inn, leaving those ingenious tricksters to continue to exploit their spiritualistic mummery.

Monsieur Delamort

In his outfit as a thorough-paced *chevalier d'industrie*, M. Delamort might be said to include all the more usual tools of his craft. He could tell your fortune by the cards, by your bumps, by the tea-cup, the crystal, or your hands; his legerdemain was a marvel of dexterity; he dabbled in hypnotism, and at times — where a particularly weak-minded individual was his subject — he achieved some slight measure of success. He practised medicine upon occasion, with results that were only a little more disastrous than those which frequently attend the efforts of duly qualified men.

Of all his accomplishments, spiritualism was the one that afforded him the deepest measure of pride. Thanks to an ingenious fraud, with which, by the aid of a confederate, he had imposed upon simple folk in almost all the rural districts of France, he had amassed a very considerable sum of money, which is an easy explanation of his predilection for that branch of his trickster's profession.

His confederate, unfortunately, took it into his head to apply to other ends the dishonesty acquired in his partnership with Delamort; and so clumsy was he that he got himself arrested for embezzling, and sentenced to a term of three years' imprisonment.

To Delamort the loss was incalculable; nor did he think it even worth while to take any steps to repair it, despairing of ever finding another who could plausibly play the part. He found himself compelled to abandon spiritualism. He no longer held forth to gaping villagers upon the mysteries of the spirit-world, no longer talked of "psychic forces" and the "obsessing flesh." He fell back upon the more vulgar and less remunerative craft of fortune-telling, and had to be content to pocket silver, where before he had taken gold.

And then — quite by accident — it came to him how he might resume his trade in ghosts, single-handed though he was.

It happened at Soreau, one evening. He was sitting in the village inn, entertaining a little crowd of rustics with an exposition of sleight-of-hand, and leaving them amazed at his miracles, when the subject of spiritualism was introduced by old Grosjean.

"There was a man of your name could raise ghosts," said the villager.

Delamort flashed him a piercing glance of his black, solemn eyes as he answered impressively: "I am that man."

There was a momentary hush, followed by a babel of questions from those of the party who were not believers in spiritual manifestations. It was the sort of challenge to which Delamort was accustomed, and one for which he had often angled in the old days.

Sheer force of habit brought him to his feet, that he might reply with fitting impressiveness, and for the next few minutes he descanted in his sharp, metallic voice upon that vexed question, causing his audience to gasp at the boldness of his statements.

A tall, lean figure dressed in clothes of faded black, aquiline of nose and clear-cut of face, with long black hair brushed back from the forehead, fiery of glance and liberal of gesture, he imposed upon those simple men of Soreau as much by his presence, air, and voice as by the things he said.

Yet some materialists there were whom neither his manner nor his matter could impress, and among them was old Grosjean, who was, in his way, a man of fair education and some reading. It was this fellow whom Delamort singled out for his special prey upon this occasion.

A quick judge of character, he had read at a glance the cupidity so plainly advertised in Grosjean's close-set eyes, in the lines of his thin-lipped mouth, and in his lean, claw-like hands. To these very apparent characteristics of the old man did he owe the notion with which he was so suddenly inspired, and upon which he set himself at once to act.

"You may laugh, you fools!" he thundered, with a fine assumption of anger. "I have been laughed at before by men as ignorant. But I have changed their mirth to terror before I had done with them; and I will do as much for you if any here has the courage to submit to the trial."

Grosjean cackled contemptuously, whereupon Delamort swooped down upon him as does the hawk upon the sparrow.

"Derider!" he cried fiercely. "Dare you undergo the test?"

"Bah!" snarled Grosjean. "You are an impudent swindler. I have heard of you."

For a second Delamort's steady glance wavered. Then he recovered, and let it rest balefully upon the speaker.

"Insult," said he sententiously, "is a woman's argument, not a man's. I am no swindler."

"Prove it and I'll believe you," was the answer.

"Certainly I will prove it," returned Delamort promptly. "You have but to name the man whose spirit you would have me evoke, and I will undertake to render it visible and audible to your skeptic senses."

"Very well" quoth Grosjean, still derisive. "Let me behold my father's ghost and I will believe you, and withdraw the term I have applied to you."

His friends, and indeed they were all friends of his — for Grosjean was as well known in Soreau as the steeple of the village church — encouraged him in his attitude of defiance.

"You shall have your ghost," Delamort promised him grimly. "But, messieurs, I am not to be insulted in this fashion by a parcel of country clods without taking satisfaction for it. It is not my way to gamble over a matter so terrible as this which I am about to embark upon, but you have said so much that before I carry out M. Grosjean's demands I should like to know how much each of you is disposed to wager that I fail to do this thing?"

"I expected that," said Grosjean, with a senile chuckle, and he lacked not for chorus.

"Did you?" sneered Delamort in his turn. "And I suppose that, as it becomes a question of risking a little money, you would prefer not to submit, for fear that I should prove you wrong?"

Grosjean's reply was to produce ostentatiously three napoleons and bang them on the table.

"I'll wager those," he cried, "that you fail to raise me my father's ghost or, indeed, any ghost whatsoever."

"Excellent," said Delamort. "And these other gentlemen — your friends — will they also manifest in gold their opinion that I am an impostor?"

"I'll wager a louis," cried one, and his example was followed by almost every member of the company, until a little pillar of twenty-six napoleons stood upon the wine-stained table.

Delamort quietly produced his purse, and counted out a like sum. Then, taking up also the money staked by the company, and having obtained a sheet of paper, he wrapped up the fifty-two napoleons and handed the package to the landlord, begging him to act as stakeholder.

"Now, *monsieur*," said he, turning to Grosjean, "if *monsieur l'hôte* will find us a room I am ready to commence my séance."

II

Grosjean paled a little before the man's assurance, and in consideration of the confidence which had led him to wager a sum of over six hundred francs. At heart, however skeptic, the old man was far from valiant, and he would certainly have backed out of the business had he seen a way of doing it without loss of prestige.

But he feared the derision of his friends. He braced himself with the assurance that there were no such things as ghosts, and that Delamort was an impostor, whom a sharp lookout on his part must baffle. With the determination to watch him very closely, and not permit himself to be fooled, he rose and announced himself ready.

The host conducted the pair to a room above, leaving the company in a state of mingled excitement and derision, to await the result of this odd experiment. Within the feebly lighted bedchamber which the landlord had assigned to them, Delamort bade his companion be seated, and approached him with eyes riveted on his, and hands busy at mesmeric passes. He had hopes of gaining sufficient influence over Grosjean to be able to mentally suggest to him that he saw the spirit of his dead father.

But it so happened that Grosjean, who, as I have mentioned, was educated above his station, had once read a book on mesmerism, and was acquainted with its methods. He recognized them in Delamort's antics and, with an indignant laugh, he rose to his feet.

"I think we have had enough of this foolery, M. Delamort," he said. "I half expected that you would resort to hypnotism to gain your ends."

"You are acquainted, then, with hypnotism?" quoth Delamort, a trifle crest-fallen, slipping his hand into his pockets as he spoke.

"Sufficiently acquainted with it to see through you, my friend," answered Grosjean. "I think that I may fairly claim to have won my wager."

"One moment," Delamort implored him. "It is an interesting topic — hypnotism. Doubtless you are aware of the effect produced by the contemplation of a bright disk or ring?"

"Yes," answered the other dubiously. "What of it?"

"I am about to have recourse to it in consequence of my failure with the mesmeric passes," was the cool rejoinder. "I beg that you will contemplate this."

Grosjean found himself staring at the bright rim of the barrel of a revolver, with which Delamort had suddenly covered him.

"*Bon Dieu!*" he ejaculated in affright.

"Ah!" purred Delamort, with manifest satisfaction. "By your face and manner I see that you are already coming under the influence. Now, be good enough to reseat yourself and listen to me."

Grosjean obeyed him with that alacrity which terror alone can impart.

"Excellent," murmured the occultist. "The hypnotic power of a pistol-nozzle has no equal. Now, sir, I think that you are sufficiently warned of the manner of man you have to deal with, to sit quietly and listen to what I have to propose."

"You don't mean to shoot me?" cried Grosjean interrogatively.

"Shoot you? By no means. You will be far too reasonable. I am exerting no more than a slight persuasion to induce you to listen to me."

"Then, will you — would you mind putting that thing away? You wouldn't believe how easy it is to have an accident with firearms."

With the utmost affability, Delamort slipped the pistol back into his pocket.

III

"Now, to business," said Delamort. "You may think, *monsieur*, that I am a rank impostor. I am not. I am a genuine spiritualist, as well as something of a hypnotist. Indeed, I have a reputation to maintain. Now, it occasionally happens that I come across a man so strong-minded, of such determination and willpower that my art is defeated and baffled. Such a man, my dear M. Grosjean, are you. I confess it with regret, for it is never pleasant to find

ourselves confronted by a stronger individuality, which will not bring itself
under our control."

Grosjean, who was recovering from his fears, smiled, with the pleasure
occasioned him by these elaborate compliments.

"While my failure, *monsieur*," Delamort continued, "makes you the gainer of
a paltry three napoleons, it occasions me the loss of over six hundred francs. As
you will readily perceive, there is no proportion in this. Besides, I am a poor
man, M. Grosjean; and, in addition to the loss of all this money, there is the
further loss of character and prestige, which will be nothing short of ruinous to
me. You understand?"

Grosjean grinned until his yellow face was wrinkled into the semblance of a
crumpled parchment.

"I understand, but I am afraid I cannot help you. It is the fortune of war."
He endeavored to give his voice an inflection of polite regret, but the pleasure
of gaining three napoleons was not so lightly to be suppressed by a man of
Grosjean's grasping nature.

"Pardon," returned Delamort. "But you can help me, and by helping me
you can help yourself. Now, if instead of three napoleons, your profit by my
failure were to be six, would it not be worth your while to save my reputation?"

"What do you mean?" quoth Grosjean suspiciously.

"Just this. If you will acknowledge to your friends that you have seen your
father's ghost, and consequently lost your wager, I will pay you nine napoleons
— that is, the three you have staked and the six I am giving you in
compensation."

Grosjean's eyes brightened with greed.

"It would be doing you a good service, would it not — saving your
reputation?"

"Assuredly."

"Also, it would be making you a profit of the twenty-six napoleons staked
by my friends, eh?"

"Why, yes. But not twenty-six, my friend. Seventeen napoleons will be my
total profit after I have settled with you."

Grosjean reflected a moment; then a cunning smile spread on his face. "I
admire your method of raising ghosts, M. Delamort," said he with jeering irony.
He shook his head and laughed. "No, no, my friend. Such a service as you are
asking of me is worth more than six napoleon. You are proposing a revolting
course to me. I can't do it. I really can't."

"You are throwing away money, *monsieur*, by your refusal," Delamort
reminded him. "Surely a gain of six napoleons is better than a gain of only
three. And you are earning it without any trouble or inconvenience. How
much better would you be if I did raise your father's ghost? It would only scare
you to death. I beg that you will seriously consider my proposal."

"I can't be a party to such a swindle. I really can't — not for six napoleons, anyhow. If I practise this wretched deceit upon my trusting friends, I must have half your profit. That is, to say, I must have thirteen napoleons."

"I'll give you ten."

"Thirteen or I'll walk out and denounce you for an impudent impostor. Make your choice."

Some one knocked at the door. His friends were becoming anxious.

"Are you all right, Grosjean?" inquired a voice, to which the old man returned an affirmative reply.

"Has he raised the spirit yet?"

"Not yet," answered Grosjean, while Delamort added: "But I hope to do so in a moment or two, if you will refrain from interrupting me. Have the goodness not to disturb us again." Then to Grosjean, in a whisper: "Now, *monsieur*," said he, "what is it to be? Will you accept ten napoleons?"

"Thirteen," was the laconic answer, delivered with finality.

"Very well, then. Thirteen be it, provided that you will follow out my instructions."

"What are they?"

"You are to scream two or three times, and then fall down and simulate a swoon as best you can, reviving only after I have admitted your friends."

"*Parfaitement*," said the old traitor, his greedy eyes shining with avarice. "Pay me the money now, so that my friends will have no suspicions."

Delamort produced his purse and carefully took thirteen napoleons from it, one by one. One by one he delivered them to his companion.

"See that they don't jingle," he admonished him; "for if any one were to hear it he would suspect."

Grosjean nodded that he understood, and pocketed each coin as he received it. When he had received the thirteenth he still put forth his hand, and upon being asked by Delamort what he wanted, he insolently replied that he wanted the return of his stake of three napoleons.

"That was included. It was to be thirteen altogether," the occultist protested. But Grosjean had not so understood it, and swore that he would not perform his part of the bargain until received another sixty francs.

They wrangled for some moments, Delamort protesting that thus Grosjean was making more out of it than he was himself. In the end he was forced to give in and pay the further money demanded, which he did with the worst grace in the world.

IV

"Now, for your part, *monsieur*," said Delamort; "and see that you play me no tricks."

It was unlikely that he would, since were he to betray the occultist he must forego the gain he was making. Rising from his chair, he awoke the echoes of the inn with a scream that was a masterpiece of blood-curdling vociferation.

"Excellent," Delamort approved. "Repeat it."

Obediently, Grosjean emitted second shriek more dreadful than the first. There came an excited knocking at the door.

"Don't touch me — don't touch me" screamed Grosjean, prompted by Delamort. "*Mon Dieu!* I am terrified. Oh!"

With that final moan he let himself fall heavily, and from his position he winked wickedly at Delamort. The occultist now turned to the door, which he opened immediately.

"What are you doing to him?" demanded half a dozen of Grosjean's friends as they sprang into the room.

"No more than I undertook him to do," Delamort replied. "I think you had better attend to him. The sight of his father has frightened him a little, but he will be all right shortly."

They hastened to the prostrate man, and raised him tenderly.

"There. He is better now," exclaimed one.

"His color is returning," announced another.

"I feared that ill would come of it," put in a third. "It is an evil thing to tamper with the dead."

"As for you," snarled a fourth, angrily shaking his fist in Delamort's face, "you ought to be hanged, you wizard."

"I am no wizard," answered Delamort, truthfully enough. "As M. Grosjean there can tell you, I have worked by perfectly natural means."

Grosjean, now feigning to recover, was giving the company an awe-inspiring account of the apparition that had visited him.

"I am punished," groaned the old scoundrel. "Never again will I laugh at spiritualism." Then to the host: "You may hand the stakes to M. Delamort," he said. "He has certainly won his wager, curse him!"

It was with an extremely ill grace that the landlord handed the occultist the package containing the money. Delamort accepted it in silence, and slipped it into his pocket. His business being thus concluded, he was on the point of taking his leave of the company, when the landlord rudely accelerated his departure by a request that he should take himself off the premises.

"I've had enough of spiritualism in my house," he swore, with a vigorous oath.

"*Monsieur* is a bad loser," was Delamort's cold answer, as he took the hint and his leave without further delay.

It was after his departure that old Grosjean felt the need of a glass of cognac to revive him. That was natural enough, but that he should invite several of his friends to a glass of something, at his expense, was a departure from the ordinary grasping course of his existence which occasioned them some measure of surprise.

Seeing ghosts was evidently a salutary occupation, if it could instill generosity into so mean a heart as Grosjean's. They profited by his mood, and accepted with alacrity the offer he made; and while they drank his health he fished from his pocket a golden napoleon with which to pay.

The landlord took the coin, glanced at it, and rang it on the table. It emitted a most unmusical timbre.

"It's cracked," some one suggested.

"It's bad," the landlord stated as he handed it back to Grosjean.

"Bad?" echoed the old fellow, with a sudden pang of apprehension. "Bad? Impossible! Anyhow, here is another one."

While he was examining the coin the landlord had returned to him, he heard the second one give out the same false sound. Dim suspicion now became sickening certainty.

With an oath he drew from another pocket a five-franc piece, to pay for the drink which in a moment of expansion he had offered his compeers.

"Wherever did you get those coins from, M. Grosjean?" inquired the host. "Surely some one has victimized you."

Deeper than words can tell were his rage and mortification. Yet deeper still was the old man's wisdom, for he held his peace touching the transaction by which those coins had passed into his hands.

Judge Foscaro's Crime

From out of a countenance withered and sallow as parchment, with its hooked nose and high cheek-bones, Judge Foscaro's eyes scowled malevolently upon his visitor.

"Lord Count," he said, in tones of finality, "my ward is not for you."

Count Mattoli shrugged his shoulders and laughed indulgently. He was a well-built man, with a frank countenance whose natural comeliness was set off by the carefully powdered wig surmounting it.

"As you will, Master Foscaro," he replied suavely; "I will wait."

"You will wait in vain, then," blazed the old man.

"Not so, sir," was the airy answer; "Giulia will not be your ward for ever. In a few months she will be free to become my countess."

The old judge rose slowly to his feet, and his face was very evil to behold.

"Lord Count," he said, in a voice of concentrated passion, "do not delude yourself. When Giulia ceases to be my ward she will be my son's wife."

"Why, so I have heard."

"Eh?" Foscaro's eyes burned evilly in their deep sockets. "Do you think to win your way by insolence?"

Much had young Mattoli endured with easy suavity, but at the word "insolence" his whole manner changed.

"Mark me, Sir Judge," he cried. "I have held my temper hard this half-hour, remembering your age; but if I am to continue to remember it, I would have you also bear in mind that I am Count Ettore Mattoli, and not some vagabond brought before you for stealing a purse.

"There appears to be little to be gained by remaining, and, maybe, I had best go, but attend to this: by your will or against it, with your sanction or without it, will I marry your ward. Believe me, you are foolish to make so much unpleasantness over a matter that is as inevitable as — as to-morrow."

Judge Foscaro's ward was an heiress, the richest by far in the Italian Marches, and for the past ten years it had been the goal of his hopes to see her wedded to his only son, the most idle, dissipated ne'er-do-well in Jesi. That in the eleventh hour this debonair young nobleman should come to thwart that pretty scheme was matter enough to account for, if not to justify, his indignant anger.

Quivering with rage, he stood now to bar the young man's way.

"One moment, Lord Count," he cried. "I would have you know that my ward is not for the first fortune-hunter that comes a-wooing."

"And yet you said that she was to wed your son," murmured Mattoli, taking up his laced hat.

In a sudden access of fury the judge snatched up a dagger from the table, unsheathed it, and flung himself like a madman upon the Count. Mattoli, taken by surprise, fell back a pace, and put his hand to his sword. But ere he could get more than half of it from the scabbard Foscaro's dagger was in his breast.

"*Sangue di Dio!*" growled the old man passionately, "take that, you fool!"

Mattoli hurled backwards, with arms flung suddenly out, and crashed down upon the floor. In falling his head struck the wall, and supported by it he lay there, with chin thrust forward on to his breast.

"You'd wed my ward by my will or against it, would you?" the old man snarled in mockery, as, still grasping his poniard, he gazed down upon his victim. Then, as he stood there, an icy terror closed round his heart, and cooled the madness in his blood.

"Dead!" he whispered — to add in a sudden frenzy — "Oh, not that, my God! Lord Count! Lord Count!" he called, stooping over the motionless body of the young man.

He noted how helpless was the attitude in which he lay, with arms fallen limp, and hands that were turned palms upwards; he marked the crimson stain oozing on the white satin waistcoat; he peered into the ashen face, over which the disarranged wig sat awry with ghastly rakishness, and through chattering teeth Judge Foscaro mumbled a long-forgotten prayer to the Madonna for aid in this extremity. With trembling hands he took up a taper from the table, and by its light again surveyed the murdered man.

"Aye, dead," he repeated.

A fresh terror took him then. He must rid himself of this horror without delay. Someone might come upon him there at any moment, for all that the hour was late. What was he to do with it? Time pressed. Softly he opened the door of his room, and crept out. No one stirred. He went back, and taking up the body in his arms he half dragged, half carried it across the chamber. At the door he paused again to listen. Silence prevailed unbroken in the house.

An old man was Judge Foscaro, and the supple young body of Count Mattoli was a stout weight, but frenzy gave him strength to bear his burden down the short flight of stairs. Below he paused exhausted, and setting down his ghastly load, he leaned against the wall to regain breath. His heart seemed to beat in his throat and to suffocate him. A step in the street almost wrung a cry of terror from his parched lips.

"*Madonna santissima*, help me; give me strength!" he mumbled — sublimely unconscious of the grotesqueness of his prayer.

Awhile he remained standing there; then he crept to the door, and softly raised the latch. Opening it by slow degrees, he leaned out and looked this way and that. No light showed from any of the houses, and in the street he saw nothing but the sharp shadows cast by a moon almost at its full. Softly he cursed that moon and the flood of light it shed. But not for long. He realised that with every second that he waited his danger was increased, and collecting what remained of his strength, he took the Count under the arms, and dragged him out into the moonlight. Out into the mid-street he dragged him — he did not want the body at his door — and there he laid him on his back, his white face turned up to the glory of the midnight heavens. Beside the body he let fall the bloody poniard he had used, whilst the sheath he flung far up the street. That done, he turned and fled like a scurrying rat back to the shelter of his doorway.

Once in his room alone, he snuffed the tapers, and went to peer through his blind at the body lying out there in the glare of the moon. He mopped the sweat from his brow, and his pulse grew more regular.

"You will marry my ward, eh?" he gibed maliciously. "*Per Dio*, Lord Count, there is no marrying where you have gone."

He would have withdrawn and betaken himself to bed, for the hour was late; but a fascination held him there to see what might befall. And presently on the still, night air there rang out footsteps. The figure of a man, showing black in the moon's white light, came into the judge's range of vision. Foscaro saw the wayfarer stoop to pick up something. It was the sheath of the dagger. Then as the man advanced he caught sight of that black heap, and with quickened steps he approached the body. He bent over the prostrate form, and moved the Count's head so that the light fell upon his face. In that instant Foscaro's quick ears caught the sound of the regular tramp of feet, and he knew it for the watch going its round.

The wayfarer heard it too, and stood upright, his cloak wrapped about him, looking over his shoulder. Then a shout went up from the approaching patrol, announcing that they had sighted the man standing over the motionless body. For a second the wayfarer seemed to hesitate; then, of a sudden, he gathered up the folds of his cloak, and, turning about, he dashed down the street at a run.

Loudly now rattled the steps of the men, who not unnaturally imagined that they were the witness of a crime. Past Foscaro's window three of them sped in hot pursuit of the fugitive, whilst a fourth paused by the body, shouting to his fellows that it was still warm.

"Fool," sneered the judge. "Why did he run?"

Meanwhile the watchman that had been left behind summoned aid, and had the body carried to the gaol, that the Governor might determine what should be done.

The Governor of Jesi gaol chanced to be Count Mattoli's dearest friend.

In the Court of Jesi sat Judge Foscaro at noon next day, dispensing that which in the eighteenth century they called justice. Impassively he listened — his grim old face set and inscrutable — to a watchman's account of the taking of Count Mattoli's murderer on the previous night. Beside him, his lips wearing an inscrutable smile of saturnine significance, was Delmonte — the Governor of Jesi gaol. His eyes never left the judge's face, and their expression was one of mingled wonder and derision. So that in the end, the judge, remarking it, could not repress an uneasy speculation as to whether this man were possessed of some knowledge of his guilt.

At last, when the watchman had done — "Produce the accused," Foscaro commanded in harsh, incisive accents.

The doors were opened, and walking between two carabineers came a swarthy young man of middle height, dressed after the manner of a gentleman. There was a murmur in the court that quickly swelled until it became a strange, indefinable cry.

Judge Foscaro raised his eyes, and as they lighted upon the prisoner they grew dull as those of a snake. His cheeks went grey and his mouth fell open, for before him stood Gennaro Foscaro, his son.

He made as if to speak. Then the hands, that had convulsively clutched the chair on either side of him, suddenly relaxed their grip. He tossed his arms to heaven, and with an inarticulate cry he sank back in a swoon.

All that night the old man lay sleepless on his bed, thinking, thinking, thinking. Towards dawn he took at last his resolve. He would keep silent and allow his son to stand his trial. Into his mind had crept the subtle argument that there was no necessity for him to betray himself. His son would be judged upon the evidence put forth, and upon that evidence surely he must be acquitted, since justice could not err.

The production of Mattoli's murderer was no part of the proof that his son was innocent. Gennaro's innocence was a thing of itself, a thing that could not fail to be established. What was the mission else of justice?

Allaying his tremors of spirit by such arguments, Judge Foscaro allowed his son to be taken to Rome. Thence a week later they brought him the astounding news that Gennaro had been found guilty and sentenced to death.

Delmonte, the governor of Jesi gaol and Count Mattoli's bosom friend, had relentlessly hunted him down during his trial. His flight had weighed heavily against him at the outset, and to this Delmonte added considerably by informing the Court that there was no lack of motive on the part of the accused, since Mattoli was his successful rival in the affections of Judge Foscaro's ward.

When Gennaro ably defended himself by pointing out with convincing force that it was precisely because he feared suspicion might fasten upon him by virtue of that rivalry that he fled upon recognizing Mattoli, Delmonte quietly replied by advancing the fact that when arrested, Gennaro had in his possession a sheath which fitted the dagger with which Mattoli had been stabbed.

Again Gennaro had urged the truth in plausible explanation of how that sheath came to be upon him, and in the moment of the judge's wavering, Delmonte rose again to finally crush the youth who denied all knowledge of that poniard by pointing out that upon its pummel it bore the arms of the house of Foscaro.

Foscaro sat with haggard face and eyes that glowed feverishly — madly almost — when he heard the fatal news. Justice, it seemed, had a strange way of going awry.

Yet there was in Delmonte's behaviour something that perplexed him. He recalled the grim, sardonic air with which the Governor had watched him that morning in the Court of Jesi, and he remembered the suspicions he had then entertained. Curiously strengthened were these now by the fact that, after having tracked down and gained the sentence of Gennaro, he had himself urged the Court of Rome to stay the execution whilst again he made such investigations as might yet be possible. He called attention to the circumstantial nature of the evidence he had himself advanced in Gennaro's destruction, and besought the Court to grant the stay he solicited until he could more positively assure them that in the execution no miscarriage of justice might there be.

The days that ensued were, for Judge Foscaro, hideous indeed; the nights a thousand-fold worse. He realised that even confession was now too late. None would believe him, deeming his statement a preposterous story invented in the attempt to sacrifice the little life that was left him in order to save his child.

In three short days he seemed more aged than might have been expected in thrice as many years. His face was drawn and haggard, his eyes bloodshot and with dark circles under them, whilst loss of sleep had so racked his nerves that every shadow caused him to start and catch his breath.

On the third night, as he sat, listless, in his room, he heard a noise behind him, and upon looking round beheld in the doorway a tall, black figure, which so startled him that he shrieked outright. The figure advanced slowly into the room. It was wrapped in a long, black cloak, and a black visor concealed the face.

"Have no fear, Master Foscaro," said a voice, that the mask rendered muffled and indistinct; "I mean you no harm."

"Who — who are you?" gasped the judge.

"That you shall presently learn. I am come to you touching the trial of your son. Judge Foscaro, why did you not tell the Court what you knew of this crime of which your child is innocent, but for which assuredly he will hang?"

"Of what do you talk?" cried Foscaro, in a voice of awe.

"I talk of what I know."

Foscaro sank into a chair like a man exhausted.

"In Heaven's name, if you know so much, why have you kept silent?"

"That I might turn my silence to account. I am a poor man, excellency, but I have a notion that you will make me rich — as rich as I shall be silent."

Foscaro's look was charged with dull surprise.

"I am a poor man, too," he said, recovering himself partly. "It seems a pity that you who know so much should not be informed of that. Go, man; I have no riches for you. Take yourself to Rome, and tell them what you know."

The man was silent for a moment; then:

"If I were to pledge myself to save your son, excellency, and yet not to divulge my knowledge, would that tempt you to find the price of my service?"

"Who are you?" cried Foscaro excitedly. "What is it you can do?"

"I will swear to do what I promise," replied he of the mask, with convincing assurance. "There is a piece of evidence whereof I am possessed, which appears to have escaped all notice. They did not go sufficiently into this case at Rome, excellency, and your own knowledge has stultified your wits perhaps. But there! This evidence I hold, and by publishing it I can save your son without yet incriminating you."

Mightily did Foscaro tax his wits to penetrate this man's disguise. Then in a flash a suggestion came to him. He remembered Delmonte's bearing at the trial and the suspicions it had suggested to him. He looked at the black figure before him now, and he saw that the height and shape were the height and shape of Delmonte. Delmonte, too, was poor. He was ambitious, and ambitious men will stoop to much that their ambitions may be gratified. No doubt of it remained to him. Delmonte had seen him carry out the body of his friend the Count, and to serve his own ends he had kept silent.

The masker's voice broke in upon his speculations. "You do not answer, excellency."

In the poignancy of his despair Foscaro stood wringing his hands before his visitor.

"I am a poor man," he repeated. "I have not the means to buy your aid."

He of the mask fetched a sigh of one who takes with reluctance a resolve.

"You have a ward," said he.

The judge looked up, inquiry in his glance.

"Common rumour accounts her the richest heiress in these parts."

"Yes," said the judge. "Well?"

"Marry her to me. I would have preferred the money without the encumbrance. Still, since there is no other way, and since I take it she is neither lame nor crookbacked, I'll marry her if you wish it."

"But my ward is to wed my son," said Foscaro dully.

"Your son, sir, will be wedded to a coffin before the month is out unless you do my will, for I shall hold my peace. Old man, be not a fool. Resign yourself to relinquish one or the other — your ward or your son. Choose."

Again Judge Foscaro's wits grew busy. A wild notion came of a sudden into his cunning mind. He feigned to ponder, then inclining his head:

"If you swear to accomplish what you promise — to save my son, and yet not to implicate me — I will do as you desire."

"I swear it," solemnly replied the other.

"When will you set about it?"

"When the nuptials have been solemnised. There is no need for haste. We had best say to-morrow night."

Foscaro bowed.

"My ward shall be bought from the convent. At this hour to-morrow I will have a priest here to wed you."

When his visitor had departed old Foscaro's face took on a grim, satanic leer. He had Delmonte, he swore, in the hollow of his hand, and the fool should learn that Judge Foscaro was something more than a match for him in astuteness.

On the morrow he caused inquiries to be made at the prison, which confirmed his assurance. Delmonte had been absent at the hour of the crime. Not a doubt remained with him but that, concealed in some doorway, the governor had witnessed the affair.

At nine o'clock that night the odious ceremony of the wedding took place. It was not easily achieved. The girl, knowing naught of the death of Mattoli, her lover, resisted them with all the power of her will, until in the end, overcome by the pressure put upon her innocent, convent-fostered mind, she went through the brief marriage ceremony in a pitiable, half-fainting condition.

Scarce was it over when Foscaro supported the almost unconscious girl to a chair. In her ear he whispered:

"Fret not, little one. You shall never see him again, and before the month is out you'll be a widow."

Then, turning to the bridegroom:

"Governor Delmonte," he cried in a firm voice, "I charge you with the murder of Count Mattoli."

The man recoiled a step.

"Are you turned witless?" he exclaimed.

"Witless?" jeered Foscaro. "Were you but half as sane you had not come here to-night. Why do you imagine that I permitted this marriage to take place? 'Twas to establish beyond doubt your motive for the crime. It weighed heavily against my son that he was Count Mattoli's rival for the hand of my ward. Do you think it will weigh less heavily against you?"

"Is that all your evidence?"

"All? No, *per Dio!* Some hours before the crime took place you visited me here — this my servants can prove. After your departure I missed from my table the dagger produced at my son's trial, and of the arms on which you made so great a point. To this I can swear. Lastly, Count Mattoli's body was discovered still warm in the street here at eleven o'clock. Can you say where you were to be found between half-past ten and eleven on that night? You shall have ample opportunity at your trial."

"*Pazzo!*" cried he of the mask; "of what do you rave?"

For all reply Judge Foscaro stepped to the curtains that masked one of the windows, and drew them back. Four carabineers stepped from the bay of the window, and at a sign from Foscaro advanced upon the accused.

"Hold!" he cried, and opening his cloak, he unfastened it, and let it slip from his shoulders, revealing a figure in a silver-laced grey riding-coat that was too slender far for Delmonte's. Then, removing his mask, he presented to the terrified gaze of Judge Foscaro the face — pale as a ghost's — of Count Mattoli, the man he had murdered!

Step by step the old judge recoiled before that apparition, his face mottled, his eyes riveted upon the Count. He recoiled until he struck against a chair, into which he sank with a helpless groan.

Then Mattoli laughed grimly.

"I am no ghost, excellency," said he; "I am Ettore Mattoli in the flesh. Your dagger did no more than scratch my breast, but it was in falling that I struck my head against your wall so vilely that I was unconscious for close upon an hour. Thanks to my friend Delmonte's help, I have sufficiently avenged myself on my supposed murderer, and your son, Master Foscaro, shall go free, as I have sworn. The fact that I was not dead at all was the evidence their excellencies overlooked in Rome."

But for all that the judge's eyes continued bent upon him out of that ashen face, they saw him not — for terror had checked the old man's heart for all time.

Receiving no answer, Mattoli turned to the startled girl.

"Giulia," he whispered, putting his arms about her, "Giulia, my wife. It was cruel, was it not, to give you so much pain? But then, *amor mio*, there was no other way to win you from that old rascal."

He drew her to him, and the brown eyes that looked up in thankfulness to his were charged with tears.

The Dream

I

Stanley Bickershaw

The colonnade is undoubtedly the most distinctive feature of Herne Place. You step from its broad shelter on to a pathway of red gravel, wide enough to admit a carriage, and beyond that there is a sweep of meadow, smooth and level as a lawn, flanked on either side by woodland, sloping gently to the river half a mile or more away.

Anthony Orpington had acquired that imposing residence on retiring from the Stock Exchange, and in the cool shade of the colonnade he was entertaining to tea, on a languorous afternoon in July, his nephew, the celebrated Stanley Bickershaw.

There was no point of family resemblance between the two men. Orpington, who was in his sixtieth year, was very tall and spare, with fine hands and an aristocratic, sallow face. He was dressed with care in a grey lounge suit, and he wore white spats — an inevitable part of his apparel — over his enamelled shoes. A soft grey hat covered his thinning hair, and a single glass in a tortoise-shell rim adorned, or assisted, his left eye.

Bickershaw was short and of a weedy, delicate build. His face was sallow, but with an unhealthy sallowness which in a man of his years — he was not more than thirty — argued sedentary habits. His nose was heavy and pendulous, his lower jaw remarkably heavy, his mouth little more than a straight line between the two. He had a bulging forehead, eyes that were too closely set, small, very dark, quick in their movements, and singularly piercing. Altogether, his was a face which the average man would find unprepossessing, and the physiognomist sinister. He was dressed untidily in a suit of flannels that had seen a good deal of wear. This carelessness of appearance was habitual, and was one of the many faults which his uncle found in him.

Stanley Bickershaw was celebrated as has been said. He was entitled to put a quite considerable proportion of the alphabet after his name, many of his degrees, however, having been conferred upon him by learned bodies as some appreciation of his distinguished services to the elucidation of hypnotic phenomena. His researches in the realm of hypnosis were vast, and much of the work he had done was unprecedented, and upon lines entirely original. This was borne out by such publications of his as "Researches in the Subliminal,"

126

and "The Rationale of Hypnosis."   Nevertheless, he remained poor, for hypnotism is hardly a marketable commodity; and whilst he won whole bushes of laurels, he made the disappointing discovery that the plant is a purely ornamental one incapable of bearing fruit of its own.

Consequently his appeals for assistance to his wealthy uncle were periodical; they recurred with the regularity of the seasons.   Such an appeal had brought him to Herne Place on the afternoon with which we are concerned, and he took the very first opportunity — as soon as his uncle's man had ceased fussing with the tea-kettle and muffin-dish and had withdrawn — to broach the matter.

There was no necessity for him to enter into particulars; nor was he afforded the opportunity.   From former experiences Orpington knew by Bickershaw's opening sentence precisely what was coming.

He sat up and dropped his eyeglass.   "What?   Again?" he exclaimed, a forbidding reproof in the question.

"I am sorry," said Bickershaw; but his tone was quite formal, his manner perfectly calm, conveying no hint of real regret.   He was, as a matter of fact, deplorably lacking in any instincts of tact or diplomacy.   His attitude towards the world was one of lofty contempt, of intolerance for a general ignorance which he was constantly flinging in its teeth.   Looking upon his uncle as an integral part of that ignorant world which he despised, he was at no pains to dissemble his contempt even when seeking him on such an errand as the present one.

"I am sorry," he said then, "but progress is very gradual in the line I have chosen.   The reward that should follow recognition is very slow in coming."

"That being the case," replied the practical uncle, "I recommend you to choose another line.   What good are degrees if you won't turn them to account?   Why don't you go into practice as a medical man?   You're duly qualified."

"Oh, please!" said Bickershaw, with a quiet scorn that was magnificent, effacing the distasteful suggestion by a deprecatory movement of his broad hands.   "I am not a practitioner.   I am a scientist.   You may not be able to appreciate the difference, but you may take my word for it that it exists."

"Obviously," snapped his uncle.   "The one can make a living, and the other can't."

"Of course, if you are going to measure merit and achievement by the standard of a mere capacity for making money, then any tradesman is a better man than I am."

"He fulfils a more useful function in society."

"The matter is one that we will not argue.   It is not given to some people to see beyond immediate returns.   To them that by which a narrow community benefits at the moment is of more consequence than the labour by which humanity in general may benefit through centuries to come.   I am afraid, my dear uncle, that you take that deplorable point of view."

Orpington screwed his glass into his eye, and scowled down upon his superior nephew. He set about returning him rudeness for rudeness, conviction for conviction.

"Your insufferable conceit," he said, "is an insuperable bar to your worldly success. Nothing else could lead you to imagine that the charlatanism and quackery which receives the applause of a few feeble-minded men and neurotic women is going to be of any benefit to humanity."

Bickershaw, entirely unruffled, smiled the lofty, tolerant smile that he reserved for ignorance too crass to merit the dignity of his scorn.

"I suppose you always consider people feeble-minded and neurotic when their notions of things do not happen to coincide with your own happy enlightenment."

"Quite so," said Orpington, intentionally provoking.

Bickershaw sighed. "I haven't your confidence — alas!"

"You've the confidence of Old Nick himself," snorted Orpington. A faint colour — reflex of his indignation — was stirring in his cheeks. "And it's just like your infernal impudence to come here and take this superior tone with the man from whom you're attempting to borrow money. What do you do with your money, anyway? You don't spend anything on clothes, as far as I can see; you're not man enough to have any dissipation; you're living at your cousin's and on your cousin; and I'm sure you don't gamble. Yet it's only three months since you had two hundred pounds from me. What do you do with it?"

Bickershaw produced a pipe, and proceeded calmly to load it. "You can't believe," he said, "how costly are my researches."

Orpington sneered.

"I am pursuing at the moment certain investigations," his nephew continued confidently, "substantiating certain theories which I have formed. I have arrived at the point where practical experiment is necessary, and for this I must have a medium. Now mediums are expensive. They demand large honorariums, and they have to be kept whilst the experiments are being conducted. These may last some time in my case. Now perhaps you understand."

"Pshaw!" was the rejoinder, undisguisedly contemptuous. "Empiricism of the rankest! Charlatanism! Neither more nor less. I was talking about it to Dr. Ross the other day when he came to see me about my indigestion. He says — "

"His opinion on such a subject," Bickershaw interrupted coolly, "is just about as valuable as your gardener's."

"He's a specialist," said Orpington.

"In gastric ailments — yes; just as your gardener is a specialist in gardens. I don't see that either is entitled to be considered an authority on hypnotic phenomena."

"Anyhow, he is able to make a living — and a jolly good one."

"We appear," replied Bickershaw, "to be arguing in a vicious circle. The point is — "

"The point is, will you earn your living if I put you in the way of doing so?"

"I desire nothing more ardently."

"Very well, then. I'll tell you what I'll do: I'll give you a thousand pounds to buy a practice."

For a moment Bickershaw's self-possession was shaken by disgust. He lighted his pipe and recovered. "Will you give me the thousand pounds without conditions?" he inquired with quiet impudence.

"No, I will not."

"Why not? What difference can it make to you? So long as you part with the money —"

"It will make this difference," was the answer. "If the money is put into a practice, and you know there is no more to come, you may work and keep yourself; whereas if you put it into this confounded hypnotic rot of yours, you'll be back again in six months, asking for more.

"Anyway, I've made you an offer. You can take it or leave it."

"You don't know what you are asking," Bickershaw protested. "Do you see me — Stanley Bickershaw — setting up as a general practitioner in some beastly suburb, spending my days and wasting my talents in treating young ladies for anaemia and old gentlemen for dyspepsia? Do you?"

The last remark was unfortunate, and it brought Anthony Orpington to his feet in a fine anger. He was extremely sensitive on the score of his age, and he saw a personal allusion to himself in the "old gentlemen with dyspepsia."

"I think you'd better go, Stanley," he said, in the voice of one who is exerting a heroic self-control. "You're wasting your time here. I'm incapable, you know, of following your mind into the fine shades of logic in which it loves to meander. You have refused the only offer I am likely to make you. I shall not repeat it. And you may as well know that if you come pestering me any more for money, I'll deprive you of the competence you are to inherit under my will as it stands at present."

"But, my dear Uncle Anthony!" Bickershaw, too, was on his feet, and belatedly he was attempting a conciliatory tone, softening the scornful lines of his mouth. "I assure you that I —"

"I don't give a durn for your assurances," was the wrathful interruption. "You can go. I've said all that I am going to say. And don't come near me again until you've put your manners through a course of training. I've done with you, and I'm glad my poor sister isn't alive to see the waster you've become."

The dismissal was final. Bickershaw picked up his rather dingy straw hat. "Very well" he said. He recovered something of his quiet insolence. "Sorry to have troubled you," he added. "Good afternoon!" And he departed.

Two red spots of anger burned in his sallow cheeks; yet through all his disappointment came a gleam of hope. He was to benefit under his uncle's will; that was news to him. A competence, his uncle had said; perhaps three or four hundred a year; that would be his uncle's notion of a competence. But the hopefulness of the outlook was discounted when he came to consider his uncle's extreme good health. Still, it was something to know that some day he would be in the enjoyment of an income that should insure him immunity from such pecuniary embarrassments as hampered him at every step. Meanwhile, however, there were his present considerable difficulties to be faced.

He considered the advisability of seeking assistance from his cousin, Major Francis Orpington, whose guest he was and had been now for some weeks past, and was likely to continue for an indefinite period.

He took his resolve upon that point, and stepped along more briskly despite the heat. He crossed the river at Romney Lock, and made his way along the towpath towards the Major's house at Old Windsor.

Coming up from the river, through the shrubbery he found Francis Orpington and the latter's sometime ward, Adelaide Burton, reclining in deck-chairs in the shade of a clump of trees on the edge of the tennis lawn. A racket lay on the grass beside Francis; he was in flannels and without a coat; there was a cigarette between his lips, and he held a long glass half-full of a beverage in which a piece of ice was floating. He was chatting gaily, and Adelaide was laughing as she listened, watching him with eyes full of affection — an affection by no means limited to what is due between ward and guardian.

Bickershaw, coming silently through the shrubbery, checked on the edge of the lawn, and stood quietly observing them, his presence unsuspected. There was no particular reason for his action. It was instinctive, a part of his rather warped nature, secretly to observe people. Had you charged him with spying or eavesdropping, it would probably have surprised him; yet, having considered your accusation, he would have brushed it aside as sentimental and frivolous.

So he stood there for a little while, considering them, listening to their lighthearted talk, and drawing conclusions of his own from what he heard and saw — fairly obvious conclusions, after all, which had none the less escaped his attention hitherto.

Major Francis Orpington was a younger edition of his uncle Anthony; he was tall, spare and active with the same high-bred, lean face, and the same habits of thought — which, no doubt, had much to do with the excellent relations that prevailed between himself and his uncle, whose acknowledged heir he was.

He was in his fortieth year, but he looked thirty and felt twenty. And this, to some extent, may account for his having permitted himself to fall in love with his ward, notwithstanding that she was twelve years younger. Nevertheless, the consciousness of the disparity in age between himself and this daughter of his old friend, Edgar Burton — who for fifteen years now, ever since her father's death, had been under his tutelage — set a certain curb upon his feelings. So far it had prevented him from making a declaration which Adelaide very ardently desired.

At times he would toy tentatively with the question of her marrying, dangle it before her, use it as a plumb to sound the depths of her feelings and inform himself how far he might navigate his own barque upon these unknown waters which allured him and yet which he hesitated to explore, dreading shipwreck.

As if for the information of that silent watcher in the background, he was toying now with that momentous question.

"You're an impudent baggage, Adelaide," he told her, laughing. "You've no proper sort of respect for me. You forget at times that I'm your guardian; that I stand towards you *in loco parentis*, as it were."

"Your French is atrocious," she informed him.

"It happens to be Latin."

"You render both unintelligible."

"This is the most obvious and noisome of red herrings," he protested. "I am referring to your want of respect for me; your want of a proper sense of the dignity of my position. It is high time I handed you over to a husband."

The mockery diminished in the brown eyes, the dark head was lowered for a moment; she studied her racket in silence. Then she laughed softly.

"If you imagine that you would thus impose obedience to a man upon me, you are hopelessly mistaken. It has gone out of fashion to obey a husband."

"And yet," said he, "in spite of that inducement to marry, you have remained single." He looked at her sideways as he spoke, his lips smiled, but his eyes had an anxious searching look.

"The right man never asked me," she answered, and faced him, laughing, almost challenging.

He turned his attention to his glass, and took a long pull through the straw. "There were suitors to spare in the old days," he said presently. "In fact, they became a confounded nuisance and a decided drain upon the resources of my modest establishment. They were a varied lot — no girl could have had a wider range of choice. And yet, like the brazen hussy you are, Adelaide, you encouraged them all, and married none. And now, when you're — Let me see, how old is it safe to say you are?"

"Twenty," she answered shamelessly.

"To be sure, now that you're twenty, the suitors are not quite as plentiful, and you are still single; by no means blessedly single. Do you know, Adelaide, that you're a great disappointment to me? In whatever light I consider you — save perhaps as tennis-player — you're a failure."

She put out a hand, slender, strong and cool, and took him by the wrist. She looked up into his eyes, smiling gently and very alluringly. "Am I really such a disappointment to you, Frank?" she asked him.

Something of his mock-seriousness departed. He flung away his cigarette. A mild excitement fluttered through him. This was his hour. In the tide of his affairs of the heart, surely this was the flood. Upon its bosom he would sail to fortune.

And then, whilst he was still pondering the words in which at last to launch his barque, a twig snapped behind them, and Stanley Bickershaw, sardonic and light-footed, stole like a snake into their Eden.

II
The Control of Adelaide

If Major Orpington was vexed by that interruption at the time of its occurrence, more deeply still was he vexed by it when he came, a week or so later, to view the matter in retrospect.

Not only did retrospection increase his assurance that the moment had been entirely favourable, but that it had been critically favourable — a moment which would not recur. For with each day that had sped there had seemed less chance of its recurring. Adelaide grew oddly reserved towards him; her manner became daily more distant.

This extraordinary change in her — this unaccountable ever-increasing aloofness — dated from the day after that upon which the Major had been so near to declaring himself; and he was intrigued to know whether the cause lay in her having suddenly instinctively guessed the declaration that had impended, or in a little difference that they had on the score of Bickershaw.

It had begun in a laughingly disparaging remark that he had made concerning his cousin's pursuits — for he very fully shared his uncle's opinion of them, and did not hesitate to set them down as so much clap-trap. It was by no means the first time that he had made such a remark to Adelaide, and it had never failed to draw an echoing laugh from her — but of a kindlier quality, in which tolerance and indulgence were blent with mockery. On this occasion, however, she did not respond to his humour by so much as a smile. The level brows were knit; the handsome dark face was overcast and brooding.

"Do you think you are quite fair to Stanley?" she inquired, her tone severe.

He was startled for a moment. Then he laughed. "Are you going to take up the cudgels for the magician?" he challenged her.

"I am not sure that it is right to mock at what we don't, perhaps, understand."

"It is intensely human," said he.

"That is the poorest excuse for shortcomings, just as it is the commonest. Of course, you haven't read any of Stanley's books."

He was astounded. "Have you?" he asked.

"I am reading 'Researches in the Subliminal' now. It is immensely interesting. It discovers for me how foolish and willful people can be in their ignorance. The book is a revelation — an astounding revelation."

He walked along beside her in absolute silence for some moments. It was after breakfast, and they were pacing the lower end of the tennis-lawn, the Major pulling at his morning pipe. To say that her words and her tone amazed him would be very inadequately to express his feelings: his surprise, his irritation, his impatience, and a sense of lurking evil that began to haunt him.

"This is a very sudden change!" he said and he said it laughingly, to conceal his true feelings.

"Sudden changes of thought are inevitable when we have been content to take our opinions at second-hand," she answered didactically. "Until yesterday it is what I have been doing so far as Stanley and his work are concerned. Last night, for the first time in all these years, Stanley came and talked to me about himself. He impressed me by his sheer honesty and earnestness. I borrowed a copy of his 'Researches in the Subliminal,' and I am afraid that I sat up until very late. It is a book that holds you — a wonderful study."

"You should hear Uncle Anthony upon the subject."

"I am capable of forming opinions of my own, Frank," she answered loftily.

It was extraordinary. He considered her attentively, half-smiling still to disguise his seriousness, his positive and inexplicable anxiety. She bore his scrutiny with characteristic calm. Yes, it was extraordinary. This handsome, straight, clean-limbed young woman, who, though intelligent and cultured, could never have been called bookish, to be suddenly caught in the toils of such morbid clap-trap. He supposed women were like that; their emotional, sensation-loving natures were easily to be ensnared by the sort of thing of which Bickershaw was an exponent. But, somehow, he had accounted Adelaide different, more virile-minded, whilst no less womanly than the average of her sex. He did not pause to consider that Bickershaw's influence was one that made itself felt not only among women and neurotic men, but amongst eminent and learned scholars. He was satisfied that his own essentially material outlook was the only outlook possible to the healthy male.

It was from that moment as if between himself and Adelaide a chasm had suddenly split itself, a gulf that widened daily thereafter, until by the end of a week of brooding and positive unhappiness, which began to mar the equanimity of his amiable good-nature, he came to ask himself whether she were not falling in love with Bickershaw.

The notion was grotesque and incredible. He flung it off in scorn at first. Bickershaw, with his unhealthy face, his stoop, his pendulous nose and beady eyes, was a type that must be repulsive to women. Then there was his personal untidiness — an untidiness that bordered upon uncleanliness — his ill-made, dusty clothes ever baggy and threadbare at the knees, and his deadly cold, forbidding manner. Surely all this must be repellant to a girl of Adelaide's pronounced fastidiousness and healthy, open nature.

And yet the conviction gained upon him; it was not to be reasoned away; and the accompanying sense of evil increased. It was unquestionable that Bickershaw exerted a singular influence over those with whom he came into contact, despite his physical disadvantages. He seemed to exude some quality of compulsion. It was difficult to resist him when he desired anything. The Major himself had experienced this and had needed all his willpower and determination on more occasions than one when forced by his good sense to deny certain things to his cousin. The servants hated him, yet were more submissive to him than to the Major himself. In fact, one could not imagine — nor did it ever happen — that an inferior ever rebelled against Bickershaw's cold authority. More than once Orpington had actually seen an angry, snarling dog suddenly crouch down with a whimper of fear, trembling in every nerve under the stare of Bickershaw's beady eyes. Beyond doubt the man exerted an unnatural, uncanny masterfulness. And as the Major came to consider all this, and saw the daily changing demeanour of Adelaide, his uneasiness increased alarmingly.

Presently he was to have proof that his fears were by no means idle — that Bickershaw's influence over Adelaide was no figment of his imagination.

Bickershaw had appealed to him for help on the day after the fruitless visit to Anthony Orpington. The Major had refused. Necessity compelled him to do so. He reminded Bickershaw that he was far from wealthy, that he had need to exercise economy, and that beyond giving the latter a home, as he was doing, he was really unable to extend him any assistance.

He had experienced the usual difficulty, the usual diffidence in opposing his cousin. But he had been quite firm about it, and Bickershaw had not insisted. He had smiled quietly to himself, a little grimly, perhaps, as one who, driven by force of circumstances, decides upon a course he would otherwise have avoided.

And then, a week later, Adelaide came to Francis one morning when he was in his study, on an errand that startled him and afforded him the proof to which reference has been made.

She perched herself on the corner of his writing-table, as she had been in the habit of doing on such occasions for the past ten years. But the manner of doing it was very different from the usual.

"I want to help Stanley," she informed him quite abruptly. "He is urgently in need of money to carry on his researches. I want you to let me have a cheque for three hundred pounds, Frank. I suppose you can manage it."

He laid down his pen, and his keen, good-natured face was troubled. He looked straight before him through the window, considering his answer. Of course, Adelaide was her own mistress, and mistress of her own finances, although he had continued to control them for her ever since her majority, just as formerly. Her father had left her a modest fortune of some six hundred pounds a year, which under Francis's stewardship had considerably increased.

He looked at her keenly, and what he observed in her face did not reassure him. She was pale and rather tired-looking; her dark eyes, usually so keen and bright, looked dull, jaded, and vacant. Vacant! That was it. It was in all her face; not pronounced, perhaps, and only to be perceived by one who was familiar with her usual vivacity. But, unquestionably, it was there.

Francis Orpington's brows came together in an angry frown. This desire to assist Bickershaw with funds was the last straw; it was the proof of the hold the man was obtaining over her, and it was an unhealthy, evil hold, as her very countenance and the change it had undergone bore witness. It would not have needed his love for her to have stirred his anger now. He must in any case have detested her intimacy with such a man as his cousin. He made a swift examination of conscience, and he found no jealousy distorting his outlook. His anger was clean and honest, and dictated purely by his affection, by his concern for her.

At last he spoke, slowly, looking her straight between the eyes.

"Has Stanley asked you to help him?"

Her eyes fell. She fidgeted nervously with the bundle of her belt. And it was not like her to be nervous or to fidget; she was frankness and naturalness personified. "No," she said presently; "he has not."

"But he has hinted that it would be acceptable — hinted pretty broadly, eh?"

"You are really very unfair to him, Frank." Still her eyes avoided his. "He has not hinted — not exactly. He has simply told me in what straits he is for funds, and how it is embarrassing his work. There is nothing small or mean in his desire for money. He does not want it for himself, to waste it on pleasure as most men do. He wants to spend it in the interests of science and of humanity."

The Major's frown grew darker. He snorted impatiently. "Yes, I've heard him talk just like that. He must find you a singularly satisfactory disciple."

She flushed. "If you don't mind, Frank, I'd sooner not discuss it with you. You are so very much out of sympathy with Stanley. You don't understand him, and you take no interest in his work." She made the slightest pause. "You'll let me have that cheque today, won't you?"

He noticed the change, the slight hardening of her tone, the altered choice of words which made of the thing a demand rather than a request. Of course, she was entirely within her rights.

"Certainly, if you wish it," he answered, and there was the least stiffening of his own tone and manner, for he was genuinely hurt. "The money's yours to dispose of as you please. At the same time, three hundred pounds is a considerable sum; as you realise, I suppose, that you stand very little chance of recovering it, once you lend it to Stanley."

"I don't mean to lend it. I intend it as a gift."

"As a gift? Oh!"

"Yes. I, too, should like to do something for — for the same cause. It's a little enough I can do. What is mere money, after all?"

"Oh, just rubbish, of course," said Francis, stung into sarcasm.

He opened a drawer and took out a cheque-book.

"If your mind is quite made up, I suppose there's no more to be said."

She didn't answer him; so he dipped his pen and wrote the desired cheque.

"There you are," he said.

She took it, glanced over it, muttered a casual work of thanks and slipped off the table.

"Can you spare me five minutes?" he wondered. "I should like to have a talk with you, Adelaide."

"Not now," she put him off. "I can't at the moment. Later on, perhaps." And she left him.

He lay back in his chair, very thoughtful and very unhappy. He was unhappy about himself and about her. The change in her attitude towards him was so extraordinary, so complete. And the proof of his fears concerning Bickershaw's influence over her she had now afforded him — it was outrageous!

He sighed bitterly, and with knit brows slowly filled his pipe. He lighted it, and then slowly put it down. Looking through the window he could see the far end of the tennis lawn, and there, on the edge of the shrubbery, she was pacing slowly with Bickershaw. She had refused him the five minutes he had begged of her that she might consecrate every moment of her spare time to his cousin.

He watched them, a very sullen anger in his heart. He observed that Bickershaw was talking; talking in that cold, impressive — horribly impressive — manner that he assumed when in earnest. The man's beady eyes scarcely left her face, and she, Orpington observed, returned his glance with one of wondering, admiring awe.

There was something abhorrent in the sight. Orpington could not define it, could not have said why it so impressed him. But it was there — something loathsome and evil that stirred his manhood and called loudly to his chivalry to hasten to the rescue.

At last he took a resolve. Bickershaw must go. There was no longer room for him in that house whose hospitality he was abusing.

"But how is he abusing it?" cried Conscience suddenly. And Orpington's honest nature stood appalled at what he believed to be his own meanness, from which such a suggestion had emanated — at the absurd jealousy that had deluded him.

That was it; he was jealous — a jealous old fool. And his jealousy was of so horrible and detestable a quality that he saw all manner of evil where none existed. Yet was it so? Again he made that examination of conscience; and this time he was left in doubt. He must bring a calm and impartial mind to give judgment upon the case. He would go and talk the matter over with Uncle Anthony. He went.

Anthony Orpington's judgment was brief and uncompromising.

"The fellow's a rotter, Frank. I've done with him myself. Turn him out neck and crop."

The Major entered into the matter of his own feelings for Adelaide, taking his uncle into his confidence. He found Anthony — a confirmed misogynist —

surprisingly sympathetic and approving.

"Why not? Why not? She'd be a fool to refuse you. I'm sure she's fond of you, and you know from experience that you can live in the same house without quarrelling. It isn't every prospective couple that has had the same chance of testing joint existence as you two have had. What's twelve years difference? Pooh! Marry her, and good luck to you."

Frank dwelt upon the signs of a change in her feelings towards him. His uncle dogmatised:

"All the more reason to get rid of the blackguard. He's at the bottom of it. Women swallow the sort of charlatanism he gives off as a baby swallows milk. Get rid of him."

"But that is just the point," Francis objected gloomily. "I am taking an unfair advantage. I am allowing my jealousy to dictate to my honesty. Stanley is rather in difficulties, and if I throw him over — "

"Serve him jolly well right," said the emphatic uncle. "Let me come and have a look at things."

"Oh, no, no."

"I'll walk over after lunch tomorrow if it's fine," Anthony insisted. "Expect me at about three."

The Major had gone to his uncle for advice; but like a good many people who in a quandary hesitate to take the only obvious course before them, he was none the better for it when he had received it. He returned home in the same frame of mind in the same state of indecision.

He took the short cut that it was usual to take in walking from Herne Place; he crossed the river at Romney Lock, followed the towpath, and turned up into his own shrubbery. Through this he came quite noiselessly by the pathway, where the soft, moist earth soundlessly received his footsteps. At the end of the lawn, just where this path debouched into it stood a spacious summer-house, or rustic pavilion, that was in constant use. As Francis was passing this, he caught a sound that brought him instinctively to a standstill. It was the sound of a human voice — Bickershaw's voice, he realised presently — speaking in soft, curiously droning accents.

Puzzled, Francis stood listening; but he could distinguish no word of what was said; indeed, he was not sure that words were being uttered; rather did the sound, on closer acquaintance, seem like the crooning with which a mother lulls her child to sleep.

He approached, and looked through one of the windows. On a cane chaise-longue Adelaide was reclining in an attitude of intense fatigue, her hands folded in her lap, her bosom rising and falling with the steady rhythm of the sleeper, her face white and vacant to the point of ghastliness.

Before her sat Bickershaw, his little eyes malignantly agleam, his hands moving slowly down over her face and body, and then outwards and round again, his lips muttering those crooning sounds which had caught the Major's attention.

Francis Orpington may have had the slightest and most superficial acquaintance with the mysteries of hypnotism; but not for one second was he in doubt as to what was taking place in that pavilion.

It was as if a bandage had suddenly been plucked from the eyes of his mind. And subconsciously — without pausing to analyse his conclusions — he understood a host of things that had intrigued and mystified him in the last few days. But for this ocular proof of the manner in which Bickershaw was gaining his ascendancy over Adelaide, the Major would have laughed to scorn the very notion of any such influence being exerted, would have classed such stories with other old wives' tales of spooks and incantations.

But here he saw Bickershaw at work, and from what he saw he realised at last the inexplicable, indefinable change in Adelaide, her aloofness from himself, her association with Bickershaw, the vacant expression he had observed in her countenance. Bickershaw had obtained control of her will, had rendered her the slave of his suggestions. The Major's strong skepticism withered on the instant, killed partly by the evidence before him, partly by very instinct.

He wrenched open the door of the summer-house and sprang into the little timbered chamber as if flung there by a catapult.

"You scoundrel!" he roared.

Bickershaw started up, and recoiled before the Major with a little whimper of fear, hands defensively raised, eyelids fluttering nervously. For Francis was truly terrific. His eyes blazed in his white face, and his hands were raised to strike.

He restrained himself, however. He took Adelaide by the shoulder and shook her roughly. A little moan was her only response. He turned on his cousin.

"Wake her," he commanded, his voice rasping. "Wake her instantly, or I'll smash you into pulp."

Unnerved, and very much afraid, Bickershaw obeyed at once. His voice was, nevertheless, quiet and cold. "Wake up, Adelaide," he said in tones that were perfectly conversational.

Obediently she stirred, the colour flowed gently back into her cheeks, and she opened her eyes. They were full of a bewilderment of one suddenly roused from sleep.

"Now come with me," the Major bade Bickershaw.

Bickershaw hesitated. He hung back, his lips tightened — the outward sign of a concentration of his will — and Francis found the man's beady eyes intently fixed on his own. It reminded him suddenly of Bickershaw's quelling of unruly dogs. But he was no poor brute to crouch down and whimper. The effrontery of the attempt to dominate him increased his anger. For an instant it overmastered him. He seized Bickershaw by the collar of his coat and shook him as a dog shakes a rat; then he flung him down the steps of the summer-house. He followed without another thought for Adelaide, slamming the door after him.

At the foot of the steps Bickershaw had recovered his balance. He saw the Major descending upon him like a thunderbolt. He edged aside out of the direct line of that descent.

"For Heaven's sake control yourself!" he cried, his voice commanding. "I — I can explain," he added weakly.

"You'll need to," was the grim answer. "Come with me." And taking him by the arm, Francis hurried him across the lawn towards the house.

III
Major Orpington Falls Asleep

Although Major Orpington recovered by an effort his outward composure, inwardly his anger continued to rage unabated. Nor could it abate whilst there abode with him the loathsome idea that Adelaide was in the monstrous power of his cousin. The picture of what he had seen in the summer-house persisted before the eyes of his mind and filled him with horror. And there was the thought that Adelaide — Adelaide, of all people — should have been a party to these abominable practices! It was monstrous, inconceivable!

So governed was he by his furious horror that when at last he found himself in the study with Bickershaw he had nothing to say. There were no words at the Major's command in which he could even begin to give expression to his feelings. And so, after a long, wrathful consideration of his cousin, he was forced to admit.

"I have nothing to say to you, after all. There are no words that will meet the case. It calls for deeds. I am tempted to thrash you — almost to kill you, I think. But — " He shrugged, snorting. "You had better go. Pack your things and leave my house at once, and never dare to enter it again."

By now Bickershaw had entirely recovered from his fright and was completely master of himself. His face wore an expression of regret. But through this, as through a thin veil, peeped the ineffaceable mockery habitual to his countenance. He moistened his lips before replying.

"You might, at least, first hear my explanation," he protested. "I don't quite know what you are imagining, Frank, but I am afraid you are doing me a very grave injustice. Of course, I will leave your house if you feel like that about it; but I think I have the right to ask you first to hear my case."

He played with consummate cunning upon the sense of justice which he knew to be inherent in his cousin.

"Can you possibly find anything to say that will mitigate the thing you have done?" There was as much pain as anger in the question.

"A good deal. In the first place, there is the pecuniary embarrassment in which I find myself."

Light blazed upon the Major's mind, and he wheeled sharply upon his cousin, interrupting him.

"So you gained an ascendancy over Adelaide to induce her to part with her money to you. That was how she came to draw three hundred pounds for you. You made her do it."

"Nothing of the sort," was the cold answer. And then Bickershaw proceeded, lying boldly and cunningly with just the lies he knew his cousin would believe. "Why, you know yourself that all that is nonsense, that there is no such thing as compelling a person to anything against his will. That is the mere clap-trap of hypnotism, as you know — as I have often heard you declare. The money she lent me, she lent me of her own free will, because she believes in me as a result of the talks we have had together. Compulsion! Pshaw!"

He laughed the notion to scorn, and the Major began to believe him, because it was the very thing he would have hoped, and because to believe it relieved him of more than half his anxiety touching Adelaide.

"All that I did," Bickershaw pursued, "was to accept Adelaide's very generous offer to supply the place of the medium I was unable to afford. With the money she insisted upon my accepting I need not have done this; but in her deep interest in the matter she was equally insistent upon that point. I was tempted by the discovery that she is gifted with quite exceptional mediumistic qualities, and I succumbed.

"But you do me more than an injustice if you suppose that I would have done this if it had been in any way hurtful. And as for my obtaining any control over her — why, it's a monstrous, foolish suggestion. I have done Adelaide not the slightest harm."

"No harm!" cried Francis. "Was there no harm in the thing I witnessed? Adelaide in a trance!"

"Well?" The coldness of the question had a singularly arresting effect. It seemed to demand the throwing over of prejudice, the opening of the mind to judgment after ignorance should be removed. "And what, after all, is a trance? It is sleep — just sleep. Hypnotism is nothing more."

"It is artificial," objected Francis, feeling rather at a loss.

"Oh, dear, no. Artificially induced, if you like, but not artificial in itself. I assure you again that I have done absolutely no harm. Still, in view of the deep-rooted objection arising from your imperfect knowledge of what the practice involves, I am quite prepared willingly to give you an undertaking never to repeat the experiments with Adelaide; but this merely as a concession to your prejudices, not as an admission that there is any harm in them."

"I can't believe you, Stanley. Adelaide has been different these last few days. Influences have been at work upon her."

"Granted. But why jump to conclusions about these influences? They are merely the influences of her newly acquired knowledge. Such influences as work upon every one of us on his way through life, and without which we should reach the grave much as we leave the cradle. To suggest that these influences have anything supernatural or occult — why — " He shrugged and laughed, contemptuously amused. "Surely you, Francis, of all men, are not going to harbour wild notions of that sort?"

The Major found himself at a loss what to think. After all, his old skepticism was more tenacious than for a moment it had seemed. "I did not mean exactly supernatural or occult," he muttered, frowning, utterly bewildered, for he feared that he had meant just that, and that he should not have meant it.

"Of what precisely do you accuse me, then?" cried Bickershaw, now master of the situation. "What evil can you suggest that I have done?"

Now, had Orpington not been in love with Adelaide, he might even at this stage have been firmer. It is odd that the very influence which should have strengthened his resolve to dismiss his cousin was the very influence that weakened it. For again, with that exceptional fairness and honesty of mind that was his own, he began to ask himself was he not perhaps doing his cousin an injustice, spurred by his jealousy to put an unnecessarily ugly construction upon the latter's relations with Adelaide.

Once he began to ask himself such questions he was lost. He still protested against the practices in which Bickershaw had indulged; but his protests became perfunctory, and Bickershaw met them in a deferential manner that was unusual in him, which, in itself, should have put the Major on his guard. For it was not Bickershaw's way to be meek or tolerant of the opinions of others where they conflicted with his own, unless he had ends to serve.

Thus it came about in the end that in view of Bickershaw's promise never again to employ Adelaide as a medium, Francis consented to forget the matter.

Reflecting upon the whole affair later in the day, he was by no means sure that he had not been a sentimental ass, and weak out of an excessive sense of justice; for he found Adelaide more distant than ever in her bearing towards him. He reflected that if he had made a mistake Anthony Orpington would perhaps correct it on the morrow when he came over, which showed an increasing weakness on his part.

He announced his uncle's coming visit that night at dinner. Adelaide showed no interest in the announcement; but Bickershaw, after a spell of thoughtfulness, looked up casually to inquire at what time Anthony was expected.

"He said that he would come over immediately after lunch — at about three o'clock," replied the Major.

Bickershaw nodded, and lapsed into thought once more; but the subject of their uncle's visit was not pursued.

That night the Major slept very badly. In fact, he hardly slept at all. He was supremely unhappy on the score of Adelaide. The events of the day ran like a perpetual panorama before his eyes. Again and again he saw her reclining entranced in the chaise-longue in the summer-house, and he was filled anew with his original horror of the spectacle. Again and again he reproached himself for not having handled Bickershaw more firmly; he despised himself for it, in fact, and still more for his dependence upon his uncle to correct that error of judgment.

In the morning he had a scene with Adelaide that was almost angry — the first approach to an angry scene between them in all the fifteen years that she had resided under his roof. He had ventured to remonstrate mildly with her for having been a party to Stanley's experiments, and she had flown out at him; she had reproached him for being domineering, ignorant and dogmatic, and for interfering in her affairs, reminding him that she had long since passed from his tutelage, that she was a woman able to judge for herself, responsible to no one for her actions. She concluded with a hint that it was her intention to emancipate herself entirely from his supervision by making a home for herself elsewhere and soon.

It all hurt him very deeply. It was so unlike her; and in her harshness there had been something that had gone very near to ingratitude; for, after all, Francis had been her best friend since her father had died — father, brother, and everything else had he been to her.

She did not come to lunch. He and Bickershaw faced each other across the table and ate in silence. Francis drank a glass or two more than usual of claret, and this may have combined with his sleeplessness of the night before to render him presently drowsy and torpid. He took a book to the summer-house, flung himself down on the chaise-longue, and loaded his pipe.

Presently Bickershaw came in.

"Awfully hot," he said casually. "Cooler in here," he added, as if to explain his intrusion. He sat down and produced his own pipe.

The Major scarcely troubled to consider his cousin's easy effrontery under the existing circumstances. His drowsiness increased; his eyelids drooped, and he found reading a positive struggle. Then Bickershaw got up.

"I think I'll fetch a book, too," he said, and went out.

The movement roused the Major; for a few minutes he read on, consuming perhaps a couple of pages of his novel. Then Bickershaw returned, a book in his hand, and resumed his chair. The place settled down. Bickershaw was quite still. On the hot, languorous air a bee sailed in through the open window, humming soporifically.

Again Francis was nodding over his book; hypnotised by the white page and the black type with which he was struggling. Two or three times he recovered and strove valiantly to keep awake; on the last occasion he grew conscious that Bickershaw was regarding him with peculiar intentness out of his beady eyes. Francis's glance returned to his book, but the eyes seemed still there on the page before him, as we see on a white sheet the image of a flame at which we have looked. His torpor grew heavier, his breathing became regular, he lost his grip of consciousness and was asleep.

Sleeping thus, Francis Orpington was visited by a dream, curiously, singularly vivid in its detail.

He dreamt that he was there in that summer-house, sitting up in the chaise-longue, a prey to a strange excitement that was quickening his pulses.

He was slow in penetrating to the cause of this. The emotion that possessed him was not immediately to be defined.

In his hand he was balancing a heavy six-shooter, and as he perceived this the motive of his excitement gradually became clear. Anthony Orpington was coming soon to visit him. He was coming to interfere between Francis and Bickershaw; coming in his offhand, autocratic way to settle this troublesome matter of Adelaide and to settle it in a manner that was bound to be distasteful to the Major. That was his delusion, and he understood that his resolve was to prevent this at all costs.

His uncle must not see Adelaide or Bickershaw. Francis must deal with him alone. His determination increased. It was an angry determination, a determination that would stop at nothing. He was filled by a frenzy, a fury of homicide. He would go down into the spinney, take cover, and wait until his uncle came. Then he would shoot him at close quarters, making sure to kill.

His course was now quite clear and definite. No thought of the consequences had any place in his dream. It carried him just as far as the shooting of his uncle. Not one step farther. All his mind, all his will, all his intelligence were focused upon just that point.

He dreamt that he rose from his seat, opened the door, and passed out of the little pavilion. He plunged into the spinney, avoiding the pathway, and making his way through the trees towards a certain point midway down between the lawn and the river, it was there that he would wait — there that he would do the thing. He moved with infinite care and without haste, for he had plenty of time. He gained at last the point that seemed in some way predetermined. He crouched there amid the tangled undergrowth to await his victim, the pistol ready in his hand, his homicidal frenzy increasing. The desire to kill, to shed blood, to destroy was overmastering. The contemplation of it filled him in anticipation with a sense of joy which he knew must reach its climax in realisation.

But when again he came to consider that it was against his uncle — against Anthony Orpington — that his hand was to be raised, some of his joy perished. He dreamt that he set himself again to review the situation, and he found that he had been at fault in his earlier estimate of his uncle's intentions.

Whatever could have led him to suppose that Anthony Orpington's interference would be distasteful to himself? He had been out of his senses. Anthony was coming because he himself had asked his help; he was coming to assist him to get rid of Bickershaw. Of course it was so. How had it been possible for him to forget that? When had his uncle ever crossed his wishes? They had always been the very best of friends; they had always understood each other as seldom happens between relatives of their degree. How, then, came he to be lying in wait for his best friend?

The wickedly joyous anticipation of the deed began to fade; a fierce struggle took place within his soul. His dream changed to the character of nightmare. He was oppressed, menaced by a deadly peril, in danger of perpetrating a loathsome deed. And suddenly he rebelled. The thing was absurd. If there was a man in the world against whom he should raise his weapon, upon whom he should vent the fury that possessed him, that man was Stanly Bickershaw — Bickershaw who was creeping like a snake between Adelaide and himself — Bickershaw who was destroying his peace of mind — Bickershaw who had been making horrible experiments with the soul of Adelaide.

Suddenly, in his dream, there came a crackle of steps in the undergrowth across the path. He felt his heart beating as if it would suffocate him. He crouched lower, until he was completely hidden behind a clump of laurels, and as he crouched the homicidal mania mounted again and overmastered him. He must kill. It was predestined that he must kill, and he would know no peace, no joy in life again until he had killed.

And then, quite suddenly, he became aware of a white, glistening face framed in the foliage beyond the path. The beady eyes were searching. It was borne in upon Francis that they were searching for him. They were the eyes of Bickershaw. Inaudibly the Major chuckled as he crouched still lower to baffle the search of those eyes.

And then the white face moved nearer. It seemed that below it there was a body — a human body. Of course there was; there was always, Orpington reflected, a body under a head. Besides, this was Bickershaw — Bickershaw standing there on the edge of the path, on tiptoe, peering about him, his livid face moist and gleaming.

Then it came to him again that it was Bickershaw who was his enemy, Bickershaw whom he hated. The homicidal frenzy surged up. It was Bickershaw whom he was to kill — Bickershaw, Bickershaw! The name boomed and boomed through his fevered brain. Of course, it was Bickershaw. However came he to imagine it was to have been his uncle?

He yielded to his furious, mad blood-lust. He rose and leapt forward from his hiding-place, leveling his pistol in the act so that the nozzle came within some few inches of his cousin's face. A second he paused, considering that livid face, the beady eyes suddenly less beady than he had ever known them — dilating widely in a curious, fearful fascination. Then he laughed, and pulled the trigger.

And on that Francis Orpington awoke.

IV
The Awakening

Francis Orpington awoke. A convulsive shudder ran through him, as it runs through those who are delivered from the thralldom of an evil dream. As the bonds of sleep dissolved themselves, and his awakening senses knew them for what they were, a great thankfulness welled up from the soul of him that this should have been no more than a dream.

And then, horror of horrors, worse horror than any that had been throughout that nightmare, his thankfulness was checked in full flow, checked by complete consciousness of his surroundings. Although now awake, nothing was changed from what it had been in his dream.

He was standing there, under the trees in the spinney, on the identical spot where in his dream he had been standing. He saw the shadow-dappled sunshine at his feet, a little wisp of smoke hung at the height of his head, and before him, on the path's edge, protruding from the undergrowth, he beheld a pair of legs in grey, baggy trousers, the toes pointing heavenwards. A gap in the undergrowth showed where a body had crashed through.

His horror and amazement grew by leaps. A sense of bewilderment paralysed him. What had happened in this place? How came he there? And then the last thread of his half-formed impressions snapped, and he realised that his hand still clutched the heavy revolver of his dreams.

He considered it stupidly. How came he to be holding it? How came he to have fired it?

On that a fresh terror clutched him. If he had fired it, then — then that thing lying there was his handiwork. He rubbed his brow in a dazed, stupid fashion. He tried to think, and he came to the conclusion that he had not awakened when he imagined — that he was not yet awake at all — that the dream was continuing. But in dreams men do not dream that they have dreamt. The queer reflection leapt suddenly to his mind to increase its torture. But, then, if not still dreaming, how came he into such a position as this? And who was the man who lay there, half in, half out of the spinney?

He advanced a step or two to obtain a clear view of the face. The sight turned him almost sick with horror; for the features were unrecognisable, so great was the disfigurement of the shot at such close quarters; but from the rest of the body he recognised beyond all doubt his cousin Stanley Bickershaw.

He felt as if an icy wind had suddenly enveloped him. On that sweltering July afternoon he was taken with a sudden chill; he was cold from head to foot, so cold that he shivered. Cold with horror and an unspeakable dread. For it was borne in upon his clearing senses that, however much of this awful affair might remain wrapped in mystery, one fact was clear: That he had killed Bickershaw, that he was a murderer.

He had been dreaming, he knew, and he had awakened; but he was no longer certain at what particular point in the sequel of events the awakening had taken place, for dream and awakening had followed each other in an unbroken, amazing continuity.

Dizzy and sick with horror he leaned against the bole of a tree, his eyes upon the disfigured face of the dead man. The pistol had slipped from his grasp, and lay unheeded by the dead man's hand.

What was he to do now?

Obviously there was but one course open to him as an honest, honourable man. He must give the alarm, make surrender to the authorities, and tell the true story of this inexplicable happening.

And swift upon the heels of that resolve came a fresh, fierce dread. The true story! The story of that somnambulistic dream! Tell a jury of sane, practical men that he had killed his cousin so? Why, it was ludicrous — grotesque. It must provoke the scorn of all right-minded folk. It would provoke their laughter but for the awfulness of the deed itself. Who in the world would believe so extravagant a story? It would be underlined in the annals of crime as the wildest and most impudent defence ever entered by a criminal. For he was a criminal — a murderer. He might not understand how the thing had come to pass; he might be quite certain that the thing had been done without volition of his own, and, therefore, that he was really innocent; but to the world, on the evidence of the facts — the only evidence the world would care about — he was a murderer, and as a murderer he would be hanged.

The thought stung him almost to anger. His outraged sense of innocence revolted at this aspect of his position. The more he insisted upon the truth of this matter, the more he would be treated as a shameless, foolish liar. The uprightness and honourableness of his past life would weigh for nothing in the scales of justice against such a tale as that.

Anthony Orpington would perhaps believe him mad. And Adelaide — what would she think? Why, surely, none would be more convinced of his guilt than she. Did she not know of his recent hostility to his cousin, of his threat to turn him out of the house, of his deep resentment on her own account?

It would not do. He dared not speak, dared not tell the world what he knew of Bickershaw's death. He must save himself by silence. So clamoured his reason, and his honour did not revolt. Since none would believe the story he had to tell, he would not tell it. He must play such a part as he would have played had he been the real murderer in intent as well as fact, comforting himself with the knowledge that he had neither desired nor consciously procured the death of Bickershaw. He must protect himself by the only means in his power from the consequences of a deed of which his hand but not his mind was guilty.

This resolve taken, much of his calm returned. He looked cautiously about; he listened intently. The deed had had no witnesses. Nothing stirred.

He moved cautiously across the path again, and plunged once more into the covert. Then he made his way towards the summer-house, swiftly yet calmly watchful, and pausing at every step to listen.

He gained the pavilion satisfied that he had not been perceived. He closed the door, and flung himself heavily down upon the chaise-longue like a man exhausted.

If he had been cold before, he was burning now. He mopped his brow, and lay back in his chair with half-closed eyes. Again he reviewed the situation, attempting to penetrate the fog of mystery in which it was enveloped. His pipe lay on a little bamboo table at his elbow, just where he had left it. By force of habit he picked it up, and loaded it. He lighted it, and lay back to give free reign to his speculation.

Suddenly he remembered the heavy pistol with which he had shot his cousin. In the confusion of the moment, in the half-paralysed state of his mind after the deed, he had not bestowed a thought upon it. Now it recurred to him, and the sudden recollection was almost like a physical blow. Whence had that pistol come? Whose was it? Not his. He owned no such pistol. He recollected the weapon distinctly; it was unlike any that he had ever possessed, and those that he did posses — his service weapons — were all locked away upstairs. How, then, had such a pistol come into his hands?

From that consideration it began to be borne in upon him that the dream could by no means have ceased at the point where he believed it to have ceased. It must have continued long after the supposed awakening, which must, indeed, have been a part of the dream itself. For since such a pistol could not possibly have existed, neither could any other part of that horrible affair have been real.

Conviction grew. It must be so — no more than a strangely vivid, a strangely unpleasant dream, resulting from his overwrought state of mind and the extra glass of claret at lunch; and part of that dream was the slaying of Bickershaw and the slinking back into the summer-house. As a matter of fact, he had only just reawakened there where he had fallen asleep, and their unpleasant vividness in his waking moments had made him believe that such a serious of events had actually taken place. It was often like that with dreams.

He breathed more freely. Much of the oppression was lifted from him. He became more and more convinced that he held the true explanation of the whole affair.

And then a shadow fell across the room, and a brisk contralto voice hailed him familiarly.

"Hallo, Frank! What have you done with Stanley?"

He jumped in sheer terror, and his movement was greeted by a burst of laughter from Adelaide, which it took him some moments to realise was reassuring.

"I declare you were asleep!" she mocked him. And her manner, as much as all the rest, filled him with a fresh amazement. For instead of the cold, aloof Adelaide of the past few days, who could scarcely find a civil word for him, here was the gay tease of a week ago restored to her habitual self.

Surely he was not awake even now. Here was but a fresh phase of this awful tormenting dream of his.

"You know," she continued, leaning her arms upon the sill of the open window, "you'll become obese if you indulge in these afternoon naps. And I should hate an obese guardian."

He smiled foolishly, vacantly. Words would not come to him in the depths of amazement into which he was plunged.

"But what have you done with Stanley?" she insisted. "He said he was coming here to read."

His course of deception began. "He was here," he answered; "but he must have gone out whilst I was asleep."

"I don't particularly want him. Only if you're too somnolent an old thing to come out and suffer defeat at croquet, I must find Stanley. He has the advantage of you in years, you know," she tormented him in the familiar way that had been so dear to him, and that he had so bitterly missed in these last few days.

He just stared at her, and thus provoked her fresh merriment.

"I really don't believe you're awake yet. I shall have to come inside and shake you. It won't do, you know."

Steps sounded, the quick steps of someone running up the path through the shrubbery. She turned to look, peered a moment, then gave a gasp of astonishment. "Why, it's Uncle Anthony," she cried. "Uncle Anthony running! He is being pursued at last by designing spinsters!"

But there was no smile on the Major's lips. A fresh fear gripped him by the heart. Anthony Orpington running! He had seen — Then the thing was not a dream, after all. It was all real. Bickershaw lay down there, in the spinney, disfigured by a shot.

The elder Orpington came up, breathless but pale for all the exertion of running, and there was a curious horror in his eyes that at once struck the banter from Adelaide's lips. The Major rose, and crossed to the window. He must continue now to play the part he had chosen; the only part possible.

"Is Frank there?" he heard his uncle inquiring between gasps.

"Yes," answered Adelaide, "he's in here. Frank!" she turned to call. Then she questioned the elder man. "What is the matter? Has anything happened?"

He hesitated a moment. "Yes," he said. "I want to speak to Frank."

"Whatever is it?" asked Frank, from the window, his voice so calm and natural that it almost surprised him.

His uncle looked at him, and then at Adelaide. Obviously he was hesitating.

"Just run indoors, there's a good girl," he said. "I want to speak to Frank alone." And then, seeing her astonishment, he began to explain. "Fact is, there's been an accident. It's Bickershaw. I'm afraid he's — ah — rather badly hurt."

"Oh, poor Stanley!" she cried. There was genuine concern in her tone, but nothing more — no transport of fear, no overwhelming anxiety, such as the Major who was watching her had been almost expecting. She scarcely changed colour; certainly no more than need any warm-hearted woman at hearing of an accident. How was this explainable? What had come to her? What had come to the world that afternoon?

The honest Major's bewilderment increased. For a week she had been more than friendly with Bickershaw, constantly in his company, taking up cudgels for him, and distant and haughty with the Major himself on Bickershaw's behalf. Yet here in the twinkling of an eye all was changed again; all was restored to the proportions that had been usual before Bickershaw had enlisted her sympathy some ten days ago. All this flashed through the Major's mind, to deepen its mystification, in the second between her expression of sympathy and his own eagerly uttered question:

"What is it?"

"You'd better just step down through the shrubbery with me," said his uncle. "Not you, Adelaide. Do run indoors, like a good girl. You'll know all about it presently."

From his grave face she saw that the matter was serious. "Stanley hasn't been killed, has he?"

The question was asked in a scared, strained voice. But no more scared or strained than was perfectly natural under the circumstances of what was feared by the speaker. Women do not find themselves beset by such suspicions without emotion. It is not in their nature, nor in man's, for that matter.

Anthony patted her shoulder. "Do go in the house," he said gravely; and it was an answer to her question as explicit as could have been given her.

The Major watched her closely. He heard her cry out, he heard her deeply pitying. "Oh, poor, poor Stanley!" He saw the glint of tears in her eyes, and approved it all; yet found it amazingly removed from what her recent relations with Bickershaw would have led him to expect.

He sprang out of the pavilion as she was making her way across the lawn towards the house. He caught his uncle by the arm.

"What is it?" he demanded, loathing himself for the deception he was forced to practise. "What has happened to him? Is he really dead?"

"He is down there," said Anthony, pointing with his cane, "lying half in, half out of the undergrowth, quite dead. He's shot himself — blown half his face away. The pistol's lying beside him. I've touched nothing, of course. Come down and see for yourself. It's perfectly horrible."

V

The Confession

The conclusion to which Anthony Orpington had jumped at sight of Stanley Bickershaw's body, proved, after all, the same as that at which the jury arrived after a careful sifting of all the circumstances attending the gentleman's tragic end.

The police had gone fully into the matter, and they submitted their conclusions to the coroner. They had ferreted out that Bickershaw was very heavily involved in speculations, his losses amounting to close upon a thousand pounds — a matter which no one had suspected — and that he was absolutely without the means of paying. They had traced a gunsmith who recognised the revolver used as one which he had sold to Mr. Bickershaw a couple of months before, and who now deposed to that effect.

The medical evidence was rather neutral. The nature of the wound was by no means inconsistent, the medical witness held, with the theory that it was self-inflicted, although the revolver must have been held at a distance of four or five inches from the forehead, which was extremely unusual. Pressed, however, for a definite opinion, the doctor on the whole inclined to the belief that deceased had shot himself. Then came Anthony Orpington, called to give evidence of the finding of the body. This he described in his clear, practical manner, adding the impression which he had instantly formed — the only tenable conclusion under the circumstances.

"Do you know," asked the coroner, "of any reason that might have led the deceased to take his own life?"

"I know of none beyond that discovered by the police," was the answer. "My nephew was certainly in financial difficulties. He had appealed to me for help some days before. I am afraid I was rather harsh with him. But, then, he made such a practice of obtaining funds from me that I was at the end of my patience. Nor was his way of asking, amounting practically to a demand, the best way of obtaining the assistance he sought. I not only refused to help him, but I threatened him that if he bothered me again I should cut him out of my will, under which he was to benefit by an annuity of two hundred and fifty pounds."

Finally, in the endeavour to clear up the last doubt, Major Orpington was called. He was perfectly calm and self-possessed when he entered his own dining-room, where the jury sat. He was the last person to have seen the deceased alive, and he was invited to submit the circumstances under which he had last so seen his cousin.

"I was in the pavilion in the garden after lunch," he deposed, "when my cousin joined me. He sat down and remained there for a few minutes; then he went out again, saying that he would fetch a book. He returned very shortly, and, in fact, he then had a book with him. I fancy we exchanged a remark or two, but I am not quite clear. I was very drowsy at the time. Soon after his return I must have fallen asleep. I awoke half an hour or so later, when Miss Burton roused me; and almost immediately afterwards my uncle ran up through the shrubbery with the news of what he had seen there as he passed through."

"You observed nothing unusual in the deceased's manner that day?"

"No. He seemed much as usual."

Asked did he know of his cousin's financial difficulties, witness replied that he knew of these difficulties, but not of their extent.

"He had applied to me for assistance, but I was not in a position to afford it. I gave him the hospitality of my house here, but beyond that I did not feel justified in going. I had, of course, no conception that he was in such straits as to be driven to so desperate an act. Nor did he at any time show any indications of it."

The end of it all was that the jury agreed that Stanley Bickershaw, harassed by his debts and driven to extremes by the attitude of his relatives — an attitude entirely justifiable, and nowise to be censured — had, in a fit of temporary insanity, committed suicide.

Nothing could have been more clear, and Major Orpington heaved a sigh of relief when he heard the verdict. The coroner came over to shake hands with him, and stood chatting for a few moments, the Major answering mechanically and absently to the remarks of this shrewd-eyed medico-legal gentleman. He was reflecting that were he now — or had he elected when called — to give the court the true facts of the case, they would treat him as insane, would regard him as the victim of a hallucination.

Indeed, there were moments in the days that followed when he did not know whether he should not so regard himself. Again and again he asked himself was he not labouring under some extraordinary delusion. He even went so far as to ask himself whether he had not been the sport of some freak of second sight, seeing in a dream an actual happening in which — after the inconsequent manner of dreams — he had imagined himself a participator.

The thing preyed upon his mind, haunted his memory by day and disturbed his nights with horrid visions. It became a recurrent dream of his that he was standing on the path in the spinney under the dappled shadow of the trees peering at a pair of limp legs in baggy grey trousers that protruded from a tangle of undergrowth, the square toes pointing heavenward. And as he looked, the body behind those legs would heave itself up, topped by the mutilated face of Bickershaw, out of which Bickershaw's beady eyes glared maliciously, mockingly, menacingly. With a scream he would awaken and lie quivering in his bed, praying for daylight to dispel the chance of these horrors.

Naturally his health began to suffer. He grew nervous and irritable under the awful strain, and he would sit for hours brooding over the matter, attempting to penetrate to the bottom of this mystery that was poisoning his existence. Had he or had he not killed Bickershaw? He no longer knew. The matter became more and more elusive. Unless light were thrown upon that dread mystery he feared, and with cause, that his reason would give way.

Adelaide he attempted to shun, but she would not be shunned. Her concern for him grew with his distemper. Her sincere affection for him manifested itself in a hundred thoughtful little ways that at another time would have filled him with thankfulness and joy, but which now served only to increase his ill-being. And then one evening, a fortnight after the inquest, she forced matters to a climax.

He was seated in a deck-chair on the lawn, near the pavilion, pulling moodily at his pipe, his brow gloomy, his mind black with ugly mystification, when she came gently behind him. She put her arms about his neck and laid her cheek against his in the affectionate manner that had persisted since the days when as a schoolgirl of fifteen she had first come to look upon him as a second father.

"Frank, dear," she murmured, "this awful affair of Stanley's is preying upon your mind. You are making yourself ill, and you are giving me a lot of anxiety. You need a change. You want to get away from this place. Supposing we were to go up to Scotland for a month. The sea-trout will be taking well on the Ythan, and in another fortnight the salmon will be running. Shall we go?"

Passionate angler as he was, the prospect tempted him. But his moral lassitude was such that the temptation could gain no hold. He sighed heavily, without answering.

She had dwelt much of late upon the things they had said on this very spot that evening, some six weeks ago now, and upon the declaration which she knew had then been trembling upon his lips, and which he must have uttered had not Bickershaw so inopportunely intruded. She loved Francis Orpington deeply and sincerely, and she had hoped and prayed that he might again find the courage to ask her to become his wife. Her quick, sensitive nature, so receptive of impressions, had long since perceived his diffidence, his fear that he was no longer of an age to be acceptable as a husband to her, his dread lest out of gratitude she should find it impossible to refuse him, and consequently his hesitation to place her in such a position by asking her.

That she read him aright she had never a doubt. She had helped and encouraged him to a declaration that evening six weeks ago. Since then the opportunity had never recurred, and in these last days she had been wondering whether perhaps that was not the matter that was preying upon his mind. Her pity for him, her sweet sympathy, her pure devotion urged her now to take her courage in both hands and force the situation.

"You need someone to take care of you, Frank dear," she murmured, a little breathless, a little pale.

He looked up at her and smiled gratefully; the smile irradiated, only to increase the wan, haggard look of his face. "I have you, Adelaide," he reminded her.

"Yes, but you never know," she answered with affected lightness, watching him intently as she spoke. "I might marry any day, and then what should you do?"

She saw the sudden frown, the darkening of the face, the painful twitch of his lips, and these signs filled her at once with pity and with joy. They were the signs for which she had hoped, and they gave her the necessary courage to proceed.

"Not that I want to leave you, Frank. There is no one like you. I could never care for anyone as I care for you. I could never be happy without you — never."

He turned quickly and looked at her very searchingly, a curious expression in his eyes, half doubt, half hope. Then he smiled.

"If I were a fool," he said slowly, "your words might tempt me to forget that you are my sometime ward and ask you to marry me."

"If you were fool enough to care for me, you mean, I suppose," she said, and she allowed her chagrin to manifest itself in her tone.

"I am," he answered, taken off his guard. "I do care. Adelaide, if — "

And then he stopped, his eyes fell, a crimson flush swept across his face, leaving it livid. "No, no," he cried. "Oh, I am mad — mad!"

She nestled closer to him. "Why?" she whispered, and then broke out, half resentful: "Must I do all the wooing, Frank? Are you to lead me on, to sound the depths of my feelings, and then to pause? Is that quite fair, do you think?"

His hand, hot as living fire, clutched her wrist a moment; his eyes blazed into her pale face. "Will you marry me, Adelaide — me?" he asked.

"Of course I will marry you, Frank. Whenever you wish."

"Oh, wait — wait!" He took his head in his hands an instant, his mind working fiercely. "Sit down," he said. "Forget what I have said — forget it until you hear what else I have to tell you. It — it is about Stanley Bickershaw."

She looked at him with dilating eyes. Alarm quivered through her soul. Already that quick receptivity of hers had caught more than a premonition of what was to come. She sank into the chair beside him, and took his hands in hers.

"What?" she asked breathlessly.

"I shot him," said the Major quietly.

She did not move; she made no sound; she just stared at him in silence, as if so great a fact needed time to penetrate in its entirety into her understanding. Then she nodded slowly.

"Yes," she said, her voice, too, curiously quiet. "Tell me about it."

A measure of relief was his already. It was as if he had flung off something of the burden that oppressed him. He went on more easily.

"I have told you the worst. I did not kill him intentionally."

"An accident?"

"I hardly know. Not quite an accident, I should say. Let me tell you." And quite quietly and naturally he told her the whole story. She listened intently, her brows knit, her mind all concentrated upon the points he made, following the narrative as a dog follows a spoor.

At the end she smiled wistfully, sympathetically. Hers was a fine, brave soul. "You did not kill him," she said. "You fired the pistol, but you were no more guilty than the pistol itself, since there was no intention on your part to kill, for you were not conscious at the time."

"But I was conscious," he reminded her.

"Yes, but your consciousness was a dream-consciousness, irresponsible, not guided by reason or will."

She grew very thoughtful. To doubt the exactness of his story never entered her mind. Nor did she suppose it an hallucination subsequent to the facts. It was all so clear, so perfectly circumstantial.

"Who shall say?" he cried almost fiercely. "Who will assure me that it was irresponsible? It seems so; it obviously is so; and yet — and yet — the thing remains with me, crushing, haunting, torturing. I remember that in those days I had come to hate Bickershaw, for he seemed to have come between you and me."

"Stanley?" she questioned. "Came between you and me? What are you saying, Frank? When?"

"When? Why, in those days immediately before his death, when you grew so very distant with me; when your every thought and every moment of your time were for him."

"Frank!" It was an exclamation of utter astonishment; and then her brows were knit and her eyes grew very thoughtful. Evidently his words had touched some chord of memory — dim and elusive, yet of a presence not to be ignored. "I do seem to remember something of the sort," she murmured. "Odd!" Slowly her face grew very white. "I wonder!" she cried, clenching her hands. "I wonder!"

"What?" he inquired.

"Nothing. Go on. You were saying how he seemed to come between us."

"Why, yes. I had come to hate him for it. I may have willed his death; and in a dream state I may have carried out the desires of my subconsciousness. Oh, I don't know. I don't understand these things. I have looked upon it all as so much empiricism, so much quackery to impose upon fools. And now I begin to fear, actually to fear, that I may have been wrong; that there may, after all, be something in the theories that Bickershaw expounded."

"I understand," she said slowly. "I can see exactly what is torturing you, Frank. You are in darkness — a terrifying darkness, and you crave light."

"That's it. I am like a child in the dark — afraid, horribly afraid. It is the mystification of it all that is preying upon my mind and driving me mad. If that darkness were dispelled — But who is there that can dispel it?"

"I think I know," she answered. "Have you ever heard of Dr. Galliphant?"

"I have heard of him, of course. An occultist, isn't he?"

"I suppose that is what people call him. But there is very little that is occult about him. He rationalises everything connected with what is known as supernal phenomena. In his hands the occult ceases to be occult; he reasons it out, reduces it almost to a material condition. What he cannot so treat he does not touch. He is the most eminent authority on hypnotism — living or dead. Bickershaw almost worshipped him, slightly though he knew him."

"But what can he do for me?" asked the Major, and there was a tinge of scorn in his voice; for convictions die hard, and the Major was reluctant to admit that a man of such pursuits could exist without being an empiric.

"I don't know. Perhaps nothing; perhaps much. It all depends where the evil lies, what the evil is. That, at least, he will soon tell you. Let me write to him."

"Do you know him?"

"No; but I know his books. Stanley gave me them to read. Besides, he knows Stanley's work, and if I mentioned that I wished to consult him — that you wished to consult him concerning certain very curious matters in connection with Stanley's death, he would come at once. He is not a professional occultist, you know. He is a man who is devoting his life and fortune to the elucidation of these phenomena and to the exposure of impostors."

Nothing that she could have said could better have commended Galliphant to Orpington. Yet still he hesitated.

"How much must I tell him?" he asked, alarmed, and added: "For we must be prepared for his unbelief of the mysterious part of it; he may jump at the conclusion that there has been just a vulgar murder and nothing more."

She shook her head confidently. "Have no fear of that. If you were a murderer, yes. But you are not, you know. And Galliphant will soon perceive that. No fraud could impose upon him; neither could a truth remain hidden where complete frankness is used. Let me write to him, Frank."

Her hand closed over his, and pressed it gently, coaxingly. He gave way; and having done so, he became infected by something of her own faith in this famous man who was but a name to him, and his case seemed suddenly more hopeful.

For some little time they remained chatting there in soft undertones, seeking for hope that this dreadful mystery would not bring another tragedy in its train.

It was dusk by now. They rose, and went indoors; and she wrote her letter there and then, fearful lest the Major should change his mind and revert to his old antipathy for all connected with the occult.

VI

Dr. Galliphant

Just after lunch next day, and whilst they were still at table, the butler presented to his master a salver which bore a card on which the Major read the name of Dr. Roger Galliphant. He took it up slowly, fingered it uneasily a moment, frowning, hesitation and dread again pervading him.

"The gentleman is waiting in the library, sir," the butler said.

He nodded mechanically. "Thanks, Smith. I'll be there in a moment."

The butler withdrew.

"It is Dr. Galliphant, is it not?" said Adelaide, faintly excited.

"Yes." Orpington rose. "I suppose we must go through with it now. You'll come, won't you, Adelaide?"

"Certainly, if you wish it."

They found him waiting in the library, as the butler had said; and at the first glance the Major was more than favourably impressed by the tall, slender, well-groomed man who stepped forward to introduce himself. His hair, which was thick and slightly wavy about the temples, was almost snow-white, giving one at first the impression that here was an old man. But a glance at the young tanned face beneath, and the keen eyes, large, and of a singularly deep blue, corrected the impression, and led people to believe Galliphant even younger than he really was. He had a deep, pleasant voice, and his tones were level and soothing; his smile was a revelation of kindliness that was entirely irresistible, and he smiled now as he asked to be informed in what he could be of service.

The Major began with apologies for troubling him. These Galliphant cut short, placing all the obligation of the affair on his own side with a courteousness that was entirely charming. There was a subtle quality in his air and manner that set the Major more and more at his ease, invited his confidence, indeed, made him come to desire to confide in one whose sympathies were so manifestly ready.

They sat down, and the Major told his story, precisely as he had told it last night to Adelaide. Galliphant heard him attentively with a face that was as dispassionate, as inscrutable as a mask. The murder left him entirely cold. He was not considering it as an act of violence, but as part of a problem to which he was desired to apply his knowledge and his intellect.

When the Major had concluded — concluded at the point where Adelaide had come to the window of the summer-house — Galliphant continued quite still and thoughtful for some moments. At last he spoke.

"Most interesting," was his comment. "Indeed, I might say, quite extraordinary. I do not think that I have ever come upon a case that even remotely resembles it. Bickershaw, I know, had certain theories — dangerous theories. I rather think they have recoiled upon him. It is highly perilous to unchain forces which we cannot be sure of entirely controlling."

"Then — then," cried the Major, "you see light! You can penetrate this riddle?"

"Sufficiently, I think, to be able unreservedly to say that you have been very wickedly abused, and most certainly that you are in no sense guilty of murder, conscious or unconscious."

"Conscious or unconscious!" echoed the Major. "But is it an hallucination, then — the whole thing?"

Galliphant shook his head, smiling faintly. He rose. "I hesitate to express my opinion just yet. I should first like an independent confirmation of my theory."

"An independent confirmation? But how is that possible?"

"Why, by means of clairvoyance. If I were to induce a good medium into a trance, and place him *en rapport* with you — "

"The medium is here, Dr. Galliphant," said Adelaide, rising.

Orpington, at once understanding her intention, made haste to protest.

"No, no, Adelaide. Not that — please!"

Galliphant held himself aloof from the threatened discussion.

"Why not?" said Adelaide. "Since it is necessary, who better than I for the purpose?"

The Major clenched his hands. "But it is a dreadful condition. I saw you in that state when Bickershaw hypnotised you, remember; and the horror of it remained with me for days."

Galliphant's eyes narrowed suddenly. "Bickershaw used you as a medium, did he, Miss Burton?" he inquired. "Was this just before your close association with him which Major Orpington has told us — which gave rise to those feelings which he fears might subconsciously have impelled him to take Bickershaw's life?"

Her brows were knit. She had grown quite white. "Really, Dr. Galliphant," she said, "my recollection of this close association is singularly faint. It exists, I admit. It was evoked by Major Orpington's mentioning it last night. But it exists rather as a dream-memory. I remember quite clearly that he interested me in his work and induced me to become his medium. But the rest is very vague and misty."

"Quite so," said Galliphant, his tone very full of understanding. "Quite so. Tell me, Major Orpington, you no doubt observed a sudden change in Miss Burton immediately after Bickershaw's decease? I take it, she would be more like her normal self — what she had been before she assisted him in his experiments, eh?"

"That is indeed so. It amazed me. It was one of the most amazing features of this case. But how did you come to know of it?"

"Oh, it is perfectly plain that Bickershaw had obtained a control over her. In a waking state she obeyed the suggestions he made to her during hypnosis.

His hold would become stronger each time he hypnotised her."

"Oh, surely, surely not!" she cried.

"How do you yourself explain your having made him a present of three hundred pounds?" asked Galliphant, bending his keen eyes upon her.

"Really," she faltered, "I am afraid you are quite right. I could not explain it. I hoped it arose from a transitory infatuation with the subject of hypnotism."

"Say, rather, a transitory subjection to Bickershaw's will, Miss Burton. That is the correct explanation. A subjection transitory because, fortunately for you, he met his death when he did, thus dissolving the bonds by which he held you."

She sat down, and covered her face with her hands. "I have been afraid to think of it," she admitted. "But that is precisely what I had begun to fear."

"I think, Major Orpington, you would do well to avail yourself of Miss Burton's offer of assistance to unravel this tangle for you."

She sprang up, too. "I think we are wasting Dr. Galliphant's time," she said gently. "By all means let me submit. He will find me a ready medium, I believe, easily to be induced. And it shall be for the last time — absolutely."

Orpington gave way, and at Galliphant's invitation Adelaide seated herself with her back to a window through which the sun was shining. On the arm of her chair, the sunlight full in his face, Galliphant took his seat.

"Please sit over there, Major, out of her line of vision, so that you will not distract her. Now, please look at me, Miss Burton."

He employed no method but that known as fascination. His bright eyes riveted themselves upon hers, and steadily held her glance for a couple of long minutes that seemed an hour to the uneasy Major. At the end of that little spell came the first droop, the first sign of heaviness to her eyelids. And now Galliphant very gently raised his hands, and made long, slow downward passes over her.

"So," he murmured, his voice caressing, droning. "So! Go to sleep! Go to sleep — to sleep — sleep! Sh-h!"

With a long, shuddering sigh she sank back into the easy chair, her breath regular, asleep.

The operator rose, and stepped back. "An excellent subject," he commented quite casually, smiling reassuringly at the Major.

He placed a chair to face the sleeping woman, and summoned Orpington.

"Sit here, Major. Now, take her hands. Hold them firmly, but not too firmly. That's it. Now concentrate your mind as fully as you are able upon the scene of Bickershaw's death. Endeavour to visualise it again."

He stepped round to Adelaide's side and placed his hand on her brow.

"You hear me, Miss Burton, don't you?" he said.

The lips of the sleeper parted. There was a pause. Then a faint "Yes" fluttered through.

"Do you see anything?" inquired the operator.

"I see the spinney, between the lawn and the river," she replied. "There are two men there, one on either side of the path, among the trees. They are approaching each other. They are watching each other. Both are moving very carefully. One of them comes forward out of the trees. It is Stanley Bickershaw. Now the other leaps suddenly toward him. He raises a pistol. He thrusts it almost into Stanley's face — "

"Wait!" rang the sharp command from Galliphant. "Who is this man with the pistol? Look at his face, and tell me."

There was a pause. The medium's breathing was quickened, her brows were knit, her lip trembled, perspiration stood in beads upon her pale forehead; every line of her betokened a terrible exertion. At last she spoke, falteringly: "I cannot see it. It is very faint, very blurred and indistinct."

Concentrate your attention upon that face, Miss Burton," Galliphant insisted. "You must see it, and tell me whose it is."

The signs of exertion increased. At last the tension was eased. "I see!" she cried. "It is Stanley Bickershaw's face. There are two Stanleys there."

"Now go on," said Galliphant.

"He — this other Bickershaw fires the pistol, and the first one falls back among the shrubs."

Galliphant's hand left her brow. He touched her lightly on the shoulder.

"Wake up, Miss Burton," he commanded sharply, and almost instantly her eyes opened, and she sat up. "That is all we require," he explained to Orpington.

The Major gasped. "But what does it mean?" he cried, more bewildered than ever.

"Could anything be plainer?" asked Galliphant. He was gently rubbing his hands, his satisfied smile showing that the medium's vision had confirmed his theories. He turned to Miss Burton and repeated for her precisely what in her trance she had told him. "Do you see light, Miss Burton?" he inquired.

"But, surely," she answered, puzzled, "the only possible meaning is that Stanley committed suicide. Stanley shot Stanley."

"True. But remember that although both had the same face, yet there actually were two men there, acting differently — Bickershaw, and another. The other's face was blurred to you at first, not clearly visible. Yet you are quite right; it was Bickershaw who killed Bickershaw; yet it was not suicide. I should call it death by misadventure. The truth, Major, is that Bickershaw hypnotised you and willed you to do a murder."

"Hypnotised me?" cried the Major. "I can assure you that he did not."

"The facts prove otherwise. You may have had no suspicion of it; but he hypnotised you nonetheless."

"How is that possible? Can such things be?"

"Bickershaw believed it possible, and to an extent has proved it possible in your own case. But we'll come to the manner of it presently. First let me relate the story of the event precisely as I now know it to have occurred."

He took a seat near the window. "Briefly, then, this is what happened: Bickershaw learnt at his interview with his uncle that by the latter's will he would benefit to the extent of a yearly competence. Along what track of thought that consideration started him it would be idle to speculate. But certain it is that he determined to improve his chances, and not only to inherit more than his uncle had provided — by removing his co-heir, yourself — but to inherit at once. To this monstrous end of his, he gains a control over you that afternoon in the pavilion. Anthony Orpington is expected presently. He has said that he will walk over, and no doubt he will come by the usual way — along the tow-path and up through the spinney. Bickershaw imposes his will upon you. He puts a pistol in your hand, and sends you to meet your uncle and to shoot him — and to shoot him at close quarters, making sure to kill.

"Thus removing his uncle and his cousin — the one by murder, the other as the murderer — Bickershaw not only revenges himself upon you both for your indifference to his wants, but, being the next of kin, he is enriched and cleared of his difficulties. The plan was diabolical in its subtle simplicity. Its one flaw was the pistol. But Bickershaw was driven to act on the spur of the moment almost, and had not time to possess himself of one of your own weapons. The subsequent explanation, had you shot your uncle, would no doubt have been that you had taken Bickershaw's pistol as being the only one at hand.

"Remember now your dream. You were imbued with homicidal mania, but you revolted when you found that it was directed against your uncle. That resulted from Bickershaw's control of you being imperfect, incomplete. He had succeeded in instilling the homicidal frenzy into your mind. But when he attempted to direct it against a person esteemed by you, he failed. Loosely controlled as you were, you obeyed the homicidal suggestion, but you followed, as it were, your own inclinations in the matter, and you vented it upon the one man you had cause to dislike and distrust, upon Bickershaw himself — your own controlling mind — who had been so rash as to be at hand, no doubt out of his anxiety to see the result of an experiment of which he was anything but sure."

"My God! How perfectly horrible!" cried the Major.

"But how perfectly just — how divinely just was the recoil that caught him in his own spring! You see now, do you not, how perfectly logical are these conclusions, how absolutely obvious, especially in the light of the confirmation afforded by Miss Burton, who saw not you, but Bickershaw himself as the slayer."

"Why?" asked Orpington. "Why did she see Bickershaw, since it was I?"

"But it was *not* you," Galliphant objected. "It was Bickershaw. You must remember that a medium does not see things with physical eyes. The medium's mind, in a super-sensitive, acute state of receptivity, absorbs the impressions of other minds; and the mind, the will at the back of your deed was Bickershaw's; therefore it was of Bickershaw that Miss Burton received an impression —

blurred and indistinct at first, precisely because blent with an impression of your own personality."

The Major rose to his feet. A man at all times reserved and un-demonstrative, he was, nevertheless, so moved in the immensity of his relief that he gave way to impulse. He seized hold of both Galliphant's hands and pressed them warmly.

"I don't know what to say, how to thank you. My nightmare is at an end. You have shown me that the finding of the jury was substantially correct, or that if it erred, it erred in mercy to the memory of Bickershaw." Then he paused, and some of his confidence left him. "But you have not yet told me how Bickershaw obtained this — this control, as you call it."

Galliphant crossed to one of the bookshelves. "Bickershaw himself shall explain that for you," he said. "I observed this volume whilst I was waiting for you." He took down a black-bound copy of Bickershaw's *Rationale for Hypnosis*, turned to the index, found what he sought, and opened the book at the page indicated. "Let me read to you this passage:

" 'Hypnosis, properly speaking, is no more than sleep, although artificially induced. The unconsciousness which supervenes is gradual; it has its distinct stages, the first of which is the withdrawal of the will power. That moment, before the subconscious faculties have ceased their activities, is the moment of control; the moment when the hypnotist thrusts in his own will to replace that of the slumberer, and obtains, as it were, a grip of his subject's mental part. The grip will be more or less firm according to the mediumistic powers of the subject.

" 'Now the fact not generally recognised is that this moment of control occurs alike whether the sleep is a natural one or the artificially induced one that we call hypnosis; and the operator who is experienced enough to judge with accuracy and to seize the chance it offers him, may obtain as complete a control of the sleeper as if the sleep itself had been hypnotically induced by him. It is for him to suggest in that moment and the control is obtained.

" 'Who has not fallen a victim to the suggestion of the knock upon his door with which he is awakened in the morning? We all know what dreams it has evoked for us — dreams in which that knock is the controlling power. Conceive, then, from that what must happen if a calculated suggestion is made by a skillful operator at such a moment.' "

Galliphant closed the book. "Now you will understand," he said. "It was a theory of Bickershaw's which received a good deal of adverse criticism at the time it was propounded. He would never have had recourse to it if any other way had offered for obtaining the desired control of you. But there was no other way; and so he adopted this, and risked its dangers."

"I understand," cried Orpington; and then he smiled bitterly. "If ever a man was punished for skepticism, I am that man."

With that he would have further expressed his deep sense of gratitude but that Galliphant stayed him.

"It has been profoundly interesting," he assured the Major; "the most interesting problem I have been asked to unravel. Also I have derived not a little instruction from this one instance — the only one on record, I believe — of the application of Bickershaw's theory touching his 'moment of control.' It quite confirms my own opinions of it, which is gratifying. And I am glad, too, to have been of service to you, Major Orpington. I need hardly say that in this matter I shall observe the secrecy of the confessional."

When the eminent occultist had departed, Major Orpington and Adelaide confronted each other in the library. He took her hand. She smiled, and attempted lightness.

"Well?" she asked. "Is it to Scotland and the sea-trout?"

Before he could answer her she was in tears. He took her in his arms.

"If you'll marry me, Adelaide," he said, "I care very little where the honeymoon is spent."

Duroc

Duroc came down the Rue de la Harpe so stealthily that his steps scarcely made a sound. He moved like a shadow, and when at last he came to a halt before the house of the Citizen Representative Clairvaux it was as if he had totally effaced himself, as if he had become part of the general gloom.

There he paused considering, his chin in his hand; and perhaps because the ground-floor windows were equipped with bars, he moved on more stealthily than ever along the garden wall. Midway between two of the lanterns slung across the narrow street and shedding a feeble yellow light he paused again.

He stood now at a point where the shadows were deepest. He listened intently for a moment, peered this way and that into the night, and then went over the wall with the swift silent activity of an ape. He found the summit of that wall guarded by a row of iron spikes, and on one of these, for all his care, Duroc left a strip of his breeches.

The accident annoyed him. He cursed all chevaux-de-frise, pronouncing them a damnably aristocratic institution to which no true patriot could be guilty of having recourse. Indeed from the manner in which the Citizen Representative Clairvaux guarded his house it was plain to Duroc that the fellow was a bad republican. What with bars on its windows and spikes on its wall, the place might have been a prison rather than the house of a representative of the august people. Of course, as Duroc well knew, the Citizen Representative had something to guard. It was notorious that this modest dwelling of his in the Rue de la Harpe was something of a treasure-house, stored with the lootings of many a ci-devant nobleman's property, and it was being whispered that no true patriot — and a Citizen Representative into the bargain — could have suffered himself to amass such wealth in the hour of the nation's urgent need.

Duroc advanced furtively across the garden, scanning the silent, sleeping house. Emboldened by the fact that no light or faintest sign of vigilance showed anywhere, he proceeded so adroitly that within five minutes he had opened a window and entered a room that was used by the deputy as his study.

Within that room he stood quite still, and listened. Save for the muffled ticking of a clock no sound disturbed the silence. He turned and very softly drew the heavy curtains across the window. Then he sat down upon the floor, took a small lantern from his breast and a tinder-box from his waistcoat pocket. There was the sharp stroke of steel on flint, and presently his little lantern was shedding a yellow disc of light upon the parquetry floor.

He rose softly, placed the light on a console, and crossed the room to the door which stood half open. He listened again a moment then closed the door and came back, his feet making no sound upon the thick and costly rugs that were flung here and there.

In mid-chamber he paused, looking about him, and taking stock of his luxurious surroundings. He considered the painted panels, the inlaid woods, the gilded chairs and the ormolu-encrusted cabinets — all plundered from the hotels of ci-devants who were either guillotined or in flight, and he asked himself if it was in this sybaritic fashion that it became a true republican to equip his home.

He was a short, slender man, this Duroc, whose shabby brown garments looked the worse for the rent in his breeches. He wore a fur bonnet, and his lank black hair hung in wisps about his cheeks and neck. His face was white and wolfish, the jaw thrust forward and ending in a lean square chin; his vigilant quick-moving eyes were close-set and beady as a rat's; his thin lips were curled now in a sneer as he considered the luxury about him.

But that attitude of his was momentary. Duroc had not come there to make philosophy but to accomplish a purpose, and to this he addressed himself forthwith. He took up his lantern, and crossed to a tall secretaire that was a very gem of the court-furnisher's art in the days of Louis XIV. Setting the lantern on top of it, he drew from his pocket a bunch of skeleton keys, gripping them firmly so that they should not rattle. He stooped to examine the lock, and then on the instant came upright again, stiff and tense in his sudden alarm.

A knock had fallen upon the street door, and the echo of it went reverberating through the silent house.

Duroc's lips writhed as he breathed an oath.

The knock was repeated, more insistent now. To the listening Duroc came the sound of a window being thrown up. He heard voices, one from above, the other replying from the street, and guessed that the awakened Clairvaux was challenging this midnight visitor before coming down to open.

Perhaps he would not come. Perhaps he would dismiss this inopportune intruder. But that hope was soon quenched. The window rasped down again, and a moment later the flip-flop of slippered feet came shuffling down the stairs and along the passage to the door. A key grated and a chain clanked — this Clairvaux made a Bastille of his dwelling — and then voices sounded in the passage. The door of the house closed with a soft thud. Steps and voices approached the room in which Duroc still stood immoveable, listening.

At last he stirred, realizing that he had not a moment to spare if he would escape detection. He turned, so that his back was to the door, snatched up his lantern and pressed it against his breast, so that while it might still light him forward, its rays should not strike backwards to betray him. Then in three strides he gained the shelter of the heavy velvet curtains that masked the window. Behind them, his back to the casement, he extinguished at last the light.

The door opened an instant later. Indeed had Clairvaux who entered, candle in hand, in nightcap and quilted dressing-gown, bestowed an attentive look upon the curtains he would have detected the quiver that still agitated them. After him came a tall young man in a long black riding-coat and a conical hat that was decorated by a round tricolour cockade to advertise his patriotic sentiments. Under his arm he carried a riding-whip, whose formidable quality as a weapon of offence was proclaimed by its round head in plaited leather with silver embellishments. He placed it upon a table beside his hat, and the thud with which it dropped to the wood further announced its quality.

The Citizen Representative, a short, stiffly built man whose aquiline face was not without some resemblance to that of his visitor, flung himself into a gilt armchair upholstered in blue silk near the secretaire that but a moment ago had been the object of Duroc's attention. He threw one knee over the other and drew his quilted dressing-gown about his legs.

"Well?" he demanded, his voice harsh. "What is this important communication that brings you here at such an hour as this?"

The man in the riding-coat sauntered across to the fireplace. He set his back to the overmantel, and the ormolu clock with its cupids by Debureau, and faced the deputy with a smile that was almost a sneer.

"Confess now," he said, "that but for your uneasy conscience, my cousin, you would have hesitated to admit me. But you live in the dread of your own misdeeds, with the blade of the guillotine like a sword of Damocles suspended above you, and you dare refuse no man — however unwelcome in himself — who may be the possible bearer of a warning." He laughed an irritating laugh of mockery.

"Name of a name," growled the deputy, "will you tell me what brings you, without preamble?"

"You do not like preambles? And a representative! Now that is odd! But there, Etienne, to put it shortly, I am thinking of emigrating."

It was the deputy's turn to become mocking.

"It was worth while being aroused at midnight to hear such excellent news. Emigrate by all means, my dear Gustave. France will be well rid of you."

"And you?" quoth Gustave.

"And I no less." The deputy grinned sardonically.

"Ah!" said his cousin. "That is excellent. In such a case, no doubt, you will be disposed to pay for the privilege. To carry out this plan of mine I need your assistance, Etienne. I am practically penniless."

"Now that is a thousand pities." The deputy's voice became almost sympathetic, yet slurred by a certain note of sarcasm. "If you are penniless, so am I. What else did you expect in a member of the National Convention? Did you conceive that a representative of the sacred people — an apostle of Liberty, Equality, and Fraternity — could possibly have money at his disposal? Ah, my good cousin, I assure you that all that I possessed has been offered up on the sacred altar of the nation."

Gustave looked at him, and pursed his lips. "You had better reserve that for the National Assembly," he said. "It may sound convincing from the rostrum. Here — " he waved a hand about him at all the assembled splendours, "it sounds uncommonly like a barefaced lie."

The deputy rose with overwhelming dignity, his brows contracted.

"This to me?" he demanded.

"Why not?" wondered Gustave. "Come, come, Etienne. I am not a child, nor yet a fool. You are a man of wealth — all the world knows it, as you may discover to your cost one fine morning. These are days of fraternity, and I am your cousin — "

"Out of my house," the deputy broke in angrily. "Out of my house this instant."

Gustave looked at him with calm eyes. "Shall I then go and tell the National Assembly what I know of you? Must I denounce you to the Committee of Public Safety as a danger to the nation? Must I tell them that in secret you are acting as an agent of the émigrés, that you plot the overthrow of the august republic?"

Clairvaux's face was livid, his eyes were bulging. He mastered himself by an effort. "Denounce all you please," he answered in a suffocating voice. "You'll leave your own head in the basket. Sainte Guillotine! you fool, am I a man of straw to be overthrown by the denunciations of such a thing as you? Do you think to frighten me with threats of what you will do? Do you think that is the way to obtain assistance from me?"

"Seeing that no other way is possible," flashed Gustave.

"Out of my house. Go, denounce me! Go to the devil! But out of here with you!"

"Take care, Etienne!" The other was breathing hard, and his eyes flamed with anger — the anger of the baffled man. "I am desperate, I am face to face with ruin. I need but a thousand francs — "

"Not a thousand sous, not a single sou from me. Be off!" And Clairvaux advanced threateningly upon his cousin. "Be off!" He caught him by the lapels of his riding-coat.

"Don't dare to touch me!" Gustave warned him, his voice shrilling suddenly.

But the deputy, thoroughly enraged by now, tightened his grip, and began to thrust the other towards the door. Gustave put out a hand to the table where his hat and whip were lying, and his fingers closed upon that ugly riding-crop of his. The rest had happened almost before he realized it; it was the blind action of suddenly overwhelming fury. He twisted out of his cousin's grasp, stepped back, holding that life-preserver by its slender extremity, swung it aloft and brought the loaded end whistling down upon the deputy's nightcapped head.

There was a horrible sound like the crunching of an egg-shell, and the Citizen Representative dropped, fulminated by the blow, and lay in a shuddering, twitching heap, whilst the colour of his nightcap changed slowly from white to crimson under the murderer's staring eyes.

Gustave stood there, bending over the fallen man, motionless whilst you might count ten. His face was leaden and his mouth foolishly open between surprise and horror of the thing he had done.

Not a sound disturbed the house; not a groan, not a movement from the fallen man. Nothing but the muffled ticking of the ormolu clock and the buzzing of a fly that had been disturbed. Still Gustave stood there in that half-crouching attitude, terror gaining upon him with every throb of his pulses. And then quite suddenly a voice cut sharply upon the stillness.

"Well?" it asked. "And what do you propose to do now?"

Gustave came erect, stifling a scream, to confront the white face and beady eyes of Duroc, who stood considering him between the parted curtains.

In a long silence he stared, his wits working briskly the while.

"Who are you?" he asked at last, his voice a hoarse whisper. "How come you here? What are you? Ah! A thief — a housebreaker!"

"At least," said Duroc drily, "I am not a murderer."

"My God!" said Gustave, and his wild eyes turned again upon that tragically grotesque mass that lay at his feet. "Is he— is he dead?"

"Unless his skull is made of iron," said Duroc. He came forward in that swift, noiseless fashion of his, and dropped on one knee beside the deputy. He made a brief examination. "The Citizen Representative represents a corpse," he said. "He is as dead as King Capet." He rose. "What are you going to do?" he asked again.

"To do?" said Gustave. "Mon Dieu! What is there to do? If he is dead —" He checked. His knavish wits were racing now. He looked into the other's round black eyes. "You'll not betray me," he cried. "You dare not. You are in no better case than I. And there is no one else in the house. He lived all alone. He was a miserly dog, and the old woman who serves him will not be here until morning."

Duroc was watching him intently, almost without appearing to observe him. He saw the man's fingers suddenly tighten upon the life-preserver with which already he had launched one man across the tide of the Styx that night.

"Put that thing down," he commanded sharply, "put it down at once, or I'll send you after your cousin." And Gustave found himself covered by a pistol.

Instantly he loosed his grip of his murderous weapon. It fell with a crash beside the body of the man it had slain.

"I meant you no harm," panted Gustave. "Do you know what wealth he hoards in these consoles, in that secretaire? You do, for that is what you came for. Well, take it, take it all. But let me go, let me get away from this. I — I —" He seemed to stifle in his terror.

Duroc's lipless mouth distended in a smile.

"Am I detaining you?" he asked. "Faith, you didn't suppose I was going to drag you to the nearest corps-de-garde, did you? Go, man, if you want to go. In your place I should have gone already."

Gustave stared at him almost incredulously, as if doubting his own good fortune. Then suddenly perceiving the motives that swayed the other, and asking nothing better for himself than to be gone, he turned and without another word fled from the room and the house, his one anxiety to put as great a distance between himself and his crime as possible.

Duroc watched that sudden scared flight, still smiling. Then he coolly crossed the room, took up the dead man's candle and placed it upon the secretaire. He pulled up a chair — there was no longer any need to proceed with caution — sat down, and producing his keys and a chisel-like instrument he went diligently to work to get at the contents of this secretaire.

Meanwhile Gustave had gone like a flash the length of the Rue de la Harpe, driven ever by his terror of the consequences of his deed. But as he neared the corner of the Cordeliers he was brought suddenly to a halt by the measured tread of approaching steps. He knew it at once for the march of a patrol, and his consciousness of what he had done made him fearful of meeting these servants of the law who might challenge him and demand to know whence he was and whither he went at such an hour — for the new reign of universal liberty had imposed stern limitations upon individual freedom.

He vanished into the darkness of a doorway, and crouched there to wait until those footsteps should have faded again into the distance. And it was in those moments as he leaned there panting that his fiendishly wicked notion first assailed him. He turned it over in his mind, and in the gloom you might have caught the gleam of his teeth as he smiled evilly to himself.

He was his cousin's heir. Could he but fasten the guilt of that murder upon the thief he had left so callously at work in the very room where the body lay, then never again need he know want. And the thief, being a thief, deserved no less. He had no doubt at all but that the fellow would never have hesitated to do the murder had it been forced upon him by circumstances. He reflected further, and realized how aptly set was the stage for such a comedy as he had in mind. Had not that fool compelled him to drop the very weapon with which the deputy's skull had been smashed?

No single link was missing in the chain of complete evidence against the thief. Gustave realized that here was a chance sent him by friendly fortune. Tomorrow it would be too late. In seeking his cousin's murderer the authorities would ascertain that he was the one man who stood to profit by the Citizen Representative's death, and having discovered that they would compel him to render an account of his movements that night. They would cross-question and confound him, seeing that he could give no such account as they would demand.

He was resolved. He must act at once. Not three minutes had sped since he had left that house, and it was impossible that in the meantime the thief could have done his work and taken his departure.

And so upon that fell resolve he flung out of his concealment, and ran on up the street towards the Cordeliers, to meet the advancing patrol, shouting as he went —

"Au voleur! Au voleur!"

He heard the patrol quickening their steps in response to his cry, and presently he found himself face to face with four men of the National Guard, who, as it chanced, were accompanied by an agent of the section in civilian dress and scarf of office.

"Down there," he cried, pointing back down the street. "A thief has broken into the house of my cousin — my cousin the Citizen Representative Clairvaux." He gathered importance, he knew, from this proclamation of his relationship with one of the great ones of the Convention.

But the agent of the section paused to question him.

"Why did you not follow him, citizen?"

"I am without weapons, and I bethought me he would probably be armed. Besides I heard you approaching in the distance, and I thought it best to run to summon you, that thus we may make sure of taking him."

The agent considered him, his white face — seen in the light of the lantern carried by the patrol — his shaking limbs and gasping speech, and concluded he had to deal with an arrant coward, nor troubled to dissemble his contempt.

"Name of a name!" he growled, "and meanwhile the Citizen Representative may have been murdered in his bed."

"I pray not! Oh, I pray not!" panted Gustave. "Quickly, citizens, quickly! Terrible things may happen while we stand here."

They went down the street at a run to the house of Clairvaux, whose door they found open as Gustave had left it when he departed.

"Where did he break in?" asked one of the guards.

"By the door," said Gustave. "He had keys, I think. Oh, quick!"

In the passage he perceived a faint gleam of light to assure him that the thief was still at work. He swung round to them, and raised a hand. "Quietly!" he whispered. "Quietly, so that we do not disturb him."

The patrol thrust forward, and entered the house in his wake. He led them straight towards the half-open door of the study, from which the light was issuing as if to guide them. He flung wide the door, and entered, whilst the men crowding after him came to a sudden halt upon the threshold in sheer amazement at what they beheld.

At their feet lay the body of the Citizen Representative Clairvaux in a raiment that in itself seemed to proclaim how hastily he had risen from his bed to come and deal with this midnight intruder; and there at the secretaire, now open, its drawers broken and their contents scattered all about the floor, sat Duroc, white-faced, his beady rat's eyes considering them.

Gustave broke into lamentations at sight of his cousin's body.

"We are too late! Mon Dieu! We are too late! He is dead — dead. And look! Here is the weapon with which he was slain. And there sits the murderer — caught in the very act — caught in the very act. Seize him! Ah, scélérat," he raged, shaking his fist in the thief's white, startled face. "You shall be made to pay for this!"

"Comedian!" said Duroc shortly.

"Seize him! Seize him!" cried Gustave in a frenzy.

The guards sprang across the room, and laid hands upon Duroc to prevent him having recourse to any weapons.

Duroc looked up at them, blinking. Then his eyes shifted to Gustave, and suddenly he laughed.

"Now see what a fool a man is who will not seize the chances that are offered him," he said. "After that scoundrel had bludgeoned his cousin to death I bade him go. He might have made good his escape, and I should have said no word to betray him. Instead he thinks to make me his scapegoat."

He shrugged, and rose under the hands of his captors. Then he pulled his coat open, and displayed a round leaden disc of the size of a five-franc piece bearing the arms of the republic.

At sight of it the hands that had been holding him instantly fell away.

The agent of the section stepped forward frowning.

"What does this mean?" he asked, but on a note that was almost of respect, realizing that he stood in the presence of an officer of the secret service of the republic, whom no man might detain save at his peril.

"I am Duroc of the Committee of Public Safety," was the quiet answer. "The Executive had cause to doubt that the Citizen Representative Clairvaux was in correspondence with the enemies of France. I came secretly to examine his papers and to discover who are his correspondents. Here is what I sought." And he held up a little sheaf of documents which he had separated from the rest. "I will wish you good-night, citizens. I must report at once to the Citizen-Deputy Marat. Since that fellow has come back take him to the Luxembourg. Let the committee of the section deal with him tomorrow. I shall forward my report."

Gustave shook himself out of his sudden paralysis to make a dash for the door. But the guards closed with him, and held him fast, whilst Duroc of the Committee of Public Safety passed out, with dignity in spite of his torn breeches.

The Mask

Bentinck's fingers took up a quill from the table at which he sat, and his prominent eyes considered his visitor with a glance that was as penetrating as it seemed dull.

"Parbleu!" he said at last. "You come most opportunely, Mr. Ranger." His voice was guttural and his accent markedly foreign, but his English was at least fluent.

Mr. Ranger bowed until the long curls of his periwig almost met across his face, and the Dutchman proceeded to deliver himself.

"You will have heard of that inveterate Jacobite, Lady Gilnockie, whose husband gave his life for King James at the Boyne. Her house in Portugal Street is the rallying ground for certain gentlemen who plot a rising to take place presently when His Majesty shall have gone to Holland. Now this plot goes a step farther than its many precursors in that it aims at the assassination of King William as a preliminary to the actual rising. Knowing so much I might send the pack of them to the Tower, but if I did that I should miss the arch-plotter, the man who has planned the assassination, and who will at need execute it himself. I speak of Lady Gilnockie's brother, Sir Stuart Rowan. So long as Sir Stuart continues at large it is not safe for His Majesty to cross to Holland where he is pressingly needed, as you may know. And Sir Stuart, realising his own importance, is careful not to come within my reach. He keeps himself abroad, and thence by letters directs the movements of the plotters here in England."

"But surely," ventured Mr. Ranger, "you have agents to track him down and seize him even though he be abroad?"

"Ah, but, mordieu! he is elusive. I do not use the word lightly. He is as difficult to seize as running water. I have employed agents to track him, but they have failed — failed utterly. Intercepted letters have given me indications of his whereabouts just as they have given me knowledge of what is afoot. He is now in Holland, now in France, but where exactly in either not all my agents, not all the money I have lavished can discover. And this is where I require your aid."

Mr. Ranger was bewildered.

"But —"

"Wait, sir. Do not interrupt. It is notorious, Mr. Ranger, that play and extravagance have brought you to the edge of ruin. You are become the very stuff out of which conspirators are made. You are in a condition to lend yourself to any desperate enterprise — even one so desperate as a Jacobite conspiracy. I desire that you do so: that you become one of the plotters who meet at Lady Gilnockie's, that you learn whatever is to be learnt of their plotting, but in particular that you discover me the exact whereabouts of Sir Stuart Rowan."

Mr. Ranger turned first red, then white. His eyes wandered through windows of that room in the Palace of Whitehall and fastened upon a stately barge proceeding up the river on the bosom of the grey tide, whipped along by the gusty winds, of March. Then they returned to bend their glance upon the periwigged Dutchman who sat watching him beyond the writing-table.

"This is catchpoll's work," he said in a voice of offended protest. "You insult me, sir. I came to you seeking honourable employment — "

"Is it to insult you to ask you to discover an assassin who aims at His Majesty's sacred life?" Bentinck smacked the open table with his open hand. "You are as tiresome with your honour as the rest. Pardieu, sir! I do not press this service on you. It is the only service I have to offer, and you shall take it or leave it as you please. Yet consider." He leaned forward, jabbing the air with his quill. "On the one hand you have ruin and the stews; on the other salvation and ease to be enjoyed in the consciousness of duty done. I leave you a free choice, Mr. Ranger."

A deal more was said, but the end of it all was that Mr. Ranger, with sweat on his brow and shame and self-contempt in his heart, chose the Judas part which was so speciously presented by the Dutchman. A drowning man clutching at straws does not pause to see whether the straws are clean or dirty.

Acting upon Bentinck's advice, Mr. Ranger went in quest of an Irishman named Roger Butler, who was notoriously one of the conspirators in question; he proclaimed himself a Jacobite eager to serve King James, and by Roger Butler was he introduced to the company that assembled at Lady Gilnockie's house. But already, before this came to pass, Mr. Ranger was filled with disgust of the service thrust upon him. And it needed but ten minutes contemplation of the beauty and charm of Lady Gilnockie, who was still on the sunny side of thirty, to complete his revolt.

He departed from her ladyship's house in Portugal Street cursing Bentinck for a foul-minded Dutchman, and reviling himself for having been so dead to honour, so basely venal, as not to have cracked the fellow's head as a gentleman's only possible answer to his infamous proposal. Now of this resentment against the servant was inevitably born in Mr. Ranger's bosom resentment against the master. From his indignation with Dutch Bentinck sprang indignation with Dutch William, until in the end he resolved to throw in his lot with the plotters, and, taking advantage of his position, forward the cause of King James, and thus come to win out of his difficulties in a more honourable fashion.

Thus, when next Mr. Ranger repaired to Lady Gilnockie's house, as he had been bidden, he was as thorough paced a Jacobite as any of the company. This company numbered a round dozen, constituting an inner circle of treason. Her ladyship, who was the only woman in this assembly, enjoyed a sort of presidency, partly because circumstance made her the hostess, partly because of her relationship with the absent ringleader, Sir Stuart.

They were an odd assortment. Half a dozen Tory noblemen of position and consequence, an impecunious Scottish laird named Glentoby, a couple of priests, the Irish soldier of fortune Roger Butler (who had been Mr. Ranger's sponsor), and a splendid fop from the Court of Versailles who seemed to be a sort of envoy extraordinary from King Louis. This last spoke English atrociously, affected a monstrous periwig and a pair of slight and quite unfashionable moustachios, and dressed with an extravagant flamboyance that was altogether out of place in England. His name was Pierre Louis de la Vilette, Vicomte de Grosmont.

The plotters met daily at the house in Portugal Street, and Mr. Ranger found himself cordially welcomed among them from the first. But his erst enthusiasm cooled rapidly in their vapid company. Out of his hot resentment he had been eager to be doing something that should oust the Dutchmen who were ruling England, and he had conceived himself to be joining hands with serious plotters. Instead, however, he found meeting after meeting alike unfruitful. There was a deal of scornful railing at the Bill of Rights, at the venality of the Whigs, and of place-seeking gentlemen who supported King William out of motives not of loyalty but of profit. There were interminable prophecies of the glorious restoration to be effected, and big talk of squeezing the rotten Orange; also there was an idle rite of assembling about a round table and holding glasses of Tokay above a bowl of water what time "The King" was solemnly toasted. But the sum total of it all was mere vapouring, intangible and unsubstantial.

Once only did things assume an air of serious purpose. A courier from France had reached M. de Grosmont with a letter from Sir Stuart, and with a vast importance the Frenchman disposed himself to announce its momentous contents. Mr. Ranger quivered with an anticipation that was presently stilled by disappointment.

M. de Grosmont notified them that Sir Stuart was at Boulogne at the Auberge de la Lune, whence he wrote that he would abide there a week for news of Dutch William's sailing to Holland, and that instantly upon receiving word of it he would himself cross the frontier to await the usurper. Meanwhile he begged his friends in London to take no measures whatsoever beyond keeping him informed of anything they judged should be made known to him.

Mr. Ranger pondered the temerity of so explicit a letter. It was of a piece, he thought, with the rest of this crack-brained plotting. And then, suddenly, he perceived that he was in a position to discharge the service required of him, and convey to Bentinck the information that should enable him to seize Sir Stuart and so prick this Jacobite bubble. But however much he might have come to despise the plotters, Mr. Ranger was firm in his newly begotten sympathy with their Cause, and in his sense of insult with the Dutchman's minister.

To his own double risk he gave no thought. He was compelled almost against his judgment to continue his visits to the house in Portugal Street, drawn thither irresistibly by Lady Gilnockie herself. He conceived by now no thought that did not gravitate about her. Knowing her suspect and in danger, his one desire was to abstract her from her peril. He conceived wild projects of carrying her beyond the reach of King William's ministers, and living in peace and happiness with her in some foreign land, himself supporting her by the fruits of such service as he might there undertake.

The love that had so suddenly flamed in this ruined gentleman's heart was fanned and quickened by the circumstances under which the pair had met, by his sense of the danger that encompassed her, and by a certain jealous fear that in M. de Grosmont he might have a rival.

At the end of some ten days he determined to put an end to a twofold suspense that was become almost more than he could bear. He was encouraged to it by the kindness, increasing ever, which from the first she had shown him, and from which he fondly argued that perhaps her heart had answered to the call of his own. Thus he went bluntly to the core of the matter; indeed, some might hold that he began at the end.

"Your relations with Monsieur Grosmont — are political and nothing more?" he asked her.

She stared at him, and confessed that she did not understand his question.

"I mean," he said, "what precisely is M. de Grosmont to you?"

"To me? M. de Grosmont?" She caught his meaning at last, and cold haughtiness leapt into her lovely face.

"I see, I see! I am answered," he cried gloomily, misunderstanding her sudden access of dignity. "This mincing Frenchman is justified of his assiduous attentions. But I — "

"By what right, sir, do you presume so far?" she broke in upon his threatened tirade of jealousy.

He made a gesture between humility and impatience. Indeed, he was the oddest wooer.

"Forgive the presumption in according me the right," said he, advancing.

He perceived the sudden agitation of her bosom, the dilation of her eyes that stared at him half in fascination, half in fear. He swept boldly on, using now her name and speaking quick and fervently.

"Mary, I am come to ask you to forsake all this, to abandon this idle and dangerous conspiracy, to withdraw yourself from these feather-headed plotters, who wilt continue to make a puppet-show of plotting until all of you are ruined together."

She recoiled a step, her face blenching.

"You speak of danger?" she cried, as if in all that he had said that were the only thing that mattered. "What danger threatens? Tell me! Tell me!"

"What danger?" For a moment he turned aside from his main purpose to answer that question. "Why, King William does not sleep, and Bentinck has as many eyes as Argus. What has been the end of all the other plots against William, and in what is this conducted better than it should end differently?"

"Then — then why, have you joined us?"

"Because where you go there must I follow. Because — oh, because I love you, Mary."

He had got it out at last, and he was consistent at least in that, having begun where he should have ended, he ended where he should have begun.

A long silence followed his declaration, and they stood regarding each other, she in the profoundest agitation, he in an agitation scarcely less profound, awaiting her pronouncement

At length her lips curled in a smile that was something between sadness and mockery.

"And this being so, you can counsel disloyalty?" she asked him.

"I do not," he answered. "I counsel the abandonment of futility, for that is all I can discover here. Plots are not for women, and were these men who gather round you worthy of the name of plotters they would not suffer you to imperil yourself amid them. But they are mere vapourers — my Lords Hamble and Sheringham are place-seekers whom Dutch Williams has disappointed; Roger Butler is a soldier of fortune whose services are at the disposal of the highest bidder, the priests have ulterior motives of their own, whilst the Frenchman — " He paused, and his jealousy flared out again. "What is King James to a Frenchman that he should imperil his neck in his service?"

"And yourself?" she asked him.

"I?" He checked a moment, dismayed by that abrupt question, and he was almost swept by the sincerity of his passion into a confession of the original motive that was responsible for his introduction there. Then, realising that to do so were to lock fast the door of hope: "I?" he said. "Oh, I am just a fool. But not such a fool as to be misled by these others, who will talk and talk, and posture and toast the king over the water, until they ruin his cause. For when their arrest results from this frivolous conspiring, terror will be spread in which King James will have lost most of the adherents that remain to him."

She sank to a chair, and leaned her elbow upon the round walnut table — the table in whose centre stood the bowl of water ready for the toast of which he spoke with such contempt.

"You are right," she said at last in a small voice. "I have long thought even as you think; but it has needed a man to make me believe the truth of what I told myself. And, yet — there is my brother, Sir Stuart, who is working diligently, and for his sake — "

He broke in impetuously:

"In what Sir Stuart may or may not do these vapourers can neither help nor hinder. Nay, now, on my faith, they will hinder more than they can help."

He dropped on one knee beside her. He caught her hand in his; he stole an arm about her waist, and passionately he pleaded, with her now to abandon all and to come away with him, away out of England. He confessed his ruined condition. He had nothing to offer her beyond his love. But he had been a soldier, and could be so again, and abroad there was no lack of service for such as he.

She listened with bowed head, sorely tempted, yet hesitating for the sake of those who counted upon her aid in this dream of King James's restoration.

He was still unanswered when approaching steps came to drive them apart. Vexed, he stood by the long windows staring out upon the garden which ran down to the Strand, all bud and blossom now in the pale sunshine of that April day.

Came a footman to announce Glentoby, the laird himself entering hard upon the lackey's heels; next followed Roger Butler, and soon thereafter all the plotters were assembled in that long paneled room with the sole exception of Monsieur de Grosmont.

The Frenchman came last, alone and unheralded, very stiff and grave for all his fopperies, and he stood just within the door scanning the company with scowling eyes until the general babble of conversation had been stilled.

Mr. Ranger looked on with a sneer at so much play-acting. The Frenchman caught the sneer and his scowl deepened. He turned, and in the general silence locked the door, and withdrew and pocketed the key. That done he came slowly forward, bowed formally to her ladyship, and took his stand by the table, one hand resting upon it, the other on his sword-hilt.

"Madame et messieurs," he said, "I have an announcement very grave to make. We are sold. Zere is a traitor amongst us!"

"What the devil's that?" said Roger Butler sharply, but his words were almost smothered in the general stir of consternation.

Mr. Ranger, standing by the window, his back fortunately to the light, felt himself turning pale. It was not that he feared any consequences with which these men might visit him when they discovered the task — the scorned and neglected task — which Bentinck had thrust upon him. But he feared — more than he had feared anything in his life — the consequences of the impending disclosure so far as her ladyship was concerned. That his love was returned her reception of his wooing had assured him, even although she had not acknowledged it in words. He held at last in his grasp the keys of happiness; it was his to mend his wasted life. And now this was all to be lost to him. Her love was to be turned to loathing by the discovery of the circumstances under which he had been introduced among them. What mattered it that from the moment he had seen her he had scornfully abandoned all idea of doing Bentinck's treacherous work, that he had gone over to King James in earnest? Who would believe it when the Frenchman told the tale he was come to tell?

In that awful moment of despair he reviled himself for not having frankly told her all — told her of the employment which Bentinck had offered him, and which in a weak moment he had accepted, to discard the next.

And now the blow was about to fall. They would kill him, of course; such men would never deal in half measures. And from his heart he thanked God for the merciful oblivion that must come swiftly to blot out the torturing consciousness of her scorn.

He found the Frenchman's eyes intently upon him; heard the Frenchman uttering his name.

"Monsieur Ranger, can *you* discover us the identity of zis traitor?

He gathered his wits together to lead them upon a forlorn hope. He would not yield without a struggle. In that resolve he grew strong again.

"Sir, how should I?" he asked steadily, under the stare of all, yet conscious, only of the wide eyes in her ladyship's deathly face. "Besides, we have yet no proof of what you say."

Grosmont showed his dazzling teeth in an evil smile.

"Zat, I zink, is to give me ze lie," said he.

"Sir," said Mr. Ranger, "if your object is to pick a quarrel with me you need take no roundabout way to gratify it. But if you are serious in this matter of a traitor, perhaps you had best discover him."

"Indeed, yes," cut in the laird, whilst Lord Sheringham and one or two others clamoured for the proofs.

"Soit!" said Grosmont. "Now listen. I have suspect zat perhaps we were betray'. A week ago in zis room I announce to you zat Sir Stuart Rowan was at the Auberge de la Lune at Boulogne. Zat was not true. Zat was ze trap. And now, Pardieu! I receive word today zat a dozen English bullies have made a raid upon ze Auberge de la Lune at Boulogne seeking Sir Stuart, whom, of course, zey have not find. It is plain — oh, quite plain — zat ze false infor-mation I give you here a week ago was convey' at once to Monsieur Bentinck, so that Monsieur Bentinck has an agent here amongst us. It remains, messieurs, for us to discover him."

Mr. Ranger gaped in his astonishment. The disclosure was far indeed from all that he had expected. It proved to him that a traitor there was in truth among them, a traitor other than himself. More it proved to him that Bentinck had employed him merely as a mask to screen the real and trusted traitor, and to be used as a scapegoat should the need arise. In swift anger against the Dutchman who had so sought to employ him, he grew eager to discover whom it was he served to mask.

"May I see the letter you claim to have received?" he asked, his voice cutting sharply into the general silence.

"Claim?" said M. de Grosmont, raising his eyebrows. "Ah, ca! But I understand. Voici, monsieur." And he proffered it.

Mr. Ranger took it, read it, scanned superscription and seals, what time several others, Butler and Glentoby foremost amongst them, crowded about him that they might see it also.

"It appears to be quite genuine," he admitted, and, having returned it, he looked the Frenchman squarely between the eyes. "Monsieur de Grosmont," said he, "ever since making your announcement, you have conveyed to me in a dozen ways that you choose to single me out for suspicion. May I beg you to be a little more definite?"

"Zat was my intention," replied Grosmont, smiling grimly. "You are so impatient, Monsieur Ranger. No doubt you wish to be relieve' of your suspense, eh? Bien! You were ze last to come amongst us, and it is my knowledge that two days before you were presented here you were close with Monsieur Bentinck at Whitehall for over an hour."

There was a general recoil of those who stood about Mr. Ranger.

"Is this true?" It was her ladyship's voice, cutting like a knife through the silence.

"Quite true," he said in a calm, level voice. For all that he had expected, no less he felt as if a hand of ice had suddenly closed upon his brain.

"And what did ye there, man?" quoth Glentoby. "We'll be needin' yer explanations."

"I went to seek employment," he answered.

"Well, man?" cried Lord Sheringham, surging forward. "And what employment did he offer you?"

Mr. Ranger drew himself stiffly erect.

"None that a gentleman might accept," he said.

Monsieur de Grosmont made a clucking sound.

"We are answer', I zink, messieurs, and you, madame. It is a confession. He was offer' no 'employment zat a gentleman might accept. Oh, ze nice equivocation! But he was offer' employment zat a scoundrel might and did accept, n'est-ce pas?"

"Monsieur de Grosmont!" Mr. Ranger thundered suddenly, his face flushing darkly.

But the Frenchman paid no heed to him. He looked at the others.

"As a consequence, messieurs, it is clear we are ruined; ze cause is lost! We must disperse, and we shall be fortunate if we escape. But before we go zere is somezing to do." He dabbed his lips with a handkerchief, two hectic spots burning in his olive cheeks. "Ze garden, I zink. We can contrive zat it shall have seem' a duel."

"But are you sure? Are you sure?" It was a cry of anguish from her ladyship, laden with a message that stiffened Mr. Ranger in his purpose to do battle to the end. It was the confession which earlier he had desired from her, wrung at last from a breaking heart.

M. de Grosmont looked at her with dull eyes.

"Alas, madame, doubt is impossible," said he. "Best make an end quickly, messieurs."

On the word there was a movement towards him, but Mr. Ranger, suddenly inspired, checked it by an uplifted hand.

"You fools!," he said. "You crass, blind fools, that think to carry through a conspiracy and can see no farther than your nose-tips. D'ye need, proof that I have not betrayed you?"

He had given them pause at least. He looked at the astonished Grosmont.

"Should I," he asked, "have sent Bentinck's bullies to look for Sir Stuart Rowan at Boulogne, knowing as I do that Sir Stuart is here amongst us; that you who call yourself Vicomte de Grosmont are in reality Sir Stuart in disguise?"

The most surprised of all was M. de Grosmont himself. He could do no more than gape and stare, like the rest of that dumbfounded company. None had ever suspected this; the disguise, thought one and all, this ponderous red wig and tiny unfashionable moustachios, completely travestied the man; besides which none save the Laird of Glentoby had ever beheld Sir Stuart in the flesh.

Two only of those present — Grosmont himself and Lady Gilnockie — knew the statement to be untrue, and of these only Lady Gilnockie realised that Mr. Ranger himself knew it to be, untrue, that his dramatic utterance was a piece of deliberate play-acting with some deep purpose underlying it. She remembered how he had come to her not an hour ago with words that betrayed his jealousy of this M. de Grosmont, and clearly he could not have been jealous of him had he supposed him, as he now alleged, to be her brother.

That swift and clear deduction of hers, upon which Mr. Ranger had counted, proved now his salvation. For even as Monsieur de Grosmont shook himself out of his amazement to repudiate the wild announcement he was checked by her ladyship. She turned to him with a nervous laugh.

"You see, Stuart, how plain it is that Mr. Ranger is not the traitor."

From the increasingly bewildered Frenchman she swung upon the company, her face still deathly pale, but her manner unnaturally light.

"Well, well, sirs, the secret is out — and the marvel is that it should so long have been kept hidden from you all."

"Oh, not quite from all, I assure your ladyship." It was Roger Butler who spoke, smiling easily. "I have known Sir Stuart, in spite of his disguise for many a day."

The smile passed from her ladyship's face; it grew hard and stony, and the eyes that flashed upon Mr. Butler were two daggers. Grosmont swore a thick "Mordieu!" under his breath, whilst Mr. Ranger laughed sardonically.

"Forgive my subterfuge, M. de Grosmont," said he, "in consideration of its inevitable fruit. Perforce the real traitor must shield himself behind this pretence of knowledge. It was upon that I counted. Here, then, is your man."

Too late Butler saw the trap that had been so cunningly baited by the desperate wits of Mr. Ranger. His hand flew to his sword. But the others bore down upon him before he could draw.

The French windows were thrown open, and through them the traitor was dragged out into the garden to receive his wages. Mr. Ranger stood aloof. Not for him to take a hand in the work, nor yet to raise a hand to save the scoundrel whom he had been used to mask.

Her ladyship and he were left alone.

"Come," he bade her. "Come at once. Let us not waste a moment."

She went with him, glad to flee from the place, and together they won to France, where they were married.

Shrinkage

Nothing in the careers of illustrious men — whether soldiers, statesmen, poets, or merchant princes — can be of greater interest than their first steps along the road by which they travelled to their ultimate eminence. No subsequent achievements, however vast, can be as striking as those early manifestations — often in the most unpromising environments — of the qualities that made for their success.

It is not to be denied that often they have been well served by chance. It is as if Fortune, perceiving in them men worthy of officiating at her altar, had reached out a hand to help them over difficult beginnings. Rarely do they afterwards acknowledge the debt. Frequently they will go so far as to deny the existence of the Goddess of Chance. That is because even great men are subject to humanity's besetting sin of vanity. To give to Luck, they would have to take from Merit, and that would flatter them not at all.

Consider, for instance, the case of the famous and enormously successful Sir Llewellyn Evans. He would be a bold man who dared to suggest to Sir Llewellyn that he owes anything to luck. Yet you shall judge for yourself the precise degree of his indebtedness and the extent to which he was afforded the opportunity of exercising those subtle and none-too-scrupulous instincts which have placed him where he stands today.

You are not to suppose that I am about to introduce you to the portly, self-confident, magnetic, dominant, crisp-voiced Sir Llewellyn, whom all the world knows — by repute, at least, and through the medium of the Press. This story does not concern the Sir Llewellyn Evans of today, the distinguished head of the great firm of Farland Singleton, Ltd., the man who has been thrice mayor of Liverpool, twice winner of the Grand National, yacht-owner, mine-owner, merchant prince, and banker.

I am about to lift the curtain of the past, and reveal to you, with the merciless candour of the honest historian, the Llewellyn Evans of thirty years ago, a lanky, pimpled, nervous young man, with untidy hair, in a ready-made suit of tweed shockingly sprung at the knees and elbows, a typical drudging clerk in the employ of one Farland Singleton, produce-broker and commission-agent, for such was the entire import of that firm in those days.

Those who have had the privilege of looking upon early photographs of Llewellyn, pretend to see in the hard lines of the mouth and the prominence of the cheek-bones the advertisement of the Welshman's exceptional abilities. It is, as we all know, very easy to perceive prophetic signs of events after the events have come to pass. The hard lines of the mouth would be lines of discontent, and the prominence of the cheek-bones was, most probably, the result of malnutrition. But let that pass.

At the time of which I propose to write, Llewellyn had already attained the position of head-clerk to Farland Singleton. Singleton, indeed, would often allude to Llewellyn as "my manager." But you are not to be misled by what was the merest grandiloquence. A survey of the establishment reduces my hero at once to his proper level. In addition to Llewellyn, Singleton employed an invoice and correspondence clerk at twenty-five shillings a week, an apprentice at ten shillings, and an office-boy at five. Our Welshman himself was in receipt of the weekly managerial stipend of forty-five shillings, out of which, he has confessed to me, he contrived to save twenty-five.

Now, it had taken Farland Singleton ten years to build up the business of the firm to the extent sufficient to justify this personnel. He had started ten years earlier with just Llewellyn, aged fourteen at the time, as his office-boy, and for the last five years the business had been at a complete standstill. Where there is no progress there must be retrogression, and, under an appearance of being stationary, Farland Singleton's business had been going back until, on the date on which this story opens, his liabilities outweighed his assets.

Unless a miracle happened nothing could avert the proceedings in bankruptcy that loomed ahead. The miracle did happen, as I am about to relate. It was supplied by Llewellyn.

On that spring morning upon which opportunity dawned for him, the young Welshman arrived at the office at half-past nine. He was half an hour late. But this troubled him not at all. What is half an hour in the time of a firm that is on the verge of bankruptcy? Llewellyn had no illusions about the state of affairs. He was profoundly depressed by it, or, rather, profoundly concerned for his own future. Forty-five shillings a week may not seem much of a figure to be concerned about, but to such men as Llewellyn opportunities to earn it are none too prolific.

He hung up his shabby bowler hat, climbed to his high stool, removed his whiskered false cuffs, and proceeded to unlock the drawer of his desk.

Daniel, the office-boy, slouched out of the private room, espied him, and bawled across the narrow space:

"Guv'nor wants yer, Mr. Evans!"

Llewellyn slipped from the stool, thrust a pen behind his ear for the sake of appearances, and went to wait upon his chief.

A few weeks earlier he might have feared a severe reproof for being late; but, with heavier matters to occupy him, Farland Singleton had refrained of late from bullying his staff about such trifles.

Six months ago Singleton had been a portly, rosy, self-sufficient gentleman of a quick and hectoring disposition. Of late he had lost a good many of these attributes. Worry had improved his appearance and his manners, and this morning Llewellyn found him thinner, paler, and more subdued than ever.

From the American roll-top desk at which he sat the produce-broker took a narrow strip of paper. He held it out in a hand that trembled.

"Just look at this, Evans," he said, his voice laden with fretful exasperation.

Llewellyn took the document and conned it, his employer watching him from under bushy eyebrows. It proved to be a debit-note from the important Belfast firm of Piper, Smith, & Co., and it ran as follows:

"To shrinkage on 5 tons lynobite, per ss. Euclid.
1 cwt. 3 qr. 4lb. ... ...   £50 4s. 3d."

Llewellyn's pallid face remained unmoved.

"Just as usual, sir," he said, turning his eyes — and they were very mild eyes in those days — upon his employer.

"Yes," said Singleton deliberately, "just as usual."

He passed a hand over his full black beard, in which a few strands of grey had lately been revealing themselves.

"It's a swindle, Evans."

"Yess, indeed," said Llewellyn, with Cymric softness, "and it hass been going on for a very long time, look you."

"It's been going on ever since we've been getting their orders," grumbled the head of the firm. "And it's proved to be an imposition. Look here, three tons by the same boat to Rea & Bartley. They agree the weights, and don't claim a farthing for shrinkage. How do you make that out? Can one parcel lose two per cent, on the passage, and the other nothing?"

"Indeed no," said Llewellyn. "For it is all out of the same lot, and it had been in warehouse for a month, and should not have lost any weight at all."

A word of explanation may here be necessary. This extremely sensitive product known as lynobite, more valuable than rubber, to which it is near akin, is so delicate of fibre that some shrinkage almost invariably takes place in transit, and it is an acknowledged rule of the trade that payment shall be made upon landing weights — a perfectly reasonable rule, for no man may be compelled to pay for more of anything than he actually receives. In the case of any extraordinary loss of weight, the matter would be investigated; but no loss of weight is considered extraordinary that does not transcend 2% of the total; and up to this percentage it is an invariable custom to accept the landing weights taken by any firm of good standing.

Now, Piper, Smith, & Co. was a very well-established and prosperous house, whose honour no man would dare publicly to impugn, although in private it was agreed that they were people who required careful watching, and that the senior partner was addicted to extremely sharp practices.

There can be no doubt that sharp practice was being pursued in these persistent and unvarying claims. With the greatest promptitude these debit notes for a 2% shrinkage were presented against each shipment made, and, with a sly trading upon commercial weakness for cash in hand, it was Piper, Smith's custom to accompany the note of claim by a cheque for the balance of the invoice, in strictest accordance with the "cash terms" of these transactions.

As a matter of fact it was entirely owing to this sharp practice that Farland Singleton had obtained Piper, Smith, & Co.'s orders for lynobite — orders which but for these claims would have been very valuable indeed. Piper, Smith, & Co. had quarreled on the subject with every other produce firm in Liverpool, until Singleton was the only broker who would accept their orders. He had accepted them with his eyes open. He was fully aware of the notorious and disgraceful practice. But he had figured it out that even when these arbitrary and unfounded claims were met, sufficient profit would still remain to make it worth his while to execute the orders.

That was two years ago. In the meantime his point of view had changed with the change in his fortunes. He had suddenly awakened to the realisation that the total of these allowances was amounting to rather startling figures. He had worked these out before calling Llewellyn, and he now held out a pad that was covered with penciled calculations.

"Look at this!" he gloomily invited his head-clerk. "We make a bare four per cent on these orders, and we have to return more than half of that to meet these infernal claims." He tapped the pad with a pencil. "In two years we have supplied Piper, Smith, & Co. with some sixty tons of lynobite — sixty-three tons to be exact. Do you know how much their claims have amounted to in that time?"

Llewellyn cast up the figures swiftly in his mind. He was quick and accurate.

"Fifteen hundred pounds, sir," he said after an instant's pause.

"Seventeen hundred and sixty-four pounds," Singleton corrected with doleful emphasis.

"I deducted the two hundred and sixty-four as the probably genuine shrinkage," said Llewellyn stolidly. "Fifteen hundred will about represent the actual — ahem — fraud."

"Call it that, then. It's — it's scandalous!"

"But you thought it worth while on those terms," Llewellyn daringly reminded his chief.

The reminder angered Singleton. It roused him to something of his old hectoring manner. "Worth while?" he fumed. He slewed round in his chair to face his clerk. "Look here, Evans, for these two years my books should show a profit of some three thousand pounds on Piper, Smith's orders. Instead of that, there's barely a thousand. Is that worth while?"

"No, sir, indeed," said Llewellyn, with decision.

"Seventeen hundred pounds!" groaned the chief. "Absolutely done out of it! And to think that if I had that money now! If I had it — " He looked at his clerk again. "Do you know that it is actually more than my original capital in business? What with our heavy losses in isinglass and rubber, the firm is in a bad way. You know it as well as I do. But if I had the money of which the wealthy house of Piper, Smith & Co. has defrauded me, we should be prosperous and flourishing."

Llewellyn considered this an overstatement. He thought that for prosperity the firm would require better management than Singleton could give it. But this reflection he discreetly left unspoken.

"Anyhow, I've done with them," said the head of the firm. "I know there isn't another house in Liverpool or out of it that will supply them with lynobite. And now you can tell them that I won't. Perhaps that'll bring them to their senses. Go and write to them." And he held out another sheet of paper, which proved to be an order from Piper, Smith, & Co., for a further four tons of lynobite to be shipped that week.

Llewellyn studied the order, and thoughtfully pursed his lips.

"Lynobite is at 5s. 2d. today, sir," he said. "And we have five tons bought at 5s. 1¾d. It's a good chance. You'd make fifty or sixty pounds on this order even if you allow the usual claim."

But Singleton was at the end of his tether. He magnified the wrong done him by Piper, Smith, & Co., he attributed his financial difficulties to this sharp practice of theirs, and he reflected again — rightly as far as it went — that if the fifteen hundred pounds of which they had swindled him were standing to his credit now, he need have no fear of ruin.

"Do as I tell you," he said shortly, and Llewellyn went out to obey him.

In the general office the correspondence clerk was giving the office-boy explicit directions about getting a shilling each way on an outsider for the Grand National with a bookie known to the enterprising Daniel. Llewellyn interrupted that important commission when he summoned his subordinate, and began to dictate a formal letter to Piper, Smith, & Co.

In the luxuriant English of commerce, he got safely as far as:

"Dear Sirs, Your esteemed favour of the 23rd inst. is duly to hand this morning, and we beg to thank you for same, contents being duly noted."

At this point he paused, and reflection brought him the discovery that his command of language was entirely inadequate to the task of delicately conveying a matter so essentially rude as that which had been entrusted to him. He was driven to ponder, and it was in the course of these ponderings that there came to him, as in a flash of inspiration, the idea which was the seed of the colossal fortune he has since accumulated. It turned him hot and cold. It made him laugh.

"Give me the invoice-file!" he cried, with a note of command so sudden and unusual that the office-boy paused a moment in sheer astonishment before obeying him.

He turned up the duplicate of Piper, Smith's invoice.

"Give me the 'Journal of Commerce!'!" was his next order, equally imperious.

He ran his finger down a column of shipping, and he found something there that caused him to smack a cloud of dust out of his shabby trousers.

He turned again to the invoice-file, and for the next ten minutes there was no sound in that dingy office but the occasional rustle of a paper as Llewellyn turned it, and the splutter of his pen when he made a note.

At last he got down from his stool, and made his way briskly back to Mr. Singleton's room. On the threshold he hesitated a moment, then boldly entered, and boldly fired his petard. A sudden access of nervousness drove him straight to the point, precluding all preambles.

"Mr. Singleton," said he, his accent more Cymric than ever, "if any one wass to show you how to get your money pack from Piper, Smith, what would you do for him?"

Farland Singleton looked up from his papers to stare at his clerk. There was a flush on Llewellyn's cheek, an unusually hard, crafty glint in his eye. He was visibly trembling, and his voice had not been at all steady.

"Not been drinking, have you?" wondered his employer.

Llewellyn drew himself up with dignity.

"I am teetotal," he announced, with pride. Alas! To-day he is renowned for his well-stocked cellars.

Singleton's frowning stare invited, if it did not encourage, Llewellyn to explain himself. Llewellyn's explanation consisted of making his proposition directly personal.

"I can do it, look you, Mr. Singleton. I can, indeed."

"Do what? Get back the fifteen hundred pounds they've robbed me of?"

"Yess, indeed, and with interest — with interest, Mr. Singleton — every penny of it."

"I'd like to see you," sneered Singleton.

"You shall if you wish," said Llewellyn, growing bolder every moment. "It would save the firm, which would be a very great service to you. What terms will you offer?"

There was a long pause, whilst Farland Singleton attentively studied the Welshman's uninteresting face. A half-sneering smile swept across the employer's heavy countenance.

"Why, Evans, if you can do that," he said, and his tone was the casual tone of one who promises something which he is convinced can never be claimed — "if you can do that I'll — I'll make you a handsome present."

At this point Llewellyn changed colour. He was intensely excited, and rather frightened of his employer. Yet he spoke very deliberately. He held in his hands the big chance of his life. He was a man who had found the opportunity to make himself, and the self-making of a man is bold work and needs to be boldly done.

"You said yourself that fifteen hundred pounds is more than the capital with which you started in pusiness," he premised. "The firm, look you, iss in a fery pad way. Fifteen hundred pounds at such a time would save it. I can save it. That iss a pig service, whatever." He paused to clear his throat, and abruptly concluded: "I want a partnership."

Singleton's first impulse was to kick him out. Fortunately for himself he paused long enough to perceive that such a service as Llewellyn proposed, rendered at a time of such dire need, would be well worth the price he set upon it. But as for the Welshman's ability to get that money back from Piper, Smith, & Co. Singleton thought it would be absurd to take him seriously. And just because of this inherent absurdity of the proposal, just because he could not think that he should ever be called upon to fulfill his part of the bargain, Singleton permitted himself to make the answer for which Llewellyn hoped.

He smiled at his clerk as one smiles at an idiot whom it is less fatiguing to humour than to engage in argument.

"It's a reasonable proposal, Evans. If you can do as you say you shall have a partnership."

"On what terms, Mr. Singleton?" quoth Llewellyn briskly, his eyes gleaming.

Singleton lay back in his chair and thrust his thumbs into the armholes of his waistcoat. His smile grew broader; the tolerant contempt of it increased.

"What terms do you propose, Evans?"

"Equal terms!" snapped Llewellyn. "Equal sharing terms!"

"You're too cursedly modest," said Singleton.

Llewellyn spread his hands.

"I save the firm, look you," he insisted.

"What's your plan, anyhow?" growled Singleton, becoming serious.

Llewellyn smiled very knowingly, and shook his head.

"The secret of that iss my capital at present," said he. "You must give me a free hand in the matter as soon as the conditional deed of partnership is prepared."

"Oh, you want a deed, do you?"

"Indeed," said Llewellyn.

In the end he got what he wanted. That very day a deed of partnership was drawn up subject to the condition that it was to come into force as soon as Piper, Smith, & Co. should have reimbursed the firm of Farland Singleton of the total amount paid in claims for shrinkage on lynobite in the course of the dealings between the two houses.

Enough has been said to indicate the contemptuously-reckless spirit in which Singleton had entered into the matter. Later on, however, he began to consider it more seriously, and to wonder what scheme Llewellyn might be evolving. Finally he actually began to hope that this way might lie the salvation of his firm.

But when in the early part of the following week an invoice was submitted to him relating to four tons of lynobite shipped to Piper, Smith, & Co., per ss.

Artemis, Singleton angrily thumped his bell. When Llewellyn appeared in answer to the summons, he was greeted with a fury of abuse that reminded him of the firm's most flourishing days.

Having sworn himself hoarse, Singleton at last came to the point.

"Didn't I expressly forbid you to execute this order?" he demanded.

"Yess," admitted the quaking Llewellyn. "But afterwards you gave me a free hand. And, anyway, the lot is shipped now."

"Shipped, is it? Well of all the infernal cheek!" He paused, and scowled at Llewellyn. "Are you running this business already?"

"This business of lynobite with Piper, Smith — yess. You gave me a free hand," he repeated.

Singleton made noises in his beard, shrugged, and finally dashed an angry signature across the foot of the letter covering the invoice.

"We shall see your fine schemes," he growled.

"We shall," Llewellyn agreed, and went out.

The interview, after all, had ended more peacefully than its beginnings had seemed to threaten. Singleton awaited events. But he abandoned whatever hopes he had founded in his clerk. He had a premonition of what would happen; and when, three days later, he opened a letter from Piper, Smith, & Co., and withdrew the inevitable debit note for shrinkage and a cheque for the balance, he called himself every conceivable sort of fool for having listened to Llewellyn. His patience was at an end. He thumped his bell, and bawled for Evans.

The young Welshman came in nervously. He was very pale, and his eyelids flickered.

"Yessir?" said he.

"Take a month's notice, Evans," said Singleton shortly.

"Bu — but what have I done, sir?" quoth the clerk.

"Done?" echoed Singleton. "Done? Look at this, and see for yourself!"

Llewellyn's fingers trembled as they took up the debit note:

"To shrinkage on 4 tons lynobite, per ss. Artemis.
1 cwt. 2qr. 11lb. ... ... £45 9s. 11d."

"The usual two per cent," was his comment. "Have they sent the cheque, sir?"

Singleton glared again.

"Yes," he snapped — "for the balance — £2,199 16s. 7d. There it is!"

Llewellyn looked thoughtful for a moment. Then he positively smiled.

"After all," he said, "you are netting something like sixty pounds on the transaction, taking the market into — "

"That's not the point!" Singleton interrupted, banging his desk. "The point is, that you have disregarded my orders. I could have sold the lynobite on the market here at a profit, as you know. You've made a fool of me!"

"Let me explain," said Llewellyn quietly.

"What is there to explain?"

"This," said Llewellyn. "When their last debit note came, I did what you should have done a year ago. I looked up the shipping intelligence in the 'Journal of Commerce.' And what do you think I found?"

"Get on with your explanation. Don't ask me silly questions."

"I found that the *Euclid* did not discharge her cargo until the 24th, whilst Piper, Smith's debit note was dated the 23rd, which was also the date on the postmark of their letter. I looked up past debit notes, and compared their dates with discharging dates, and I found the same thing on three occasions in the past year. It is quite evident that Piper, Smith, & Co.'s staff have standing orders always to put in a claim for the full two per cent shrinkage against each invoice. This has been going on for so long and has become so habitual that they have grown careless, and don't even trouble to verify the landing date of their goods."

Farland Singleton sat up, with an oath.

"You had this clear proof of the swindle, and you never told me?" he demanded. "Why, man, we've got them in a cleft stick! They'll have to disgorge."

"They've done so already," said Llewellyn, "and with interest, as I promised you. That cheque is drawn on the Liverpool branch of the Bank of England. It will be as well to get it cashed without delay. Just to make quite sure, look you."

Singleton looked at his clerk, and his face was blank.

"What the dickens do you mean?"

Llewellyn took up the debit note.

"This claim for shrinkage amounts to an acknowledgment of the goods. They couldn't weigh the lynobite unless they'd got it, could they?"

"Well?"

Llewellyn permitted himself to wink at his employer.

"The four tons of lynobite, per ss. *Artemis*," he said slowly, "were never shipped at all. They are still in your warehouse."

Singleton's eyes bulged.

"But — but the bills of lading?"

"They were advised, as usual, by the ship's mail. But they never went. There were none to go. And Piper, Smith, & Co. can hardly write to ask for them, seeing that they've not only taken delivery of the goods, but actually weighed them, and verified a shrinkage of — "

"But it's a swindle, Evans!" his employer protested.

"A little sharp, look you," Llewellyn admitted. "But we've only been recovering the money out of which they've defrauded us. And they can't protest. They daren't, for they would be exposing their own dishonesty. They're fairly caught, and I have no qualms of conscience whatever."

"Oh, you haven't, eh?" growled Singleton. "And who the blazes are you, anyway?"

"Your partner from to-day," said Llewellyn cheerfully. And, mistrusting the look that crossed Singleton's face, he added, lest the other should say anything he might afterwards regret: "Of course, if you don't care about fulfilling the engagement, you can return Piper, Smith, & Co.'s cheque, with an explanation. But if you do that, I don't think you need trouble to give me a month's notice — for, indeed, the firm won't last a month."

Constrained to it thus, Singleton did what was good for him, and the firm of Farland Singleton & Co. — as it then became — entered upon a career of swelling prosperity, and rose steadily to the eminence which it occupies today.

Such is the true story of the founding of the fortunes of the illustrious Sir Llewellyn Evans, Bart., and it is greatly to be doubted if commercial history can supply another instance of a man having erected so fine an edifice upon so elusive an element as shrinkage.

The Pretender

I was glad enough, in all faith, to call a halt at the inn at Rosthwaite in obedience to the importunities of my men, Peter and Andrew, who had borne with me the burden of the day at the horse-fair at Keswick.

It was approaching sunset when we gained the little hamlet, and there was still a good hour's ride home before us, so that it behooved us not to tarry overlong. Just time to wash the dust from our throats and give our legs an easing-space from the saddle stiffness that was besetting us.

Half reclining on the cushioned window seat of the empty inn parlour, I called to Blossom for a draught of October. A garrulous old soul was this vintner, who suspected me — as for that matter did the whole countryside — of an imprudent attachment to the cause of Prince Charlie, and it was of that lost cause and the prince's alleged wanderings in the heather that he was discoursing to me when the advent of a stranger set a sudden bridle on his foolish tongue.

The newcomer was a tall, fair young man, wrapped about in a cloak and wearing a three-cornered hat so far forward upon his brow that it masked the upper portion of his face. He bore himself with an easy, graceful carriage rarely seen in our country parts, and through the dust that overlaid him one perceived his garments to be of a quiet elegance that suggested the South as his likely origin.

He paused at sight of me, and for a moment seemed to hesitate. Then, having paid me the honour of a close scrutiny, to my surprise he suddenly advanced upon me with a glad eagerness. He thrust back the hat from his brow, and the youthful face which he now disclosed, with full lips, prominent eyes and a flaxen tie-wig — was elusively familiar. He halted before me, leaning slightly towards me across the deal table, whilst I looked up and waited for him to speak. A moment or two he stood as if expecting some movement from me. Seeing that none came, his level brows were slightly knit, and a look of hesitation that amounted almost to alarm flitted across his face.

"Surely, surely, sir," said he, at length, and his voice was fresh and pleasant, and softened by a slightly foreign enunciation, "surely I have the advantage to address Sir Jasper Morford?"

I smiled agreeably — his air and manner all compelled the friendliness — as I corrected his impression. "My name, sir, is Dayne — Richard Dayne of Coldbarrow." And again moved by the gallantry of his air, I added courteously — "your servant, sir."

He continued to stare at me, between astonishment and unbelief. "Why, surely — " he began; then halted, and — " 'Tis very odd!" he muttered. "I see I am mistook. Your pardon, sir." And he dropped me a congee, all very brave and courtly.

"What is no less odd," I said, "is that not only should you have mistook me for one of your acquaintances, but that there is about yourself a something with which I seem acquainted."

He drew back sharply, and again alarm peeped at me from his eyes. Then, recovering: " 'Tis very odd, as ye say," he answered, and now there was a note of coldness in his voice, an imperious note, that seemed to forbid the pursuance of my curiosity. "Again, I crave your pardon, sir." He turned away, and crossing the room to the table remotest from me, called the landlord to supply his needs.

I sipped my ale and mused, my eyes upon his graceful back, until presently my attention was caught by a shadow that fell athwart my table. Idly I turned to seek the cause. For just one instant I had a glimpse of a face — blotched, villainous and unclean — pressed against the leaded windowpane, and of two red-rimmed eyes, evil and intent. The next moment, in a flash, even as I turned, the apparition vanished.

That a man should peer into an inn parlour was no great matter for astonishment; but that the man should be at such pains himself to avoid being seen was a circumstance sufficiently suspicious. Instantly the thought occurred to me that the ruffian's business might be with my young gallant across the room.

I resolved to watch, in the hope of learning more, of making sure; and to this end I set my pewter a little to the left, where the whole of the window was reflected on its polished surface. And now I sat on and smoked, my eye upon that reflection. Nor had I long to wait. Presently the face reappeared slowly and cautiously, and for all that it was too diminished and distorted by the pewter's surface to enable me to gather anything of its detail or expression, yet it was enough to inform me that the watcher had returned. I rose with leisurely nonchalance, and without turning, took up my measure and sauntered across the room to the young stranger.

"Ye'll forgive the liberty," said I, "but are ye like to be worth watching? Have ye cause to fear being watched, I mean?"

From the start and the expression of his eyes, 'twas very clear he had.

"I beg that ye'll not move. There is at this moment the most rascally face in Cumberland pressed against the window-pane."

His uneasiness grew so that my every suspicion was confirmed. Not a doubt but that here was some poor fugitive Jacobite with, as like as not, a price upon his handsome head.

He looked at me a moment with eyes that seemed to be seeking to fathom my very thoughts. Then he lowered his glance. "It is very kind in you to warn me, sir. 'Twere idle to pretend that I am in no danger, since in the pass to which things are come, you, sir, an entire stranger, are now my only hope. I have no claim upon you," he continued, his tone growing halting, as if fettered by a certain shyness, "and ye may marvel at the temerity — the effrontery that impels me to implore your aid in the desperate case in which ye find me."

"Sir," I answered readily, more and more assured with what manner of man I had to do, "I beg that ye'll command me freely. In so far as I may be able, I am most ready to assist you."

Again he looked at me, long and searchingly. "That, sir, is as kind as it is rash. Were I less hard-pressed I must refuse the service you so generously offer. But, being desperate, I have no other course but the selfish one of taking you at your word." Then in an altered, brisker manner — "You are well known in these parts?" he inquired.

I made answer that I was.

"And no doubt ye'll be a person of substance and reputation; to be seen in your company might mean the disarming of suspicion against me — for surely it can be no more than a suspicion at present. Were he certain, he'd not be content to watch. Will ye not join me, sir?" And he waved me to an empty chair by the table, and raised his voice to call the landlord.

Anon, when the latter had fetched me a fresh can, and had withdrawn, the stranger — as I thought at first, for lack of other subject wherewith to entertain me — raised his measure to propose a toast. "The King!" said he, watching me very intently as he spoke.

I paused a moment before replying. Had he named the king he pledged, his meaning could not have been plainer than it was. Now, as I have hinted, for all that I had taken no part in the ill-starred rising — having been restrained from any such rashness by my far-seeing uncle, the sheriff — yet my heart was entirely with the Stuart cause, my sympathies all against the Dutch usurper. Nor had I in the least dissembled these feelings of mine, and if any surprise I caused in Cumberland at the time, it was at my remaining passive during the strife that was but lately ended. That passivity was mainly begot of my affection for my uncle, which was very deep, and tempered with a gratitude that compelled my obedience to his wishes in the manner.

Notwithstanding, in the presence of this stranger a certain caution beset me now and I hesitated. Then, drawn to him by the anxious, almost pathetic, glance with which he watched me and awaited my reply, I raised my pewter, and in the same significant tone that he had employed — "The King!" I answered, and would have drunk, but that leaning across, he set a hand upon my arm, and checked me.

"Which king?" quoth he, his voice dropping almost to a whisper. "Which king — de jure, or de facto?"

I met his glance, and answered his eagerness with a smile. My heart went wholly out to him, and "The King de jure!" said I, to assure him that in me had a friend upon whom he might depend.

His eyes brightened on the word, and then there was the click of a latch behind him; the door was thrust slowly open, and a burly ruffian, wearing the evil countenance and the red-rimmed eyes I had seen at the window, shuffled into the room. My companion flung a glance over his shoulder at the new comer, and the other returned the glance with interest, a sneering smile investing the corners of this loose-lipped mouth. Then the fellow turned aside, and shuffled slowly away to the seat which I had lately vacated, where he thumped the table for the landlord.

My Jacobite looked at me with eyes eloquent with apprehension, whereupon I immediately fell to talking loudly of commonplaces such as should lead a stranger to suppose him other than he was. I expounded to him upon the seasons, upon the excessive rains that we had lately had, and the urgent need of fine weather to bring on the crops. I discoursed of the horse-fair at Keswick, and to some extent of the business I had done there, airing opinions upon the breeding and rearing of horses, upon the tricks of horse-dealers, and the manner in which they made gulls of townsfolk. My Jacobite entered into the spirit of my little comedy, and played his part in it with a quick and ready wit, now agreeing, now disputing, and generally conveyed the impression that he had no interests in life outside of crops and cattle. But his appearance was prone to belie the suggestion. His laced hat, his tie-wig, his fine boots of Spanish leather, with their silver spurs, to say nothing of the dress-sword that hung on his thigh, were all so many contradictions to his talk of husbandry. Out of the corner of my eye I watched the spy — for that I now accounted him — and to my dismay observed the growth of that sinister smile of his as he sat there, his eyes upon us, his ears attentive.

The suspense grew to a pitch that was unendurable. Better force him into action, and learn the worst that was to be expected from him, rather than prolong the present state of things. I resolved upon the bolder course, and rose.

"Come, Jack," said I, giving my Jacobite the first name that entered my mind, to show the spy that we were by no means chance acquaintances, "it is time we were getting homewards. The nags will be rested by now."

"Why, yes, Ned," said he, very promptly following my example. He stood a moment to finish his ale, entirely at his leisure, then turned to cross with me to the door. But at the same moment the spy rose too, and casting aside all further attempt to dissemble his purpose, he gained the door ahead of us, and set his back to it.

"Not so fast, sirs," said he, leering his wicked relish. He was the cat, and we were the mice that had made sport for him.

"Why, what's this?" said I, covering my fears in a display of angry astonishment. "The door, sirrah!"

"Pooh!" said he, eyeing me contemptuously. "You may go your ways, Mr. Dayne of Coldbarrow. My business is not with you. None has bethought him yet of setting a price on your head. My affair," and he turned to my companion, "is with your Royal Highness."

His Royal Highness! I fell back in my amazement, doubting at first, and then convinced, and marveling how it came that I had been so long in doubt. Indeed I should have put a name long since to that pale, oval face, those prominent eyes and full red lips. Here, in the flesh, stood "Bonnie Prince Charlie" himself. So convinced was I that I had not the presence of mind to laugh, as did the Prince — disdainfully as at an egregious blunder.

"Lackaday!" said he. "D'ye address me as 'Royal Highness'?"

"Yourself, Charles Stuart," answered the other grimly.

" 'Tis a jest, to be sure," the Prince assured him, frowning, "but I find little humour in it. Ye'll be letting us pass, sir."

The ruffian leaned forward, leering still. "If I'm wrong, the constable of Rosthwaite shall tell me on't; or, if not the constable, why then the sheriff."

"D'ye dare detain me?" demanded my companion, and he drew himself up with a great dignity.

"Ye see," quoth the other, at his ease, "there's a matter of a thousand guineas on your head. I'm a poor man, your highness — "

"Tush, sir! Ye're mistook, I tell you," the Prince broke in impatiently. "Out of my way there!" And he clapped a hand to the silver hilt of his sword.

The ruffian flashed a pistol from his pocket. "I'm not mistook," said he, and laughed. "Ye'll be stepping as far as the constable with me. And not an inch of that steel of yours, or I'll shoot ye first, and drag you by the heels to the constable afterwards. I'm a plain-spoken man, your Highness. I like to be understood."

At that the Prince's self-possession entirely left him. He turned to me a face that was blank with dismay. Then, with a nobility and a forgetfulness of self in such a moment that won my heart entirely — "Very well, sir," said he. "The game is yours. But this gentleman, at least — I have but met him by chance — you'll not wish to embroil him with me."

The fellow shrugged his massive shoulders. "As for him, why let him go his ways and be hanged." He stood away from the door. "There, sir," said he.

"Not I," I answered, my resolve taken not to abandon this poor prince who had ever had my heart, thankful that at last and in his need I should have this chance of serving him. "This gentleman comes with me, and — "

"Chut!" he interrupted angrily, and set his pistol on a level with my breast. "If ye're for turning troublesome, young sir, your account is soon settled. D'ye dream I'll let you come between me and a thousand guineas?"

"Leave me, sir, I beg," put in the Prince., "You cannot help me. Here is a mercenary villain in quest of blood-money. What arguments do you suppose could prevail with such a knave?"

The answer to the question flashed at once into my mind. In a belt about my waist I had two hundred guineas — the fruits of my dealings at Keswick, the price of the horses I had sold.

"The argument of gold," I answered, and under the Prince's astonished eyes I turned to the spy. "Look you, sir, what is your price?"

"My price?" He blew out his cheeks and laughed. "Say his price, rather — and that's a thousand guineas."

I shook my head. "Too much, my friend.. Allow his Royal Highness to depart in peace, forego your pursuit of him, and you shall have two hundred guineas here and now."

He looked surprised at first; then laughed contemptuously. But the Prince caught me by the arm.

"No, no, sir!" he exclaimed. "I could not — I will not permit it."

"Sir," I answered very deferential, "you shall. Indeed, it is scarce your right to refuse the service of a loyal subject, who so far had done naught but talk to show his devotion to your cause. To others it has been given to fight your battles with steel. I would I might have been one of those; but since I was not, grant me at least the honour now of fighting this with gold."

"Sir, it is very noble of you — " he was beginning, when the other broke in again.

"Not noble enough by many a hundred pounds if he's to carry the victory," he sneered.

I turned to him with arguments based on the philosophy that a bird in the hand is worth several in the bush, and urged him to accept my offer, since it amounted to all the money that I had upon me.

"What security have you that the government will pay you the reward?" I asked him. "I have never heard it urged that it is an over-honest government; nor sir, with all respect," I added, sardonically, "d'ye look a man with a clean conscience, to whom the government might show a becoming deference." I saw him wince, and I pursued the argument. "What, for instance, if the government, reluctant to part with its money, were to set up an inquiry into your ways of life, and were to find in them a pretext on which to gaol you and so save its guineas? What then, my friend? I taunted him, perceiving that my thrust had gone home. "Bethink you of the risk you run; consider the certainty I am offering you. What is it to be?"

He hesitated a moment, considering me with a gloomy eye. " 'Tis not," said he presently, "that I am moved by your talk, but that neither do I, myself, desire the Prince's death. It is just that I am a poor man, else would I not be at the task in which ye find me. Pay me five hundred guineas and his Highness shall go free; more — I'll even help make good his escape. I swear it."

"I have but two hundred guineas on me. But stay! You shall have these now, and another three hundred when you bring me word to Coldbarrow that his Highness is safe."

He pondered my proposal; then leered, and shook his head. "Ay," he growled, "and set a trap to catch me when I come. Nay, nay. I'm not to be taken in that gin."

"Bethink you," I returned impatiently. " 'Tis I shall be in your power. You have but to inform against me if I fail you." I unbuttoned my waistcoat, unbuckled the heavy belt, and dropped it on the table with a resounding clink. "There!" said I. "Will the government prove as prompt a paymaster, think you?"

But in that moment another sound beside the chink of gold had caught his ear, and he stood in a listening attitude, a strange, startled look upon his evil face.

"What's that?" he snapped, almost under his breath. "Hoofs!" He leapt to the window seat, flung up the window, and thrust out his dirty head. The Prince, standing beside me, looked alarmed and uneasy, as well he might. And if it crossed his mind to profit by the ruffian's attention being momentarily engaged elsewhere, he must have dismissed the thought as unavailing until he knew what fresh peril was approaching. To make a dash for the open now might be to fall into a worse plight than the present one.

"A posse of sheriff's men!" cried the ruffian, turning.

"In Heaven's name, then, resolve yourself," I besought him. "Take this belt, and come to me at Coldbarrow for the rest, as I have said."

He cogitated me a moment, what time the hoofs came rapidly nearer. "Come, man," I cried, "there is need for haste."

He advanced slowly — with a maddening slowness. "Very well," he said. "I'll trust ye, Mr. Dayne." He took up the belt and buckled it about his waist under his ragged coat.

The Prince turned to me, holding out his hands, thanking me and blessing me, and overwhelming me with his graciousness. Perforce I had to cut him short. I turned again to the other.

"Remember," I said, "it is part of our bargain that ye help his Highness to safety."

He nodded. "Ye may trust me. A bargain is a bargain, and ye'll not find me fail in my part on't. Quick!" he cried to the Prince, very brisk now in his manner. "They are almost here." He plucked a second pistol from his pocket, and thrust it into my hand. "Secure the landlord," he bade me. "See that he doesn't blab; that he denies having had other guests than yourself. Come, sir," he resumed to the Prince. "Our way lies by the back. I shall need a horse — "

"Take mine," I cried in a frenzy. "Bestir! Bestir! Leave Borrowdaile behind you with all speed."

He opened the door, and held it for His Highness. The Prince turned to me again to recommence his thanks, perhaps to protest. I thrust him unceremoniously forward. "Away, sir," I bade him, "or we are all lost."

And so, at last, they went. I heard their feet go pattering down the passage; I heard a door open and close, just as the landlord, coming out of the room opposite, would have inquired into the unusual manner of their departure. He knew me well, and entertained friendly feelings towards me, and in half a dozen sentences he was won over to my side.

Then in a cloud of dust and with a thunder of hoofs, the sheriff's posse swept up to the door of the inn, and shouted for old Blossom. He would have gone at once in answer to their call, but I detained him. Every moment was of value now, as every moment increased the start which the Prince had got, and his chances of winning through to safety. In vain did Blossom remind me that it was no good to keep the sheriff waiting, in vain did he implore me to let him go in answer to their impatient calling. I kept him where he was, and let them shout themselves into a rage. I even went the length of threatening to shoot him if he disobeyed me. Thus were some precious minutes gained — enough at least for the purpose which I sought to serve. Then the door was flung open, and the sheriff himself, in a very fury of impatience, stood on the threshold.

"Why, what a devil's here?" he cried, very red of face, very angry of eye. "Why am I kept waiting when I call?"

I came to the landlord's rescue, and myself answered my uncle with the truth. " 'tis my doing, sir. 'Twas I detained him."

"You?" he thundered at me. "And to what end, pray?"

"Why, if you must know, sir," I answered boldly, in a burst of loyalty to the Prince, whom at last I had the honour of serving, "to the end that his Royal Highness might get safely away."

"His Royal Highness," he echoed, like a man dumbfounded. Then his brow cleared, and his eye flashed between mockery and anger. 'So!" he cried. "Then he was here!"

The landlord flung himself forward in a panic. "Sir James," he cried, "I swear I never knew him for the Prince, else I had never harboured him."

"The Prince!" echoed my uncle, with a short angry laugh. "Gad a' mercy, fool, 'twas no prince — 'twas Mike Coleman, Captain Coleman of the hightoby. 'Tis a fair trade he has been driving with silly Jacobites by his likeness to the Pretender; ye're not the first gull he's bubbled with his gooseberry eyes and yellow wig. His Royal Highness, forsooth! Pah!" He shriveled me with the scorn of his glance. "What draft, now, may he have made upon your purse, sweet nephew? — he and his fellow-rogue, Tom Lindsay?"

If I looked foolish as I felt, I must have looked very foolish.

" 'Tis no matter for that," I answered glumly, dissembling my loss that I might avoid still keener gibes from him. "They'll be away by now, I fear."

He looked at me with undisguised contempt. "Ay, they'll have a deal to thank you for. Get you to Coldbarrow, nephew, to mind the farm, and give thanks that ye've an uncle for sheriff, or it might go hard with you for this. Ay, and leave politics to shrewder heads."

Ambs–Ace

Mike Coleman — alias Captain Coleman of the hightoby — was in full flight from the North and the unpleasant attentions of Sir James Dayne, Sheriff of Cumberland.

Tom Lindsay, the associate with whom so long and so successfully he had contrived to practise his famous swindle upon secret Jacobites, was already caged in Keswick gaol; and Coleman himself had had so near a shave of it that a cold sweat broke over him at the mere recollection.

Whilst it had lasted theirs had been a most diverting and remunerative game. Coleman's striking likeness to the fugitive Prince Charlie — a likeness heightened by certain supplements of art, including a flaxen tie-wig copied from one of the Prince's own — had imposed itself upon many a conspiring Jacobite fool, and many an amiable gull had submitted to a merciless plucking in so excellent a cause. But it was all over and done with, and here was Coleman spurring wildly along the heights between Rydal and Windermere, thankful to be over the border of Cumberland, but knowing that he dared not ease his pace nor account himself beyond the reach of the terrible Sir James this side of Lancashire. And the game itself, since it could not be played alone, could be played no more. For where should he find him such another associate as Lindsay? Poor Lindsay! He was done for, together with the game of "Bonnie Prince Charlie." Henceforth, if he would live, Captain Coleman must abandon the high histrionics by which his purse had swollen and support himself by the coarse and direct methods of "Stand and deliver!" — taking what purses came his way after the manner of any common scourer of the pad.

So he rides on a fair May evening along that mountain road, three-cornered hat hard pressed down over scowling brows, cloak flung carelessly about him. Ahead and far below him lies — a violet and orange tinted mirror — the long expanse of Windermere, studded with the black bulks of its luxuriant isles. But the scene's fair beauty held no glamour for the captain's eye. A glimpse of the desolate waste of Morecambe sands would more rejoice his heart with its assurance that a whole county lay between him and the plaguily diligent Sir James Dayne.

The view of the lake was shut out by a sudden bend and dip of the highway. Ahead the lonely road was split in twain. On a grassy mound at this junction, under a grey, battered signpost, stood two ragamuffin horsemen, who at sight of Coleman moved forward to block his way. A duet of harsh voices bade him stand.

He took their measure and assumed them to be sheriff's men — as ill-kempt and foul a pair of ruffians as you would meet on any road in England. One was short and thick-set, built like an ape with short legs and long arms; like an ape's, too, was his head with its massive, brutal jaw and shallow brow, whilst his coarse, pock-marked face was red and bloated. The other, by contrast, was long, and cadaverous, and wore a patch over one eye — either from necessity or for purpose of disguise.

They were not a pair whom it was good to meet on a lonely road, much less to have a holding against you. But Coleman was not a man easily daunted. He advanced boldly.

"Your pardon, sirs. I am pressed," said he, and as he spoke he reached for one of the pistols in his holsters.

That rash act precipitated matters. The cadaverous horseman emptied a barker at him on the instant. The shot went wide, but it so startled his mare that she plunged, came down upon her knees, and flung Captain Coleman headlong upon the road.

For a moment or two he lay dazed and half stunned where he had fallen. Then recovering, he sat up to find himself between his two assailants.

They had remarked his fine clothes, the gold lace on his green riding-coat, the ruffles at his wrist, his handsome jack-boots with their silver spurs and his silver-hilted colichemarde. Here for certain, they opined, was a bird worth plucking — for our captain had been entirely mistaken in his estimate of their quality.

Coleman sat up, winded and sore, his flaxen wig displaced and hanging rakishly over his left eye.

"Come now, sweetheart," croaked the hoarse voice of the red-faced rascal, "let me be relieving you of any burden you may be carrying on your travels."

"In plain English," the cadaverous one elucidated, "out with your purse."

The difference in their speech was as marked as that in their appearance. The, shorter gallows-bird spoke with the soft accent of the home counties; the other spoke with the rough burr of the North.

To Coleman's clearing brain the challenge brought relief. If they were not bum-bailiffs, he had been needlessly alarmed. He even could find a certain streak of humour in the situation of a tobyman unhorsed by tobymen. But what time he was turning it over in his mind, they were turning over the contents of his pockets; and before he had sufficiently recovered to resist them, the cadaverous one had relieved him of a purse that held close on fifty guineas.

Well content, they were departing, when Coleman, now fully master of his faculties, detained them.

"Hold, you muckrakes!" said he, and staggered to his feet.

They halted instantly out of astonishment at the truculence of his address. He stood confronting them squarely, and straightened his wig. In that moment the tall ruffian's single eye dilated, his mouth fell open and he clutched his comrade's arm.

"Tim!" said he, hoarser than ever in his sudden excitement, "Look at him, Tim. Look at him!"

The burly thief considered Coleman's pale oval face with its full, scarlet lips, gooseberry eyes, arched brows and flaxen tie-wig. A scowl denoted his mental labour of recollection.

"Now where have my glasiers lighted on that gentry-cove afore?" he wondered slowly. And then quite suddenly, he smacked his thigh so that the dust flew from his greasy breeches, and he blasphemed volubly to express the amazement with which he was filled by the sudden solution of the riddle.

On the instant Coleman perceived the situation. The extraordinary likeness to Charles Stuart, by means of which he had bubbled so many Jacobites out of their money, was imposing now upon these rogues. He waited for developments before determining upon a course. The ruffians looked at each other, startled at first by the magnitude of the thing before them, then leering evilly.

"Thirty thousand pounds be t' price on him, Tim," said Ned. "Thirty thousand pounds!" He mentioned the sum with the respect that was due to it, in a voice becomingly hushed.

"And we all but left him there!" growled Tim. "Him with thirty thousand pounds on his nab! Now stab me for an owl!"

Very quickly came they back, and Tim stretched out one of his long arms, and took the captain by the shoulder, grinning. "Ye'll come with us," said he.

"Whither, pray?" quoth Coleman indifferently. He had considered matters and resolved to make what capital he could out of the mistake, until he found a chance to recover his fifty guineas.

"Where your Highness will be safe," said Tim, making a leg very elaborately. "Fetch the prancers, Ned."

Long Ned went obediently for the horses, what time Tim clung to the supposed prince's shoulder with one hand, brandishing a great pistol in the other and entertaining him the while with lurid threats of how he would deal with him did he attempt to escape.

Two minutes later the three of them were in the saddle, Coleman between the highwaymen, his holsters emptied, his sword appropriated by Ned.

He realised that his case was one for cunning and patience; that a sudden attempt of evasion, or even of resistance might drive them to extremes. Moreover, he assumed that they would ride to Kendal, to take him before the sheriff of Westmoreland, and as that lay along the southward road it was his aim to travel, he would lose nothing by waiting for a chance to best them.

To his dismay, however, they faced northward instead and rode back with him towards Rydal, the very way by which he had come, the very way to meet his possible pursuers. Alarmed, he demanded to know whither they were taking him.

"Till Keswick," said Ned, "and t' sheriff o' Cumberland."

The Sheriff of Cumberland — Sir James Dayne, whom he feared more than any man living! That would not suit his ends at all. Every step in that direction increased the imminence of his peril. But he cloaked his fears under a false calm.

"What sense is there in that," quoth he, "when Kendal lies so much nearer? Besides, my nag is spent, and will never stay the journey to Keswick."

"We'll be resting t' night on r' way," said Ned reassuringly. "We've maybe reasons of our own for no' ganging till Kendal."

Coleman understood. The Sheriff of Westmoreland was as dangerous to them as was the Sheriff of Cumberland to himself, hence this reason for the longer journey. But it made all the difference to Coleman. It quenched his hopes and made him curse himself for a fool. There remained the truth. He essayed it.

"You fools — you ugly, addle-pated fools!" he said, and laughed so heartily that he alarmed them by it.

"Stow you that," growled Tim, his red face swelling and empurpling. "Stow it and be done."

"Why, look at me, you louts!" spluttered Coleman. "Look at me — closer. I am Mike Coleman."

Their stare grew broader, their looks more puzzled. Then Tim sneered:

"Not a doubt but that your Highness will have been many things since Culloden."

Coleman's laughter perished suddenly. If his name went for nothing with them, then was his plight desperate indeed.

"What?" said he. "Have ye never heard of Mike Coleman — Captain Coleman?"

"Never," said Ned gloomily.

This — thought Coleman as many another has thought before him and since — this was fame! In his vanity, he had conceived that all England rang with his exploits. Yet here, in the very county adjoining that in which he had conducted his operations, two men of his own profession had never so much as heard his name.

"Ye'll be telling us presently ye're a gentleman of the pad yourself," said Tim the humourist.

" 'Tis what I am telling you. I am Captain Coleman of the hightoby — all Cumberland knows Captain Coleman by now."

"And you're he?" quoth Ned.

"I am he," said Coleman. And, thereupon his captors were both taken with laughter, each after his own fashion — Tim noisily, Ned silently.

"Very well," snapped Coleman. "Take me before Sir James Dayne. Attempt to pass me off as Charles Stuart, and if he doesn't hang the pair of you for your pains, then I'm a calf."

They grew more serious at that, and Tim, who was the quicker-witted of the twain, bethought him of a test to which he might put this self-proclaimed highwayman.

He leaned towards him. "Cut benar whiddes, bene cove," said he, "or bing we to the queer cuffin," which, Englished, amounted to an invitation to explain himself more clearly if he would avoid being taken before the justice.

Had Coleman understood, even without being able to reply in that same thieves' cant, all had been well with him. Unfortunately — for all his sins — he was a man of gentle rearing, who, though a rogue, had never sought the company of rogues and, therefore, had never learned their language. He knit his brows and stared at Tim, as much bewildered as if he had been addressed in Greek.

"You say?" quoth he.

"That your Highness is a liar!" he was answered by solemn Ned. "We'll be pushing on till Keswick, for we are loyal subjects o' King George, we are."

Night had fallen by the time they came to make the steep ascent of Dunmail Raise. They went afoot, leading their horses, the tobymen pistol in hand and very watchful of their prisoner.

Up to the top of Dunmail Raise they came, and saw the distinct face of Thirlmere like a sheen of phosphorescence in the light of the young moon that had meanwhile risen. By Dunmail's grave they mounted again and ambled carefully down to the valley, then quickened their pace until they came — a mile or so short of Witheburn — to a lonely cottage whose windows were alight. Here they drew rein and Ned got down to knock. The door was opened instantly by a middle-aged woman, spare, strongly-built and — as Coleman was quick to perceive — of a certain harsh comeliness.

Ned stood in muttered talk with her, what time Tim was bidding the prisoner dismount, informing him that they would lie the night here. Coleman submitted silently to the inevitable, but his hopes of finding an opportunity of evading them were being lessened. What was difficult to accomplish on the open road must become impossible from within four walls.

None the less, however, he continued to preserve his outward ease as Ned ushered him at pistol-point across the threshold into the candle-light of that shabby parlour-kitchen where he underwent a swift, sharp scrutiny from the woman's hard blue eyes. He was invited to sit, and he flung himself carelessly upon a settle that stood at right angles to the hearth and the cold ashes of a dead fire.

The woman continued to observe him in wonder and some awe. She had been informed of his quality, and it was not every night that princes came to sit by her fireside. Her wonder arose from the fact that, as far as she could judge, he was a man like any other.

"Come, wife," came Ned's gruff voice. "We be fair hungry."

"I warn't expecting you," said she, and being experienced in the quality of his appetite — "There be nowt to drink i' t' house," she added.

"Naught to drink!" roared Tim, who entered at that moment, having put up the nags.

"Ye warn't expected," she repeated.

Ned turned to him. "Away wi' thee till Witheburn for a gallon, Tim," he urged, and Tim departed with alacrity upon an errand so pleasant, having enjoined Ned to have good care of the prisoner.

"Never doubt it," said Ned, and scarce had Tim closed the door than the one-eyed ruffian had taken a length of rope from a drawer of a chest that stood against the wall. With this he advanced upon Coleman.

"Stand up," he bade the supposed prince.

Coleman, perceiving his intent, retained his seat. "Sir," said he very loftily, "I beg you to consider that already I have suffered more than enough indignities at your hands without this. Be content, therefore, if I give you my parole not to attempt an escape."

With his assumption of dignity, he had almost unconsciously lapsed into the grand manner he affected when he played the prince. Ned's single eye narrowed shrewdly, a grin overspread his face. "Soho!" he crowed softly, "Here's a change o' tone. Ye've forgot your part — forgot that your highness preferred to travel incognito — as they say — Captain Coleman o' t' hightoby."

Coleman shrugged, and his very shrug was princely. His speech, he reflected, might in one sense have been ill-considered; yet in another, it might do him good service. They might accept the prince's parole, and leave him unbound, in which case he would have not the slightest scruple in breaking that same parole on the first opportunity. Bound, his last hope was quenched.

Ned breathed noisily and smiled. "Your highness has not been above seeking to abuse t' confidence o' two poor devils by falsehood. How then can I take your parole? I prefer to have you bound — if ye please, sir."

"But," began Coleman desperately, when the fierce ruffian interrupted, thrusting his pistol under the captive's nose.

"Enough said," he snarled. "Look ye, sir — t' price set on tha head'll be paid till any what takes thee living or dead — living or dead, bethink thee o' that?" He laughed silently. "I'd as soon make sure and have thee dead, save that thou'lt ride better nor thou'lt carry. So up wi' thee or I'll be showing my loyalty to King George by putting a plug of lead in tha silly Stuart brains."

Coleman realised that there was no more to be said. He rose, maintaining with difficulty his air of haughty insouciance. Turning as he was bidden, he placed his hands behind him. It was the woman who pinioned him, first at wrists and then at ankles, whilst Ned stood guard.

When they had done with him he resumed his seat in the corner of the settle a very despondent man. Ned and his wife went to sit at the table, facing each other with never another glance in the prisoner's direction. From his pocket Ned took the pistols of which Coleman had been relieved, and placed them on the board; next, he produced the bulging purse of fifty guineas. It dropped with a fat, mellow chink, that set the woman's blue eyes greedily agleam. Her fingers caressed it. They would have fastened upon it, but that Ned restrained her.

"T' half is Tim's," he reminded her.

"And t' half o' yon, too, no doubt," said she, with a jerk of her head to indicate the supposed prince.

He nodded; and then as if responding to something suggestive in her tone:

" 'Twere a rare jest," said he, "to carry him off afore Tim gets back. Lord! How he'd stare to find t' nest empty and himself bubbled o' his share o' thirty thousand pounds!"

She considered him cunningly. "He'd ride after us," said she.

"I but jested," Ned reproved her, shortly.

"Is thirty thousand pounds a jest, quotha? Ha! Thirty thousand pounds! We could gang o'er seas, turn honest and become gentlefolk wi' yon!"

" 'Twill still be a mort o' money when it's halved," said he. But his brow had grown dark with thought.

"He's a fool that takes the half when he can have all," she replied.

Ned fixed her solemnly with his one eye. "But I have told thee he'd be after us," said he, "And if he o'ertook us — faith! he's an ugly fellow to thwart."

She leaned across to him and dropped her voice so that Coleman could catch no more of what was said. But he could see the wicked glitter of her hard eyes, and when presently he had a momentary glimpse of Ned's face, he saw that it was yellow, the brow agleam with sweat. It was easy to conclude that they were plotting no good for the absent Tim.

Suddenly the woman clutched her husband's arm. "Hist!" And Coleman strained to listen as did Ned.

In the far distance sounded the faint clatter of hoofs. It was Tim returning. Nearer and louder they came; and the thud and beat of them seemed to cast a spell over the man and the woman at the table. In utter, frozen silence they sat listening as intently as if they were counting every beat.

At long length the horseman came to a clattering halt before the door. Ned and his wife rose. The door was pushed open, and a jar set down within. "I'll stable the nag, Ned," came Tim's voice, and from his utterance it would seem that he had filled his skin as well as the jar at the alehouse at Witheburn.

Ned lifted the vessel to the table. Then in utter and deathly silence they awaited Tim's coming, and in that portentous pause, Coleman felt his heart thudding as if it would suffocate him, already prescient of the thing he was about to witness.

Tim's feet stumbled outside. The door was flung back violently and the fellow blundered into the room, his huge face aflame, his glance foolishly amiable. He closed the door as noisily as he had opened it. "I took my fill at the bowsing-ken," said he, and added with a humorous glance at Coleman — "Been drinking — health — King George!"

They were his last words, for in that moment Ned emptied a pistol point-blank into his breast.

The deafening noise of the shot was succeeded by the crash of Tim's fall, as he tumbled sideways and rolled over on his face.

The murderer stood a moment in a crouching attitude, a look of fear on his evil yellow countenance. At his elbow, his wife, crouching, too, peered through the lifting smoke at the fallen man. Then Ned dropped the pistol, flashed a glance at Coleman, who had been a silent, stricken witness of the deed, and looked quickly away.

He coughed, oppressed by the stench of powder. "Come," he said to his wife, "fetch glasses. A draught to wash this filth from our throats, and then we'll gang."

She turned to a cupboard — quickly, as if glad to have something to engage her — produced two earthenware jugs. With shaking hands she set them on the table. Her wide eyes stared at the prostrate Tim out of a pinched and suddenly haggard face. He was moving. One of his hands faintly flapped the floor, presently it steadied, and he slightly raised himself upon it.

Ned poured the ale, taking no heed of him. The woman clutched his sleeve. "Look! Look!" she gibbered, and pointed tremblingly.

Ned shrugged. "What odd's?" said he gruffly. "He's crippled anyhow. He'll not interfere wi' us." He lifted his mug and emptied it at a draught.

Coleman, looking from one to the other in fascinated horror of the scene, surprised a distortion of extraordinary and horrible mirth upon Tim's ashen face. The dying man was regarding Ned with a glance that was evilly exultant. The climax came as Ned set down the cup, in a splutter of awful laughter from Tim's writhing lips. He coughed and choked on it, sank down again abruptly and lay quite still. Ned and the woman regarded him in an astonishment that held some terror. Then Ned suddenly clutched his breast and swung round gasping. An oath broke from him.

"I burn!" he screamed, and bent himself almost double in his agony.

In alarm she caught him, and thrust forward a chair. He dropped to it, sweating, groaning and rolling his one eye horribly. A moment he flung his head about like a man fighting for breath, and clawed the air with his hands.

"What ails thee, lad? What ails thee?" cried his wife.

He made no answer, but in that moment collapsed upon the table, his arms flung out before him, his head pillowed on them, and so lay still.

She took him by the shoulders and shook him. But he made no response. She stared into his ashen face and recoiled aghast. Her wild eyes fell on Coleman, who was looking on with wondering interest.

"Help — help me!" she panted. "He is ill. See what ails him, wilt tha." And snatching up a knife she slashed through the prisoner's bonds.

Coleman rose, stepped up to Ned and looked at him closely to confirm that which Tim's infernal laugh had already told him.

"What ails him?" came the woman's voice, shrill and querulous. "What ails him?"

"Naught ails him," said Coleman.

"Nowt!" she echoed.

"Naught," he repeated, and added the explanation — "He is dead."

"Dead?"

Coleman looked at her. "Men drink as they pour," said he.

She took him literally. "Drink?" said she. "Was it drink? Did — did Tim — "

"Each played the same game as the other," said Coleman slowly. "Each cogged the dice, and each has thrown ambs-ace." He took up his purse and pistols, which still lay upon the table, the woman making no attempt to hinder him. "And the irony of it is," he added, "that there was no stake at all upon the board, for I am not the prince. They wasted labour when they killed each other. Give you good-night."

He passed out of that foul chamber, took the best of the three horses in the stable, and rode it so hard that by dawn he was in Lancashire.

Sources

"Wirgman's Theory," *London Magazine*, July 1906

"The Face of the Clock," *The Realm*, August 1904

"The Red Mask," *The Ludgate*, December 1898

"The Evidence of the Sword," *The Royal Magazine*," September 1900

"The Valet Mystery," *The Storyteller*, September 1914

"His Last Chance," *American Illustrated Magazine*, December 1905

"The Spiritualist," *Pearson's Magazine*, July 1905

"Monsieur Delamort," *The Cavalier*, August 1909

"Judge Foscaro's Crime," *Pearson's Magazine*, July 1904

"The Dream," *The Storyteller*, August 1912

"Duroc," *Weekly Tale-Teller*, October 2, 1915

"The Mask," *Cassell's Magazine of Fiction*, February 1916

"Shrinkage," *London Magazine*, October 1914

"The Pretender," *The Lady's World*, August 1911

"Ambs-Ace," *The Lady's World*, August 1912

The Evidence of the Sword

The Evidence of the Sword and Other Mysteries by Rafael Sabatini, edited by Jesse F. Knight, is set in Garamond (for the text) and Harrington (for the chapter titles and running titles), and printed on 60 pound Natural acid-free paper. The cover is by Tom Roberts, and the Lost Classics design is by Deborah Miller. *The Evidence of the Sword* was published in April 2006 by Crippen & Landru Publishers, Norfolk, Virginia.

CRIPPEN & LANDRU, PUBLISHERS

P. O. Box 9315, Norfolk, VA 23505

E-mail: info@crippenlandru.com; toll-free 877 622-6656

Web: www.crippenlandru.com

LOST CLASSICS

Crippen & Landru is proud to publish a series of *new* short-story collections by great authors who specialized in traditional mysteries. Each book collects stories from crumbling pages of old pulp, digest, and slick magazines, and most of the stories have been "lost" since their first publication. The following books are in print:

Peter Godfrey, *The Newtonian Egg and Other Cases of Rolf le Roux*, introduction by Ronald Godfrey. 2002.

Craig Rice, *Murder, Mystery and Malone*, edited by Jeffrey A. Marks. 2002.

Charles B. Child, *The Sleuth of Baghdad: The Inspector Chafik Stories*. 2002.

Stuart Palmer, *Hildegarde Withers: Uncollected Riddles*, introduction by Mrs. Stuart Palmer. 2002.

Christianna Brand, *The Spotted Cat and Other Mysteries from Inspector Cockrill's Casebook*, edited by Tony Medawar. 2002.

William Campbell Gault, *Marksman and Other Stories*, edited by Bill Pronzini; afterword by Shelley Gault. 2003.

Gerald Kersh, *Karmesin: The World's Greatest Criminal — Or Most Outrageous Liar*, edited by Paul Duncan. 2003.

C. Daly King, *The Complete Curious Mr. Tarrant*, introduction by Edward D. Hoch. 2003.

Helen McCloy, *The Pleasant Assassin and Other Cases of Dr. Basil Willing*, introduction by B.A. Pike. 2003.

William L. DeAndrea, *Murder — All Kinds*, introduction by Jane Haddam. 2003.

Anthony Berkeley, *The Avenging Chance and Other Mysteries from Roger Sheringham's Casebook*, edited by Tony Medawar and Arthur Robinson. 2004.

Joseph Commings, *Banner Deadlines: The Impossible Files of Senator Brooks U. Banner*, edited by Robert Adey; memoir by Edward D. Hoch. 2004.

Erle Stanley Gardner, *The Danger Zone and Other Stories*, edited by Bill Pronzini. 2004.

T.S. Stribling, *Dr. Poggioli: Criminologist*, edited by Arthur Vidro. 2004.

Margaret Miller, *The Couple Next Door: Collected Short Mysteries*, edited by Tom Nolan. 2004.

Gladys Mitchell, *Sleuth's Alchemy: Cases of Mrs. Bradley and Others*, edited by Nicholas Fuller. 2005.

Philip S. Warne/Howard W. Macy, *Who Was Guilty? Two Dime Novels*, edited by Marlena E. Bremseth. 2005.

Dennis Lynds writing as Michael Collins, *Slot-Machine Kelly: The Collected Private Eye Cases of the One-Armed Bandit*, introduction by Robert J. Randisi. 2005.

Julian Symons, *The Detections of Francis Quarles*, edited by John Cooper; afterword by Kathleen Symons. 2006.

Rafael Sabatini, *The Evidence of the Sword and Other Mysteries*, edited by Jesse F. Knight. 2006.

FORTHCOMING LOST CLASSICS

Erle Stanley Gardner, *The Casebook of Sidney Zoom*, edited by Bill Pronzini.

Ellis Peters (Edith Pargeter), *The Trinity Cat and Other Mysteries*, edited by Martin Edwards and Sue Feder.

Lloyd Biggle, Jr., *The Grandfather Rastin Mysteries*, introduction by Kenneth Lloyd Biggle and Donna Biggle Emerson.

Max Brand, *Masquerade: Nine Crime Stories*, edited by William F. Nolan, Jr.

Hugh Pentecost, *The Battles of Jericho*, introduction by S.T. Karnick.

Mignon G. Eberhart, *Dead Yesterday and Other Mysteries*, edited by Rick Cypert and Kirby McCauley.

Victor Canning, *The Minerva Club, The Department of Patterns and Other Stories*, edited by John Higgins.

Elizabeth Ferrars, *The Casebook of Jonas P. Jonas and Others*, edited by John Cooper.

Anthony Boucher and Denis Green, *The Casebook of Gregory Hood*, edited by Joe R. Christopher.

Anthony Boucher and Denis Green, *The Casebook of Gregory Hood*, edited by Joe R. Christopher.

Philip Wylie, *Ten Thousand Blunt Instruments*, edited by Bill Pronzini.

G. T. Fleming-Roberts. *Lilies for the Iron Cross and Other Stories*, edited by Monte Herridge.

Erle Stanley Gardner, *The Adventures of Señor Lobo*, edited by Bill Pronzini.

SUBSCRIPTIONS

Crippen & Landru offers discounts to individuals and institutions who place Standing Order Subscriptions for its forthcoming publications, either all the Regular Series or all the Lost Classics or (preferably) both. Collectors can thereby guarantee receiving limited editions, and readers won't miss any favorite stories. Standing Order Subscribers receive a specially commissioned story in a deluxe edition as a gift at the end of the year. Please write or e-mail for more details.

Lost Classics